THE MORTAL FALLS

Other Books by Anna Durand

The Mortal Falls (Undercover Elementals, Book One)
The Mortal Fires (Undercover Elementals, Book Two)
The Mortal Tempest (Undercover Elementals, Book Three)
The Janusite Trilogy (Undercover Elementals, Books 1-3)
Obsidian Hunger (Undercover Elementals, Book Four)
Unbidden Hunger (Undercover Elementals, Book Five)
Cyneric (Undercover Elementals, Book Seven)
Echo Power (Echo Power Trilogy, Book One)
Echo Dominion (Echo Power Trilogy, Book Two)
Echo Unbound (Echo Power Trilogy, Book Three)
Passion Never Dies: The Complete Reborn Series
Banished in the Highlands (A Hot Scots Prequel)
The Notorious Dr. MacT (A Hot Scots Prequel)
The British Bastard (A Hot Scots Prequel)
Dangerous in a Kilt (Hot Scots, Book One)
Wicked in a Kilt (Hot Scots, Book Two)
Scandalous in a Kilt (Hot Scots, Book Three)
The MacTaggart Brothers Trilogy (Hot Scots, Books 1-3)
Gift-Wrapped in a Kilt (Hot Scots, Book Four)
Notorious in a Kilt (Hot Scots, Book Five)
Insatiable in a Kilt (Hot Scots, Book Six)
Lethal in a Kilt (Hot Scots, Book Seven)
Irresistible in a Kilt (Hot Scots, Book Eight)
Devastating in a Kilt (Hot Scots, Book Nine)
Spellbound in a Kilt (Hot Scots, Book Ten)
Relentless in a Kilt (Hot Scots, Book Eleven)
Incendiary in a Kilt (Hot Scots, Book Twelve)
Wild in a Kilt (Hot Scots, Book Thirteen)
Lachlan in a Kilt (The Ballachulish Trilogy, Book One)
Aidan in a Kilt (The Ballachulish Trilogy, Book Two)
Rory in a Kilt (The Ballachulish Trilogy, Book Three)
Brit vs. Scot (A Hot Brits/Hot Scots/Au Naturel Crossover Book)
The American Wives Club (A Hot Brits/Hot Scots/Au Naturel Crossover Book)
A Novel Secret (A Hot Brits/Hot Scots/Au Naturel Crossover Book)
One Hot Chance (Hot Brits, Book One)
One Hot Roomie (Hot Brits, Book Two)
One Hot Crush (Hot Brits, Book Three)
The Dixon Brothers Trilogy (Hot Brits, Books 1-3)
One Hot Escape (Hot Brits, Book Four)
One Hot Rumor (Hot Brits, Book Five)
One Hot Christmas (Hot Brits, Book Six)
One Hot Scandal (Hot Brits, Book Seven)
One Hot Deal (Hot Brits, Book Eight)
One Hot Favor (Hot Brits, Book Nine)
Natural Obsession (Au Naturel Nights, Book One)
Natural Passion (Au Naturel Trilogy, Book One)
Natural Impulse (Au Naturel Trilogy, Book Two)
Natural Satisfaction (Au Naturel Trilogy, Book Three)
Fired Up (standalone romance)

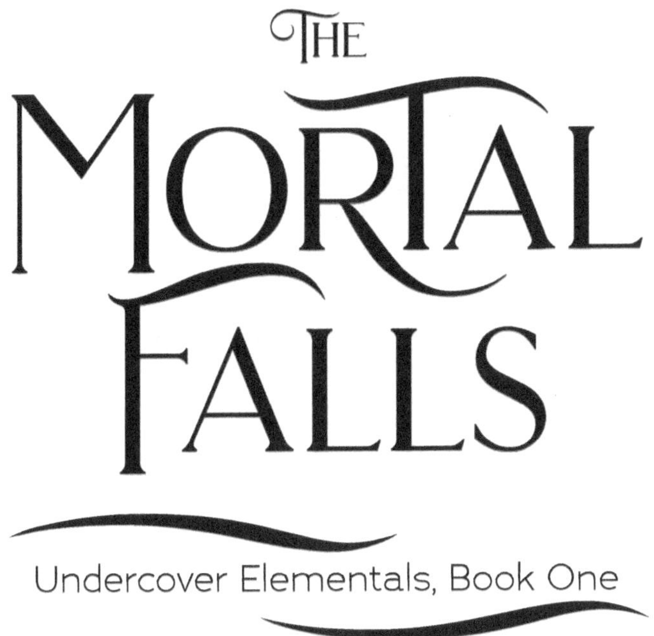

THE MORTAL FALLS

Undercover Elementals, Book One

ANNA DURAND

JACOBSVILLE BOOKS · MARIETTA, OHIO

THE MORTAL FALLS

ISBN: 978-1-934631-88-1 (pbk.)
ISBN: 978-1-934631-89-8 (ebook)
Library of Congress Control Number: 2017936798

Manufactured in the United States.

Jacobsville Books
www.JacobsvilleBooks.com

Publisher's Cataloging-in-Publication Data
provided by Five Rainbows Cataloging Services

Names: Durand, Anna.
Title: The mortal falls / Anna Durand.
Description: Lake Linden, MI : Jacobsville Books, 2017. | Series: Undercover elementals, bk. 1.
Identifiers: LCCN 2017936798 | ISBN 978-1-934631-88-1 (pbk.) | ISBN 978-1-934631-89-8 (ebook)
Subjects: LCSH: Magic--Fiction. | Spirits--Fiction. | Fairies--Fiction. | Shape-shifting--Fiction. | Women heroes--Fiction. | Romance fiction. | BISAC: FICTION / Romance / Paranormal / General. | FICTION / Romance / Paranormal / Shifters. | FICTION / Romance / Fantasy. | GSAFD: Love stories. | Occult fiction. | Fantasy fiction.
Classification: LCC PS3604.U724 M67 2017 (print) | LCC PS3604.U724 (ebook) | DDC 813/.6--dc23.

CHAPTER ONE

I TROTTED OUT THE DOORWAY OF THE ROCK SHOP AND HURRIED AROUND the corner of the barn-red metal building, past the rock garden with its whimsical statues frolicking among the boulders and flowers. My boots clomped as I hustled down the path through the woods, straight into the area marked by a big wooden sign. White-painted letters declared "HEALING VORTEX." Three boulders, shaped like benches, hunkered in a semicircle around the empty space that was the so-called vortex of mystical energy. I stopped in the middle of the space. No spiritual effects lightened my psyche, or whatever the thing was supposed to do.

Maybe the vortex shunned me because I'd stopped believing in the supernatural. I liked the charming idea of an invisible energy field that healed what ailed you, but ridicule from school kids had squelched my fascination with the paranormal. I'd long since given up on caring what others thought of me, yet I couldn't quite get back to those beliefs.

Glancing around, I realized no one was here. My customers must've left already, or meandered down the trail to the waterfall. If I returned to the shop without speaking to the customers, or at least verifying they'd left the premises, my boss would chew me out good. "Go act like a tour guide," Stan Lagorio had commanded, and I obeyed. A thirty-two-year-old woman should not have to schlep rocks and chase down tourists for minimum wage. Still, with my lackluster work history, I was grateful to have any job.

Sultry air stuck to my skin as I trudged down the trail. I swiped a bead of sweat from my temple. Summer on the Keweenaw Peninsula—the way-way north of Michigan's Upper Peninsula—shouldn't scorch. I mopped more perspiration from my brow, plodding onward. Up ahead, out of sight, the waterfall drummed a dull rhythm. Something else moaned beneath the rumbling, something like…

The throaty bellow of a human in agony.

1

I slid to a stop. My heart raced. Adrenaline electrified my every nerve as I struggled to peer through the trees, but the foliage blocked my view. The urge to flee blasted through me, but someone needed to check this out. If I galloped back to the store for help, the injured party might bleed to death or stumble into the water and drown. I inched forward.

A strangled cry reverberated through the woods.

I slipped my right hand under my blouse to close my fingers around the grip of the Bond Arms derringer holstered on the inside of my waistband—legally, thanks to my concealed carry permit and the permission of my employer. The pistol's grip felt warm in my cold hand, heated by my body temperature. The two .357 rounds, one in each barrel, could stop a bad guy or at least slow him down. *Never a victim again.*

A chill seeped into me, penetrating to the very depths of my being. The air crackled with invisible energy that skittered across my skin. The trees towered above me as before, the sun still blazed overhead, and the waterfall still thundered further down the trail. But the atmosphere had shifted, like a shadow snaking across my soul.

Baloney. Energy didn't crackle. No shadows infected me. I'd let my imagination mushroom into paranoia.

I pulled out my derringer and tiptoed two steps. Hesitated. Took another step. Listened.

The falls rumbled. Jagged breaths hissed from my lips. The weight of another gaze squirmed down my spine, but I saw nothing except aspen and maple trees, and wildflowers sagging under the weight of morning dew. I would've accepted I was alone and had confused the cry of a fox or bear for a human scream, if not for the worm of doubt burrowing into me.

A raven swooped down out of the high trees.

The bird squawked as it passed within inches of me. I ducked down. When I raised up again, the raven was gone. Had it been aiming for me? Christ, I was losing my mind.

I jogged down the trail and broke through the screen of trees into the clearing surrounding the falls. The water gushed over the twenty-foot-high red sandstone cliff into the small pool below, where it disgorged into a stream. No one stood on the wooden bridge that arched over the stream. I dragged in a breath, inhaling the clean scents of water and grass, but a sharper smell, almost metallic, lurked beneath the woodland aroma. The trail angled left, away from the falls and into the deeper woods. I sprinted around the curve, into the trees.

And tripped over the man sprawled across the trail.

My derringer popped out of my grasp as I stumbled sideways. Blood dripped from the man's forehead onto the ground. The fluid stained his red hair and congealed as a dark puddle in the dirt. One arm lay twisted under his body. His eyes stared at nothing. His mouth gaped open, caught in the final scream.

I crouched beside the man, extending a trembling hand to check his pulse, but I sensed the truth before my fingertip dug into his flesh.

The man was dead.

CHAPTER TWO

A FORCE AS POWERFUL AS A BLACK HOLE HAULED MY ATTENTION TO the body. The man. Christ, he was still a human being, not a slab of meat. I collapsed to my knees, unable to tear my gaze away from the lifeless body of the man whom—less than an hour ago—I'd caught shoplifting a pair of copper ore bookends, stuffing them into his backpack. Baffled at why a grown man would risk jail time for slabs of polished rock, I'd seized his arm and demanded he give up the items.

He'd bared his teeth and hissed, "Go to hell, bitch."

Now the shoplifter lay dead at my feet. The police would probably think I'd argued with the guy, chased him through the woods, and murdered him in cold blood. The sheriff already thought I was a psycho. He'd dream up some kind of motive, just like last time.

I swallowed hard. The dead man's eyes. They stared into nothingness. Into eternity. I jiggled the body. He didn't rouse. I shook him hard and shouted, "Wake up!"

The head lolled at an unnatural angle. I yanked my hands away. What had I expected? The man was stone dead.

A shiver coiled down my spine. *You have to call the cops.* I jammed a hand in my jeans pocket, yanking out my cell phone, and punched the 9 key. The inescapable pull of the dead man tugged my gaze back to the body at my feet, to the blood pooled around his head and the vacancy in his eyes. My fingers twisted around a clump of grass, clenching it until the blades crumpled. Dew seeped over my fingers. *Rein it in, Lindsey.* I drew in a long breath and let it out slowly.

My other hand gripped the phone so tight my fingers ached. *The phone.* I lifted my damp fingers to the keys.

A crunch pierced the silence.

I whipped my head around. The noise originated behind me, in the woods. Goose bumps erupted up and down my arms and I snatched up my gun, scrambling to my feet. The stench of blood suffocated me. Straight ahead, a three-foot-wide pine tree loomed.

Rustling. Behind the tree.

I bit my lip. "Who's there?"

A figure leaped out. The naked man loped down the path away from me, toward the falls. His footfalls thwapped. He craned his head around, shot a grin at me, and sprinted faster.

Maybe he killed my shoplifter. By the time the cops arrived, the stranger would've escaped into the wilderness. I bolted after him.

It was like a crazed spirit had possessed me, propelling me into a reckless pursuit. *Chase a naked man through the woods. Brilliant plan.* I'd mutated into the dumb chick from a B horror movie, but I could not stop. Something in my soul drove me onward, legs pumping, blood rushing. My veins burned with adrenaline. My breaths huffed so hard and fast my head started to spin, but I drove my body on and on. I closed the distance between us just as the man touched down on the main trail. The stranger swerved right and vaulted over the wooden railing meant to deter people from jumping into the water. He sailed through the air, powerful, graceful, beautiful. His feet whomped down on the rock ledge at the cliff's base and he trotted toward the falls.

I hollered through cupped hands. "Stop right there!"

The man dived straight into the torrent.

At the railing, I stopped so fast I almost toppled over headfirst. The waterfall pummeled the pool, churning up foam that dissipated as it oozed across the surface. Drops spattered my face and I blinked at the sting in my eyes. The rumbling of the falls, though far from deafening, drowned out my thoughts and obliterated my intentions. Why had I run here?

The man. He'd fled the scene of a crime, or at least a possible crime. My shoplifter died from a severe head wound and the naked man I'd chased must've either been a witness or the killer. The sheriff would never believe I'd seen a naked man unless I delivered him on a silver platter with the recipe for roasting him pinned to his chest. I must track him down.

Where? He'd vanished into the waterfall.

"Hello again."

I yelped, scrambled sideways, tripped over a rock. My arms flailed. I caught a peripheral glimpse of the stranger as I staggered backward. My heel dropped into a hole. My feet flipped out from under me and I sailed toward the ground.

The man snagged me around the waist. He hoisted me up, hugging me to him. My derringer thumped onto the ground beside his feet, but his only reaction was a quick glance at it and a faint lift of one brow.

Panting, I gaped at my savior. The murder suspect. Or witness. Or… something. His arms, roped with taut sinews, pressed me to his muscular body. Despite his jump through the falls, he wasn't wet. *Impossible.*

I wriggled against his grip. "Let me go."

He released me, stepping back. "You should exercise more care, darlin', or you'll crack that lovely head of yours."

"What?"

He nodded toward the ground. I followed his gaze down to a fist-size rock situated right where my head would've struck. *Ouch.* I gulped.

The man watched me, his brows furrowed.

Not a man. A murder suspect. I scuffled away from him, drawing out a distance of several yards. My gaze flicked to the gun, but I couldn't retrieve it without approaching him. "Why did you run away?"

"So you would follow."

His Irish brogue tickled my senses like a feather grazing my skin. I gave myself a mental shake, but the sensation lingered. "Excuse me?"

My suspect sighed, as if I were the dumbest human on the planet. Maybe I was. Right at this moment, I wouldn't have bet money on my intelligence. Still, I had my pride.

I crossed my arms over my chest. "Why did you run?"

The man hooked a thumb over his shoulder, toward the trail. "To draw you away from the body. It seemed to upset you."

When I leaned to the left, I glimpsed the trail but not the dead man. The stranger blocked my view, which made me wonder if he'd positioned himself there on purpose. Him. The strange man who'd leaped into the falls only to pop up behind me a split second later. *Impossible.*

He glided one step closer, into a shaft of sunshine that painted his face in hues of gold. The shadow from his elegant nose kissed the corner of his mouth. The sun's rays ignited his amber eyes, gracing them with a vividness beyond the normal. I roved my gaze up and down his golden body, soaking in the alien beauty of him. He wasn't actually naked. A tan loincloth clung to his flesh, but since the scrap of fabric covered his buttocks and groin and not much else, the impression of nudity wasn't entirely unfounded. The loincloth's color blended into his complexion. The way it hugged his body accentuated his male physique, the way it clung to his lean hips and the upper swathe of his powerful, tanned thighs.

My gaze fell across a long scar on his chiseled torso, right over his heart. I wrestled against the bizarre urge to lunge toward him and run my hands over that glorious chest. Heat swept through me, the suddenness of it shortening my breaths.

Get a grip. I was suffering from shock. Nothing else explained this. I should not be ogling a murder suspect twenty feet away from the victim's corpse. I wasn't like this, not ever, especially not since—I severed the memory before it swallowed me whole. Nothing supernatural was going on here. I had a half-naked murder suspect to question. Once I knew the answers, I'd subdue this guy—somehow—and call the cops. Only then might the sheriff believe me.

Okay. Time to grill the suspect.

Straightening, I lifted my chin. "Did you kill that man?"

The stranger shook his head. The light glimmered on his shadow-dark hair. The breeze tousled his wavy locks around his face, brushing them across the tops of his ears. His lips, thick and luscious, cinched together. Strands of glossy hair fanned across his eyes, but he seemed not to notice. "You ask the wrong question."

"Did you see what happened to the dead man?"

The stranger shrugged. His broad shoulders undulated. "Not really, darlin'. But I wasn't on the lookout...for a man."

"What are you talking about? Who are you? And what are you doing out here dressed like—" I flapped a hand toward him. The loincloth, and what it concealed, snagged my attention and warmth rushed through me anew. I clamped my upper lip between my teeth. Zeroing in on his face, I said, "Nobody dresses like that in the woods."

"Is that so." A statement, not a question.

"Yes. It's not proper." Cripes. I had more urgent matters to worry about, like the corpse rotting in the woods behind this crazy man. Since the moment I found the body, nothing made sense. It all seemed...paranormal.

My gaze fell on my derringer, where it lay in the grass near the stranger, so close yet so far beyond my reach. I needed the hard metal in my hand, an anchor to reality.

I cleared my throat. "What do you know about the dead body? Who are you? Where did you come from?"

"Again with the questions."

"I'd quit asking if you'd answer."

His mouth slid into a wide grin and he strode toward me. One step closer. Two steps. Three. I stumbled backward as ice frosted over my skin, leeching into my flesh. His long legs spanned the distance faster than my feet could travel. My spine smacked into a tree. His body blockaded my view, a wall of muscle and bronzed flesh. Pinned there, I clutched at the trunk. Bits of bark crumbled under my nails, fluttering to the ground. I flattened against the tree. Breaths gusted out of me in sharp huffs. *Brilliant, Lindsey, get yourself trapped between a tree and a weirdo.*

He slanted his head down to whisper in my ear. "Take it easy, darlin'. I won't harm ye."

Did I fear him? No. The realization shivered through me. I should fear him. I ought to hurl him away and flee back to the shop. But I didn't. Call it intuition or a sixth sense, but I understood he meant me no harm, even before he spoke the words.

Wait. I didn't believe in intuition. I'd gone insane. Snapped, at last.

He fingered a lock of my hair, studying it as if he'd never seen such a thing before. "Lovely. Like chestnuts powdered with gold dust." He switched his gaze to my eyes. "And your irises are pale as glacial ice, but with substance behind them. Fire. Spirit." He squinted, angling his head side to side. "Something else too. Can't quite place it. An energy bubbling up from a hidden well."

"Cut the poetics, pal." Wow, I'd actually sounded forceful. I tried to glare at him, but chewing the inside of my cheek probably ruined the effect. My ears rang and I suddenly realized I'd forgotten to breathe. "What on earth are you?"

He clapped his palms on the tree, straddling my shoulders. His body radiated heat. It poured over me like liquid sunshine. I sucked in a breath. The scent of him devoured my senses—an earthy tang, underlaid with exotic spice and a sharp sweetness that evoked thunderstorms. His breath whispered over my lips. "What are *you*?"

"Uh…" I squirmed. "I'm a woman, a human being, like you."

He chuckled. "We are nothing alike."

His laughter twanged a nerve inside me, breaking the spell. I blinked three times and hauled in a deep breath, letting it out slowly, overcome by the need to clear my senses. I stared at his chest, desperate to banish all thoughts of the supernatural. I needed to get back to the interrogation. "A man is dead. You must've seen something. Don't you care about that, or anything?"

"Another question."

"Which you aren't answering. Again."

"I regret I'm unable to become involved in mortal affairs."

"Mortal affairs?" I shook my head, dumbfounded. "How can you be so heartless?"

A strange expression flickered across his features and he bowed his head. "Because I am. You would do well to stay away from me and my kind."

His kind? That implied he was—No. Oh-no-no, I would not go there. I cleared my throat. "*You* approached *me*."

He looked up, but his shoulders slumped. "Alas, I don't always do as I should."

"Don't you feel anything?"

"This has nothing to do with emotions." He rubbed my hair between his thumb and forefinger, his attention riveted to the lock. "But to answer your question, I do feel. More than I should, in fact."

I craned my neck to scrutinize him across the six-inch gap in our heights. A tightening around his eyes, coupled with a falter in his smile, led me to believe—or maybe hope—he did feel. He bent his head to peer at me. Those eyes. They smoldered from within. Shades of gold, bronze, and silver swirled inside the irises. No one's eyes swirled. But heaven almighty, his did.

He dropped my hair. "Have ye lost the power of speech, love?"

"N-no. Why?"

His tone rife with amusement, he asked, "Don't ye ever speak a declarative sentence?"

I snapped my spine straight, glared into his supernatural eyes, and said, "You're an obnoxious twit. How's that for declarative?"

"You astound me with your charm and slay me with your wit."

Slay. The word plucked me out of this bizarre conversation and back to the reality of why I'd pursued this man in the first place. Someone was dead. My damn intuition, or whatever it was, refused to let me believe he had killed the shoplifter, but I must get an answer from him. A concrete, rational answer. "Did you kill him?"

The arrogance flooded out of the stranger's expression. His lips angled downward in a slight frown. "Kill him? Oh, you mean the poor fellow out there."

He tipped his head back and to the side, indicating the trail through the woods.

"Yeah," I said. "I mean the guy with his head bashed in. The one lying dead at the scene you fled from—which is a crime, by the way."

At least I thought it was. I didn't know for sure, but the statement sounded good.

"I'm not bound by your rules."

"They aren't my rules. It's the law."

"Not my law." He jerked his head, glancing past me, past the tree. I listened, but my ears detected nothing except the soft rumble of the falls and the thudding of my own heart. His gaze shifted to the water. "I wish I could assist you, but I'm afraid I must go."

"You can't. We have to call the police."

He pushed away from the tree. "Sorry, darlin'. Can't help ye with that."

"You must've seen something."

He shrugged, his shoulders flexing. "I saw what you saw, nothing more."

"You have to stick around and tell the police your story."

Humor glinted in his eyes and his lips twitched into a half-repressed smirk. "My presence would do nothing to help the situation. Take my word on that."

Well, he did have a point. A half-naked man with freaky eyes corroborating my story probably wouldn't console the sheriff. Oh hell, given my relationship with the sheriff, he'd slap cuffs on me for being in the vicinity of trees, never mind my stumbling onto a corpse.

The stranger swung his head to the left, diving his face into my hair, and inhaled deeply. Sniffing my hair? What the hell? I slapped my palms on his chest and shoved. He didn't budge. I pushed harder, but I might as well have wrestled with a giant redwood.

He lifted his head, eyes clouding with confusion. "How odd. I thought it was your hair, but it isn't. You smell of—I must've imagined it."

"I don't understand a word you've said."

He fingered my hair, then withdrew his hand. "At least I succeeded in distracting you from the poor dead fellow."

The stranger pulled back and opened one palm. A flower appeared there, as if by magic. A daylily, its white petals blushed with pink. His other hand spread open, revealing my gun balanced on his palm. He pressed the derringer into my hand and curled my fingers around it. "Thought ye might like to have this."

I stared at him. "Uh…yeah."

He tucked the flower behind my ear, planted a kiss on my forehead, hopped back a step, and vanished.

A gasp burst out of me. He hadn't scampered away, or even flown up into the sky. He had vanished. Poof. Gone before I could blink. A dream? A hallucination?

Great. I *was* insane.

I tossed the flower on the ground and blazed down the trail, back toward the shop. Where the path forked, heading off into the woods, I halted. A chill sprouted in my chest. It branched out until the tendrils invaded every cell in in body. I swiveled my head—and gasped again.

The dead man had vanished.

CHAPTER THREE

A COPPERY ODOR BLUSTERED OVER ME ON THE WIND AS I CROUCHED over the blood stain. I gagged and coughed, one hand flying up to cover my nose and mouth. My brain refused to process anything I'd experienced since leaving the shop. I squeezed my eyes shut, took long breaths until my ears stopped ringing, and stared at the stain again. The blood proved a corpse had rested here. I hadn't imagined it.

Well, it proved *something* bled here.

I'd touched the body. Now it had vanished, or been moved. Without a witness to corroborate my story, no one would buy it. I had to report it anyway. *Suck it up, Lindsey.*

Holstering the derringer inside my waistband, I spotted my phone on the ground where I'd dropped it and snatched it up.

Sirens wailed, muted as if far away. I knew the woods could swallow sounds, tricking the ear into believing the source lay distant. The cops might've been coming for me, or they might be rushing somewhere else, called out on another matter. I punched 9-1-1 into my phone.

The crack of a twig snapping reverberated off the trees. Someone was coming.

My went dry. I pulled in a breath, counting to ten as I released it. A tourist, that's who approached from down the trail. A goofball intent on visiting the vortex.

The breeze kissed my face. A familiar scent teased my senses. Earth and thunderstorms—and blood.

I bit down hard on my lower lip. A salty, metallic flavor seeped onto my tongue and I ran my finger across my lip. Blood slicked my fingertip. Great. I really would have blood on my hands when the sheriff arrived. I licked it off, wiped my hands on my jeans, and flipped my phone open.

Darkness draped over me. I hesitated, my finger hovering over the keys.

"What the blazes are you doing?"

The gruff voice arrowed straight into my chest. I jerked my head up, yet even before my eyes met his, I knew whose face I'd see. My heart pounded against my ribs, the air froze in my lungs, and every muscle in my body turned rigid. I clapped the phone shut.

Sheriff Travis Blackwell towered over me from several feet away, the apex of his shadow engulfing me. The sunlight imbued his dirty blond hair with a harsh glint, like tarnished gold. When he planted his hands on his hips, the dark brown shirt of his uniform stretched taut over his broad shoulders and chest. His tan pants mirrored the color of the dry earth. In one sinewy hand, he held a black box by its handle.

"Were you planning on calling me?" His Texas drawl reshaped the words.

I stretched my neck back to meet his gaze. He squinted his slate-gray eyes at me, head listing to the side, lips compressed. Sunlight glanced off his badge, spearing my eyes. My brain struggled to form coherent thoughts, but my words emerged in disjointed clumps. "Yes. I was. Going to report. Uh, what happened."

"Somebody beat you to it."

One of his deputies raced up behind him. Kal Ruoho was breathing hard, his face red.

"Get back to the shop," Travis told him, setting his black box on the ground. "Interview the staff."

The staff consisted of me, Stan, and Stan's brittle wife who filled in on my days off. Travis knew this, yet he made it sound like his deputy would have a passel of employees to question.

Kal trotted back toward the shop.

Travis settled a hand on the gun strapped to his belt. "Who'd you kill this time, Lindsey?"

Anger seared through me, evaporating my anxiety. Travis must've had magical powers, the way he always turned up at the worst moments in my life. But how in the fires of damnation did he hear about the body?

I heaved myself to my feet and, hands on hips, drummed my fingers. "What are you doing here?"

His mouth twitched downward. His Texas twang thickened a little when he said, "My oh my, ain't this the highlight of my day. Seeing the sweetheart of Mandan County."

Though I didn't overlook the sarcasm in his tone, I did let it go this time. After all, I'd torn him away from the rampant crime in the tiny village of Lutin Falls, the county seat ten miles from here, where right now someone was probably stepping on an endangered wildflower. "Why are you here?"

He slanted his head and rolled his eyes toward the ground. The blood stain. Right. "I assume that's the alleged crime scene."

"It's not alleged. I saw the body." How he knew about it mystified me. "Who called you?"

"Anonymous tip. The caller said you killed a man. That true?"

"Of course not."

"Not like it'd be the first time."

He locked his burly arms over his chest, tilting forward just enough to project menace. I stiffened. Tried not to, but this man had a way of triggering my fight-or-flight instinct. My stomach churned and the sourness of bile rose into my mouth. *Dammit.* I'd sworn Travis would never intimidate me again.

Yeah. How many times had I vowed that? Ten, twenty, a million?

"The better question," he said, "is why didn't you call it in?"

He shifted his weight. The .40-caliber Sig Sauer strapped to his hip bounced. I scratched my arm and stared at the white bark peeling away from a birch tree, but my gaze drifted back to the sheriff.

Travis cleared his throat, scowling. "Well? What's your excuse this time, Porter?"

I ground my teeth. Travis had used my last name, like he was interrogating a damn suspect. I cranked my face into a glower of my own. "I don't need an excuse. As usual, I've done nothing wrong." I jabbed a finger toward the blood stain. "I found a dead body there."

He quirked an eyebrow. "An invisible dead body?"

"No. Someone took it."

"Who? The corpse fairy?" His lips contorted, as if he struggled not to laugh. "How much cash you get for tucking a dead body under your pillow?"

Jackass. I choked down the word and said, "I left for a minute and when I came back, it was gone."

"Where in tarnation did you go?"

Aw hell. I ransacked my brain for an explanation, because no way could I tell him the truth. I hugged myself and fixated on the birch tree again.

"Spit it out," he said.

"Um, I..." *Took off after a half-naked man I thought might've been the murderer, but he vanished, and then he came back and sniffed my hair. You understand, right?* Sure, I'd say that. A straitjacket might flatter my figure. "I thought I saw someone fleeing the scene."

Good. That almost made sense.

He scrutinized me, squinting again. "Hmmm."

I dropped my arms and huffed a breath out my nose. "What do you mean *hmmm*?"

"Your story sounds like a load of horse shit." He narrowed his eyes. "Ain't like this is the first time I found you standing over a blood stain yammering about a disappearing victim."

My nerves bristled, as if he'd scraped a stiff brush up my spine. "There was a body, goddammit."

His expression blanked. His eyes widened, though only for a second. My glacial tone had shocked me too. Though he tried to frown, his eyes crinkled with a repressed smile. "The ice princess returns. Or maybe she never left, huh?"

The wind rustled the trees and the aspen leaves sizzled with a phantom fire. My hair feathered across my face, tickling my nose. I sneezed.

"Gesundheit," Travis said.

"Thanks." Why on earth was he being polite, I wondered, but discarded the thought. "Can I go, please? I have a job, you know."

He lodged one hand on his cocked hip. "I see a dark patch over there that might be trace evidence. I got a tip there was a murder committed and I find you admiring the crime scene."

A viscous chill oozed over my skin. *I can't go through this again, please no.*

"Listen up, Porter. Things'll go a lot easier on you if you tell me what you did with the body."

"You really think I could drag a body off by myself?"

He shrugged one shoulder. "Maybe you got an accomplice. Or maybe you planted some fake blood here and called in the tip yourself, just to rile me up. The caller had a funny voice that coulda been a man or a woman."

"Don't be ridiculous. There was a body."

"Nobody but you saw the alleged victim."

I clenched my teeth so hard pangs jolted through my jaw. "The body was real. I can't help that no one else noticed the man bleeding to death on the trail."

Travis blew out a breath, his cheeks swelling and deflating. "That's all you got for me?"

"Yes."

"All right then." He whipped a pair of handcuffs from his belt. "I'm taking you in for questioning."

I shuffled backward two steps, checking left and right for an escape route. The trail led to the falls or back to the shop, and tearing off into the woods without a map or GPS terrified me more than a jail cell.

"I got no choice," Travis said, and sounded almost sorry about it. "See, I know you're not telling me everything. There's been a report of a death, so I gotta take some action."

The handcuffs glittered in the sunlight.

I flicked a finger toward them. "Are the cuffs necessary?"

"No, but it's more fun for me this way."

"You're a bastard."

His scowl slackened into a blank expression, his lips parting. His gaze zeroed in on a sight beyond my shoulder.

"Perhaps I can be of assistance," a cheerful Irish voice said.

My heart skipped. Anticipation chased across my skin. *Him.*

The stranger who'd sniffed my hair traipsed out of the woods behind me to halt at my side. His hand brushed against my wrist. A tingle coursed up my arm and outward into my body, suffusing me with his warmth. The scent of him enveloped me and every hair on my body prickled with awareness. I resisted the urge to glance at him. My strange, bronzed god.

Not that he was mine. We weren't…anything to each other. I didn't even like the guy, really. But I itched to peek at him, and so I risked a sideways glimpse. I choked on a breath. Instead of a loincloth, jeans and a cotton dress shirt cloaked his chiseled frame. The sun glistened on his dark hair, swept back into a conservative style. He winked at me.

Was I still hallucinating? Part of me prayed I was, since that would make the dead body a figment of my mind too.

The stranger slipped his right arm around my waist. His hand bumped my gun and he ran his middle finger around the outline. His touch teased my skin through the fabric of my shirt. He drew me close, tucking me into the crook of his shoulder. Though I tried to wriggle free, but he kept his arm around me in a hold more supportive than threatening, as if we were intimately familiar with each other.

I flitted my gaze from the stranger to Travis. Wait a minute. Travis saw the other man. My Tarzan fantasy was real? Relief sluiced through me, but panic swept in behind it. There was, after all, the minor matter of the wayward corpse.

His fingers moved over my hip in a light circles. *Real.* I wasn't totally insane, at least.

Travis eyed my new friend with his best policeman glare. "Who are you?"

"Nevan. And you?"

"Sheriff Travis Blackwell. You got a last name, buddy?"

"I demand to know why you are threatening Lindsey."

Nevan knew my name? Duh, he must've overheard Travis using it. I poked Nevan with my elbow and muttered under my breath, "Shut up and let me go. I can handle this."

He ignored me and spoke to Travis. "While you've been harassing my Lindsey, I've been searching for the body."

Travis's gaze bored into me for a few seconds, then he squinted at Nevan. "You saw the alleged victim?"

"Indeed," Nevan said. "I saw the poor dead fellow. Lindsey's telling the truth about that."

Travis swung his attention back to me. "Is she now."

"Absolutely," Nevan said.

"Did you see an individual fleeing the scene?"

"I did."

Travis rammed his tongue into his cheek. His gaze never vacillated from me, though he aimed his words at Nevan. "Can you describe the suspect?"

"Not really. We saw the back of him, nothing more."

"Uh-huh. And what happened to the body?"

"Not a clue," Nevan said, his expression overflowing with innocence.

Travis glowered at him with such ferocity I expected flames to shoot out of the sheriff's eyes. Nevan matched Travis's eye contact with unwavering intensity, yet managed to hold onto his look of utter innocence.

I waved my hand between the men's faces. When Travis rotated his eyes toward me, I asked, "Are we done here?"

"Hardly," Travis said. "You're still a suspect."

"I didn't do anything."

"Gotta take you in for questioning. None of this adds up and I want some frigging answers. From both of you."

My mystery man bounced on his heels, jostling me against his firm torso. My stomach fluttered, but I coerced a calm demeanor from my traitorous body. His voice took on a decisive edge, though somehow he imbued his words with politeness. "Lindsey has answered enough of your questions."

Travis curled his lip at Nevan.

I jabbed a finger in Nevan's side. He either didn't notice or didn't care. I poked him again and hissed out the side of my mouth, "Cut it out. You're not helping."

He ignored me. Again.

Travis crouched beside the blood stain. He cracked open the black box he'd brought, which held plastic bags and other equipment.

I rose onto tiptoes for a better angle. "What are you doing?"

"Collecting evidence." He donned a pair of latex gloves and set about his work. When he'd finished gathering a sample of the blood-soaked dirt, he closed up his kit and rose. "No tire tracks or drag marks, no footprints other than yours."

No footprints? But Nevan had run past the body. *Impossible.*

Travis sighed. "You're coming with me, Lindsey."

"But—"

Kal jogged up the trail, halting at the edge of the clearing. Travis held up one finger to me. "Wait here." His lip curled once more as he told Nevan, "That means you too."

Travis retreated to the clearing's edge to chat with Kal, their backs to us, their voices too indistinct to make out.

I murmured to Nevan, "Thank you."

"Are you expressing gratitude to me?" Surprise tinged his voice.

"Yes. Thank you for sticking up for me with Travis."

"You're most welcome." He hesitated, and when he spoke again, I swore I detected a note of anxiety in his voice. "But in the future, take care when thanking me. It may have unforeseen consequences."

"Such as?"

Another pause. "Take my word for it, that's all I ask."

His clothes dissolved. No other way to describe it. They simply evaporated into nothing—save for the loincloth, which coalesced around his hips. His skin burned hot against mine as his arm shifted up to my shoulders and one fingertip traced a circular path on my upper arm, carving a trail of sensation in its wake. It felt so good I wanted to snuggle into him, lost to the tingle his touch ignited.

No. I did *not* want to.

I could not be attracted to a man I'd just met who had swirling eyes and the ability to poof in and out of view, who was arrogant and annoyed me. Then again, he had lured me away from the dead man because I seemed upset. And he distracted me from the problem until I calmed down. And he saved me from cracking my skull on a huge rock. He stood up for me with Travis too. Maybe I did know a little bit about him.

But not nearly enough.

I disentangled myself from his hold, scurried a few steps away, and spun to confront him. "Why did you do it?"

He sauntered to the nearest tree, a couple yards away, and leaned his long body against the trunk. "You'll have to be a bit more specific, love, if you want me to answer."

"Are you saying you will answer my questions?"

"Possibly." He raked a hand through his hair and his biceps bulged from the movement. His voice dropped to a husky whisper. "If you're nice to me."

"Nice?" I stomped closer. "What the hell do you mean?"

"If you'd quit swearing at me, that'd be a start."

I clenched my hands into tight fists. My nails dug into my palms and pain shot through my knuckles. "I'm so sorry if my language offends you. I'd think a guy who can poof in and out of sight would have a thicker skin."

"My, but you are fetching when you're vexed."

I scrunched my lips, fuming with an anger rooted in more than this man's sarcastic, blasé attitude. Yet I had seen glimmers of deeper emotions under the surface, which made me wonder if his nonchalance was a cover. For what, though?

He arched an eyebrow. "Are ye all right?"

"Fine." I forced my hands to unclench. "What are you?"

"A man. Has it been so long since ye had one that you're unsure?"

"I—wh—" My thoughts disintegrated, but I gathered the bits and pieced them back together. My brain ached from the effort. "My personal life is none of your business."

He pushed away from the tree. Strode toward me. Stared into my eyes. The molten metal of his irises feathered a tingle down my spine.

I floundered backward. "What do you want from me?"

"To understand," he said in a sultry tone, as his eyes towed me down into their depths. "You intrigue me and I must deduce why."

"Huh?"

His gaze stroked over me from head to toe. "Shall we play, darlin'?"

"This isn't a game."

"It could be. If you'd loosen up a bit."

"Loosen up?" The spell shattered, I shot my best glare at him. "Forgive me if I have trouble relaxing around a complete stranger."

"It was a suggestion, not a command. Though I cannot comprehend how a person could be so tense and not snap like a twig underfoot."

I had the most ridiculous urge to explain myself, but I bit it back. "This conversation is over. Thanks for the assist, but I hope I never see you again."

His face pinched and he glanced away. When he turned back to me, the nonchalance swept in again. "I suppose you'll be returning to the shop then?"

"Not that it's any of your business, but I plan to scarf down an insanely fattening lunch, gain five pounds in the process, and then go back to work and pretend none of this ever happened."

"Your friend the sheriff seems intent on detaining you."

"He's not m—Ugh, forget it. Maybe I can talk him out of arresting me." Riiiight. And then I'd take my pet unicorn for a stroll.

Amusement tugged at one corner of Nevan's mouth. "Good luck with that, darlin'."

I whirled on my heels and stomped toward Travis. I felt Nevan's gaze tracking me, like a warm breeze tickling the back of my neck. *Don't look back, just keep walking.*

A raven squawked overhead.

I shielded my eyes to spy the bird swooping in front of the sun. Its head angled in my direction, those coal-dark eyes sharp on me. I had the strange sensation the bird was sizing me up.

The raven flew out of sight.

I tapped Travis on the shoulder. He started, half turning toward me. How he missed the weirdness unfolding right behind him baffled me, but I didn't have time to worry about that. I held out my hands, wrists together. Right now, a jail cell sounded like a haven from the insanity around me. The supernatural around me. "Arrest me or let me go, please."

Travis's brows shot up. He nodded to Kal, who set off down the trail toward the shop. Travis hooked the cuffs around my wrists, each locking shut with a metallic *snick*. My stomach twisted. My fingers grew cold, despite the sweltering day.

"You ain't under arrest—yet." Travis placed a hand on my shoulder to guide me down the path in front of him. "But I am taking you in."

A pang tightened the back of my throat.

Travis's brow furrowed, his gaze scanning the woods behind us. "Where'd your friend go?"

Good question. Nevan was gone, again. "He had to leave. Urgent personal business."

"How the hell'd he get past me and—Never mind." He cursed under his breath. "I'll track him down if I have to comb the whole county to do it."

I bowed my head. A bead of sweat rolled down my temple to splat onto my chest.

Travis gave me a little shove, urging me to move faster. "You won't see the sun again, Porter, till I get answers to every damn one of my questions."

—

"COULDN'T FIND A BODY, IF THERE EVER WAS ONE," TRAVIS SNARLED. HE slammed the driver's door of the vehicle. A sticky breeze surged in through the open windows. I slumped into the backseat, a sour taste infiltrating my mouth. He'd left me here for an hour—inside his Ford Expedition marked with the sheriff's logo, branding me a suspicious character by association—while he, Kal, and Stan searched for the missing corpse.

They found nothing. No body, no tracks, no evidence aside from the blood stain. For a moment, I feared I'd imagined the whole incident. But Travis had met Nevan, which meant I wasn't crazy. Probably. Hormone-addled, yes. Crazy, not so much.

Revving the engine, Travis rolled up the windows as the air conditioner rushed cool air through the car. "I'm sending the blood sample off to the state lab for analysis. If it comes back as porcupine, you're in big trouble for wasting police time."

"There was a body." My attention wandered to the rear of the rock shop and the woods beyond it. I pitched sideways, straining for a better view. "Nevan corroborated my story, remember?"

He twisted around to nail those cool, gray eyes on me. "Yeah, I'm sure your boyfriend wouldn't lie for you or anything."

"Nevan is not—" I'd almost blurted out he wasn't my boyfriend. *Don't tell him the truth, dummy, it'll blow your alibi.* Yeah, because I had such an ironclad one. "Nevan's not a liar."

But I was. Nevan hadn't exactly lied to me. He refused to tell me much of anything.

Travis's lips flattened into a thin line. He let out an exasperated sigh. "I don't get it. Why'd you hook up with a sleaze like Nivea?"

I clamped my lips between my teeth for a second to avoid laughing. "His name is Nevan. And it's none of your business who I hook up with."

Jeez. For the first time in my life, I'd uttered the phrase "hook up." Not that I'd done any such thing.

"Guess you're right," Travis said. "And I reckon I should worry more about what you'll do to him than what he'll do to you."

"You have no clue what really happened with Calder."

"Enlighten me."

I ground my teeth, which only made my jaw ache.

He draped one wrist over the steering wheel, his fingers coiled into his palm. "No body, no crime. If you won't talk, I can't help."

I fidgeted, the cuffs biting into my wrists. "I didn't ask for your help."

"But ya sure as hellfire need it."

Maybe I did need help, but I positively did not want *his* assistance. So I changed the subject. "Why did you follow me here?"

"Somebody called in a tip, Porter."

"No. Why did you follow me to Michigan?" I'd moved here to get away from the Blackwell clan and everything I'd suffered in Texas. Six months after I came here, Travis showed up and wouldn't explain why or how he'd found me. "How'd you even track me down?"

He scratched his neck, eyes averted. "I'm a cop, Lindsey, and you ain't exactly an experienced criminal. Tracking you down wasn't that complicated."

"Why bother? You hate me." I'd avoided asking him for three years, because I avoided contact with him as much as possible and I avoided conversation with him at all costs. He might think he wanted the truth about his brother, but he'd never believe me if I told him what Calder had done.

Travis stared into space for several seconds, while I squirmed in an attempt to scratch an itch on my back by rubbing it against the seat. At last, he looked at me over his shoulder. "I gotta protect the good citizens of Mandan County from the likes of you."

He steered the vehicle out of the parking lot onto the highway, taking me back to his office for an interrogation. I glanced behind the car, into the woods. My life had changed irrevocably and I still had no idea how or why.

I wrinkled my nose at a strange odor wafting over me, something like cat urine but not quite. Did Travis never clean this car?

A sensation of pressure slithered down my neck, almost like fingertips closing around my throat. Tighter. Tighter. I fought for breath but couldn't budge a muscle. My pulse thundered in my ears. In the rearview mirror, Travis's eyes stayed focused on the road ahead. The pressure choked my throat and a voice growled in my ear.

"Mine forever, sweet thing, or no one's."

Dark splotches encroached on my vision. I struggled to shout for help, but it came out as a strangled hiccup.

The phantom fingers sprang free of my neck. I sucked in a wheezing breath.

"You okay back there?" Travis asked, studying me in the rearview mirror.

I coughed, rubbed my eyes with the back of my hand, and drew in a slow breath. "Just got a little overheated, I think."

He cranked up the AC and cool air flooded into the backseat. The blessed relief of it calmed my nerves, but a lingering doubt niggled at me. Maybe I'd had a panic attack due to the stress of the day, or my mind snapped under the strain of paranormal shenanigans. I might've believed that, except the words I'd heard a moment ago were familiar. Calder Blackwell issued the same threat on the night that destroyed my life.

I tucked my hands between my thighs, my fingers suddenly chilled. He wasn't here. He couldn't be.

Calder had been dead for three years.

CHAPTER FOUR

THE SHADE OF A TALL ASPEN TREE BLANKETED ME, SHIELDING MY SKIN from the sun's heat. With the late-afternoon air temperature in the high eighties, though, and the humidity almost as high, sweat oozed out of my pores to dampen my flesh and hair. I rested against the tree trunk, an uneaten turkey sandwich in my hand and an unopened bag of baked potato chips on my thigh.

Travis had relented on his promise I wouldn't see the sun again. After three hours of interrogation, he'd let me go. I honestly couldn't provide the answers he wanted, because I had no clue what was going on. The memory of those hours replayed in my mind, still fresh. Travis had ordered me to sit in a chair beside his desk, which abutted the wall, and then he dragged a folding chair in front of me, flipped it around, and settled his large body onto it with his forearms resting on the back. His knees grazed mine.

Once he uncuffed my wrists, Travis started in on me. "Come on, Lindsey. Fess up."

"To what? I didn't even know the guy."

His fingers moved as he spoke, punctuating his words. "I'm not buying any of this. You were first on the scene and all you can tell me is some *person* fled the scene."

"Nevan told you. He saw the suspect."

"Right." Travis elongated the syllable into a sarcastic insinuation. "Nevan. There's a high-quality witness. He skedaddled and left you high and dry."

He kind of had. But as Nevan had warned me, his presence did nothing to alleviate my predicament. Instead, he chafed the sheriff even more. There in his office, Travis's questions had run in circles, a tornado of accusations and demands for answers I either didn't know or didn't dare give.

"Who's the suspect you claim fled the scene?"

"Are you sure the alleged victim was dead?"

"Where did the body go?"

"How come you didn't call nine-one-one?"

"If somebody fled, why aren't there any footprints besides yours?"

He'd insisted on verifying I had a permit to carry a handgun, though he damn well knew I did, adding more time to the ordeal.

The grumble of car engines roused me from the memories. The noise originated just over a little rise that hid the shop building from my view. Customers rarely visited this part of the woods, because the only trail leading to it was a narrow track worn down by deer. This was my little sanctuary. Every day, I tromped out here on my lunch break to escape the stress of work—and the incessant watchfulness of Stan Lagorio. Today, Stan had given me honest-to-God permission to take a late lunch, even though I'd been gone for hours in the middle of my shift. He knew the sheriff had taken me in for questioning and I swore he was…sympathetic.

The world really had flipped upside down and inside out.

For the umpteenth time, I lifted the sandwich to my mouth. Although my stomach growled at the prospect of food, I stared at the layers of meat and cheese with a growing sensation of nausea. I dropped my hand to my lap.

"Your meal doesn't look particularly fattening."

The sandwich popped out of my grasp as I jumped at the masculine voice emanating from behind me. The sandwich flew apart. The bread landed on the grass while the meat and cheese plopped onto my jeans.

Nevan ambled from behind the tree and halted near my feet. "Not that I have much experience with mortal food, but from what I've seen, that sort of meal is considered healthy."

"Could you please quit scaring the daylights out of me?"

"I do apologize. I had no intention of frightening you."

"Hmph." I plucked the tatters of my sandwich off the ground and tried to reassemble it. "What do you want this time?"

"I see your gratitude has waned."

Flicking bits of grass from the sandwich, I raised it for a bite. The scent of turkey and swiss cheese wafted into my nostrils and my gorge rose in my throat. I stuffed the sandwich back into its plastic bag. "I was grateful, yes, but that's done and gone. You split before Travis could interrogate you and he took his frustration out on me."

"I'm deeply sorry for abandoning you."

"Yeah, whatever." I played with the zipper seal on my sandwich bag. "Why are you here?"

"To be quite honest, I'm not certain."

I glanced up at him. Big mistake.

From this angle, his loincloth provided me with a glimpse of what lay beneath it. Just a glimpse. A hint of flesh. But I recognized the shape of the flesh and my cheeks flamed at the realization. I'd caught a peek at his manly parts.

Squeezing my eyes shut, I clamped my lips between my teeth. The spark of pain did nothing to free me from the knowledge of what I'd seen. Almost seen. Sort of seen. Oh jeez. Why me? Why did I have to stumble over a tele-porting corpse? And out of all the billions of women on earth, why did I have to acquire a supernatural stalker who pranced around in next to nothing?

Burying my face in my hands, I groaned. The heat of my blush warmed my fingers.

"Are ye not well, darlin'?" His voice sounded too close.

I peeked out between my fingers. He was crouching so near me I could've extended one finger to poke his nose. His face hovered inches from my hands, his expression concerned. He laid a hand on my upper arm, the touch light and casual, but it stirred something inside me. A want I'd sup-pressed for too long. The sensation wasn't sexual, not entirely. I longed for more than a kiss or a sensual caress. I longed for connection, belonging, for someone to need me. But a stranger could not need me.

"Lindsey."

"Everything's fine." My hands muffled my voice.

"Why, then, are you hiding in this manner?"

"Um…" *Blast it all.* I was acting like a teenager who'd sneaked into her first R-rated movie with nudity and sexual content. I lowered my hands, the fire in my cheeks somewhat abated. "Really, I'm fine. Thank you for your concern."

His eyes widened a hair, enough to remind me of what he'd said earlier about thanking him. The statement had made no sense. Gratitude exacted no consequences, at least none so dire it justified his fear. Then again, I was talking to a half-naked man who popped into and out of sight whenever he felt like it.

I drew my knees to my chest, erecting a barrier between us. "Sorry. I know you hate it when I say thank you."

He sat back on his heels. "On the contrary, I enjoy your gratitude."

A hint of sensuality warmed his tone. I hugged my knees. "But you said I shouldn't be grateful. It would have unforeseen consequences."

"I said you should take care when expressing gratitude to me. Feel as grate-ful as you wish, but refrain from voicing it. You'd likely come to regret it."

"That makes no sense. If I'm grateful, I say it and I don't backpedal later."

"You misunderstand." He edged closer, his firm chest bumping my knees. "I'm not suggesting you'll regret thanking me. I'm saying you'll re-gret letting me know you're appreciative."

I cracked my mouth open, tapping my tongue on the bottoms of my front teeth. "I don't get it. What is the big deal about being polite?"

His voice grew wistful. "Alas, you may never understand the rules of my world. I'm not at all sure I'd want you to."

I had the weirdest urge to slide my fingers through the dark, sleek curls tum-bling over his ears. "You keep saying your world, like we live on different planets."

He tilted his head up, his eyes seeking mine. "Not different planets. Separate realms of reality."

"You've got to be joking."

"Ah, but you know I'm not." He released my arms, but tension lingered in his body. "I should have said nothing. Don't know what I was thinking."

"Hmm."

He canted his head, regarding me with curiosity. "Afraid I don't understand your noises, love."

"Sounded an awful lot like you were apologizing for telling me the truth."

"Yes, I was. I should never have told you anything."

I snorted. "That's rich. You apologize for honesty, but not for evasion."

His body shifted as he settled onto his buttocks, one leg outstretched and the other bent to support his arm. The pose also shifted his loincloth, but I resisted the temptation to look. The last thing I needed was my cheeks on fire again.

Nevan balanced his wrist on his knee. His fingers rose and fell like swells on the ocean. "What would you have me do then?"

Another snort ripped out of me. I really couldn't control it. How could any man be so dense? I stretched my legs out alongside him, clasping my hands on my lap. "If you want me to be nicer to you, then try being a little more cooperative with me."

"I can't."

A half-strangled roar of frustration erupted out of me and I threw my hands in the air. "You follow me around but won't explain anything. Do you have any idea how infuriating that is?"

He tilted his head, eyes alight. "I'm beginning to see."

A shorter roar broke out of me and incited a closed-mouth smile from him. I seized my bag of chips and tore it open. Crispy potato slices sprayed up, pattering down on my jeans and the grass.

Nevan chuckled. Little stars glittered in the whorls of his eyes.

I crushed the now-empty bag in my fist and tossed it aside. The foil unraveled with a crinkling noise. "Why do you keep showing up?"

He shrugged. "You intrigue me."

"I'm not that interesting."

He stretched his foot out to nudge my calf. His bare sole was dirty, but then he did apparently live in the woods. "I disagree. You are the most unusual mortal I've ever encountered."

Unusual? Intriguing? Baloney. I was the most boring person on the planet, a hermit nobody liked. Except my family. And this…man, or whatever he was.

Another term he'd used circled back around to the front of my thoughts. "You called me a mortal, and earlier you said something about mortal affairs. But everybody's a mor—" The words died on my tongue, annihilated by an insane revelation. "You can't mean that you…"

"At last you're beginning to see."

"No. It's not possible." I clung to my preconceptions for one second longer, then I flung them out into the universe. "You're immortal."

Nevan's smile was mischievous. "I am immortal, yes."

My thoughts floundered. I opened and closed my mouth, shook my head, and gaped some more at the creature seated across from me. No. Not a creature. I had to think of him as a man, albeit one with incredible powers, because the alternative was terrifying.

I resorted to my comfort zone—asking annoying questions. "Are you really Irish?"

"Well now, I was born on the island currently known as Ireland. But I'm more of an ancestor to the humans living there today."

"Ancestor?" The earth wobbled under me. I clutched at the grass, my nails cutting into the blades, bleeding moisture from them. "How old—"

"Tell me about yourself. Where do you hail from? This place?" He made a sweeping gesture with his arm.

"I'm from nowhere. My family moved around a lot for my dad's work."

"Tell me more. I'm enthralled."

I rolled my eyes. "You are so full of it."

"At times, I'll admit. But not now." He settled a hand on my knee and squeezed lightly. The warmth of his flesh penetrated my jeans. "Do you see your family often?"

"No." An ache pulsed in my chest. "I haven't seen them in over three years."

His hand slid a couple inches down my thigh, braced by his wrist on my knee. The action seemed unconscious, so I pushed aside the notion it meant anything. He tapped my thigh with one finger. "You miss them."

"Yeah." Why was I confessing all to him? I couldn't explain it, but talking to him eased some of the weight in my chest. "Every summer, they travel the country in a big RV. They keep wanting to visit me, but I put them off."

"Why is that?" He watched me with deep interest.

The paranoid part of me, admittedly sizable, wondered why he was asking these questions. "Enough about me. What does being immortal mean? You can't ever die?"

"I can." He wiggled his fingers, eliciting a tickle that spread up my thigh. "But if you're investigating ways to get rid of me, I'm afraid I'm rather difficult to kill."

His fingers. They teased.

"Please stop that." I reached for his hand, to shove it off, but he withdrew it before I could touch him. His intense scrutiny made my skin itch. I picked at the hem of my shirt. "Can anything hurt you?"

"I'm immortal, not invincible. Many things can injure me, but I heal rather swiftly." He hesitated, rubbing his chin. "To destroy me requires extraordinary power. An endued sword, a magically enhanced poison, things of that nature."

"Endued?" I asked.

"Invested with power."

I straightened my posture, which pressed my gun into my belly. I must've winced, because he surged toward me. In the space of a second, maybe less, he went from lounging at my feet to kneeling before me—too close, just like before.

His hand settled on my shoulder. "What causes you pain?"

"Nothing." I shrugged away from his hand. "And please quit touching me."

His lips twisted into a half frown.

I tried to look stern. "You're sure you don't know anything about the dead man."

"My, you are a suspicious one."

"You've got that backwards. You're the one acting sus—"

My phone warbled. I wrestled it out of my pocket. Nevan's gaze held mine as I muttered a greeting.

"Porter, where the hell are you?" Stan's voice bellowed through the speaker, rattling my whole ear, inside and out. "Your lunch break ended six minutes ago."

Checking the time on my phone, I saw he was right. "Be there in a minute."

I disconnected the call before he could scream at me anymore. My brain couldn't handle another shock. I hauled my body off the ground, brushing chips and bread crumbs off my jeans. Nevan rose too, his expression unreadable.

Shoulders hunched, I snatched up my lunch. "I have to go."

He executed a little flourish with his hand, the fingers curved toward the palm. Then he opened his hand to reveal a perfect peach seated in the center. He offered the fruit to me. "Do eat a little something before you go."

"Not hungry."

"Humor me."

I grumbled, but accepted the peach.

He nodded and vanished.

I didn't know which bothered me more—that he could disappear in an instant, or that I was getting used to it. My fingers rubbed across the peach's fuzzy surface. I lifted the fruit to my mouth. The fairy tale about Snow White sprang to mind, the poison apple glimmering in my inner vision. Poison peach? Maybe Nevan intended to drug me and abduct me to his "separate realm." Whatever that meant. Deciding I didn't care to find out, I tossed the peach into the grass.

Once again, Nevan had evaded my questions. He told me next to nothing, except how to kill him. I couldn't figure out why he divulged that info. Of course, it wasn't like I could visit MagicalDeathWeapons.com and order an endued sword.

As I topped the rise, headed down to the parking lot, a shadow swept across the ground in front of me. I looked up to see a raven swoop low overhead. Its wings pumped up and down, whooshing with each down stroke. For a second, I swore the bird locked eyes with me, its gaze probing, before it soared out of sight.

Twice today, I'd been convinced ravens were spying on me. The idea sounded ludicrous, but then so did vanishing corpses and men with swirling eyes.

I shivered, and trotted back to the store.

⁓

"THE HEALING VORTEX IS AROUND BACK. HEAD OUT THE BACK DOOR, through the rock garden, and follow the signs." Over the past two hours, I'd given the same directions to a dozen tourists and smiled at each and every one of them. My dimples hurt. I longed to rub my temples, to stop the seed of a headache from sprouting, but Stan was surveilling me from the other side of the shop. I pasted on my professional smile for the young couple standing across the counter from me. "When you're done there, please stop back in to check out our wide selection of native rocks and semiprecious gemstones."

The brunet man nodded. "Thanks, ma'am. We'll do that."

I opened my mouth respond but a visceral recognition of an alien presence shivered across the back of my neck and swept over my entire body, freezing my voice. My pulse pounded in my ears, drowning out the hum of the industrial fans and the chattering of my customers. The sensation unleashed a repressed memory. Calder Blackwell on top of me. Eyes wild. Teeth scraping down my throat.

"You okay, ma'am?"

I jolted back to reality. The brunet man gazed at me with concern in his topaz eyes. Heart still racing, I cranked up my smile again. "I'm fine. May I help you with anything else?"

What was wrong with me? Why did I keep feeling Calder's presence, to the point it hurled me back into the memories I'd locked away in the deepest vault of my mind? I scratched the back of my neck, but the icy tingle endured.

The man's blonde companion batted her mascara-laden eyelashes at him. Seriously, she batted them. And then she focused her denim-blue eyes on me. "Does, like, the vortex spin you? I get seasick."

I tilted my head. "Spin? Uh, not as far as I know. It's invisible."

A man sauntered into the shop through the front doors. The sun shimmered on his glossy, platinum-blond hair, a startling contrast to his olive skin. He scanned the shop, head swiveling, until his gaze landed on me. His lips skewed upward, but the expression failed to reach his eyes. The man rolled his broad shoulders back.

My scalp prickled. Though I tried to convince myself I was overreacting, I sneaked a hand to my waist to pat my gun through my shirt.

"But you can feel it, right?"

At the blonde girl's voice, I jumped. "What?"

"The vortex. You can feel what it does to you, right?"

"Uh-huh." I caught sight of Stan peripherally, his squinted eyes trained on me with the precision of a sniper sighting his target. No more sympathy for me, my duty called. I squared my shoulders and cleared my throat. "The healing energies wash over you like a cool breeze, infusing your body with ancient wisdom."

The brunet guy tucked an arm around the blonde. "Awesome."

Her gaze drifted past my head. Pencil-thin brows crinkled as she struggled to mouth the words emblazoned on the wall—Rock the Keweenaw, the Copper Country's Geology Superstore.

"What's a Kay-wee-now?" the girl asked.

I smiled again, for real this time. "It's pronounced Kee-win-aw. Don't worry, nobody gets it right the first time."

The girl's mouth hung ajar, like an oven door cracked open to release the hot air. Her brain must've overheated. "I thought we were in Michigan."

Oh jeez. Stan owed me more than minimum wage for this. "It's kind of confusing. The Keweenaw is part of Michigan's Upper Peninsula, but it's also a peninsula of its own." I pulled a map out of a drawer, unfolded it, and flipped it around to face the girl. I tapped a sliver of land protruding from the U.P.'s northwest corner. "Right here. It's attached to the U.P."

"Cool."

"Yeah, it is. And it's a beautiful place to be." Not to mention a great place to hide—until your past caught up with you and got himself elected sheriff. An image of the missing dead body ruptured my thoughts. Maybe this wasn't such a great hideout after all. I should've left the second Travis turned up in Lutin Falls, but something about this place kept me rooted to it, as if I belonged here. *Now you're believing in fate? So much for logical Lindsey.*

Vanishing corpses. Half-naked men who blipped in and out of sight. The fingers of Calder Blackwell, my dead fiancé, gripping my throat…Logic flew to Tahiti a while ago.

The brunet tugged his companion's arm. "Better get moving if we wanna see the vortex today."

The couple thanked me and walked out the back door. I ducked my head, rubbing my neck.

A shadow distended across the counter to engulf me.

I popped my head up. The man I'd seen in the doorway loomed before me, his smile duller now. His polo shirt and khaki pants barely contained his marble-hard muscles. His dark eyes, fixated on mine, glimmered with hints of metallic hues.

My feet tried to take a step back, propelled by the thumping of my heart, but I restrained the impulse. I was probably being paranoid. Nevan's eyes were metallic, but they swirled with vivid ribbons of color. And I never feared him. This man…

He bent his head left and right, scrutinizing me. "Are you all right?"

"Fine." I aimed to lay my hands on the counter but missed. My knuckles banged into the counter's edge. A little "ah" hissed out of me.

"You don't seem well."

His eyes, they curled out invisible tendrils that collared my neck, choking me. *For Christ's sake, rein it in.* I coughed, massaged my neck, and mustered a cheerful voice. "May I help you, sir?"

"Yes, you may." He leaned forward, his body a hulking mass. "Might I share a meal with you?"

"I don't date anymore."

"What a pity." Lips pinched, he tipped his head to stare down at me. He was huge, taller than Nevan. His focus migrated to my breasts, hidden beneath my blouse. "You are a tolerable specimen, worth bedding once, or perhaps twice."

"Excuse me?"

The metallic sparks in his eyes erupted into seething torrents of green and orange. "My watcher sees all. The guardian is bound to me, mortal. Remember that."

He winked out of existence, right there in front of me.

I swung my head left and right, desperate to spot him dashing out one of the doors. The huge fans blustering air through the shop seemed to roar like jet engines, jarring my eardrums. I stared numbly at the doorway, certain of nothing anymore. The man, or whatever he was, had vanished just like Nevan did.

Plunking my elbows onto the counter, I cradled my forehead in both hands. A guardian. A watcher. And one creepy son of a bitch who apparently wanted to "bed" me. This day kept getting better and better. The headache seed behind my eyes shot roots out to burrow into my brain. I shuffled out from behind the counter and headed toward the nearest aisle. The heat sweltered around me in an unwelcome embrace.

Movement flashed in the corner of my eye.

Across the store, an elderly gentleman observed me. Sunshine streamed in the open back door to bathe him in a golden, almost ethereal glow. The door swung shut behind him, severing the light. Cloaked in shadows, he scuffled forward, supported by a metal cane. His attention stayed fastened on me.

Though Stan had returned to his office, I recalled his command from earlier today that I get out to the vortex and inform our customers of its healing wonders. My feet heavy, I headed toward the back door. The old man's gaze transfixed me and goose bumps pricked my arms. I walked closer. And closer. He held his position, his face a mask of serenity. Closer. My shoes scraped on the rough concrete floor. The old man winked, a faint smile on his lips.

I bumbled into the corner of a display table, lost my footing, and flailed forward. My hands grasped the table's edge just in time, sparing me from smacking into the concrete face-first.

The old man took a step toward me, clutching his cane harder. "Are you all right, miss?"

He spoke without an accent, yet something in his voice twanged a memory inside me, though I couldn't latch onto it. With a clumsy effort, I righted myself. "Fine. I'm a klutz, that's all."

He moved forward another step. The sunlight from the front door struck his eyes.

My hand flew to my chest. *His eyes.* They burned a golden amber, as if lit from within. He stared at me with such intensity my breath caught in my throat. Shades of gold, bronze, and silver twirled in his irises. No. It couldn't be. But those eyes. They drilled into me, down to my very core. Into my heart, my soul.

Nevan. Somehow, he was the old man.

Footsteps clapped behind me. I whipped my head in that direction, in time to see the blonde girl I'd helped earlier, the one who wondered if the vortex spun you. She flapped a manicured hand at the old man. "Are you coming? I thought you wanted me to show you the vortex."

"I do," the old man replied. "Thank you, child."

The old man wandered past me, leaning on his cane with each step. He glanced at me as he shambled past. I stood immobile, my gaze trailing him out the door. It couldn't be Nevan. The man I'd met was young and virile, not elderly and frail. But it *was* Nevan.

I dashed out the door. My shoes cracked on the gravel. I didn't stop until I'd cleared the corner into the parking lot. At the far side of the building, the blonde tugged the old man's sleeve. He followed her down the path through the rock garden, and soon, the pines and blackberry bushes swallowed them.

Wind gusted over me. My hair fell into my eyes and I blew it aside.

Nevan had the power to alter his appearance. I shuddered. What else could he do? And what was he doing with the girl? If he hurt her...

Never trust a man.

I sprinted after them.

CHAPTER FIVE

A CARAMEL SCENT RUSHED OVER ME AS I PASSED A GROUP OF BLACK-berry bushes at the other side of the rock garden. Up ahead, through the bushes and trees, I glimpsed a blonde head.

Nevan would not hurt the girl. I wouldn't allow it. My hand instinctively went to my gun. Maybe I couldn't kill him, but I could damn sure injure him.

My pulse thundered. I pumped my legs faster, despite the pains in my thighs. *Got to catch up. Stop him, help her.* A small branch thwacked me in the face. The sting made me wince, but I forged onward. This girl wasn't me. Nevan wasn't Calder. I knew these facts, but none of it mattered. I had to stop him from—doing whatever the hell he was planning to do to her. I sped past the vortex and its stone benches. Feminine laughter echoed through the woods from ahead of me.

An instinct impelled me to glance at the spot where I'd found the dead man. My throat tightened, but I had no time to spare on those thoughts. I stopped at the railing beside the falls. Foam sprayed up to tick on my skin and clothes. Where were they?

Laughter. It bubbled out of the woods to the left of the falls. A narrow game trail wended through the trees there. I rocketed down it. Weeds lashed my legs and I raised my arms to block branches from hitting me. Partway down the trail, I halted. If I wanted to discover Nevan's true intentions, I ought to sneak up on him—conduct a little surveillance, catch him in the act. I might intervene before he…did whatever.

My heart pounded so hard I could barely breathe. I tiptoed down the trail. Voices murmured, too far away for me to make out words. Soon though, I spotted a clearing straight ahead and slowed my pace even more. I took care with each step, so I wouldn't snap a twig or smack a branch in my face again. At the clearing's edge, I ducked behind a thick aspen, peeking around its bulk.

Weeds, tall and fragile, quivered in the breeze. High above, a squirrel chattered a warning call. The blonde knelt on the soft grass on the opposite side of the clearing, her back to me. The "old man" leaned on his cane a few feet from her, near a fir tree.

The image of the old man crumbled away, revealing Nevan.

Holy heaven. What was he?

Nevan posed with one arm extended, his palm braced on the tree and one ankle crossed over the other. A shaft of sunlight blazed across his muscled chest.

He reclined his head, impassive. "Don't be afraid, Sandy. I mean ye no harm."

The gentleness of his tone didn't match his assumed posture. I studied him, noting the way his free hand clenched and loosened repeatedly. His shoulders were stiff and he avoided Sandy's gaze, his own darting here and there.

Sandy's features had slackened, her lips parted. She pitched forward, eyes large. Her full lips split into a dazed grin. "Whoa." She drew out the syllable into a long, breathless word. "What are you?"

"Ah…" He dragged a hand over his cheek. "We'll have time for that later."

Her grin mellowed. She undulated a little, like a cobra enthralled by a snake charmer.

Nevan coughed and scratched his head. I watched his chest inflate with a deep breath, which he let out little by little. I'd expected him to be confident and easygoing, as he had been with me. The man across the clearing from me behaved the way someone would if he were…ashamed.

No. I had to be misreading him.

With a quick nod, as if he'd reached a decision, Nevan closed the distance to Sandy. He cupped the girl's chin in his hand. "I need to ask you a question. Consider it carefully. Can ye do that?"

"Sure."

His long body descended as he knelt before her. Sandy's head blocked most of my view, so all I could glimpse was the top of his head. I must see his face. The reason baffled me, but the need clawed at my chest. I lowered into a crouch and crept around the clearing's edge, behind the trees and bushes, until I found a good vantage point. My skulking brought me closer to the duo, alongside them at slight angle that granted me a better view of her face than his. Sandy's pupils had dilated into black disks, nearly consuming her irises. Her hand rose to her throat and her fingers lightly caressed her flawless skin.

One corner of Nevan's mouth crimped downward.

Sandy, oblivious, puckered her face. "What's the question?"

His shoulders buckled forward. He ducked his head and his fingers dug into his thighs. I had the weirdest urge to hug him.

Dammit. I refused to empathize with him. This man—creature, thing, whatever—was manipulating Sandy. I didn't know how or why, but I was witnessing the effects.

Nevan lifted his head and squared his shoulders, his face now a mask of polite detachment. Yet when he spoke, sensuality infused every word. "I want to take you somewhere you've never been before. A special place. You belong there." He took hold of her hands. "Will you come with me?"

She blinked a few times in slow motion. Her tongue sneaked out to moisten her lower lip. "Can my boyfriend come with us?"

Nevan's gaze was nailed to hers, but a muscle in his jaw twitched. His voice stayed sultry, if a bit forced. "No, child, you will return to your lover afterward. This is for you alone."

"What's your name?"

He huffed out a breath, his gaze switching to the trees on my side of the clearing. His gaze homed in on mine and my heart thudded. He saw me.

Sandy, lost in her own realm of reality, said, "Don't you have a name?"

Nevan shut his eyes briefly, then swiveled his focus to me for a heartbeat before he turned back to Sandy.

I hugged the tree, desperate to see but dreading what I learn.

Grasping Sandy's shoulders, Nevan tugged her closer. She tilted her head back, her lips open, eyes unfocused. He bent his head and pressed his mouth to hers.

He was *kissing* her? I ground my teeth. I shouldn't care. I didn't care. Only one thing mattered—protecting an innocent girl from a predator.

I stormed into the clearing, yanked the derringer out of its holster, and whipped it out from under my shirt. I flipped the safety off, leveling the muzzle at Nevan. "Get the hell away from her."

My shout ricocheted off the trees.

One half of his mouth cinched up into a smirk.

With my right hand clamped around the Colt, I braced it from underneath with my left. "I mean it. Move or I'll shoot."

My gun was a few inches from his head. I poised my finger over the trigger, tensed, ready to take hold and squeeze if necessary.

Nevan touched one fingertip to the derringer's muzzle. "Your little weapon will do no good. But you know that, don't you?"

"A couple slugs in your skull might slow you down."

"I've caused no harm to the girl."

I planted my feet wide. "Let Sandy go."

He spread his hands, palms up. "She came here freely and she may leave whenever she wishes."

The girl still rocked in place, hands on her thighs. She licked her recently kissed lips, as if anxious for another taste of Nevan.

"Bastard," I muttered under my breath.

"Lay down your weapon and let me explain."

I indicated Sandy with a jerk of my elbow. "She's hypnotized or enthralled or whatever. Release her."

"The enchantment will wear off in a moment."

My gaze boomeranged from Nevan to Sandy and back again. His arms fell limp at his sides. He looked away and gave a half-hearted shrug.

I sank to my knees beside Sandy. Setting my pistol on the ground, I grasped her shoulders and shook. Her pupils had returned to normal, but she kept mooning at Nevan.

"Wake up!" I jostled her again. "Snap out of it, Sandy."

Her eyelids fluttered. Her slack expression solidified. She touched a finger to her lips, surveying the surroundings, then rubbed her forehead. "Where am I?"

Nevan flinched when I glared at him. "Would you care to tell her how she got here?"

He slid back into a sitting position, his legs bent before him, and fiddled with a weed.

My face tightened, a sure sign I was frowning. "Will she remember any of this later?"

"No." He ripped the weed out of the earth, tossing it aside. "The enchantment ensures no memories of me remain in the mind of the…uh…"

"Victim?"

He murdered another weed, but crushed this one in his palm. "If you give her instructions, she will follow them with no recollection of any of this later."

"How convenient for you." At least I could spare Sandy the memory of being used, for whatever Nevan wanted from her. I snapped my fingers to get Sandy's attention. "Listen. You went for a walk and got lost, but found your way back to the main trail. Go back to your boyfriend and forget this ever happened."

Sandy nodded, chewing her lip. She pushed up onto her feet, shuffled around, and hiked back down the game trail. I grabbed my gun and started after her.

Nevan sprang up to seize my arm. "Where are you going?"

"To make sure Sandy gets back okay." I grated the words out between my grinding teeth. "Not that you give a damn."

"You've got the wrong impression of me." His fingers relented a bit. "Please, Lindsey, allow me to explain. This is my duty—"

"Screwing with a woman's head and kissing her while she's half-conscious? That's your job?" My skin crawled at the thought of what he might've done if I hadn't intervened. I threw my arms up to shed his hands. "When you have a crappy job, you quit."

"Have you resigned from yours?"

"I have no choice. I need the money." I backed away several steps. "Besides, I don't abuse vulnerable women for a living."

"Believe me, I have no choice either."

My hand ached. I realized I'd been gripping the gun tighter. Loosening my fingers, I stomped closer to Nevan, until I had to crane my neck back to glare at him. "My job may suck, but I don't do anything morally reprehensible."

He wiped my spittle from his chin. "I am bound to my duty, by magic. Skeiron, my king, forced me into a bargain from which there is no escape. He throttled back my powers to prevent me from disobeying him."

"What a fabulous excuse." I raised the derringer, muzzle aimed at the sky. "Stay away from Sandy—and me."

I spun away from him and stalked off down the trail. In what seemed like seconds but must've been a few minutes, at least, I broke out of the woods into the rock garden. Once in the parking lot, I paused to collect myself.

Good luck with that. Nevan's voice echoed in my mind, his words from earlier even more relevant. My dignity and self-control shredded the instant I found him with Sandy. Maybe he lured women to clearings all the time to hypnotize them into making out with him. Afterward, he probably lugged them off to a cave and shackled them to the wall so he could debase them in private. Whatever his motives, I refused to engage in his machinations anymore.

Across the parking lot, Sandy's boyfriend was helping her into the passenger seat of a Jeep Cherokee.

Nevan had *kissed* her.

I stomped to my car, a cherry-red Chevy Malibu parked at the periphery of the woods, just inside the gravel parking lot. I moved to unlock the door, only then realizing I didn't have my keys or purse. I'd left them in the shop, because my shift wasn't over yet.

A creature squawked.

My every muscle went rigid at the familiar cry. I scanned the sky for the source. Where in blazes had the noise come from? The hairs on the back of my neck lifted. I swung my head to the right, to a pine tree at the forest's edge. A raven perched on a low branch, its weight dragging the limb down to within feet of the ground. The fading sunlight glinted off the bird's black eyes. Its gaze bored into me, ripping a shiver through my body.

I tried to pry my attention from the raven, but I couldn't. Its eyes pinned me in place, freezing my will. The raven squawked again.

"Shoo," I said, unable to move my eyes, much less wave a hand at the beast.

The bird swooped down onto the roof of my car. It waddled toward me, its talons ticking on the roof. The bird approached so close it could've snapped my nose off with its beak if it wanted. Instead, the raven pitched its head left and right. Its beak popped open.

The creature screamed.

My ears rang. I stumbled backward, tripped, and plummeted onto my ass. I struck the ground hard and I choked back a cry.

Red flames exploded in the depths of the bird's eyes. It leaped onto my chest. Talons sank into my breasts. They would've punctured my flesh, if not for the barrier of my shirt and bra. I dug my fingers into the gravel, but my body ignored my commands to move. Gravelly sounds emerged from the raven's open mouth. My mind insisted they were words, scrambling to comprehend them. The noises coalesced into clipped syllables.

"Guardian—not—yours." Its talons penetrated deeper, pulling a gasp out of me. "Stay—away."

The bird launched off me with a thrust that forced the breath out of my lungs. The beast swooped low over me. Its wings scraped the crown of my head.

The raven blasted off into the sky, out of sight.

CHAPTER SIX

STAGGERED BACK INTO THE ROCK SHOP A FEW MINUTES LATER, MY thoughts whirling, adrenaline heightening my senses and sharpening my paranoia. A bird assaulted me? Really? Pinpricks burned on my breasts where the raven scratched me. Today sucked like a vacuum-powered toilet.

The raven had spoken to me. Actual words. I had no clue what they meant, but I was certain the bird uttered them. A few years ago, I'd watched a documentary about ravens that explained how they could mimic human speech. The attack bird must've been mimicking…someone. Maybe the sinister guy in the shop. He talked about a guardian and issued a similar warning I didn't understand.

The guardian wasn't mine. Okay, whatever.

I dragged my feet, heading back behind the counter. The soles of my tennies scraped across the concrete. In my absence, the store had emptied. The huge fans stood silent, their blades motionless. The air hung stagnant and humid around me, redolent with the odor of human bodies on a hot day. I pushed a lock of damp hair away from my eyes, lodging it behind my ear.

An odd sensation wisped through me. Fiery, but with a frosty undercurrent and a low-voltage bite. *He's watching.*

I gnawed the inside of my cheek as I scanned the shop. Nevan was not observing me. Oh hell, maybe he was. A being who vanished at will might also possess the ability to go invisible. Then again, my stalker might be my favorite customer—Mr. Tall, Blond, and Menacing. He had delivered a vague threat. I slipped a hand under my shirt to fondle the derringer's grip.

"Porter!" Stan shouted from his office doorway. "Time to close up. Get a move on."

His gaze flicked down to my shirt, and his brow scrunched the tiniest bit. I'd retrieved my emergency scarf from the car, strategically positioning it over the blood stains my raven pal caused. The bright floral print was a bit gaudy for my taste, but it distracted the eye from any stains peeking out from under the fabric.

Stan flapped a hand at the cash register. "Count 'er out."

Next time I changed careers, maybe I could choose a duty like Nevan's and kiss attractive men every day as my job. Switching from paralegal to rock peddler, via a string of temp jobs, wasn't a lateral career move. If I'd never moved to Texas, if I'd gone to grad school instead and stayed with my parents and brother then—No, I couldn't get lost in regrets and what-ifs.

By the time Stan and I finished closing the shop, and I settled into the driver's seat of my car, the odd sensation of being watched had dwindled. Sunset plunged the day into a deep twilight. I revved the engine, flooring the accelerator as I guided the car onto the highway. Two cars whizzed past in the other direction, but soon the night closed in around the car, severing me from the rest of humanity. I usually enjoyed the freedom of feeling like the last human on the planet. Tonight, the notion scraped my nerves.

The AC blasted crisp, dry air over me. The twilit sky descended into blackness sprinkled with stars. The headlights pierced the night to lay bare the road ahead as trees zipped past. The yellow line blurred.

Unseen currents of energy pulsated through the air, stirring the hairs on my arms. The scent of damp, virgin earth tantalized my senses. I clenched the steering wheel and fought against the excitement fluttering through me.

A shape materialized in the passenger seat.

I should've yelped or jumped, but I wasn't the least surprised. The disturbing realization prickled my nerves. I didn't bother looking at my newly arrived passenger. "I told you to stay away from me."

Nevan draped an arm across the back of my seat. I risked a quick sideways glance to spy his bronzed body a few feet away, then I nailed my gaze to the road. His fingertips trailed over the nape of my neck. My belly tightened, arcing delicious tension down between my legs. *Get a grip.* Though I tried to obey my own command, the itch deep under my skin begged to be scratched.

"You anticipated my arrival." He sounded far too certain of himself.

I considered lying, but it offered no advantage. "I felt something. Don't pretend to understand what."

"You felt me, naturally."

The words danced over my skin like fingertips. I cleared my throat. "What do you want?"

He leaned closer, his face inches from my cheek. "I want you, of course."

Numbness tingled over my scalp, down through my face, to paralyze my mouth. Oxygen, I needed oxygen. I swallowed. Bit my lip. My lungs refused to work, but I mentally yelled at the bastards until they drew in air spiced with his essence. When I'd regained mastery of my lips, I said, "Tell me why you're here. I told you to stay away."

In my peripheral vision, I couldn't help but notice his every move. His head slanted left and right, his gaze hot on my skin. A squadron of butterflies took flight in my stomach and fanned out into my chest.

"Have you eaten?" he asked. "You look a bit peaked."

I hadn't eaten since breakfast, but for darn sure I wouldn't tell him that. My stomach growled. *Traitor.* "I repeat, what do you want?"

"We need to talk, love."

"No." My hands tightened on the wheel. "We don't, *love.*"

A twinge of guilt pinched me at the sarcasm dripping from my voice on the last word. But dammit, if he called me "love" or "darling" one more time, after what he did to Sandy…

His tongue flitted over his bottom lip.

I fidgeted in my seat, unable to get enough clearance from him. The far side of the moon wouldn't have been enough. I threw a sideways glance at him. "I saw what you did."

"I don't understand what you're implying."

"You know damn well what I'm implying." I blustered a breath out my nose. "Sandy. She could barely speak, she was so out of it. You claimed you enchanted her, whatever that means. For all I know, you drugged her."

He pulled away, withdrawing his arm. "I've no need of drugging anyone. I may have whatever woman I choose, whenever I choose."

I bristled. "Great. Go pester one of those hordes of women who throw themselves at your feet. I'm not one of them."

"No, you are not."

The silken tone of his words slid over me like velvet on bare skin. "I am positively not interested in cavorting with a woodland lothario. Poof out of here immediately."

"Poof?" He lifted one eyebrow.

"Yeah." I slowed the Malibu for a curve before speeding up on the straightaway. Silhouettes of trees whizzed past, the headlights flashing over them. "Poof. As in disappear."

"Ahhh, I see." He adjusted his position with a sideways rock of his hips. I successfully resisted the urge to glance at his crotch. *Score one for me, ten thousand for him.* He sighed. "I will gladly poof away once we discuss what you witnessed earlier."

"I keep asking and you keep deflecting."

His gaze settled on me with physical weight. Crazy, but true. The intensity of his stare aroused certain parts of me and chilled others. I longed to look at him, to drown in those alien eyes, but I feared what I might find there.

Instead, I concentrated on the highway and locked my hands around the steering wheel. The headlights glanced off a road sign up ahead. Black letters on the rounded, triangular sign declared this highway U.S. 41. The sign marked one mile from the rock shop. One mile closer to home. If a cheap little apartment with peeling wallpaper counted as home.

The Malibu raced toward the highway sign.

Nevan bolted upright. "Stop the car."

"Excuse me? Why on earth would I—"

"Stop the car!"

"I will not."

Nevan seized the steering wheel and yanked it to the right. The car fishtailed. It straightened out, veering straight toward the roadside ditch. I rammed my foot on the brake. The tires screamed, the car skidded and slammed to a stop. The force thrust me forward, my seatbelt tore into me, pain ricocheted through my shoulder and stomach. The car's bumper just missed the highway sign.

Nevan released the wheel. He grabbed my face in his hands, turning me toward him. My breaths huffed hard and fast, my mouth was agape. He ran one hand up my face to my forehead and back down again. "Are you hurt?"

"No." I shook free of his grasp. "What the hell were you thinking?"

"I..." Unidentifiable emotions, dark and intense, flickered across his features. He bowed his head, exhaled a long breath, and lifted his face. The tension eased out of his shoulders. His features relaxed into the familiar expression of serene confidence. He eased his arm across my seat's back. I folded my hands on my lap and his big, warm palm enveloped them. "I don't wish to talk while you're driving."

"Gah!" I threw my head back, bumping the headrest. "Are you kidding me? You nearly got us both killed. Brilliant plan, Romeo."

Lines creased his forehead. "Romeo?"

"You know, like Romeo and Juliet. The play. Shakespeare wrote it."

"I understand the cultural reference. I have visited playhouses." A hint of annoyance colored his tone, but it dispersed into the ether as he threaded his fingers between mine. "I'm asking why you called me Romeo. It didn't strike me as complimentary."

"I meant to call you Casanova."

"Unflattering as well, I gather. As is the term lothario, yes?"

I wrestled my hands out of his. The cool air erased the heat of his touch. "Do you always lurk in the woods hunting for women to seduce?"

"No, I lurk in the shop." He flattened two fingers over my lips to silence my objection. "And I had no intention of seducing the girl."

I batted his fingers away. "Why were you enchanting her? Assuming I believe in any of this nonsense."

"You do." He captured a lock of my hair and twirled it around his forefinger. A shadow seemed to enshroud him, weighing down his shoulders. "My duty requires me to seek out mortal women who possess a touch of the Unseen realm. I sensed the energy within her. The next step is a test, to determine if she is the one I'm tasked to find."

"I don't get it."

He combed his fingers through my hair over and over, clearly fascinated with the task. "One hundred years ago, a prophecy was issued. It told of a human female who would become the gatekeeper of the realms. This mortal is known as the Janusite."

"Janusite? Sounds like a disease."

His fingers skimmed up my neck and began to massage my nape. The headache stabbing pangs into my skull fled at his ministrations. It felt so good I almost moaned, but choked it back just in time. Score another one for me. *What exactly are you competing for, huh?*

I peeled my lids apart and shrugged his hands off. "Thank you, but I'm okay."

"You dislike accepting help of any kind, don't you?"

"None of your concern." I propped my elbow on the window frame and rested my head on my fist, my face aimed toward Nevan. "What is a Janusite?"

"The one I seek." His teasing smile elicited a tickle in my chest. "Janus was, in your world, the Roman god of doorways and transitions, beginnings and endings. Have you ever seen a Janus coin?"

"A picture of one, yes." I scratched behind my ear. I could at least get rid of this tickle, if not the strange one behind my ribs. "On the coins, Janus is shown with two faces looking in opposite directions. Sometimes, though, he was depicted with four faces, pointing to the four corners of the world—the cardinal directions. North, south, east, west. This represented his dominion over the whole world."

His hand on my nape went still. "Are you a scholar?"

"I'm a minimum-wage slave."

He looped a lock of my hair around his finger, lifted it to his face, and inhaled deeply. His eyelids drifted half shut.

I coughed—loudly.

His eyes sprang open and he released my hair. The lock unwound, falling to brush my neck. "Few mortals, aside from scholars, know so much about Janus."

"I like mythology." I yawned, shielding my open mouth with one hand. "You mentioned a test."

He spread his thumb and forefinger wide over his forehead. "Yes, the test. Once I detect a touch of the Unseen realm, I must determine if the energy I sense in the candidate is strong enough to warrant taking her to Skeiron."

"What is the Unseen realm?"

"The place I come from. A world of magic."

"The separate realm you mentioned earlier."

He nodded.

"And what does this test involve?" I worked my fingers under my shirt collar to pull it away from my skin. The air in the car seemed to have gotten warmer, though the AC still blasted away.

Nevan traced the glowing numbers on the dashboard clock with one finger. "The test is a kiss, which you already knew. Why does it bother you so?"

"Doesn't bother me. You can suck face with anyone you please." Heartburn simmered in my chest and I had the sudden urge to punch something. "When we first met, you claimed you sensed energy in me. But you didn't kiss me."

His head swiveled toward me. Those eyes flared hot. His lips curved into a slow smile. "Would ye like me to?"

"Would I like you to what?" I could be evasive too. *So there.*

Nevan edged closer. His hip brushed mine. He sneaked his arm over the back of my seat, the hollow of his shoulder too near my body. His voice smoldered like his eyes. "Would ye like me to kiss ye?"

"No." A part of me said yes, but I shut that slutty girl up quick.

"Don't be jealous, darlin'."

"I am *not* jealous." Was I? No, absolutely not.

His hand slid down the seat. His fingers lighted on my shoulder. "You are a feisty one. I can't for the life of me deduce why the sheriff called you an ice princess. Unless you're of royal blood and hail from a cold climate."

"I'm far from royal and I hail from nowhere."

Ice princess. Travis's words lashed my mind. I'd battled long and hard to earn that insult and my practiced restraint had rescued me more than once. Yet Nevan stripped it all away with two words—*hello there.* The ease with which he'd unraveled me made my stomach churn. Me off balance was exactly what he wanted. Therefore, I would not give it to him.

Not often, anyway.

I ratcheted my spine straight. "Why did you help me with Travis? The sheriff, I mean."

Nevan's smile crumbled. He gave a tiny shake of his head. "I don't know."

"What are you? I demand you explain yourself."

His face pinched. "Love to, but I can't."

"You already told me about the Janusite and your duty."

"That I did." He groaned, his gaze distant. "I oughtn't be here at all."

"Drop the cryptic bullshit." I nodded toward the highway sign. "Or I'm driving past that sign. You don't want me to do that, do you? It's why you freaked out when you saw it."

"Can't tell ye that either."

I shoved his arm off my seat. "I want answers. Pronto."

He stared at me for several seconds. His attention shivered powerful currents through me. Cool as fall air. Crisp as green grass. Strong as hurricane winds. I flattened my back against the door and hugged my shoulders.

His expression morphed into stone. "I must go."

"Wait. You have to tell me—"

I was speaking to empty air.

I TRUDGED INTO MY APARTMENT AND SLUNG MY PURSE OVER A COAT hook. The door clicked shut. The faint scent of burned toast wafted over me, a remnant of my scorched breakfast. The only thing I'd eaten today. Toast flambé, drowned in cinnamon and sugar.

The lights outside my door cast a wan glow through the windows. I flicked a switch on the wall to power on the floor lamp by the sofa. Its pinkish-white light soothed my nerves. I flopped onto the sofa, tossed my phone onto the table, and sank into its overstuffed cushions. A sigh whispered out of me as the padding cradled my throbbing head. I removed the holster and gun from inside my waistband, setting both on the table.

Finding, then losing, a dead body could really damage a girl's brain. Mine hurt like somebody stabbed a trio of red-hot pokers into the base of my skull. I shut my eyes and succumbed to the weariness. I should've dragged my butt into the bedroom before passing out, but my muscles vetoed that idea. I let my body go limp, my thoughts draining away into the oblivion of sleep.

The phone rang.

With a groan, I flailed a hand out to grab my cell phone from the table. My fingers knocked it off and the phone clattered to the floor. It rang again. *Ugh.* Without getting up, I bent over to fumble for the phone until my closed around it. Two more rings assaulted my tired ears before I lifted the phone and grumbled, "Hello."

"Lindsey, honey."

My mom's voice blared through the receiver, her cheer twanging every nerve in my head. I rubbed my eyes, yawning. "Hey, Mom."

"You sound tired. Have you eaten anything?"

Why did everyone keep asking me that? I must look, and sound, worse than I thought. The mere idea of hauling myself into the kitchen to reheat some leftovers made my limbs ache. "I'm okay. How are you guys?"

"We're fine. Your dad's meditating and Ash is reading his comics, but he wants to say hi. I need to talk to you first, though." Her voice got muffled as she, no doubt, held her hand over the phone while shooing my brother away. "Ash says he'll text you. Lindsey, I've got wonderful news."

"Mmm?" My eyelids drifted shut, beckoned by the allure of sleep, wonderful sleep.

"We're coming for a visit, sweetie. We'll be there Friday."

I bolted upright, punching my fingers into the cushion so deep my nails almost punctured the fabric. "The day after tomorrow? Oh, uh, it's not a good time for me."

"Why?" Mom's voice took on a suspicious, mother-knows-all tone. "Is something going on? You don't sound like yourself."

I found a dead body that poofed out of existence and met a Tarzan wannabe who poofed into my car and nearly crashed us both into a tree. Other than that, I'm peachy.

My mind flashed back to this morning, in the woods, when Nevan cornered me against a tree, his vortex eyes blazing. I envisioned his sculpted chest, his broad shoulders, the loincloth draped around his hips, and those luscious lips tantalizingly close to mine. Tarzan wannabe? No, not him. He was my UFO—an unidentified flirtatious object.

"Lindsey? Are you still there?"

Mom's voice shattered my fantasy. "Yeah, I'm here. I've got to work Friday, all day and way late into the evening. Maybe you guys could stop by another time."

"Your aura is practically screaming at me through the phone. Something is not right, honey. We're coming Friday and that's that."

"How does an aura scream?"

"Don't get smart with me."

I gave myself a mental slap and rubbed my temples again, but I couldn't ward off the headache drumming through my brain. "I'm sorry, I didn't mean to be testy. It's just that this week's really, really not a good time."

"Eat a good dinner, get plenty of rest, and we'll see you soon."

"But Mom—"

"Good night, Lindsey."

What was the use? Parents did what they wanted. "Good night, Mom. Say hi to Dad and Ash for me."

We hung up and I tossed the phone onto the table. It skidded, thunking into the lamp's base. I leaned my head back, closed my eyes, and sighed. Just what I needed, a visit from the gurus of all things metaphysical. I'd never told them the truth about Calder, too ashamed to broach the subject, which was the reason I'd kept them at a distance—literally—for three years.

Static electricity sizzled over my skin, from toes to scalp.

I jerked my head up, glancing left and right. Goose bumps flared up on my arms. The sensation skittered up my spine, chilly at first, then warming into a curtain that enveloped me like a large, muscular body. Oh hell no, it couldn't be. I did not sense—

An electrical charge jolted me. I recognized this feeling. Inexplicable, undeniable, and unique. I sat forward. "Nevan?"

Silence answered me. Maybe I was insane after all.

Three crisp knocks rattled the front door.

I sprang to my feet but stared at the door, my feet glued to the frayed carpeting. Seconds elapsed, with nothing but my heartbeat to break the quiet.

Three more knocks, quick and precise, resounded through the door.

I sucked on my upper lip, then freed it with a smacking sound. My intuition—a faculty I'd long ignored, and worse, scoffed at—told me the identity of the person on the other side of the door. But it couldn't be. I mean, he'd zipped off to who-knew-where to escape my questions.

Another surge of electricity zinged through me. Hell with it. I marched to the door and yanked it open.

Nevan smiled that sensual smile, the one my body lapped up like an alcoholic swigging booze. He wore nothing but the loincloth. The interplay of shadow and light accentuated every hard line of his body. My breaths grew shallower, the air thicker, and my breasts heaved up with each intake of air. He caught sight of them and wet his lips. I fought my every impulse, because I'd learned the hard way impulses led to bad, bad things. At last, I peeled my gaze away from his body.

That's when I noticed the wooden tray he balanced on one palm, waiter style. The tray held a plate and two small bowls, each shielded by a half-dome lid. He gestured at the tray. "May I come in? I've brought you sustenance."

He offered me food, but his tone promised so much more. My mouth watered. "Not hungry."

Somewhere between lashing out at him after witnessing his encounter with Sandy and experiencing the inexplicable rush of anticipating his arrival, my anger had reduced to a simmer. I kept flashing back to his shamed expression when he enchanted Sandy and his defeated tone when he explained his duty. Looking at him now, I couldn't stop the simmer from fading away. Maybe he was his king's pawn.

"You're pale." He brushed the backs of his fingers across my cheek. "You must eat. But if nothing else, please accept this food as recompense for my poor behavior in your car."

"Are you apologizing?"

His eyes burned into mine, suffusing me with a liquid heat. "In this world, I might express gratitude. But alas, I'm simply stating a fact. I frightened you and nearly caused you harm." He reached for my hand, but when his grazed mine, he pulled his hand away. "I've no wish to ever harm you."

A door slammed further down the concrete walkway. I leaned out the door to peer down the length of the second-floor walkway hemmed in by metal railing. A gray-haired woman toddled toward us, heading for the stairwell beside my apartment. Oh great. Mrs. Kantola, a busybody of the first order, was about to see me conversing with a half-naked man.

A flicker of movement made me glance at the parking lot below. I didn't see anything, though, and returned my attention to the problem at hand.

"Lindsey, dear, is that you?" My neighbor flapped a hand at me.

I waved back. "Have a good night, Mrs. Kantola."

Teeth gritted, I snagged Nevan's arm and towed him inside. The door clapped shut.

He raised one eyebrow. "Pleased to see me, are ye?"

"You can't walk around dressed like that." I pointed at the door. "If my neighbor had seen you, I'd be the subject of town gossip for days, maybe weeks."

"Why do you care what others think?"

"I don't." I ran a hand over my forehead, back and forth. "Maybe I do."

"Relax, love." He cupped my elbow and guided me to the sofa. "You're far too tense. Sit and eat. I created this meal just for you and I'm certain you'll feel much better once you've gotten some food into your belly." He patted my behind. "Sit."

I made a half-hearted attempt at a scowl, then gave in and collapsed onto the sofa. He set the tray on my lap. I pushed up out of my slouch, tipping forward to examine what he'd brought me.

Nevan plucked the lids off the plate and bowls. Steam curled up from the food, flooding my senses with heavenly aromas—spicy and sweet, with a hint of berries. My mouth watered again, for a very different reason this time. The plate seemed to hold a meat dish, though I didn't recognize it. One bowl contained leafy stuff reminiscent of spinach, though with an unusual golden tinge. In the second bowl, what resembled fruit overflowed from a flaky, pastry-like shell.

Head down, I peeked up at Nevan. "You cooked this?"

"I did."

"For me."

"Yes."

He lowered his body onto the sofa beside me, the cushion compressing under his weight. My cushion tilted slightly toward him. My cheek skirted his mouth. I bounced backward and the dishes slid across the tray.

He tapped my chin. "Eat, before your meal gets cold."

"You sound like my mother."

His finger glided up my jaw, his touch feather-light on my skin. His fingertip traced soft circles under my ear, teasing the lobe. Every inch of my flesh awakened to the sensations around me. The soft, but uneven, texture of the sofa cushions. The weight of the food tray. The heat of his skin.

Slanting toward me, he splayed his fingers over my cheek, the heel of his hand rough against the corner of my mouth.

I struggled to keep from turning my face into his palm. "What do you want from me?"

"*From* you? Nothing." The exhalations from his husky murmur stirred the gossamer hairs on my cheek. "*With* you…I'm uncertain."

"Why do you keep coming back? I said awful things and told you to stay away."

"I deserved your words."

"But why come back?"

"Can't explain it." He dragged his hand down my face. His fingers trailed over my skin, falling away one by one. "I sensed an energy in you, but it's nothing like the touch I seek out as part of my duty." He lingered close to me, a gap of inches between us. "That's why I neglected to kiss you. I've wanted to, believe me, but I can tell you aren't quite ready for me."

I stammered, but couldn't form coherent words. My breaths quickened. I moistened my lips, as if I might taste his withheld kiss.

His gaze roved over me. "There is an unusual power in you, buried deep. Have you not felt it?"

"All I feel is you." I slapped a hand over my mouth. My fingers muffled my voice. "Forget I said that."

His lips parted, then closed. He canted his head. "Do you mean you've sensed my approach, as you did in the car?"

My limbs refused to budge.

Nevan pried my fingers away from my mouth. "Lindsey—"

"Yes, okay, yes." I locked my hands over my midsection. "Happy now?"

His chuckle rippled through me with physical pleasure. He patted my knee. "Happier, yes. But I won't be fully satisfied until you eat."

"Only if you promise to explain a few things while I stuff my face."

He drew a cross over his heart with one finger. The lines bisected the scar. He raised his hand, palm out. "I swear it on my very existence."

A brilliant smile enlivened his features, lighting him up from the inside. A matching glow ignited inside me. In spite of myself, I relaxed into the sofa and dug into the meal he'd prepared specially for me. I discovered a fork and knife hidden under the plate's lip. The meat dish melted on my tongue, rife with exotic spices, and I moaned my appreciation.

Nevan tensed, his eyes narrowed on me.

"What?" I asked with food in my mouth. Good thing Mom wasn't here.

He swallowed visibly. "Your noises confound me."

"*Mmm-mm* means I like it." I forked a hunk of meat glistening with savory sauce.

"I see."

The faint growl in his voice made me glance up at him. A hint of white teeth gleamed behind his parted lips. I froze with the fork halfway to my mouth. "Stop looking at me that way."

"What way might that be?"

"Like you want to…uh…"

"Kiss you?" The pink tip of his tongue danced behind his teeth. "As I said, I won't do it until you're ready."

"I suppose you're going to decide when I'm ready."

His gaze tracked down to my throat and he pulled in a heavy breath. "Perhaps you are ready."

"There you go, making assumptions about me again."

"No assumptions." He nodded at my chest and his Adam's apple bobbed. "The way you're touching yourself speaks to the truth."

"Excuse me?" I glanced down—and froze. My right hand hovered over my breast, concealed by my blouse and scarf. My fingers feathered over my breast, stroking along the inner slope. The slight tickle of my own caress hadn't registered in my brain, overwhelmed by the tingles coursing up and down my body, triggered by Nevan's proximity. I jerked my hand, clamping it tight, but my wrist chafed my nipple.

"Take it easy, darlin'. I won't kiss ye." He bent closer still, his skin a hair's breadth from mine. "Not tonight."

My chest pumped out quick, shallow breaths and my body hummed with a need I refused to acknowledge. "Keep your lips away from mine, please."

"As you wish."

He ducked his head to mine, his lips a millimeter from my cheek, and blew a steamy current across my skin. He moved his mouth down my face, never making contact but eliciting hard shivers with every whisper of his breath across my flesh. A tiny noise burst out of me, a cross between a gasp and a moan, so soft I prayed he hadn't noticed. His muscles tightened, his shoulders bulged. As his lips approached the corner of my mouth, he exhaled a soft, erotic breath that unleashed a crushing need within me.

I tried to speak with authority, but it came out breathless. "What are you doing?"

"Keeping my lips away from yours." His breaths fanned across my cheek to my ear. I heard nothing except his exhalations and my own pulse throbbing in my ears. He brushed his mouth across my lobe. "Is this far enough?"

He nibbled my earlobe.

A memory blasted through my mind. Teeth biting down, tearing, nails scraping down my neck, fingers grasping my throat, a voice snarling in my ear. *You're mine forever, even beyond death.*

I slapped my palms on Nevan's chest and shoved him away. I shook my head with such violence my hair flapped around my face.

Eyes wide, face blanched, Nevan searched my gaze with his own. "What in the name of the stars is wrong?"

"I—" Words clogged my throat, trapped there. I squeezed my eyes shut to banish the memory to the recesses of my brain, where it belonged, before I looked at Nevan again.

He rubbed his hands on his thighs. His smile was bitter. "I pushed too far too soon. You may have noted my tendency toward taking liberties."

I was too shaken to appreciate his attempt at humor. Other men I'd known would've gotten angry if I physically ejected them from my personal space. Nevan seemed to understand.

Right. After knowing him for less than a day, he understood me. Juiced up by hormones, I willed my voice to stay calm. "It's not you. I have…bad memories."

He nodded slowly. "I'm beginning to appreciate that."

I cleared my throat. "You should go. I'm seriously damaged, which means you're wasting your moves on me."

"Nothing is wasted on you."

Slumping into the sofa, I closed my eyes. "You seem nice enough, in a strange way, but I met you this morning. I have no idea who or what you are."

"I'm Nevan." He tipped his chin up, pride evident in his voice. "And I'm a sylph."

I whipped my head sideways to stare at him. "A what?"

"Sylph. I believe your kind describes us as elemental spirits of the air."

I poked his chest. His firm flesh resisted the pressure of my finger. "You seem pretty solid to me, not at all airy."

"I am not made of air. I was forged from the earth and the air, but I'm as corporeal as you."

"Sure, that makes perfect sense."

His lips twisted in a half smile. "After everything you've seen today, how can you not believe in the Unseen realm? I am an elemental being from another world parallel to yours. A land of magic."

"Uh-huh." Maybe I just wasn't smart enough to get it. I felt dense as a steel brick right now.

"You've seen some of what I can do."

"Yeah." I closed my fist around the knot in my scarf. "You can change your appearance. How do I know this is the real you?"

"Because it is. You have to trust me, but I've come to realize you have trouble with such things. Since you first began working at the shop, I've seen you every day while I carry out my duties. I would never approach you in glamour. Never."

"You've been stalking me for three months?"

"No." He rubbed the back of his neck. "I saw you, in the course of my duties."

From what he'd said about his duty, and what I'd seen of it, I believed him. "Okay, you're not a stalker. But what's glamour?"

"An incantation to disguise my appearance." He touched a fingertip to my jaw. "I've never hidden myself from you."

"Yes you did. When I saw you with Sandy, you were an old man."

"Ah. That." He scratched his cheek. "Our encounter then was an accident. Besides, you recognized me. I would never intentionally deceive you."

I wanted to believe him. Though the reason why eluded me, the compulsion was strong.

His finger fell away from my face, his gaze diverted to the floor.

I took in the lines of his profile, then my attention drifted lower, sweeping down to the waist of his loincloth. I jerked my gaze up to his face. "Earlier today, a creepy guy turned up in the shop and he sort of threatened me. He had weird eyes a lot like yours. Do you know anything about him?"

Nevan snapped bolt upright. He grasped my shoulders. "This man, how did he threaten you?"

"Well, first he called me a tolerable specimen worth bedding once or twice." I wound the end of my scarf around my fingers. "Then he said the guardian is bound to him and I should remember that."

Nevan's fingers clamped harder around my arms. "What else?"

"I'm pretty sure he poofed away."

"He said nothing else?"

"Nope."

He let go and sagged against the sofa.

"You know this guy?" I asked.

"Skeiron."

A cold serpent wriggled down my spine. "Your king Skeiron?"

"Correct."

"I've never met him. He has no reason to bother me."

"Protecting the sanctity of the Unseen realm is reason enough for him."

I closed my eyes, my head drooping. Sylphs. Kings. Magic. My brain spun its wheels, unable to find traction in this new reality. I cracked my lids apart.

Nevan leaned forward, elbows on his thighs. "Interfering in the mortal world is forbidden. You are forbidden."

He infused the word forbidden with both bleakness and sensuality. I was forbidden. Until today, nobody ever cared enough to label me off limits. I rested my chin in my cupped hand, my fingers partly covering my mouth. "I don't understand any of this."

Nevan shoved a hand through his hair. "I cannot explain further, I'm sorry, wish I could. The risk is too grave now that Skeiron has discovered my interest in you."

I squinted at him and let my hands fall. "What do you mean the risk is too grave?"

"The danger to me, not you." He grazed a thumb across my lips. "Please forgive me. I should never have revealed myself, but when I saw you weeping over the death of a man you'd never known, I had to intervene." He rose to his feet with the fluid grace of water flowing over a boulder. "I must go."

"You haven't finished explaining."

He pecked a kiss on my forehead. "Sorry, love. I have duties to fulfill."

"More women to kiss, you mean." Why did I sound grumpy?

"Don't worry," Nevan said, eyes sparkling. "I'll be testing no more women."

"Won't you get in trouble for shirking your duty?"

"Perhaps." He nuzzled the top of my head. "But not immediately."

He stepped back and I sensed he was about to disappear. "Wait. I have more questions. What about the missing body—"

Nevan vanished.

I was left to cuddle up with my confusion.

CHAPTER SEVEN

THE SUN STABBED INTO MY EYES THROUGH MY LIDS. A HEADACHE raged behind my eyes and cold sweat chilled my chest. The remnants of a gut-wrenching nightmare receded, leaving behind impressions of blood and anguish and terror. I pulled in breath after breath until my heart slowed its rapid thumping.

Rubbing the sleep from my eyes, I dragged myself out of the bed. My raven-attack wounds burned when I moved and the satiny fabric of my nightie brushed across the deep scrapes and punctures. I chose my softest cotton bra, but it still chafed. After dressing, I got a bowl of cereal and sat cross-legged on the sofa munching on the whole wheat biscuits. The glaze of frosting didn't fool my taste buds. They longed for more of Nevan's sinfully succulent offerings.

Oh crap. I stopped mid chew. I'd eaten his food, without balking, without thinking. *Calm down, if it was poisoned, you'd be dead.* Sure, but what if the food was cursed or enchanted or whatever? I might be magically bound to do his bidding.

If that were true, why had he left last night? He would've stuck around to play with his new toy. Maybe…the food was just food. Which implied he cared about my well-being. Why else bring me dinner and insist I eat it? He kept saying he shouldn't have been here with me, he shouldn't have told me anything, and yet he came back.

Even supernatural men had a knack for confusing me.

I finished my breakfast and drove to the shop. This was Thursday, my day off, but I needed to check out the crime scene again. If Travis found out about this, he'd laugh at me and tell me there was no crime scene, then handcuff me for the hell of it. Big mystery why I couldn't stand him.

A man had died. I witnessed the result of the foul play. If the sheriff wouldn't investigate, I would.

Stan's Toyota was tucked behind the shop, in his private parking area. I stowed my Malibu in the far corner of the gravel lot, under a sprawling pine with sagging branches that shielded my car. Nobody liked to park there, so I wouldn't be taking up a space a tourist might want. The morning was relatively cool, considering the heatwave, but humidity made the air sticky on my skin.

As I slunk across the parking lot and through the rock garden, I heard the hollow metallic rattling of Stan opening up the big front doors. Upping my pace, I hurried down the trail through the woods. Sweat dribbled down my chest to sear my wounds. I stopped at the healing vortex and perched on one of the stone benches. I might've been delaying because the thought of the blood stain, and what it signified, shivered dread through me. When had I become a coward?

I dug a wadded-up tissue from my jeans pocket. Lifting the neck of my T-shirt with my thumb and forefinger, I dabbed at the sweat on my chest, careful to avoid my wounds. The antibiotic ointment I'd applied to them last night didn't seem to do much.

Warmth suffused my breasts where the raven had punctured me, spiraling out into the rest of my body. I gulped air and the warmth infused my lungs. I slapped my palms on the rock beneath me, overcome by a sudden wave of dizziness. The woods twirled around me, yet the sensation sweeping through my body soothed me. The dizziness abated with a suddenness that left me slumped on the bench, breathless.

My wounds no longer stung. I palpated my breasts but no pain ensued. I snagged the hem of my shirt and whipped the fabric up to expose my chest. An iron fist hardened in my gut, heavy and cold.

The wounds were gone. Healed, as if they'd never existed.

I sat motionless for a moment, staring into space. The healing vortex was real. Why that revelation hit me so hard, after everything I'd experienced in the past twenty-four hours, mystified me. I just couldn't acclimate to this new world, or rather, this new version of the same old world.

Wake up, you're on a mission, remember? Right. My investigative mission. With a cleansing exhalation, I pushed up off the bench and headed for the crime scene.

The blood stain came into view. My throat tightened and my step faltered, but I kept my footsteps on a trajectory for the crime scene. My brain superimposed a vision of the body over the vacant dirt plot punctuated by the dark stain. I knelt beside the blood. The dried puddle seemed smaller than yesterday, or else my memory inflated its original size.

Christ. A man had died here.

Scanning the area, I spotted no signs of a struggle. Yeah, like I was a forensics expert. I had to try. I tiptoed over to the railing along the pool at the base of the falls. Though I searched the ground for any clues, nothing popped out. None of the rocks near the railing bore any blood stains and the railing itself was intact. If the man had fallen and hit his head on the railing or the rocks, surely a sign would remain. There was nothing.

I returned to the site marked by dried blood. Here he'd lain—and here he'd vanished.

A strange, yet familiar, sensation fluttered through me. I shut my eyes, struggling to decide if I wanted him to appear or hoped he'd give up and go away.

"What are ye doing?"

Every single hair on my body rose at his deep voice, and my skin tingled as warmth flowed over my skin, soaking in down to my bones. I took a breath, let it out, and faced Nevan.

He stood several feet away, arms folded over his chest, broad shoulders relaxed, a faint smile on his lips. Water dripped from his powerful body, spattering the ground. His hair was dripping too, the wavy locks drenched but springing back with amazing virility. He shook his head, drops sprayed out, and in an instant every speck of water evaporated from his toned flesh and skimpy loincloth. Waves of silky hair, now dry, settled around his face.

Nevan drank in my appearance with a long, slow appraisal. His lips curved up at the corners and he stroked his tongue over them in a languid lick. The memory of his mouth on my earlobe careened through my thoughts. Last night, I'd freaked out at the contact, but today my skin flushed at the prospect of his slick tongue and soft lips teasing my skin.

I clasped the back of my neck with one hand, fingers knotting in my hair. "Hi."

"Hello, darlin'." He strode one pace toward me, consuming half the distance between us. "What are you doing here? I thought this was your day of rest."

"Yeah, this is my day off."

"Why are you here then?" His arms fell to his sides, slack, yet he inched ever nearer.

I scuffled backward. "Checking out the crime scene. If Travis won't investigate, I will."

"I shall aid you." He glanced at the blood stain and pursed his lips. "Don't expect we'll uncover meaningful evidence. Whatever stole the body clearly had the power to cover its tracks."

"How come you say 'whatever' and 'its'? This must be a person."

"You persist in assuming the universe is home to humans alone."

"And you."

"I am not the only sylph, or immortal being, populating the realms." He slanted his torso toward me, his body suddenly too close. My feet refused to budge, though I wanted to move away. I did want to, didn't I?

He captured a lock of my hair, threading it between his fingers. "This is your day of rest, a time for fun. Why waste it on a fruitless search for answers you'll reject?"

"This could be a mundane crime, no immortals involved." My brain did a U-turn back to his two comments about my day of rest. I pointed a finger at him. "How do you know this is my day off?"

"Well now, I—"

"Oh right. You've watched me for three months, but not in a creepy stalker way."

He managed to seem offended and amused at the same time.

"Porter!" Travis's bellow bounced off the trees and the sandstone cliff, rattling my eardrums. He'd skulked up behind me while I had my back turned to the trail, my attention trained on Nevan. Travis, in his sheriff uniform, stomped up to us. His lip curled when he glared at Nevan. "Thought my mind was playing tricks on me last night, but no. You actually prance around in that getup."

Last night? Fury rose hot in my chest and I slugged Travis's chest. "That was you last night. In the parking lot outside my apartment. You've been spying on me."

He grunted. "You're a suspect in a crime, Porter. It's called surveillance."

I planted my hands on my hips. "Yesterday you said there's no body, so there's no crime."

"Not talking about the alleged body you claim to have found." He rocked on his heels. His forefinger tapped the grip of the Sig Sauer holstered on his hip. "Told ya, I gotta protect the populace from the likes of you. George of the Jungle here better watch out." His gaze swiveled to Nevan. "She's a man-killer."

Though I tried to speak, my voice abandoned me.

"I'm watching you, Porter."

Travis stalked back down the trail toward the shop.

Nevan rotated his head sideways to monitor Travis's departing silhouette. When Travis disappeared around a bend in the trail, Nevan harrumphed. "Why does the sheriff persist in maligning you with such lies?"

Okay. Time for full disclosure. I shoved my hands in my jeans pockets. "It's not a lie. I am a man-killer."

Nevan's gaze snapped to mine. "Impossible."

"You don't know me." I wouldn't look away, no matter how much I longed to break the connection. I must make him understand. "I killed my fiancé, Calder. Travis's brother."

"No."

I stepped up to him, so close my breasts nudged his bare chest. Standing tall, I tilted my head back to zero in on his eyes. "I shot Calder six times in the chest and once between the eyes."

His head whipped back. His eyes widened, the colors flared and whorled. He shook his head.

"I did it, Nevan. I emptied a full clip into the man I thought I loved and I don't regret it." I flattened my palm on his chest, feeling his heart hammer beneath it. "Listen to Travis. I am no sweet, innocent girl. I'm a woman who killed an unarmed man, and in the same circumstances, I'd do it again without hesitation."

He gave a weak shake of his head.

"Believe it, Nevan. I'm a man-killer."

I turned my back on him and marched down the trail.

Stalking around the bend, I caught sight of the rock garden twenty feet ahead. A tear rolled down my cheek, hot on my skin. I wiped it away, my breaths hitching, and stared at the ground as my feet pounded out a hard rhythm on the earth. What was wrong with me? So what if I told Nevan about my past—a part of it anyway. That gave me no reason to feel...exposed. Raw. Humiliated.

I tripped over my own toes, flailing forward in an uncontrolled zig-zag. With a little hop and a grunted curse, I regained my balance.

"Best take it easy, love."

My stomach fluttered. I halted and swung my head up, a breath caught in my throat.

Nevan lounged upright against a tree, ankles crossed. One arm hung slack, while the other rested on his thigh. He studied me with an intensity that belied his casual demeanor. "I'd prefer ye don't make a habit of tripping and falling."

"I didn't fall."

He pushed away from the tree and strode closer, consuming the distance between us, stopping an arm's length away. A repressed smile tugged at his lips. "Congratulations. Ye managed not to crack your lovely skull, and without any assistance from me."

I grasped my shoulder with the opposite hand, my arm a diagonal bar across my torso, as if that might deter him from coming closer. "Did you not hear me before? I'm a man-killer."

He moved in, his breaths ghosting over my face, teasing me with enticing scents I couldn't identify. "Fortunately for us both, I am not a man."

"Would six shots to the head kill you?"

"No." His fingertips trailed down my arm. I sucked my lips between my teeth, overwhelmed by the pleasure of his caress as he danced his fingers back up my skin. "Bullets in my brain might slow me down a bit, but I would heal."

"Good to know."

He drew lazy circles on my skin, with his fingertips barely touching me. "Are ye plotting to murder me?"

"If I said yes, would you leave me alone?"

"Do ye truly wish me to?"

His husky tone, and the delicate stimulation of his fingertips, drove out rational thought. Slick heat pooled between my thighs and I felt light, as if I might float away—yet rooted to the ground, helpless to move. "Why are you here? I'm a killer and I'm annoying. You've said you shouldn't be with me anyway, so go. Save yourself a lot of trouble."

"You are neither trouble nor annoying. If you killed a man, I'm certain it was self-defense." His hand glided up, over my shoulder to my throat, and higher, to cup my cheek in his smooth palm. "You are intelligent, brave, beautiful, highly sensual, and thoroughly bewitching."

"Oh. Is that all."

I angled my face away, but he hooked a finger under my chin to coax me into meeting his gaze. He stroked his thumb over my bottom lip, back and forth, back and forth. My legs got wobbly and I locked them for stability, though my inability to break eye contact ensured my legs wouldn't firm up anytime soon. God, those eyes. They cast some kind of spell over me, twirling my thoughts until they scattered out into infinity. Even spellbound, I couldn't manage to keep my big mouth shut.

"Have you fulfilled your duty for the day?" I asked, with no desire at all to know. The image of Nevan's lips on Sandy's plagued me and I didn't need more unwanted visions. Especially since they made my gut twist and my chest ache and my fingers curl in preparation for clenching into fists.

Christ. Maybe I *was* jealous.

Nevan gave a small shake of his head. "I cannot."

"I thought you were magically bound to hunt down special women and shove your tongue down their throats."

He flinched. "They are not special. You are."

A bizarre little thrill shivered through me. I was special. Shouldn't care. *Didn't* care. But right then a memory exploded in my mind of Nevan pressing his lips to Sandy's, and I gritted my teeth hard enough to cause pain. *Rats.* I did care, more than I wanted to, more than reason permitted.

"The bargain with Skeiron," he said, "requires me to search for the Janusite. It does not require me to unleash my ethereal senses every time I encounter a mortal woman."

"I don't understand. If you hate your job, why did you agree to the bargain? And why do you stick to it, instead of saying 'to hell with this stupid agreement'?"

He slipped his hand into mine, twining our fingers. It felt so good I let my fingers wrap around his hand, and his sealed around mine in response. "Magic is new to you, love. You've no conception of the power a bargain wields."

My gaze became glued to his mouth, those luxurious lips, my mind fixated on the notion of what it would feel like to crush my mouth to his and take the flavor of him into me.

"Your lips are awfully close to mine," he purred, his eyes hooded and glowing with unfurling tongues of flame.

I blinked. Holy crap. My mouth was millimeters from his, my lips were parted, and—oh God. I was licking my lips with slow strokes. Somewhere in the middle of my fevered imaginings, I'd leaned toward him, risen onto my tiptoes, and gotten into position to smack one on him.

Hopping back a step, I shoved my hands in my jeans pockets, shoulders hunched. "Sorry about that." I bristled at his half smirk and hastened to add, "Not like I was about to kiss you or anything."

"Why do your desires frighten you?"

No, I wouldn't answer that question, so I chewed the inside of my cheek. "Have you done something to me? Like what you did to Sandy?"

"If you believe I would do such a thing to you, why are you still here?"

"Keep telling you to go away."

"And yet, you could walk down this trail and leave me behind."

Oh. Yeah, I probably could do that. "Won't you just pop up in front of me again?"

"Not this time." He lifted my hand and rubbed his thumb across my knuckles. "You were upset before, when you ordered me to leave you. This time, if you tell me to go, I will. Do you wish me to leave?"

I stared at his bowed head. His shoulders had sagged, his hold on my hand had weakened. *Aw hell.* "No. I don't want you to go."

His head came up. A faint smile lifted the corners of his mouth. His expression was almost...grateful.

With my hand still in his, I cleared my throat. "You, uh, could walk me back to the shop. If you want."

The smile brightened and he straightened. "I will accompany you."

He led me down the path at a leisurely pace, our hands linked. As we strolled toward the rock garden, he spoke, hesitantly at first. "Perhaps in your world it's possible to walk away from an agreement such as mine with Skeiron. But in the Unseen realm, a bargain is sealed by magic. If I fail to fulfill my portion of the bargain, Skeiron may mete out whatever punishment he sees fit, even destroy me."

"Destroy? You mean kill?"

"Worse. To destroy an immortal means to tear him apart at the most basic level—what I believe mortals call molecules—and scatter his essence and powers to the Four Winds. That is what the other gods did to Janus, because they feared his ever-growing power. It took all their combined magics to eradicate him."

I strengthened my grip on his hand. "In my world, we have a saying about a fate worse than death. Sounds like you immortals made it literal."

"We have."

At the edge of the rock garden, he stopped and turned toward me, blocking my view of the garden and the shop beyond. The sun lit him from behind with a halo effect, his body outlined in a golden glow. Though numerous birds twittered in the trees, a dove's voice rose above the rest, its mournful call tugging at my soul.

"Nevan, why would you make this awful bargain? What did Skeiron promise you in return for doing his bidding?"

The breeze tousled his hair, but he ignored the strands blown into his face. "The king agreed to spare his daughter's life."

"What's that got to do with you?"

Though his arms hung at his sides, his shoulders were tensed and his fingers worked as if untying invisible knots. His gaze drifted far away from me, from this place, this time. "I engaged in a dalliance with Skeiron's daughter."

"Oh." I stuffed my hands in my jeans pockets, refusing to think about him cavorting with yet another female.

When he shuffled around, angled sideways to me with his profile illuminated by soft sunshine, the pain in his eyes evaporated my jealousy. He scrubbed a hand across his mouth. "It was…a rather long dalliance involving numerous liaisons. When Skeiron found out, he commanded us to marry but she refused. Skeiron grew quite angry and threatened her life."

"He threatened to kill his own daughter? What a sweetheart." My dad was a good man who worked long hours to make sure we had everything we needed. I couldn't envision any circumstance in which he'd murder me. Nevan's world really was another realm of existence, alien in every way.

Alien in almost every way. He seemed more human than an awful lot of the people from my world.

"It was his right," Nevan said. "Though I did not love his daughter and had no more wish to marry her than she did me, I could never allow harm to come to her. I pleaded with Skeiron to spare her, vowed to accept any bargain in exchange for her life. He'd learned I've indulged in many amorous encounters with other females, even during my acquaintance with his daughter."

"Ouch. That must've seriously ticked him off."

"I was a cad in those days, had been for thousands of years. I deserved to be punished, but his daughter did not." Nevan's chin dropped to his chest, his hair flopping down in a curtain to shield his eyes. "Skeiron agreed to a bargain, but his price for her life was my enslavement. My rank as a general in his army was stripped and I became guardian of the falls, bound to this precise location, never to wander free again."

For a roving Casanova to be tied down in a near-literal sense must've been like, well…castration, I supposed. *Double ouch.* "And you were coerced into hunting for the Janusite."

"Yes." He absently touched the scar on his chest. "To seal the bargain, he imprecated my heart."

"Imprecate?"

"Cursed it. Cursed me to have no heart, no feelings, nothing but a yawning abyss in my soul." Nevan picked at the scar, but his gaze had retreated into the past. "To complete the imprecation, he cut my flesh."

"But you do feel."

"Only since I saw you." His fingers on the scar stilled. "Perhaps the energy I sensed in you diluted the curse."

What could I say to that? I couldn't have anything to do with it. Maybe Skeiron lied about cursing him, but I doubted he'd accept the suggestion. Thanks to his guilt over Skeiron's daughter, he'd become too invested in believing he couldn't feel.

"How long ago did you strike this ass-backwards bargain?" I couldn't help the disgust in my voice. Forcing a man to enchant and kiss innocent women, day after day, was repellent—even for a man who'd thoroughly enjoyed the company of women before the bargain.

Though I despised the deal he'd been forced into, I did not despise Nevan, in spite of his past and his current—er, occupation. I loathed Skeiron. Kill his own daughter? Enslave and curse Nevan? If I ever crossed paths with the king of the sylphs again, I'd empty my derringer's clip into the bastard's head and see how long it took for him to heal. Then I'd do it all over again.

A question popped to mind, one I was fairly certain I didn't want answered. But sometimes a girl has to ask anyway. "What will Skeiron do the Janusite if you find her?"

"I take the Janusite to him. My duty ends there and I am not privy to the remainder of his plan."

Rustling erupted overhead. A raven cackled and cawed.

I zeroed in on the frenetic motion partway up the trunk of an aspen tree. Leaves tumbled down from the branches. The raven flapped its wings in a tight arc, its glistening eyes trained on me.

Nevan shoved me behind him. His every muscle was tight, his body poised for battle. Head thrown back, he shouted at the bird in an alien language.

The raven laughed. Swear to God, it did.

With a final cackle, the bird launched into the heavens. Branches flapped and leaves showered down on us.

Nevan spun around to grasp my upper arms. The intensity of his expression, rife with fury and anguish, made my chest constrict as if he'd clamped iron bars around my ribs. He gave me a gentle shake. "Have you seen a raven before?"

I folded my arms over my belly. "Yeah. So what?"

He shut his eyes for a heartbeat. "Has the raven threatened you in any way?"

"I guess. If you call slamming me to the ground and digging his talons into me a threat. He told me the guardian isn't mine, the same thing Skeiron said." Comprehension blew the breath out of my lungs. "The bird meant you."

Nevan nodded.

"You are the guardian of the falls." I shook my head. "Why does Skeiron's pet raven—and I'm guessing it's more than a nasty bird—why does it care if I hang out with you?"

"I've no time to explain. I must go, if I'm to catch him."

"Him? Do you mean the b—"

Nevan vanished.

With no idea what else to do, I went home and scoured the Internet for information about sylphs and magical bargains, staring at my computer screen until my eyes burned and head ached. Cyberspace gave up nothing more intriguing than myths and legends, interspersed with New Age-y theories. None of it enlightened me. None of it clued me in on the motivations of a real-life sylph king. Or the motivations of a one sexy, mysterious male in a loincloth.

At sunset, I carted my trash bags down to the dumpster in the parking lot. The shadow of a skyborne object flashed across the pavement. I bent my head back to study the heavens, where a bald eagle sailed off into the distance. Not my raven friend after all. The sun sank lower every minute, though, heralding the darkness and dangers of the night. Of course, it wasn't like I could see my enemies coming in the daytime either.

I rubbed my arms in a futile effort to ward off a chill originating from deep inside. Kings and bargains and angry ravens. All those things would haunt my nightmares tonight.

CHAPTER EIGHT

THE NEXT MORNING, TRAVIS WAS WAITING FOR ME WHEN I ARRIVED at the shop. Ambushing me when I climbed out of my car, he penned me between his body and the open driver's door.

I hugged my purse to my belly. "What do you want?"

"Answers."

"You have no evidence I've done anything. This is verging on harassment."

Travis, his eyes flinty, slapped a hand on the roof of my car. "Dammit, Lindsey, I've got reasons to be suspicious of you. Not only did I catch you fooling around with some weirdo, but I also couldn't verify your report of a dead body."

Strange that his first thought had been about Nevan, aka "some weirdo." Why did Travis give a hoot about my relationship with Nevan? Not that I had a relationship with him. Hell, I didn't know what Nevan and I were to each other.

"You don't get to clam up on me, Porter." Travis grabbed my arm. "I gotta explain this crap to the state police."

My scalp prickled with a cold realization. "Something happened."

"A downstater is missing."

"So?"

"The last time his friends saw him, he was walking into this shop. He wanted to see the vortex, but his pals thought it was hokum. They dropped him off here and went over to the museum to check out the big honking steam hoist. Their words, not mine. Anyhow, they haven't seen him since. They reported his disappearance to the state police." He let go of my arm, backing up a couple paces. "Guess they don't trust us yokels. Point is, the fella they're looking for matches your description of the alleged corpse."

"I told you there was a dead guy."

"Yeah, I know." His gaze snapped to the surveillance camera behind me, mounted on the shop's exterior wall. "Stan emailed me the footage from the security camera. I know you had an altercation with the alleged victim."

"The creep was shoplifting."

"Your altercation looked pretty hostile."

I slammed the car door. "What are you hinting at?"

He lodged his hands on his hips, adjusting his belt and the gun holstered on it. "I have to search your car."

"What? Why?""

"Got an anonymous tip." He glanced away, working his shoulders up and down. "You're a person of interest in the case. And I got a warrant."

He plucked a folded sheet of paper from his shirt pocket and thrust it at me. I snatched up the paper. A sick feeling in my stomach, I unfolded the sheet and skimmed the text. Yep, a search warrant.

"It's a routine search," he said, his tone conciliatory. "You've got nothing to worry about, unless you're hiding a body in your trunk."

A cloud scudded in front of the sun. The heat of the sun abandoned me, supplanted by a frigid foreboding. Wind blustered over us, lashing my hair into my face. Behind the rushing of air, I swore I heard a faint cackling, strangely reminiscent of the cry of a jungle creature. Probably a barred owl. They made weird, monkey-like noises.

"Let's check your car," Travis said, "and go from there."

The empathy in his voice disturbed me more than I would've expected. This man despised me, had for years, a fact he'd proved two days ago with his hostile interrogation.

His search began with the car's interior, which he pawed through without expression or comment. "Pop the trunk for me. Please."

I reached through the open window and punched a button. The trunk clicked and floated open a few inches. Travis shoved it up the rest of the way.

His expression blanked. His eyes widened for a second, until his cop demeanor regained its hold.

I took a halting step toward him. "What is it?"

He backed away from the trunk, his gaze glued to whatever lurked inside it.

I couldn't breathe. Every instinct warned me not to look, but I had to know. Trotting forward, I whirled toward the trunk. *No, no, no.*

There, swaddled in a blanket from my bedroom, lay a human body.

Red hair. Pale skin. Green eyes gaping. The dead man from the woods. In my trunk.

Travis pulled out his handcuffs and moved toward me.

I bolted for the woods, blasting through the rock garden, careening around concrete statuary. Gravel crunched under my feet. The thorns of wild rose bushes nicked my arms and hands, but I ignored the stinging, intent on one goal. Stay out of jail. But how?

Nevan.

Only he could help me. Despite the quivery sensation in my gut at the idea of trusting a man—any man—with my safety, I recognized I needed him right now. Travis would arrest me. He'd have no choice. Who would believe my story? Nobody. I was the ice princess, a liar, the ruthless and crazy girl who fabricated stories.

I crashed through a hydrangea. White petals sprayed up around me. A faint perfume teased my senses, but it was whisked away on the wind kicked up by my flight. I punched through more bushes, leaping onto the dirt trail that led to the falls.

"Lindsey, stop!"

Travis shouted from far behind me. The crack of his footfalls on the gravel of the rock garden told me he'd catch up soon. Too soon.

I pumped my legs faster. I'd told the truth, always, yet none of it mattered. After what happened with Calder, no one would trust a word I said. Except Nevan.

A raven squawked overhead, the sound registering dimly in my panicked brain.

The raven swooped low in front of me. Its wings thwap-thwap-thwapped. Feathers scraped my face an instant before the bird rocketed up, out of sight.

I veered toward the sound of the thundering falls. My thighs burned, my chest ached, grit stuck in my eyes, water splattered my face. I tried to stop, skidded, and toppled over backward. My butt hit the ground with a splat. I gasped as pain shot through my tailbone.

Behind me, twigs snapped. Boots clomped. Voices hollered.

They'd catch me. I had nowhere to run.

Scrambling to my feet, I whirled in a circle. "Nevan!"

What kind of witless damsel in distress had I turned into? Screaming his name again and again, praying for him to appear and rescue me.

Boots clomping. Branches snapping. Water rumbling.

No Nevan. No escape.

I fell to my knees on the grass, my head sagging forward. Scents tantalized me. Sweat, grass, damp earth—and the sweet, sharp aroma of an approaching thunderstorm.

My head sprang up. Earth. Thunderstorms.

Foliage rustled. Footfalls pounded. Travis and his cohorts were seconds away.

A familiar sensation rippled through me. *He's coming.*

Relief and joy tumbled through me like a landslide. I leaped up and spun toward the falls.

A raven slammed into my chest. The full weight of its body, propelled by the kinetic energy of its flight, combined to flip me off my feet. I smacked into the ground flat on my back, my feet in the air. Lights exploded in my vision as pain ricocheted through my body.

The bird squatted on my chest and thrashed its head, its razor-sharp beak slicing my cheek, igniting searing streaks of pain. The raven's talons sank into my shoulders.

A figure reared up behind the bird, casting a shadow over me and my avian attacker.

Nevan latched onto the raven with one hand and pitched it aside. A thump resounded somewhere to the left. The raven must've hit a tree.

My savior knelt beside me, his face pinched, body stiff, eyes scanning up and down my body as he assessed my condition. He slid his hands into my hair to probe my scalp with unexpected gentleness, then bent close to peer into my eyes. His body relaxed on a long sigh and he raked a hand through his hair, but his expression remained tense.

Nevan slipped an arm under my back to raise me into a sitting position. Pain pulsed in my skull and I groaned. Nevan braced me against his body, cradling my face in one palm. "Are ye hurt, love?"

"No." I slurred the syllable a bit, but after a brief pause, I managed a steadier tone. "I saw stars for a minute, but I'm okay."

A flapping noise pulled my attention to the area past my feet.

The raven squatted there, its beak ajar, wings elevated and spread. The creature's black eyes darted up and down, left and right, as if measuring me up.

I huddled closer to Nevan. He folded an arm around my shoulders.

The bird's body glimmered and blurred, liquefying into an oily mass that hovered in the air. Ribbons of prismatic blue unfurled and writhed within the mass, as it swelled and lengthened into an elongated blob taller than Nevan at his full height. With a snap of electricity and a burst of sparks, the roiling mass coalesced into a humanlike being with male attributes.

The thing rolled his shoulders back, tightening his pitch-dark flesh and flexing his gargantuan shoulders. Thick sinews corded his torso and arms. Nevan boasted an impressive physique, but this man—or bird-man, or whatever—dominated my view with his mountain of muscles, devoid of any cellulite. His skin, from his bald head down to his bare feet, glistened with an iridescent blue sheen. His biceps were thicker than my head.

Nevan rose, though he stuck close to me. His voice seethed when he said, "Brennus."

The raven-man smiled. His lips peeled away from white teeth, each tapered to a blunt point. No amusement emanated from him, but rather his smile conveyed a menace that chilled me down to the deepest atoms of my being.

"Guardian," Brennus said, his voice as deep and dark as his fathomless eyes. "You act against your duty, and Skeiron will know of this. Inciting his wrath is unwise."

Nevan stalked toward Brennus. Hands balled into hard fists, his jaw tight enough to pulverize steel, he incinerated the raven-man with a glare so hot I swore it singed my skin. "If I rip your head from your body, you filthy shapeshifter, you won't have the chance to tell Skeiron."

Brennus laughed. Without mirth. Without pity. He sniggered like a demigod certain of his supremacy over all foes.

It was the most terrifying sound I'd ever heard.

Nevan clamped a hand around Brennus's throat and hurled him across the clearing. The monstrous raven-man whacked into a birch tree. The trunk shivered. A wide fissure splintered the trunk from the ground straight up to the lowest branch.

Brennus surged to his feet and took a single step toward me.

I dug my fingers into the damp earth, as if I might anchor myself there against the shapeshifter's assault.

The raven-man extended his arms to the sides and tipped his head left and right. The shivering branches of the birch tree cast undulating speckles of sunlight on Brennus's skin, sparking on the blue streaks in his flesh. "My master also wants your mortal whore and I am forced to obey his will. As you must obey your king."

Nevan stood a dozen feet from the raven-man, his stance wide. "I perform my duty. That is all Skeiron need know."

I stomped past Nevan to halt between the two supernatural beings. "Jesus, even immortal men have pissing contests. Since this conversation clearly involves me, how about including me in it?"

Brennus speared me with his jet-black gaze, and for a frozen second I wished I could reel my words back into my mouth. Until he spoke again.

"Guardian," he snarled, "silence your female before I do."

I stamped my foot. "Talk to the female, asshole. I'm not deaf."

Nevan grasped my shoulders from behind and whispered, "Allow me to handle this."

Brennus stretched out his fingers. The sunlight glanced off his wickedly sharp nails.

I gulped. Nodded. Sidled around Nevan so his body shielded me. Even I understood when to retreat.

Brennus let his arms fall to his side. "Beware, guardian. Protecting the female may bring about your own destruction. She will be his in either case."

Every muscle in Nevan's body had gone taut, sculpting him into a bronzed statue more beautiful than Michelangelo's David and more imposing than any Greek god. He squared his shoulders and met Brennus's cold gaze head-on.

Despite eclipsing him by more than two feet, Brennus paled next to the sylph. Even the raven-man's Himalayan Mountains of muscle could not compete with the awe-inspiring presence and raw sensuality of Nevan in his full glory.

And God, was he magnificent. Anger molded him into a spectacle straight out of ancient legends.

"Leave," Nevan said. "If any harm comes to this female, I will unleash my wrath upon you. Do you recall the power of my wrath, Brennus?"

The raven-man shuffled backward.

Hell, I would've too if Nevan had aimed his threat in my direction. Everything about him, from his stance to the seething undertone of his voice, screamed danger. Somehow, though, his anger didn't frighten me half as much as Calder's had, when he'd morphed from nice guy to demon incarnate.

Brennus turned his hands palm up, raising them to shoulder height. "These are not my commands, guardian. Heed them or do not, it makes no difference to me."

Nevan peeled his lips away from his clenched teeth. "Leave."

The raven-man shimmered and dissolved, his mass shrinking into a blob the size of a raven. Within a heartbeat, the figure solidified into a bird. Brennus took off into the sky.

Nevan turned to me, and the second our eyes met, his fiery tension was doused. His expression, once forged from wrought-iron, softened. I softened too, overcome with a need to throw my arms around him and kiss him until we were both mindless. I'd dived headfirst into romance with a deadly man once before, though, and I couldn't do it again.

"Can you explain to me," I asked, "what that insane conversation was all about?"

"I believe Brennus was threatening you as a means to control me. He is Skeiron's assassin and spy. Why he would claim Skeiron wants you, or for what reason that might be true, I cannot say."

"I see." Didn't really, but with the confrontation over, the electrical surge of adrenaline that had bolstered me snuffed out. I let my head fall onto his chest.

He smoothed my hair away from my face. "It's all right."

"No." I tilted my head up to stare at him. "It's not all right. A scary bird-man called me a whore and threatened to hand me over to an even scarier guy. All right is a distant planet and I don't have a rocket to take me there."

"Since I am from another world, you may consider me your distant planet." He splayed his fingers over my shoulder, gliding them down to my elbow. "And you have already touched down."

Oh, the idea sounded so good I wanted to melt into him. As badly as I longed to seek solace in him, I couldn't. "This is really bad, isn't it?"

"Yes."

I moved away from him. "I'm glad you don't feel the need to sugarcoat things. It's awfully comforting."

He narrowed his eyes. "What would you have me do, lie?"

"Of course not." I kicked the dirt with my toe and watched a little clod fly up. "Don't know what I want. Supernatural threats make me irrational. You'd think I'd be used to it by now, but no."

He took hold of my chin with a warm, strong hand, compelling me to look up at him. "Lindsey, has someone else threatened you? Someone besides Brennus or Skeiron?"

"Not lately."

His face went as taciturn and implacable as stone, though a muscle in his jaw ticked. "Tell me when. And who."

A command, not a request.

His hand still gripped my chin. I shied away from his touch, backing up another pace. "I don't want to talk about it."

Fingers twitching, he blew a breath out his nose.

The memory of Brennus's attack reeled through me. His beak piercing my cheek. His talons knifing into my shoulders. I yanked up my T-shirt to check for wounds, exposing the low-cut bra that shielded my breasts. The raven's talons hadn't broken the skin.

Nevan averted his eyes and winced.

"You're embarrassed? Seriously?" I rolled my eyes. "Nibbling my ear is okay, but one glimpse of my bra and you're humiliated."

He cleared his throat. "I am not humiliated. I'm simply trying to…respect your privacy."

"Whatever you say." I dropped my shirt and it fluttered down to cover me again. I glanced around the clearing, where the evidence of the Brennus tumult marked the ground and trees. The pounding of approaching men had silenced. "Wait a minute. The cops were coming for me and they were almost here."

"I made them believe you'd run the other way."

"You—How?"

"Magic, naturally." He strode toward me. "However, my illusions rarely last long. The fae from whom I acquired the spell refused to give it endurance."

"Oh. Sure. I get it." In a warped reality where magic made perfect sense, I would've gotten it. Confined to my world, I suffered from a pressure headache triggered by thinking about this insanity for too long.

"We must go." Nevan proffered a hand. "Well, darlin'? I haven't got all day. Even a sylph has work to do."

"Porter!"

Travis's voice bellowed through the woods. He burst out of the trees and stopped twenty feet away, breathing hard, his face red from exertion. "Why the hell'd you run?"

"You were going to arrest me. I can't go through that again. I won't."

Between huffing breaths, Travis said, "I wouldn't do that."

"You took out your handcuffs."

"Force of habit. I wouldn't arrest you."

"But you'll haul me in for questioning."

"Had to, and I kinda thought—" He shifted his weight from one foot to the other and back again, while his fingers plucked at the strap on his gun holster. "Never mind. I'm sorry."

I fumbled for a response but came up empty.

A shuffling noise jerked me out of my confusion. Nevan traipsed around me, planting himself between me and Travis, who leaned sideways to keep an eye on me. Every couple seconds, he'd shoot a dagger glare at Nevan, but the sylph ignored it.

Nevan, shoulders back and head held high, gazed down on us mere mortals with austere confidence. I was struck once again by the power he exuded, his aura of otherness, beautiful and yet so far beyond my reach.

Realizing with a start Travis had spoken again, I blinked rapidly and tried to focus on him. "Huh?"

The sheriff stared at me for a few seconds, then his gaze tracked to the loincloth-clad elemental being stationed between us. His hand on his holster, he tapped one finger on the Sig berthed inside it. "What's this freak doing to you? Drugs? Hypnosis?"

Travis stalked toward me, veering around my self-appointed protector.

Nevan thrust out an arm, blocking him.

"Outta my way," Travis snapped.

Nevan regarded Travis with remote interest, like a scientist observing a microbe—and preparing to squash it.

A minute ago, I'd reveled in his incredible power. What had I been high on? The last thing I needed was Nevan pummeling the county sheriff. I'd get blamed for it, for sure. "Nevan, cut it out."

He ignored me, though a single, dark brow ticked upward.

I shot for a reasonable tone, despite my hammering heart and the sweat dribbling down my temples. "Please let Travis go by. He won't hurt me. Will you, Travis?"

"Course not." Travis raised a fist at Nevan. "But if this freak don't get outta my way, I will pump six rounds of hollow-point ammo smack into his brain."

Great. That would defuse the situation for sure.

"Let's all calm down." I directed a serene smile first at Travis, then at the sylph. "Please, Nevan."

He stepped aside, but kept his steely gaze on the sheriff.

Travis rushed toward me, seizing my shoulders. "Wake up, Lindsey, shake it off. Let me help you."

Nevan's mouth angled into a cool smile. "Perhaps she doesn't trust you."

Travis slung a sidelong glare at Nevan. "Stay outta this."

"Afraid I can't, son."

Travis tore his hands away from me to stab a finger in Nevan's direction. "I am not your son. For one thing, you aren't old enough to be my dad, and believe me, I'm real grateful for that." His hands fisted so tightly the muscles in his arms bulged. "Back off. This is between me and Lindsey. I don't know who the hell you are, but I guarantee I will find out."

"Highly doubtful." A derisive smile tautened Nevan's mouth. "But go on and try, son. It'll be amusing."

Travis shook his fists in the air, his face flushing bright red. "You son of a bitch—"

"Gah!" I shouted. "Enough. You two are acting like cavemen."

Both men swung their gazes to me. Expectant. Questioning. Irritated.

I huffed. "Don't give me that look, either of you. I do what I want, remember? It's called free will."

Nevan looked suitably chagrined, but Travis stared at me like I'd grown three extra heads—tiny gargoyle heads that were making rude faces at him.

Travis scrubbed a hand over his face, straightened, and held out a hand to me. "Listen, I know we ain't exactly been friends, but I never lied to you. Come back with me."

Something flickered across Nevan's features, something reminiscent of disappointment, but it dissipated too fast for me to be sure. He slackened his shoulders, cocking one hip. "Do what you want."

Despite his aloof pose, he fixed his gaze directly on mine. The metallic hues in his irises blended and twirled, diverging and joining, hypnotizing me for a second too long. I neglected to notice he'd moved closer, edging up beside me, until I realized—thanks to a muscle spasm at the base of my skull—I'd craned my neck back to maintain eye contact.

"Lindsey," Travis said, in his most commanding cop voice.

I ripped my gaze from Nevan, returning my attention to Travis.

The sheriff held his arms stiff at his sides, fingers coiled into his palms. "I know you don't trust me. Why would you? I shoulda believed you about Calder, shoulda supported you, but I couldn't accept my brother had turned into some kinda…monster." He tugged at his shirt collar, rolling his shoulders in jerky movements. "I shouldn't have arrested you three years ago. I won't do it today. You gotta believe me."

"Am I supposed to be grateful?"

Travis shuffled up to my other side, scowling at Nevan, his anger easing up as he snaked his hand around mine. His skin was cool, his hold awkward. "We can fix this together. Just stay."

Though Nevan said nothing, his lips had flattened and his nostrils flared the tiniest bit. When he curved one corner of his mouth into a faint attempt at a grin, the expression stopped short of his eyes.

I glanced back and forth between the two cavemen before me. How could I turn away from Travis, a man I'd known for five years, in favor of someone I met yesterday? Travis had always despised me—or so I'd thought. As for Nevan, I had no clue what he felt.

Standing rigid beside me, Nevan spoke in a low voice. "You know I am the only one who can protect you."

Travis had turned his back on me three years ago, when I needed a friend the most. In the past two days alone, Nevan had aided me more than anyone else in my whole life. Anyone except my family.

I slipped my hand into Nevan's. He squeezed gently. A genuine, if muted, smile relaxed his lips.

"No," Travis said, shaking his head vigorously. "You can't be serious. *Stay here.*"

I moved closer to Nevan, my shoulder bumping his chest. "I can't stay. Nevan's right. He can help me a lot more than you can."

"Are you kidding me? You can't run off with Kevin the jungle fairy."

Nevan shot ramrod straight, his gaze narrowing on Travis. "I am not a fairy."

Travis ground his teeth. "I ain't letting you take her."

What drug was he on? Travis had treated me like a criminal until abruptly deciding to help. "I'm going with Nevan."

Travis bolted his hand around my arm and I flinched at his steel grip. "I won't let you go, Porter. You're a suspect in a murder."

"You're giving me vertigo with your constant one-eighties. Make up your mind, Travis. Hate me, help me, you have to pick one."

Spittle spraying from his lips, he snarled, "I'll do whatever it takes to keep you away from—" He punched a finger in the air toward Nevan without looking at the other man. "Away from that *thing.*"

Confronted with Travis's vehemence, I sidled closer to Nevan. Travis's behavior had grown so erratic I had no clue what he might resort to next.

He wrested the cuffs from his belt. "This is for your own good, Lindsey."

Nevan flicked his wrist.

Travis's feet flipped out from under him and he sailed backward through the air. His body thwacked down at the far side of the clearing. Prone on the ground, Travis jacked his head up, grimacing, his eyes dull and his hair mussed.

I wrested my hand free of Nevan's. "What are you doing? You could've killed him."

"The sheriff is unharmed." Nevan grazed his knuckles across my cheek. "He threatened you."

"Now who's jealous."

"I said I'd protect you and I keep my promises." He dragged one fingertip down my jaw, a faint smile on his lips. "I seem to recall a certain mortal screaming my name, begging for my help."

Crap. I had. Worse, I didn't regret it. But still…

I studied Travis. He'd pushed up into a sitting position and was fingering the back of his head.

Nevan hauled me into his arms, pressing me into his body, suffusing me with his primal heat. He had hidden layers to his personality and I didn't know if I could or should accept his darker side. In this moment, though, he represented my best hope.

He spanned the small of my back with his large hands, tethering me to him. "Ready?"

"For what?"

"To cross the veil."

Sheesh, his world had screwy terminology. "To what the what?"

"You'll see."

The world evaporated into a roiling mist, the ground fell away beneath us, and we plunged into blackness.

CHAPTER NINE

ICE CLAWED AT MY FLESH. I CLUNG TO NEVAN WITH BOTH ARMS around his neck. His biceps flexed and tautened around me as he adjusted and strengthened his hold. I tried to speak, to ask where he was taking me, but couldn't. If my body still existed, my mind must've detached from it. I rocketed through an abyss, numb except for the pinching, slashing ice.

Whump. My feet touched down with a gentleness incongruous with the noise I'd heard. Or sensed. Or something. Sunlight swaddled me in its delicate warmth. A forest encircled us and I understood, on a visceral level, we had teleported to another spot in the same woods, in the vicinity of the falls. I strained to hear the rumbling of the water, but detected nothing more than birds twittering.

Nevan's embrace crushed me. No wonder I couldn't catch my breath. With my face mashed against his chest, I croaked, "You're squishing me."

He loosened his hold. "Sorry, love, I don't often travel with a passenger. And I assumed ye wouldn't appreciate it if I dropped ye."

"Absolutely not."

"I will never let you go." He combed his fingers through my hair. "Are ye all right?"

"Yeah." I propped my chin on his chest. "Glad to be back on the ground."

A relieved smile accompanied his sigh. "As am I."

I hesitated for a moment, entranced by the odd safety of being in his arms, before I pushed away. "Travis found the dead guy. In the trunk of my car."

A vein throbbed in his forehead. "Did he now."

"Could Skeiron have put it there?"

"I've no idea. Can't imagine why he'd bother mucking about with a corpse." His brows cinched together. "Someone else must've killed the poor fellow and waited for the right moment to plant the body, to place the blame squarely on you."

"Great." I rubbed my arms, scratching my elbow. "I have at least two mortal enemies. I love being popular."

"Your enemies aren't mortal. I'm quite certain, given the body thief's actions, he or she is no more mortal than Skeiron is."

"Thanks for the awesome pep talk."

His forehead wrinkled. "Pep talk?"

"Forget it." I surveyed the vicinity, arms belted around me like a strait-jacket. "I shouldn't have run. It was stupid, I know. I should've trusted the law to straighten out this mess. That's what normal people do."

Nevan harrumphed. "The innocent often suffer at the whim of any legal system."

"Do elemental beings have a legal system?"

"Of course." He canted his head, lips parted slightly. "When you mentioned the law, were you referring to the sheriff?"

"Not sure. Travis did seem halfway sincere when he offered to help."

With a *hmt* noise, Nevan began to scrape his finger across his thumb in repetitive jerks.

It was my turn to smirk. "Jealous much?"

"Of a human? Bah." He waved a dismissive hand.

If he wanted to swim in denial, fine. "You said you can help me. How?"

"Hmm," he said, with a teasing glint in his eyes. "Let me think."

"You don't have a plan?" I was in no mood for jokes. Panic amped up my volume and elevated my pitch to a higher octave. "You swept me away, promising to fix things, and you don't even have a—"

Nevan snared me in his arms. I sucked in a sharp breath. He cradled my face in one hand, his thumb caressing the corner of my mouth, eliciting wave of heat that bloomed out into my whole body. "Hush, darlin'. I have a plan."

The intimacy of our position had me squirming against him. "You do?"

"Resurrect the dead fellow."

"You can—I mean, you seriously could—bring someone back from the dead?"

"I cannot do it personally, mind you, but I can access the magic." He pulled me hard against him, both arms folded around me. "We've got a journey ahead of us."

"A trip? Where to?"

"Through the veil. Into the Unseen realm."

"I thought we already crossed the veil thingy."

"Not quite. I brought us a short ways from the scene of the crime, as it were. We have yet to pierce the veil—the barrier between your world and mine."

My head throbbed, most likely from information overload. More than my head throbbed, thanks to the disconcerting way he'd bound our bodies together. The way Nevan exposed my deepest needs, inflaming them beyond reason, scared me more than being framed for murder.

"Are ye ready?" he asked.

Too many discomfiting layers to that question. I ignored all but the most obvious. "Take me there."

Nevan studied me for a moment, apparently uncertain whether I meant what I'd said or if I comprehended the gravity of my decision. Maybe I didn't. He'd explained and presented me with the option. I'd granted my permission. More than that, despite vowing never to do it again, I'd made the decision to trust a man.

A breeze fanned over us, feathering my hair across my shoulders and my chest. A stray lock flew across my lips and spilled down again to tickle my collarbone and stray over Nevan's hand, where it still rested there on my bare skin.

His gaze skipped down to my breasts, then blazed straight into my eyes. His chest heaved once. The swelling length of his erection strained against his loincloth but somehow stayed contained beneath it.

A bolt of searing need tore through me. Images rolled past my mind's eye, vivid to the point of making my skin tingle and my sex throb. I hungered for him to see me exposed before him and lay those big hands on my naked body. I craved the rasp of his tongue on my—

Noooo, I would not finish that thought. Passions of all kinds, sexual and emotional, must be restrained or bad things would follow.

His tongue rolled over his lower lip. "Tell me one thing first. Why does the sheriff call you ice princess?"

"You have to know now?"

"I would like to know, that's all."

I knotted a lock of my hair around my finger. Why not tell him? Maybe the truth would squelch his desire and I'd be safe again. *Do you want to be safe?* I wound the lock tighter, until it strangled my finger, then shook it off. "After I shot Calder, I told Travis everything that happened. Everything. Even the incredibly personal stuff, because I thought he needed to know in order to help me. Back then, I still believed he would help."

Nevan turned his hand over, skating the back of it down my breastbone until it encountered my T-shirt's neckline. He hovered his hand there, a millimeter from my skin. "He arrested you."

"Yeah." I linked my hands over my belly, only to let them drop away. "Weird thing is, he didn't yell at me about murdering his brother. He started calling me ice princess instead."

Nevan withdrew his hand. "Why?"

"Because I…well…" *Spit it out, you coward.* "When I told Travis what Calder had done to me, I also told him what I am. For some reason, it enraged him."

"And what precisely are you?"

My stomach churned, but I took a deep breath and told him what I'd never told anyone else except Travis and Calder. "I'm a virgin."

Nevan's mouth fell open and quickly clapped shut. His brows arched before knitting together. As the lines smoothed out of his forehead, he gave a slow nod. "That explains quite a few things."

"Really. Such as?"

"Why you forbade me to kiss you, for one. And why you're uncomfortable with my lack of clothing."

The ache in my head spread to my neck. Once again, he'd bared my secrets without the slightest effort. It made me feel as transparent as glass.

He rubbed his chin. "But your virginity hardly makes you cold and remote, as the term ice princess implies."

I stuffed my hands in my jeans pockets. "According to Travis, I string men along with tacit promises of sex, only to shut them down when they make a move." I cast my gaze to the ground as the old knot cinched tight in my gut. "He said I like to torture men and that's how I drove Calder over the edge. I deserved what happened, he said. I'm a rotten tease."

Was that my voice, so small and pathetic? I'd thought I could bury the past, but it kept rising up like a zombie to terrorize me.

Because I let it. Because keeping it alive gave me a fantastic excuse to hide inside myself. *Never a victim again.*

"Lindsey—"

"Forget it." I lifted my gaze to Nevan's and swung my hands at my sides. "I told you I'd cross the veil with you. Take me already."

His lips twitched with suppressed humor. "Well now, I thought it'd take far longer for ye to beg me to take ye."

My rebuttal turned into a choked grunt. After a few seconds, I managed to speak. "I didn't mean it like that. And I was not begging."

"I heard a note of…" He gave a soft chuckle, his mouth forming a slight smile. "Desperation."

"What you heard was frustration."

His smile broadened into a grin that set off glittering sparks in his eyes. "I'd be more than happy to assist ye with your *frustration*."

Cripes, I'd done it again. I had to start thinking before I spoke. Maybe I ought to write the words down and read them three times first. "Let's get this veil-crossing thing over with."

With one fingertip, he charted a path down my breastbone until my shirt's neckline interrupted the journey. "The next time you beg me to take you, best make certain of your meaning, because I will take you at your word."

The sight of his penis peeking out from under the loincloth ripped away any response I might've formulated. I gave myself an actual shake, like a dog shedding water, but the discomfort lingered. "Take me to the damn Unseen realm."

Nevan surveyed the tree branches as if hunting for something, but then gave up the search. "Before I can take you there, I must make certain you have the touch. If you don't, the veil will not open for you."

"I don't understand."

"You must have a touch of the Unseen realm in you."

"And how do you figure out if I have it?"

"With a test." He twisted his mouth into a grimace. "You may not like what's involved."

"Just tell me."

"I must enchant you."

"Enchant?" My throat tightened, my jaw too. "That's what you did to Sandy."

His grimace dug in deeper. "Yes."

The blonde girl's face, dazed and befuddled, flashed in my mind. My muscles seemed to calcify, freezing me in place. "How is it any different from what you've been doing to me all along?"

"I've done nothing—to you." He slanted forward, his face hovering above mine, his breaths slow and deliberate. "I have never enchanted you, I swear it."

His fevered gaze bounced from my eyes to my lips and back again.

I laid a hand on my chest, but the tickle behind my ribs refused to quit.

"Not once," he said, "have I used magic on you. I wouldn't, unless I sensed the touch in you. And I haven't sensed it—yet." He closed his hands around my upper arms. "I do not wish to do this, but it's the only way. You must believe me."

Though the silent *please* in his tone had my lips straining to smile, I clamped them between my teeth. He was all but begging me to believe him, and if I wanted to fix the mess I'd stumbled into, I had no choice except to trust him. To let him enchant me. And kiss me.

My lips tingled. I became acutely aware of my hand on my chest—the warmth of it on my bare skin, the way my wrist brushed against my breast— and the feel of his hands on my arms. God, I wanted him to kiss me, like I'd never wanted anything.

He let his hands fall away from my arms and shifted his weight to one hip. "If you still wish to cross over into the Unseen realm, we should do this quickly. The sheriff, that persistent beggar, will soon find us."

Boy, my two cavemen totally despised each other. I couldn't understand the depth of their dislike, because it struck me as jealousy, which made no sense. Nevan being jealous, I could see. But Travis?

No time to worry about it. I had to fix my life, and a single viable option was available to me.

"Okay," I said. "If enchantment's what we have to do, I give you permission to go ahead with it."

He marveled at me as if I were a goddess incarnate, descended straight from the heavens, shimmering with remnants of stardust.

A rock settled in my gut. He'd called me intriguing and unusual, but then he also said he didn't want to enchant me. Maybe he didn't want to do it because I wasn't Sandy. I lacked the va-va-voom all men seemed to crave. Then again, he had gaped at my breasts.

He gripped the nape of his neck in one hand, his head lowered. "There is more."

"You can tell me."

His fingers, woven with mine, tensed. He expelled a ragged breath and wrapped his other hand around our joined fingers. "The test requires intimate contact."

"We are not having sex right here in the woods."

"Not that intimate." He started to chuckle, but stifled it. He watched me with uncertainty in his eyes. "You know of what I speak."

I let out the breath I hadn't realized I was holding. "A kiss."

"Yes. But I promised to keep my lips away from yours."

My mouth watered as my body began to ache in places I wished it wouldn't. "You have my permission. One kiss."

He took one large step backward. Though the gap between us measured less than an arm's length, the withdrawal of his body seemed to strip the oxygen from the air. His eyes burned with twirling flames of every color, spinning faster the longer he beheld me. My gaze traveled down to his lips, full and ripe and parted for a deep kiss. He swiped his tongue across his lower lip, leaving it glistening and slick.

"What are you doing?" I breathed.

"Unleashing my ethereal senses."

The erotic undertone in his voice brushed warmth across my skin, stirring the hairs on my arms and the nape of my neck to rise. With his hands on my shoulders, he drew me to him. My head fell back as my gaze sought his. My whole body seemed to lighten and lift off the ground, though my feet stayed glued to the earth. I battled to resist the allure of total surrender, but the part of me that yearned for it swelled larger and stronger every second.

"Can ye hear me, love?" he purred.

"Yes." A dreaminess infused my tone, matching the floaty sensation in my body. Dimly, I realized I should probably worry about my altered state, but the notion flitted away from my consciousness. "Am I enchanted?"

"Not yet." He ran a hand through my hair, trailing his fingers down to my neck, across my jawline, to curl under my chin. "I want to take you to a special place few mortals have ever seen. Will ye come with me?"

Someplace special. A thread of anxiety wound tight around my heart. "You told Sandy the same thing."

He bent his head nearer to mine, his voice barely a whisper. "That was my duty. This is my choice."

"In that case…Yes, I will go with you."

"Are you certain?"

Although my brain might've still been a bit muzzy, I understood what I'd agreed to and what he'd meant when he said this was his choice, not his duty. He'd asked for my trust again and reminded me, in his own way, he'd chosen me—against his duty, against the decree of his king.

I slanted forward until only a whisper of air separated our lips. "I'm sure."

His pupils flared wide, the metallic irises shrinking to a narrow ring.

"When's the enchantment start?" I felt warm and fuzzy, but nothing like what I'd witnessed in Sandy. She'd seemed…mesmerized. "I'm not really feeling—"

"Quiet." He exerted a light pressure, urging my chin up. "Look into my eyes."

"Already am."

He growled out a sigh. "Look harder."

I rolled my eyes. "What exactly am I supposed to be looking for?"

"Nothing. Just *focus*."

"On what?" I tried to shake my head free, but his thumb and forefinger locked my chin in place. "If you don't want to do this, tell me. I realize I'm not as hot as Sandy, or probably any of the other hordes of women you've—"

He thrust his thumb up, sealing my lips. "There are no hordes of women. I've told you that before and you claimed you believe me. Perhaps you're the one having doubts about this."

"No." It came out muffled and squashed, thanks to his thumb over my mouth.

"All right then. Look in my eyes, and relax."

I looked. And relaxed. Well, as much as I could under the circumstances.

Sparks ignited in his eyes, white hot against the warm, liquid shades of his irises. His heat enveloped me, soft and searing at the same time. A breeze tousled his hair and transported his scent to me, tantalizing my senses. His thumb traced circles on my lips, the brush of skin like satin, arousing me with a slow-building desire, until my skin felt tight, my breasts swollen, my lips engorged and aching for his kiss.

I flicked my tongue out to steal a taste of him. Salty. Earthy. With a spicy undertone. Hunger shivered through me. Seconds ticked by. *Tick, tick, tick,* went the clock in my head. I dared to lave the pad of his thumb.

He went stone still, the roiling currents in his eyes the only motion within him.

Tick, tick, tick.

A mosquito lighted on my nose. I tried to blow it off, but his damn thumb blocked my breath. I swatted the bug away.

He released my chin, withdrawing his hand.

I scratched my nose. "Did you start it yet?"

"Did I start?" His brow furrowed on a slight frown. "Of course I started, minutes ago. Yet you don't seem enchanted. How do you feel?"

"Peachy. What's supposed to happen?"

"You should experience a mild euphoria and…" He looked down at his feet. "An overpowering desire to be near me and to please me."

Laughter exploded out of me on a snort. I held up a hand, struggling to recover from the inappropriate outburst. "I'm sorry. Please don't take this the wrong way, but if that's how I'm supposed to feel then I don't think you're it right."

"Of course I'm doing it right," he all but snarled. "This has been my duty for a century. I know how to enchant a woman."

I shrugged. "Guess it just doesn't work on me."

His mouth flattened into a line as his eyes tightened into a squint. He nostrils flared on an explosive exhalation. "Enchantment never fails."

I raised my hands in supplication. "Hey, it's not my fault you've lost your mojo. Maybe I don't have any magical energy in me."

"Even if you don't, I should be able to enchant you. But clearly, I cannot." He locked his hands behind his back, rocking onto his heels. "My magic does not fail."

I patted his shoulder. "I'm sure it happens to every sylph at least once in his life."

"Bloody hell." He jammed a hand into his hair, scratching furiously. "You must be blocking it."

"Typical. Blame it on the girl."

"I sensed an energy within you when first we met. It must be the touch, but you've repressed it. It is unprecedented." He rubbed his eyes with the heels of his hands. When he lowered his hands, he stared at me blankly for a few seconds before shaking his head as a look of sheer wonder overtook his features. "You, love, are a unique human."

"Thanks. You're pretty unique yourself."

He cleared his throat. "Remember what I told you about thanking me. Gratitude can be dangerous, and you would do well to beware of expressing it. Please heed me on this, Lindsey."

"Fine, whatever. Now shut up, will you?" I slanted my body nearer to his, tipping my head back. "Try the kiss thing. Maybe that'll do the trick."

I shut my eyes. No longer able to see him, I felt the wisp of air displacement as he bent his head toward mine. The breath caught in my throat. I burned to fan my fingers across his chest, to slide up and down that silken skin.

He cupped his hands around my elbows, gliding them up my arms. His lips skimmed across mine, warm and soft and oh so tempting. I melted into him as he enfolded me in his arms, the embrace tender at first, intensifying little by little, his arms pressing me firmly against him. Plastered to him, aware of every hard line of muscle and his rigid shaft crushed against my belly, I trembled with a desperate hunger that eclipsed anything I'd known before, an all-consuming lust for his touch, his kiss, his body, his—

My knees threatened to buckle. I clung to him, rocked by the realization of what I burned for most. Him. Inside me.

His mouth coasted over mine one last time, then retreated.

I moaned, clutching at his biceps, reveling in the sensation of his sinews tautening under my fingers. His chest rose and fell erratically and he seemed as incapable of catching his breath as I was. I let my head fall back, my lips parting on another moan, guttural and wanton.

Crushing me to him, his hands fisting in my shirt, he scraped his mouth over mine once, twice, and with a rough, drawn-out groan he possessed my lips with his. I opened to my mouth to him, pleading for more, surrendering my will and my body without reservation.

"Lindsey," he breathed into my mouth, his lips still on mine. The vibrations from his mouth—from the uttering of that single, reverent word—reverberated through my entire body.

"Nevan," I murmured, moving his lips with mine. "Please."

He sealed his mouth over mine, thrusting his tongue inside, our lips molded together as our tongues tangled, as we devoured and tormented and inflamed each other with ever slick glide of flesh over flesh. Famished for the taste of him, I plunged deeper inside his mouth, loving the way he opened more for me and growled low in his throat.

Slow down, a muffled voice in my head urged. *Shut this down before it goes too far.*

But God, I couldn't.

Nevan's hands dropped to my ass, kneading with ravenous strokes, and I was lost. I flung my arms around his neck, holding on like I'd disintegrate without his arms to bind me together. He raked a hand up my back to spread his palm over my spine, between my shoulder blades, while his other hand clutched my ass, tugging my hips forward, angling them up and into him perilously close to his raging erection.

"Mm." I tunneled my fingers into his hair, pulling his head lower, opening wider for the kiss. Currents crackled around us, inside me, alive and electric, fueling an irresistible fervor. My head swam. We barreled toward an inescapable destination, about to blast away my barriers—and my virginity—and Christ, I wanted to go there. Right now. With him. With a man who wasn't even a man.

He wrenched away from me, staggering backward. The loss of his heat, his scent, his flavor, cast me out into an emptiness so vast my thoughts echoed back to me.

Mouth agape, eyes wild and fiery, he bored his gaze into me.

A chill frosted over my skin. "What's wrong?"

He staggered backward another step. The flaming hues in his eyes quieted to a faint glimmer, though he stared at me without blinking.

Shoving my hands in my pockets, shoulders bunched. "Kissing me was that bad, huh?"

Whatever panic had gripped him sluiced out in the space of a breath. He folded me in his arms, cradling my head to his chest. I closed my eyes, relishing the *thump-thump* of his heart beneath my ear. He did care for me, in some way, even if our kiss hadn't left him thunderstruck, the way it had me.

He nuzzled my hair and caressed my back. "You misunderstand my reaction."

My heartbeat accelerated, revved by a dangerous hope—and a hint of fear.

"Kissing you," he said, pressing his lips to my forehead, "transcended anything I've experienced in my entire existence. It was perfection."

Elation swelled in my chest and I curled my fingers against his chest. "Nobody's ever kissed me like that."

"Then every man who's touched you has been a bloody idiot." He threaded his fingers through my hair, the tips dancing across my scalp. All the remaining shreds of my anxiety fled and I snuggled into him. He sighed, as if the greatest pleasure of all was holding me. "Your bravery and intelligence impressed me, but your passion…You astound me."

What he'd said a moment ago resurfaced in my mind and I had to ask. "If kissing me was the highlight of your existence—" A knot hardened in my gut, but I lifted my head and finished the question. "How old are you?"

"I'm immortal, remember?"

"You must've been born, or created, or something."

The tips of his fingers found my nape and rubbed with a slow, sensual rhythm. "How old are *you?*"

"Thirty-two. Now it's your turn."

He fidgeted and coughed.

I rested my chin on his chest. "Please tell me."

He nodded and drew in a long breath. "Well now, I lost count after five thousand."

Chapter Ten

I STOPPED BREATHING, CERTAIN MY HEART HAD CEASED BEATING TOO. I COULD do nothing but gawk at him—with my mouth open, I suspected, given the draft coming in between my lips. Five thousand years old? Five *thousand*? More, even, since he claimed he'd lost count. This man was older than Stonehenge or the pyramids of Egypt. I had just made out with an ancient being.

Damn if that wasn't the hottest thing ever.

And sort of ooky at the same time.

"There's more," he said. "I sensed none of the Unseen realm in you."

My heart sank to the ground and I swore I heard it splatting at my feet like the limp, clammy rag into which it seemed to have morphed. "I'll go to prison for the rest of my life if we don't do this."

"I wasn't finished." He tickled my earlobe with his finger, an amused smile on his lips. "There is an energy deep within you, hidden even from your own perception. I've tasted it."

The idea of him tasting energy that lurked inside me shot an erotic thrill straight into my core. I licked my lower lip, the velvety feel of my own tongue triggering a sense memory of his mouth, his tongue, ravishing me with wild abandon.

His fingertip teased the skin behind my ear, summoning a little shiver of delight.

"This energy of yours," he said, "I don't know if it's the right kind to get you into the Unseen realm. It's like nothing I've ever felt before, but we could try."

"How?"

"I shall take you to the doorway. If it opens for you, we'll know."

"Okay, I'm ready. Take me."

Oh damn. I'd done it again. *Stupid mouth, stupid brain.*

His lips eased into a languid grin. "Since ye granted me one kiss only, I can't take ye in the manner I'd most like."

I opened my mouth to speak, but couldn't muster words.

His grin closed into a smirk. He knew damn well what kind of effect he had on me and he enjoyed pushing that button. If I were honest, I'd admit I liked it too. I tapped my toe on the grass, creating a faint swishing sound. "You know what I meant."

"Ah yes, I do." He slid his hands down my back to rest on my hips.

"Has your test ever not worked before?"

"Never." A darkness scudded over him, like a gray cloud obscuring the sun. "Everything about you is unprecedented."

"Do I get a gold medal or something? For being the most difficult human on earth?" After what we'd shared a moment ago, I shouldn't have let him put his hands on me. I ought to pull away right now. If I planned on keeping my wits, I had to maintain a distance from him. But the contact felt soooo good.

"If you attempt this," he said, "and you don't have the requisite trace of elemental energy, you will die."

I pushed away from him. "I have to risk it."

He folded his arms around me.

I squeezed my eyes shut. Padlocked my arms around him. Held my breath. And prayed.

The ground dropped away. The silence of a vacuum engulfed us as we spun round and round, up and up. Icy needles pricked at my skin. I gripped Nevan so hard my arms trembled from the effort. Whirling. Soaring. Shattering and reforming.

My feet plunked down on solid ground. Nevan's embrace loosened, though his hands lingered on my hips. The solidity of his touch grounded me, more than the actual earth beneath my boots.

The throaty roar of a waterfall pelted my eardrums. Light glowed on the other side of my lids. I peeled them apart.

And yelped.

We perched on the rock ledge alongside the falls. My right toe caught in a depression and I stumbled sideways, flailing my arms to regain my balance. My boot slipped off the edge, skewing my center of gravity. I lurched toward the precipice.

Nevan seized me around the waist, hoisting me up and over to plunk me down on the ledge. He braced my body with his, both arms snug around me, his hands fastened over my belly.

Terrible visions assailed my mind, of my body plummeting and crashing into the water, of bones fracturing, of water choking my lungs.

Nevan gave me a gentle shake and hollered to be heard above the thundering cascade. "Are ye damaged, love?"

"No." I mashed myself into him, my toes frighteningly close to the edge. "Terrified, but not damaged."

"It's a six-foot drop. Far from life threatening."

I peered at the pool below, at its water churning and foaming. "I don't like water."

"Then we have a problem." He nodded toward the gushing cataract behind us. "To reach the Unseen, we must first breach the falls."

"I don't like deep bodies of water, like ponds and lakes. A waterfall is doable."

He squinted at me, searching my face, a question poised on his tongue and evident in his eyes—but then he nodded, seeming satisfied. Nudging me away, he grasped my shoulders and rotated me to face the waterfall. "Jump."

The hairs at my nape bristled and my skin went clammy, not entirely from the water droplets peppering my arms and face. Jump into the falls? What if I blundered off the edge? Or smacked head-on into a rock wall?

"I've taken many mortals through the water," he said, his body blockading me from behind, leaving me no escape route. "This is not the dangerous part."

Great. That eased my mind. *Not.*

"I'll show you." Nevan hopped around me. His feet slapped onto the ledge in front of me. Water sprayed over his bronzed flesh, glazing it with a faint sheen. I stretched out my fingers to skate them over his damp skin, but just as I touched him, he spun away from me.

And leaped into the falls.

"Hey, wait!" I lifted my hands, as if I might hold back the raging waters or maybe part them like Moses. No such luck. I inched closer and my boots skidded on the wet rock. I flung a hand out to the solid sandstone cliff beside me, thwarting my fall, sparing my skull from a bone-splitting impact.

I took a fortifying breath. Straightening, my hand firmly on the stone wall, I edged toward the cascade. Drops spattered my face, raining particles of a chill on my skin as the liquid evaporated. The clean scent of water mingled with the dankness of wet dirt and the racket of water pummeling rock pulsated through my skull with deafening force.

What on earth was I doing? I worked in a rock shop, serving tourists who thought agate was the name of a teen pop singer. I did not allow strange, half-naked men to lure me into waterfalls.

Except today, apparently, I did.

From my position mere inches from the falls, I noticed the ledge extended behind the curtain of water, where I could just make out a yawning darkness indicative of an empty area beyond. Nevan hadn't thrown himself into the cliff of sheer stone behind the water. He'd leaped through the falls, into whatever space lay behind it.

Okay. I could do this. Saving myself from prison required a literal leap of faith, with Nevan on the other side to catch me. I tensed, bracing for the impact of hard, cold water. Clenched my fists. Shut my eyes.

"Porter!" Travis and his deputies rampaged toward the railing. The sheriff's voice echoed off the trees. "Porter, get the hell offa there! What in blue blazes are ya doing? Trying to break your fool neck?"

My attention diverged, like a TV displaying two feeds in a split-screen effect. My nails scraped at the rock, but my left foot skidded sideways. My fingers grasped at depressions in the stone, steadying my balance. I pushed away from the wall and confronted the curtain of water.

"Lindsey, no!" A note of panic quavered in Travis's voice.

I jumped.

The water swallowed me. Cold. Sharp. Tiny nails driven into my flesh. I cleared the falls and my boots struck solid rock.

Panting, but with both feet flat on the ground, I struggled to orient myself in my new environment. The frigid water left me shivering, my teeth chattering. My hair and clothes clung to me, sodden and heavy. I stood within a small cavern, from the outside hidden by the falls but now revealed before me. To my left and right, rock walls rose up to meet the ceiling, where it arched across the space at least five feet above. Water-filled depressions pockmarked the sandstone floor.

The thundering of the water had faded into a dull rumble. I glanced backward, but the cascade still blocked the entrance. I couldn't explain the dulling of its roar, though the effect reminded me of wearing foam earplugs.

To my left, a few feet away, Nevan braced his body with one hand on the wall.

"Why is the noise quieter in here?" I asked.

"Magic."

I supposed that was all the explanation I'd get, so I returned to surveying the cavern. The floor was level, if pockmarked, and strands of green copper ore weaved through the arching ceiling. In front of me loomed an unnatural darkness. It shimmered and swirled, in a striking echo of Nevan's eyes. In contrast to the bright metallic hues of his irises, this whirlpool gyrated with a fathomless blackness, as if it were made of crude oil sprinkled with starlight, a wall of glittering emptiness stretching into eternity.

The closer I approached to the shimmering void, the more colors I detected inside it. Thin ribbons of iridescent blue, green, and purple twirled within the black. I lifted a hand to touch it but felt nothing, as if I'd tried to caress the air. My fingertips disappeared into the opalescent shadows. Goose bumps materialized on my arms, heralding a tingling chill.

Get out of here.

My subconscious had a point. I ought to run. Right this instant.

I couldn't. I had to know.

Nevan's fingers wound around mine. He sidled past me, partway into the shimmering abyss. One side of his body vanished.

I stood paralyzed before the portal to another world.

He tugged my hand in quiet invitation.

My gut clenched. *Ohhhh, this is a really bad idea.*

I did it anyway. I marched straight into the blackness.

Light blinded me. Radiant warmth chased away the chill of the cavern, calming my shivers. I squinted into the brightness, which emanated from above like the sun. As my eyes adjusted to the change, I noted the source of the light. It was the sun.

Which made no sense. I'd walked into darkness. Yet here I stood, bathed in sunshine with a tepid breeze tickling my face.

Nevan strode past me, freeing my hand.

I turned in a circle, awed by my surroundings. Behind me, where the cavern and waterfall should've been, a six-foot-tall boulder hunkered. Water burbled up out of the boulder's top, spilling down its sloping sides and onto the ground, where the water collected in a pool about ten feet in diameter. Tiny waves lapped at the pool's edge, inches from my feet.

Everywhere around me, thick trees hulked at least a hundred feet overhead. In place of leaves, stringy stuff reminiscent of moss dangled from the branches. The sky shone an ethereal blue, as dark and lustrous as a sapphire. The sun blazed within the blue, a flaming diamond embedded in the sky. Unseen birds chirped and twittered, their songs like nothing on earth. Indescribable scents wafted on the breeze, tantalizing and mysterious, delicious and dangerous. Everything here struck me as beautiful but *wrong*.

Nevan leaned his hip against a tree trunk on the other side of the pool, his arms folded over his chest. Our trip through the waterfall had drenched him too, molding the loincloth to his flesh and slicking his hair back. My gaze tracked the lines of his muscles down his body, over his hips, along those powerful thighs. His skin had become a glistening tapestry, dappled with beads of water, kissed by the unearthly gleam of the sun.

My hand rose to my throat of its own volition, my fingers stroked my skin.

God, he was as beautiful and strange as the surroundings. The memory of our scorching kiss rocketed through me, my body reliving the bliss of his hands groping and his tongue milking every ounce of passion from me.

"Come back to me," Nevan murmured, suddenly right in front of me.

I blinked rapidly, but couldn't shake the lightheaded awe—of him, of this place, of the surreal dream my life had become. "Imposs—wha—"

His lips curved in a closed-mouth smile and lines of amusement crinkled around his eyes. "You'll need to finish a sentence, or at least a word, if you're wanting me to respond."

Rationality burst back into me with a jolt. I'd have to wait until later to process everything I'd seen and experienced. As for the lust-inducing memory of Nevan's mouth…Best not think of that at all.

Nevan studied me with his glowing, amber eyes. His tongue slipped out to wet his lips.

I repressed the urge to squirm under his scrutiny. "I gather this whole 'touch of the Unseen world' stuff is designed to keep pesky mortals out of your precious realm of magic and creepiness."

"Naturally." He brushed a lock of hair from my shoulder, his fingers teasing my skin. "If it were easy to enter the Unseen, marauding droves of your kind would overrun our world."

I stifled a laugh, sort of. It broke out as a wet snort. "Come on, we lowly humans aren't that bad."

"*You* aren't bad at all." He ran his finger along the top of my ear, tucking my hair behind it. "Allowing the teeming hordes free entrance would rather negate the *unseen* aspect of this realm."

"I see your point." But another thought occurred to me, and I scrunched up my lips. "But you guys have free entrance to our world. That's not fair at all."

"Not free entrance." He twined a lock of my hair around his finger, winding it loosely, letting it fall, and winding it again, his gaze trained on the task. "There is a boundary which limits our egress."

"Your egress?" My derisive grunt turned breathless as he trailed his fingertips down my throat. *Not fair at all.* "Nobody talks like that. Besides, I haven't seen any walls or fences blocking your way."

"It is a magical boundary," he said on a sigh, as if I'd questioned the existence of gravity. "We cannot travel more than one mile from any of the gateways between the worlds."

"The waterfall. It's a gateway."

"All bodies of water serve as doorways."

"Hmm." I thought back to our encounter in my car, when he'd freaked out at the sight of a mile marker up ahead. "That's why you nearly got us into a car crash. We were approaching one mile from the falls."

"Ah...yes."

"Jesus, why didn't you just say so?" I rolled my gaze up to the heavens, shaking my head. "Could've saved us both a lot of grief if you'd told me the truth right then."

"Perhaps." He winked, grinning. "But where's the fun in that?"

"Do you honestly think it's fun to almost get me killed?"

His grin crumbled. "I would never harm you, if I could prevent it. What happened in your vehicle was an accident, one for which I have apologized."

"Yeah, I know." I paused, then said, "But you've been in my apartment. It's outside the boundary."

"Outside one boundary, but inside another. There is a small, secluded waterfall nearby."

"Guess I'll take your word for that. What happens if you try to cross one of these invisible lines?"

"Annihilation."

"Of the world?" I squeaked the question, my heart surging into my throat.

"No, love." He patted my cheek. "Annihilation of the immortal being who tries to violate the boundary."

"Oh." I yanked my hands out of my pockets to rub my arms. "Guess I can understand why you flipped out in the car."

"I did not flip either out or in." Nevan backed away, tripped over a rock, and staggered forward, about to collide with me. Sputtering a curse, he righted himself with a little hop. "I requested you stop the car."

"Requested?" I laughed. "Oh, come off it. You totally flipped your lid."

He frowned, brushing himself off. "We'd best track down the bloody leprechaun, if we're to have any hope of resurrecting your deceased friend."

"Shoplifter."

"Pardon?"

"The dead guy. He was a shoplifter, not my friend. I didn't know him and I damn sure didn't like him."

"I appreciate the clarification." In one swift movement, he planted a firm kiss on my cheek, stepped away, and tugged my hand to urge me into motion. "But I wasn't concerned about your relationship with a corpse."

As we headed across the clearing, I bumped my shoulder against his arm. "And what about when he's not dead? Will your green beast rear its head again?"

He froze, forcing me to stop with him. "You think of me as a beast?"

"No, it was a joke." I'd nicked a nerve, but why? An instinct warned me not to pursue the topic further, at least until I'd learned a little more about my would-be savior. Pasting on a smile, the one I wore so often it hurt, I said, "Let's find this leprechaun, okay? I'd really prefer not to go to prison."

"Leprechauns are terribly unpleasant."

Enunciating each word with exaggerated lip movements, I said, "Take me to the leprechaun."

"As you wish."

Nevan shepherded me into the shadows of the forest, down a dirt path veiled in shadows. The further we traveled, the more his smile faded and his body stiffened. I struggled to keep up with his brisk pace. Underneath his flippant disguise, he must've been annoyed at the prospect of visiting a leprechaun. Pardon me, a *bloody* leprechaun.

Jeez, I hoped he hadn't meant that literally.

The path dead-ended at a small clearing. Nevan stopped at the edge of the trees, his body blocking my view. He turned sideways, his expression no longer amused but tight with tension. Whoa. He must've really disliked leprechauns.

"There," Nevan said, jerking a thumb toward the clearing. "You'll need to do the talking because the leprechaun won't speak to me."

"What did you, sleep with his sister?"

Nevan flinched. "Indeed I did."

"Oh." I'd been joking, but his confession spurred a stab of jealousy. I didn't want to know, not really, but my mouth seemed to have a mind of its own. "Of course you did. How many women have you screwed?"

He rubbed his forehead with his thumb and forefinger. "I have lived for thousands of years, and for most of that time, I recklessly indulged my baser instincts."

"In other words," I said, "you've boinked thousands, maybe millions, of women. Lovely."

He dropped his hand from his forehead, clenching it into a fist. "I make no excuses for my behavior, but never once have I forced a female into my bed. They came to me willingly. Tris's sister pursued me, in fact."

I tore my hand out of his and stomped toward the clearing, ducking under a low-hanging branch. Tendrils of mossy stuff drooped down from it. A clump of the gunk lodged in my hair and I batted it away. "I was right, wasn't I? You are a woodland lothario."

He growled in frustration, punched his fist into a tree, and shook his hand as if the motion could quell his temper. He breathed in and out, in and out, until the dark tension in him ebbed. "All you need know is that for the past century I have been celibate."

"A century?" I looked straight into his eyes, one part of me unable to accept his statement, another part wishing it were true. He hadn't lied to me so far—that I knew of—and I couldn't believe he would lie about this. Being a thirty-two-year-old virgin didn't sound so bad compared to a century of celibacy.

Nevan gave a curt nod.

"Okay then." I swung my arms at my sides, slapping my palms together each time they met in front of me. "I have no idea what to say to that."

"Say nothing. For once." He moved closer, taking my hands in his, and fixed an earnest gaze on me. "Listen to me, Lindsey. On this side of the falls, you cannot trust anyone."

"I trust you." No clue why, but I did.

"Don't." He leaned in, his voice infused with a quiet intensity. "Anyone you meet may try to trick you into a bargain. Do not speak the words 'please' or 'thank you' in this realm and never—*never*—agree to anything. Do you understand?"

"Not really." My throat constricted at the pain in his eyes. "But I'll do what you want. I prom—Is it okay to say 'promise'?"

"I'd prefer you didn't risk it." He freed my hands. "I know you will do as you say. There's no need for promises."

"How about if I pinky swear?"

Nevan's lips twitched. "Also not necessary, but not dangerous either."

He gestured for me to head for the clearing and walked alongside me as we entered the open area. Nevan slowed his pace, lagging by a couple paces. When I halted, he stayed behind me.

In the clearing's center, seated atop a flat boulder about two feet tall, hunched a rangy teenager. His brown hair, clipped into a buzz cut, matched the freckles dotting his peaches-and-cream skin. The clomping of my footsteps stirred him from his contemplation of a rock he gripped in one hand. His bright green eyes locked onto me briefly, but then his attention zipped straight past my shoulder. His lips contorted in annoyance.

"Go away," the kid said, his accent reminiscent of Chicago or the Bronx. "I ain't interested in the sylph's latest bimbo. I'm busy."

"I am not a bimbo." How many girls had Nevan brought here? *Thousands of years, remember?* "I don't appreciate the sexist jibe, you pubescent rat."

His brows shot up. "I been called lotsa things, but never that. Least Nev brought a sassy one this time."

The kid wiped his free hand on his ripped and faded blue jeans. He lifted the rock to inspect it. I recognized the chunk of green-tinged stone as copper ore, much like the chunks we sold in the shop. Two of the rock's edges had been sanded to a smooth surface and polished to a glassy shine.

My jaw fell open. No, not *like* the ore we sold in the shop. The rock had come from the shop. The kid was holding one of the float copper bookends my now-deceased shoplifter had tried to swipe. He must've sneaked back into the shop to finish his heist. But how did the leprechaun get the bookend?

The top edge of the stone, once curved and smooth, now looked ragged and raw.

My new friend raised the copper bookend to his mouth and bit into it. *Crunch.* Bits of copper ore peppered his green flannel shirt.

"Lindsey," Nevan said, nodding toward the boy, "meet Tris."

"He doesn't look like a leprechaun."

"If you were expecting a stout little fellow wearing a green outfit and a big smile, I'm afraid you've come to the wrong place. Tris doesn't do colorful or cheerful."

Tris threw a hot glare at Nevan before zeroing in on me. "We do not wear lame hats or dole out luck. Got it?"

"Yeah, I get it." Thinking I'd better ingratiate myself if I hoped to resurrect the dead man, I added, careful to avoid any dangerous niceties, "I didn't mean to offend you."

His glower softened, though only a smidgen. "I blame the sylph. If I could, I'd sue him for libel and I'd win." He bit off another mouthful of copper, munching it with great relish. "What do you want, lady? You're busting in on my lunch."

I decided to take the high road and assume rudeness was a defense against the weird magic rules. "Do you know what happened to the dead man?"

Tris gulped down the last of his copper ore. "Look, I don't got a clue what you're yammering about. Go away."

He flapped a dismissive hand in my direction.

To hell with ingratiating myself. If this kid was guilty, I wanted to know.

I marched three steps toward him, narrowing the gap between us to a few feet. His eyes, though glowing like Nevan's, lacked any motion or fire in the irises, imbuing them with a coldness. Yet behind the flat green light something sputtered, faint and well hidden, visible only from the right angle. He might not be as cold as he wanted me to think. "The man you stole that copper from is dead. Somebody bashed him in the head. I'm guessing it was you."

Tris made a thumbs-down gesture. "You guess wrong."

He hefted the bookend for another bite.

I snatched it from his hand.

Tris let out a loud hiss. "That's mine, sister. Give it back."

He thrust out a hand, waggling his fingers in the universal gesture for *gimme-gimme.*

I clutched the bookend to my chest. It was oddly warm, probably from the leprechaun's hands around the stone. "You stole it."

From another thief, but that was immaterial.

The kid shook his head, not as if denying what I'd said, but as if he knew I wouldn't leave him alone until he told the truth. Good. Let him stew.

Nevan bounded up behind me. "Tell her what happened, Tris. This one is willful. Ignoring her won't do you one bit of good."

Tris refused to glance at Nevan or acknowledge the man had spoken. Instead, he slumped forward to rest his elbows on his knees. "All right, all right. But I didn't kill nobody. He was dead when I found him. Seeing as how he didn't need the copper anymore, I sorta claimed it. As abandoned property."

I tapped my fingers on the bookend, still hugged to my chest. "Why should I believe you?"

"It's the truth, lady," he snarled. "Believe it or don't, what do I care?"

Actually, I did believe him. Couldn't say why. The kid was annoying, insolent, and must've suffered from a bizarre mineral deficiency. I didn't like him. And yet, I believed his story. "If you didn't kill the guy, who did?"

"Dunno." His glazed eyes fixated on the bookend and he licked his lips. "I'm still hungry. Can I have that back?"

Considering the way he kept moistening his lips, and the greedy sheen in his eyes, he must've really been hungry. For copper ore? Oh well, I'd given up on trying to understand anything that happened since I found the dead man yesterday.

I handed the bookend to Tris. He bit off a mouthful. His teeth pulverized the rock with an audible grinding noise and powdered copper dribbled from his lips. He swiped the back of his hand across his mouth.

What kind of teeth did this kid have?

I shoved the question to the back of my mind, returning to the issue at hand. "I believe you. Which means I need to ask for your help."

He made a rude noise. "I don't do favors. 'Specially not for stinking mortals."

A snide quip popped to mind, but I bit it back and tried my damnedest to look relaxed and nonthreatening. Not that anyone had ever accused me of being threatening. Just seemed like a good idea to minimize the hostility. "If I could ask anyone else, I would, but according to Nevan, you're it. Resurrect the dead man for me."

"Ah," Nevan said, a finger raised. He gave me a look that suggested he thought I was tiptoeing too close to the P-word. "Perhaps I should take over from here."

"I need his help and you said he wouldn't talk to you." I turned back to Tris. "Will you do this for me?"

"Help a mortal?" Tris cackled. Like a witch from a bad horror movie. Leprechauns were not supposed to cackle. In that moment, I realized I'd better adjust my preconceptions—or better yet, dump them altogether—if I hoped to survive in my new reality.

I raised both hands, palms together, letting my gesture beg where I could not. "Bring back the dead man and I'll owe—"

"No-no," Nevan said. He strode between me and Tris, a massive blockade composed of tight muscles and burnished skin. "She doesn't care to finish that sentence."

"Sure I do."

Nevan shot me a dark look. "Trust me. You don't."

Tris lowered the bookend, letting it rest on his thigh. He tilted his head up to glower straight at Nevan, who met his gaze with a blank one of his own. Tris spoke directly to the sylph. "Don't this broad know nothing? What kinda morons are you bringing in here these days, Nev?"

My sylph companion feigned surprise. "Now you're speaking to me, eh?"

The kid snorted. "Not cuz I wanna. But what's the point in talking to this broad when she don't even know about debts? Teach these dames the basics before you drag 'em in here."

I peeked around Nevan's shoulder. "Debts? What do you mean? Does this have anything to do with not letting me say the P-word?"

"Never mind," Nevan said, shifting sideways to keep me blockaded. "Tris, Lindsey asked for your help. Will you voluntarily perform the service?"

Voluntarily perform? I marveled at the deft way he tap-danced around these magical land mines. No please, no implication of owing anything. He asked the leprechaun to volunteer.

"What's in it for me?" Tris demanded.

Nevan gritted his teeth, blustering a breath out his nostrils. "I won't throttle you."

I curled a hand over Nevan's bicep. It bulged under my palm, hardened by a barely contained anger. His eyes fluoresced in shades of red, bronze, and white, while his skin seemed to toughen like leather stretched taut. He had the aura of a wild beast preparing to pounce. Whatever happened between Tris and Nevan must've involved way more than the sylph enjoying a simple roll in the hay with the leprechaun's sister.

I gave his arm a light squeeze. "Nevan, chill out. I can handle this."

His radioactive eyes swerved to me.

I let my hand fall away from his arm, chilled by the eerie sense of gazing into the soul of an ancient, ruthless warrior. I bit back the first word that wanted to come out of my mouth—"please"—and scoured my brain for a safer phrase.

Nevan crept closer to the leprechaun.

"Stop this," I said. "You've done enough for me and I can handle one snotty twerp. I'm grate—"

Nevan slapped a hand over my mouth.

I pushed his hand away. "What are you doing?"

"You were about to incur a debt." His gaze flitted to Tris and back to me. "All debts must be repaid, by whatever means the owed party desires."

By whatever means. He'd told me Skeiron forced him into a bargain that enslaved him to the king's whims. Nevan repaid that debt every day, humiliated by his duty. I did not care to wind up bound like that.

"You vowed to do as I asked," Nevan said. "Do not incur a debt. Obey me on this."

The gravity of his tone stopped me. His grip tightened, his nails slicing in my flesh. "Ouch. You're hurting me."

He yanked his hands away and held them in mid-air, as if he weren't sure they belonged to him. Breathing hard, he slowly lowered his arms. "I should not have held you so tightly."

"No shit." I lifted my right hand, palm out. "I won't thank anybody or say I owe them ever again. Satisfied?"

His shoulders flagged, looking suddenly weary. "Yes."

"I almost heard a thank-you in that yes."

"Owing you would not be a trial."

Tucking my hands in my pockets, I rocked forward on my toes to smile up at him. "I'll remember you said that."

His mouth slid into half smile, but then he reminded me, "No bargaining. And no gratitude of any kind."

"Got it." I angled a little closer. "You're bossy, but I've decided it's in a good way."

His voice dropped to a husky rumble. "How good am I?"

Despite the distance between us, his radiant heat soaked into me like sunshine. Our gazes intersected, drawn together by a gravitational force. My thoughts and desires revolved around him—I, the satellite trapped in the orbit of him, the planetary body. If I gave in to the pull, our passion would explode like a supernova. The mere thought of it shuddered anticipation through my entire body.

I was in so much trouble.

The leprechaun cleared his throat, regarding me with a canny gleam in his eyes.

Oh yeah, sooo much trouble.

CHAPTER ELEVEN

"I DON'T GIVE A RAT'S ASS ABOUT YOUR TENDER MOMENT," TRIS AN-nounced. "If you're wanting me to resurrect somebody, better gimme one whopper of a reason. I ain't the generous type."

He dragged a finger down my arm, from the hem of my sleeve down to my wrist. I ached to drown in the fire of our kiss one more time. Instead, I tromped over to the leprechaun, who grunted his derision.

Nevan, sidling up beside me, trailed his middle finger down the back of my forearm to tease the sensitive skin of my inner wrist, unleashing a riot of sensations. My body yearned to lean back into him.

None of that now. I linked my hands behind my back.

"Well?" Tris said. "You gonna convince me or what? I told ya I ain't in the habit of doing favors for mortals."

Nevan bent forward to loom over the seated leprechaun. "You'll be wanting to grant this favor. Unless you're in the mood for a thrashing."

"Shush," I said, elbowing him in the side. "I can handle this."

He grumbled.

I turned to the leprechaun. "Someone is trying to frame me for murder."

"That's my problem how?"

"Because…" My lips moved, I knew they did, but my train of thought derailed. Nevan and Tris must've heard the engine of my mind chugging, the wheels spinning, because they both studied me with bemused humor. I bounced on my heels and told Tris, with no attempt at all to disguise my self-satisfaction, "Because Nevan'll beat the crap out of you if you don't."

Nevan balked. "Pardon me, love, but I thought you were handling the dilemma yourself. Woman's liberation, eh? I believe that's what your kind calls it."

"Yeah, it is—and yeah, I am handling it."

"But you told him—you threatened I would—" Nevan's words disintegrated into exasperated noises. He threw his hands in the air. I muffled a giggle, but lost the battle with my grin. My reaction seemed to smother his temper and he let his arms drop. "I will never understand mortals."

"The feeling's mutual, Mr. Elemental Spirit of the Air." I tried to glare at Tris, but the humor slowly fading out of me hindered the attempt. "Will you do the resurrection thing or not?"

Tris worked his lips as if torn by the decision. "All right. But I'm only doing this to shut up your yammering. And so's I don't gotta watch you two drool over each other anymore. I'm getting nauseous."

"Maybe it's the raw copper ore you've been wolfing down."

He fixed me with a sly stare. "You want your sack of flesh and bones brought back to life or not?"

"I do."

"Let's get on with it then."

"Thank—" I clapped my own hand on my mouth this time, cutting off my words one syllable short of thanking the weaselly leprechaun. I chastised myself silently and removed my hand. "How's it work? This resurrection thing."

Tris chomped a bite of copper ore. "Use the vortex."

"Excuse me?"

"The vortex." Tris made a swirling gesture with his hand. "The one with the big sign next to it that says *healing vortex* in big white letters."

Realization rushed through me, stealing my breath and leaving me speechless. I'd known the vortex could heal minor wounds, but resurrect the dead? Holy heaven.

Tris eyed Nevan. "She illiterate or something?"

"No," Nevan intoned, "but she can be a tad slow to comprehend. We should excuse her, since this is her first trip through the falls."

The flapping of wings made us all jerk our heads skyward. A raven orbited overhead, banked lower with each circuit of the clearing. Though ravens all looked the same to me, an instinct warned me I'd met this one before. Brennus was back.

The raven dived into a tree, landing on a low-handing branch, and cawed three times.

Nevan stared down the bird.

The creature canted its head, coughing. Brennus casually fluttered his wings.

I inched toward Nevan. "Am I right in assuming that's—"

"Brennus."

The raven launched his body off the branch. It flapped wildly as Brennus rocketed up into the heavens to circle higher and higher until his dark figure shrank into a dot, winking out of sight.

Nevan pulled me snug against his side. He didn't have to tell me Brennus's appearance signaled bad news for us. Thanks to his spy and assassin, Skeiron would soon know where we were.

Thunder grumbled. A storm cloud blossomed in front of the sun and a chilly wind whipped through the clearing. I rubbed my bare arms as my gaze drifted up to the sky and the black mass consuming the blue. A crack of thunder detonated overhead.

I jumped.

Tris froze mid chew.

Nevan scowled at the cloud, his arm clinching me tighter.

An explosion of thunder rolled across the heavens, fading into silence, but I swore I heard laughter rumbling beneath it.

Nevan's breaths heated my cheek as he hunched to whisper in my ear. "No one will harm you. Not Brennus, not Skeiron, not even one of the gods will dare lay a hand on you. I will not allow it."

I longed to believe him, but though his words carried the weight of conviction, the sight of the raven soaring across the sky had slithered doubt through my heart. Nevan would try to protect me.

He would fail.

The certainty of it shimmied a chill down my spine, despite the warmth of Nevan's arm around my shoulders. He held me fast, his arm rigid.

Tris snapped off yet another bite of copper. "What's Brennus want with you two?" Nevan opened his mouth to answer, but Tris waved a hand. "Forget it. I don't wanna know."

"Are you sure this will work?" I asked. "The resurrection thing."

"Drag the mook into the vortex and it'll heal him." Tris scratched his chin. "Probably. Depends on how long it's been since he croaked and how busted up he is. Assuming his head ain't lopped off, it oughta work."

Earlier I'd learned firsthand the vortex had real regenerative power. Still, of all the shocking revelations I'd been hit with in the past twenty-four hours, somehow the notion of a genuine healing vortex stung worse than anything else. I'd spent three months denying such a thing could exist—hell, I'd spent years denying anything supernatural existed—and now my freedom depended on mystical healing energies.

Does it spin you?

Sandy's question about the vortex echoed in my brain. Yesterday, I'd told her no. Today, I felt my head spinning at the very mention of the blasted thing.

I resisted the impulse to tap my heels together and pray to go home. Instead, I leaned into Nevan just a little. "All I have to do is drag the body into the vortex?"

"Mm-hm," Tris mumbled around a mouthful of rock. "And let me finish my lunch. Gotta get the vortex up to full power for this one." I must've crinkled my brow or given some other sign of confusion, because Tris held up the copper bookend. "I eat this, it gives me power. The vortex gets it power from me. Get it?"

No, I didn't really, but I'd take his word for it.

I considered my options for a couple seconds, then said, "You didn't have to help me, Tris, but you did. You are a much nicer boy than you want everyone to think."

He looked up at me through his eyelashes, his mouth warped into a half grimace, half smile. Couldn't expect a teenager to admit he was a good boy. So not cool.

Was he a teenager? If Nevan could change his appearance, maybe Tris was older than he let on.

Tris shrugged one shoulder, returning his attention to the copper ore. "Whatever."

I swore I detected a faint blush on his cheeks.

As Tris kept on crunching ore, I twisted out from under Nevan's arm. He raised his brows but didn't try to stop me.

Tris, mouth stuffed with rock, mumbled, "You gonna save the dead guy or what?"

"Yes. Right now." I spun on my heels and bolted down the path back to the pool and the water-spouting boulder. Another pair of footfalls clapped up the path behind me. No need to glance back. Nevan was tailing me, I knew—or rather, I *felt* it.

Breaking out of the trees, I veered toward the boulder and its burbling water, certain the way home must lie somewhere in the vicinity of the tiny cascade. I'd wound up standing in front of the rock when I leaped through the darkness into this alien place.

Great, more water.

I halted at the pool's edge, mere feet from the big rock, my eyes drawn to the fountain spurting from it. Would I have to dive into the pool? My skin crawled at the idea.

Nevan sprinted past me, straight up to the boulder. Though I panted from exertion, he hadn't even broken a sweat.

"I'm assuming," he said, "you haven't the faintest idea how to get back from whence you came."

"Nope."

"It'll be easier this time." He slid his hand into mine, lacing our fingers. "Water is the doorway. When I say jump, do it. No hesitating. It is imperative you follow my instructions."

The seriousness of his tone convinced me. I nodded, but my gut clenched when I glanced back at the water.

Nevan dipped his free hand into the little fountain. The boulder dissolved into a darkness teeming with worm-like bands of blue, green, and purple. "Jump."

Hand in hand, we jumped.

The impact as we hit the floor in the cave made my knees buckle, punching them into the stone floor, shooting pains through my legs.

Nevan landed flat on his feet, steady as a mountain.

As my vision adjusted to the dimness, I raised a hand to my forehead and strained to make out my surroundings. Ahead of me, the waterfall cascaded over the cave's mouth in a rumbling, silvery curtain, muted by…uh…magic.

I glanced over my shoulder at the portal whatsit spiraling into infinity. Would I ever get used to the supernatural being real?

Nevan crouched beside me, lashed an arm around my waist, and jacked me up off my ass. Once he'd set me on my feet, he cradled my neck in his hands. "All right, love? No permanent damage?"

A playful lift of his brow contradicted his concerned tone. He was the most confusing man I'd ever met. "I'm fine. Let's go."

To my left, a shadow stirred. My attention swerved toward it just as a figure trundled out of the darkness in the depths of the cave.

Sheriff Travis Blackwell passed in front of the curtain of water, shoulders slumped, his clothes and hair rumpled and drenched and splatting drops onto the ground. Scrapes on his arms turned the skin a raw red. His mouth was open, his breaths came hard and fast. Eyes narrowed to slits, lips compressed into a line, he planted his feet wide to bar our path out of the cave with one hand positioned on the butt of his Sig Sauer.

His voice was hushed, his tone eerily cool. "Where have you been?"

I scuffled backward, bumping into Nevan. His body pressed against my back, buttressing me there. His hands, coiled around my upper arms, staked a claim. I had no time to consider whether I liked his dominant stance or the possessiveness it communicated, because Travis intervened.

With one wide step, he closed the distance between us and stabbed a finger in the air in front of my face. "I said where the hell have you been?"

His voice boomed in the confines of the cave, ricocheting off the walls. He repeated his question, with even more volume. I suppressed a cringe—damned if I'd show him any fear, no matter how insane he was acting—and told him in a dead-calm voice, "We explored the cave."

Travis's gaze swung past me, past Nevan, straight to the disk of blackness behind us and the multicolored tendrils corkscrewing within it. His eyes flew wide, his face blanched, and the fury crumbled out of him like a fragile shell broken by the wind. His hand fell away from his gun. He rocked back on his heels.

I wondered how long he'd hidden in the shadows, how much he'd witnessed.

"What is that stuff?" Travis asked, his tone far too even.

He was putting on a front and I couldn't fault him for it. The otherworldly hole in reality had thrown me for a loop too. His voice may have been even, but his eyes beseeched me for a rational explanation.

"I saw that thing when I first came in here, chasing after you two. I tried to touch the stuff, but it—" He jerked a hand toward the whirlpool hovering in midair, his lips trembling, infecting his voice with a matching quaver. "It floated away."

"Long story." One I really, really did not want to tell him. He'd drag me off to the loony bin for sure and maybe sign up for his own stint in a padded cell.

I tracked his gaze as it zeroed in on the churning darkness and its ribbons of luminous color unreeling into eternity. The abyss telescoped down to a pinpoint and winked out with a sizzling snap and a puff of air. Where once the portal had hovered, I saw only the mottled, uneven rock of the cave's rear wall.

Travis blinked twice in slow motion. He shook his head with such ferocity his head seemed to flap like a flag in the wind. He sank his face into hands, and after a moment, looked up at me. "If it's all right with you, I'm gonna pretend I never saw...whatever I thought I saw."

"Do what you want."

He squared his shoulders, straightening. "Why'd you run, Porter?"

Just like that, we were back to the cop-versus-suspect dynamic. Not more than half an hour ago, I'd panicked when Travis whipped out his handcuffs and suggested he might arrest me. Now—backed up, in the literal and figurative sense, by a sylph who could whisk me away in a heartbeat—I discovered it had gotten much easier to defy the sheriff.

"I won't go to jail again," I informed him. "Not ever."

Nevan's fingers pressed into my skin. Whether his gesture signified support or a warning, I couldn't say for sure.

Travis drummed his fingers on his leather belt. "I offered to help you."

"You mean the way you helped last time?" I shrugged out of Nevan's grasp to take a single step forward. "Why should I trust you?"

My fingers curled claw-like toward my palms but did not ball into fists. The memory of those days, of the most horrifying time in my life, ratcheted up my tension until my entire body ached from the pressure of rigid muscles.

Nevan kissed the top of my head. His hands stroked my arms, the realness of his touch banishing the ghosts of the past. He nuzzled my hair, murmuring phrases of comfort too soft for Travis to hear.

Thank you. Did gratitude expressed in thoughts count? Nevan had said debts accrued in the Unseen realm, not here, so I supposed I was safe.

"Well, Travis?" I said. "Why should I trust you?"

He rubbed his eyes and his voice grew strained as he met my gaze head-on. "I'm sorry for how I treated you back then. More sorry than you could possibly know. Took me six months to track you down, Lindsey. I came here to try and mend our friendship. I screwed that up too. Won't ask forgiveness, 'cuz I don't deserve it, but I will say this. I failed you three years ago. I won't make the same mistake today."

I should've felt vindicated by his admission, but it left me hollow. "Why didn't you tell me any of this when you turned up in Lutin Falls two and a half years ago?"

He aimed a long-suffering look in my direction. "You wouldn't speak to me unless it was in an official capacity. I've been fixing to tell you lots of times, but I chickened out. It's still hard to admit my brother went psycho on the girl he loved more than anything in the world. Hard to admit, to believe, I didn't see it coming. He was my *brother*."

Nevan glided a hand up my back, settling his palm between my shoulder blades. I'd almost forgotten about Nevan. He had become a pillar of strength for me, and though I'd leaned into him moments ago, his presence had faded into the background of my consciousness. Another item had also lapsed from my thoughts.

The dead body.

Enough distractions. Travis's admission confused me, but I had no time to consider its implications. I moved away from Nevan, toward Travis and the waterfall behind him.

"I appreciate your honesty," I said and shoved him aside, clearing my path to the falls. "But I've got work to do."

"Work? What the blazes are you talking about?"

Spray from the waterfall misted over my face and my hair, pasting strands to my cheeks. I swiped them away. "I have a dead man to resurrect."

Travis scuffled sideways, distancing himself from me even as he glared at Nevan. I glanced around in search of the sylph and found him standing behind me, motionless and erect, his gaze remote yet fastened on Travis. Despite his aloof demeanor, Nevan's irises burned with a tempered fire. He'd withdrawn from the battle, but not from the war.

What exactly the two men were fighting for, I had no clue.

"I'll retrieve the dead fellow," Nevan said, and vanished in the blink of an eye.

Travis took a hesitant step toward me. "Retrieve? What the hell's he talking about?"

"Nevan has gone to find the body and bring it here."

Travis's mouth puckered. "He's stealing a corpse?"

"Guess so."

The vibrations from the pounding water of the falls numbed my brain, driving out thoughts. Weariness descended upon me and my shoulders caved under the phantom weight. It felt like decades had elapsed since I leaped into the other world in search of a copper-eating leprechaun. I closed my eyes, more weary in mind than in body, yearning for a rest from all this craziness.

"You were gone a long time."

I came back to reality with a mental start, rolling my eyes toward Travis. His voice had sounded too close, which made sense considering he'd crept to within a foot of me. Worry lines creased his forehead.

"Don't be so dramatic, Travis," I said. "Half an hour is not a long time."

"Half an hour?" His mouth opened and his upper lip lifted, exposing his teeth. "Lindsey, you were gone for three hours."

Chapter Twelve

Y OU'RE DEMENTED." MY VOICE SPIKED AN OCTAVE HIGHER. THREE
hours? No way. As a little girl I'd read stories—legends—about people
who were taken by the fairies and returned years later, but they hadn't aged
a day because, for them, mere hours had ticked by in the fairy world.

Travis nodded solemnly. "It was three hours."

He tipped his wrist toward me to reveal his watch, the hour hand a black
sliver on the pale face. Three hours had passed. *Three hours.*

I laid a hand on my chest, over my racing heart, unable to process the
shock. Time truly did move slower in the other world. No legend after
all. Why hadn't Nevan warned me?

As if on cue, Nevan popped back into the cave between me and the falls,
the dead man slung over his shoulder. I yelped and hopped back, my feet
splashing in a puddle. "You scared me. The way you zip in and out is not
good for my health."

He tilted his head down, lowering his voice to a whisper meant only for
me. "You can feel my approach."

Good point. Why hadn't I this time?

I lolled my head into his chest, exhaling a soft groan. "Travis told me
something I couldn't believe and it kind of knocked me off kilter."

"He did what?" Nevan enunciated each word with the hardness of an
ax splitting bone.

Looking up at him, I gave his chest a light smack. "Don't go all caveman
on me again. This is your fault."

"My fault?"

I backed away a few steps. "You didn't warn me time passes slower in
the Unseen realm."

"Ah, that." He gave me a sheepish smile. "I simply didn't think to mention it. Besides, the time difference is usually minimal."

"Usually? We were gone for three hours."

He tapped his wrist. "Sylphs don't wear watches."

"But you knew this would happen. Why didn't you tell me?"

Travis chuckled, appearing far too pleased with himself. "Not so gaga over jungle boy anymore, are ya?"

As one, Nevan and I swung our heads toward Travis and shouted, "Shut up!"

"This is none of your business," I added, and Travis raised his hands palms out, backing away. He watched us with smug amusement.

Nevan turned his attention to me. "Time passes more swiftly in the Unseen realm when magic affects the continuum."

"You swore you wouldn't use magic on me."

He shot ramrod straight, chin up, gazing down at me over the tip of his elegant nose. "I never break a promise. Perhaps whatever allowed you to cross the veil caused time to pass more quickly. Besides, what would I have to gain by stealing hours from you?"

Good point. The missing time had served only to tick off Travis worse than before and saddled me with an absence I had to explain away. If Nevan had planned this, he would've known I'd realize how much time passed. I'd be mad at him, which I currently was. He gained nothing from the missing hours.

A nasty thought occurred to me and I whirled on Travis. "How do I know you didn't set your watch ahead three hours?"

He slapped a hand on the rock wall. "Christ, if you're gonna believe a freak who wears a dish towel for clothes, I don't know you at all."

"We finally agree on something."

Nevan hefted the dead man off the floor, slinging him over his shoulder again. "Shall we take care of your deceased friend, or should I hand him over to the sheriff?"

"Let's fix this. Please."

Nevan crossed through the falls and out of sight. I tiptoed closer to the water, envisioning the cliff one step beyond it and the roiling pool below.

"Porter," Travis grated through his locked teeth, "think about what you're doing. Who you're trusting."

"I have."

Holding my breath, I steeled myself for what lay ahead and marched through the silvery curtain of the falls.

I halted just in front of the falling water, my toes sticking out over the ledge. Nevan grasped my hand. I accepted the support and inched along behind him as he strode down the ledge with the dead man on his shoulder. When he stopped a few yards from the falls, I aimed a questioning look at him. He draped his free arm around my shoulders, snuggling me against him.

The world plunged into darkness. We sailed down, down, down into the clawing abyss, crashing through energies that scraped at my flesh. My arms bolted around Nevan's waist, I hooked my legs around his and prayed his hold on the dead man wouldn't weaken his grip on me, sending my body reeling out into the void.

Light stung my eyes. Warm, humid air clung to my skin. I blinked my blurry eyes, my arms still welded to Nevan. His muscles moved beneath me and his weight shifted as something thumped nearby, then his other arm wrapped around me. The brilliance that had blinded me diminished into sunlight streaming down through the thick canopy of foliage.

We emerged in the clearing alongside the pool. The dead man lay on the ground at our feet.

Nevan cleared his throat. "Ye might want to unhook yourself from me, darlin', before I get the wrong idea about your intentions."

"Huh?" I glanced down. My legs were intertwined with his, my arms belted around his waist, and my hips tilted into him in what might've qualified as a seductive pose under different circumstances. *Oops.* I disentangled my body from his. "Sorry. Here I order you not to kiss me, and then I go all drunken-slut-at-a-frat-house on you."

His features scrunched into the most adorable look of bafflement. "What in the name of the stars are you rambling about?"

"I—Oh, to hell with it. Think whatever you want."

Spinning away from him, I waved an arm to indicate the dead man. "Grab him and let's get moving. Travis won't be far behind."

"The sheriff is of no consequence to me, love."

His imperious tone had returned and it rankled. "Stop calling me darling and love."

"Whatever you say, dearest."

"Gah!" It was my turn to throw my hands in the air. "Maybe I'll start calling you honey-pie. How'd you like that?"

Nevan collected the body, and as we headed down the trail, I thought I heard him mutter under his breath, "Mortal women are insane."

I broke into a sprint, hurrying past Nevan, anxious to reach the vortex and resolve my legal problems. The slapping of footfalls to the rear assured me Nevan had picked up speed too and I risked a glance over my shoulder. He loped along in my wake with his usual grace and fluidity, the literal dead weight bouncing on his shoulder. Nary a speck of perspiration marred his skin.

My breasts flopped up and down with each heavy step I took, my breaths quickened into gasps, and sweat dribbled down my face into my eyes and mouth. The salty flavor made me oddly hungry. When had I last eaten? My stomach grumbled, as if answering my question with a stern *too long ago*. Every step pushed my holstered gun into my side. I'd gotten so used to carrying it every day that I tended to forget about the weapon unless I needed it.

I rubbed my burning eyes, but kept my attention riveted to the path ahead, not stopping until I reached the vortex.

Nevan laid the dead man on the ground in the center of the circle de-lineated by the rock benches. He lowered himself onto one of the benches, crossed his ankles, set his hands on the rock, and leaned back.

I huddled at the entrance to the vortex, incapable of moving or tearing my gaze away from the corpse. The man looked too pallid and…well, too dead to spring back to life. Tris might've lied. Or too much time might've passed.

Please, God, let this work.

The dead man groaned.

I crouched beside him, knees bent, hands gripping my thighs. *Come on, come on.*

The man's chest heaved once, twice.

Please, please. I leaned over him, counting the seconds.

The man's breathing normalized. His eyes darted back and forth behind his lids and then, as his chest rose on a deep breath, his lids eased open. He blinked slowly, gaze unfocused. Lifelike color suffused his cheeks and his lips warmed from blue to a dusky pink. Pushing up onto his elbows, he rubbed his eyes and turned to me. His dark eyes, though still a smidge bleary, shim-mered with life.

The vortex had resurrected him. I sat back on my heels, lost for words.

The man fingered his earlobe, glancing from me to Nevan and back again. His gaze sharpened on me. "I remember you."

A memory of our first encounter, back in the shop when he tried to pilfer the bookends, replayed in my mind. He'd told me to go to hell, wearing much the same expression. I locked my arms over my chest.

He bared his teeth in a sneer. "You're the bitch who grabbed me in the store."

"And you're the slimy thief who tried to make off with stolen mer-chandise."

The shoplifter wrinkled up his nose as if I smelled awful. "What'd you do, whack me over the head and drag me out here to torture me into con-fessing?"

I strongly resisted the urge to slug him. *You died, you nasty little toad, and the vortex brought you back—thanks to me and my pet sylph.*

Okay, I was not going to tell him that.

Tipping backward a few inches, needing more space between me and the angry jerk in front me, I said, "Don't you remember what hap-pened?"

"Whatever it was, must've been you did it." He scrambled to his feet, swayed for a second, and regained his equilibrium in time to snare my arm. "You had it in for me from the start. Lying bitch."

He yanked my arm.

Nevan seized the man by his shirt collar, hefting him off the ground until his toes dangled in the air. The man thrashed but couldn't break free.

For the first time since we entered the clearing, I noticed Nevan's appearance. He'd conjured up the outfit he'd worn yesterday when he corroborated my story about the dead man for Travis.

Calm as the eye of a hurricane, Nevan told his captive, "This woman knows what you are and decided to save your life anyway. Perhaps you should be grateful to her, or else perhaps I will reverse the decision."

Threatening and polite at the same time. Impressive. And the way his biceps swelled and stretched every time the toad-man wriggled, yet his grip never faltered…Well, that was even more impressive.

The toad-man went pale and limp. He dared a sideways glance at me before bowing his head to stare at his dangling feet. "Sorry."

"And?" Nevan hefted the man a little higher, extracting a whimper.

The toad looked at me. "Thank you."

Nevan dropped the man, who struck the ground on his ass, legs splayed before him, arms slack.

Since the jerk appeared suitably defeated, I offered him a hand up. He cringed as if I'd held out razor-sharp claws, or maybe he thought I'd toss him over to Nevan, but after a couple seconds he accepted the aid.

On his feet again, he scratched at his arms, avoiding my gaze. "What happened to me?"

"Someone hit you on the head."

"Hit me?" He ran a hand through his hair, catching his fingers on the blood caked there. His face blanched. His fingers came away with dried blood stuck under the nails. His brow furrowed and his eyes widened. "Why don't I have a wound? I've got blood but—"

"It was a scratch," Nevan said. "Scalp wounds bleed like the dickens."

The toad-man closed his eyes briefly, relaxing. "Yeah, that's right. They do bleed a lot."

I forced my lips into my professional smile. I did need this guy to stay grateful, so he wouldn't blab to Travis about the imagined slights I committed against him. "I'm Lindsey, and this is Nevan. What's your name?"

"Brad." He spread his hands wide, scanning the ground. "Where's my bag?"

"Your backpack?" When he nodded, I counted to five before answering. *Oh, you mean the backpack you tried to shove stolen merchandise into right before you called me a bitch?* No, that would not do. "I guess somebody took it."

"What? I had important stuff in there."

Important stuff like the bookends he pinched. I shrugged. "Maybe it'll turn up."

Brad stretched his neck, rolling his head this way and that until something cracked. Appearing relieved, he said, "I really need to get out of the stinking woods."

"Better see a doctor, just to be safe."

"No thank you. Hospitals give me the willies." He stretched again, yawning. "Besides, I feel fine."

Although I was relieved to hear it, I couldn't quite believe he felt fine. Sure, the vortex had healed my lacerations, but those had been minor. This man had died.

Brad turned his head left and right, eying the rock circle. "How'd I get here? Last thing I remember is walking out of the store, to go wait for my friends in the parking lot."

Slinking out of the shop, he meant, with his booty stashed in his backpack. Still, I had to come up with a believable explanation of how Brad wound up here.

"You must've crawled here," Nevan suggested, sounding quite reasonable, "and then you passed out. A bump on the noggin can cause short-term amnesia."

He spoke with a tone of authority, as if he knew everything about head injuries. I gave him a quizzical look, but he wasn't paying any attention to me.

"Crawled?" Brad said. Lips parted, he tapped his tongue on his upper teeth. "I suppose that could've happened."

"I'm sure that's how you got here," I said. "Nevan's a doctor. He knows all about head injuries."

Hooking my arm around Nevan's, I beamed up at him with only a hint of sarcasm.

Nevan hit me with his smoldering smile, the one that always shifted my pulse into overdrive.

"A doctor?" Brad asked. "Couldn't he look me over?"

Full of gravitas, Nevan squinted down at the other man. He laid his palm on Brad's head, patting all around his scalp, then felt under the man's chin. "You seem quite fine."

"Thanks, doc." Brad held out a hand to Nevan, who shook it once. He nodded to me. "Thanks for watching over me while I was out."

He had no idea how "out" he'd been.

Brad took three steps past us.

I whirled, capturing his arm.

"Wait, I—" *Can't let you leave because you know too much.* Oh yeah. That'd go over swimmingly. "Could you wait here for a minute? Please."

A trace of suspicion flickered across his face. "Something wrong?"

Explanations deserted me, swept away on an icy tide of panic. "Please. As a favor to me, the woman who saved your life, stick around for a minute. While I talk to my, uh, friend over there."

Nevan arched an eyebrow at my use of the term friend.

Thankfully, Brad took a seat on one of the stone benches. "Okay. I'll wait."

I moved off to the side, out of Brad's earshot, and motioned for Nevan to follow. He waved a dismissive hand, returning his full attention to the formerly dead guy, over whom he stood sentry—tall and imposing, face blank and posture relaxed, but exuding a *don't mess with me* aura. When I stomped my foot and crooked my finger at him, Nevan finally obeyed and strode toward me.

His lips quirked, anxious to form a smirk, but to his credit he suppressed the look. He made no such effort with his playful tone of voice. "Can't wait to get me alone, eh?"

Since we had more pressing issues at the moment, I ignored his innuendo. "You have voodoo powers, right?"

"I believe you're confusing me with a witch doctor. Voodoo is not among my powers, nor is it a pastime of mine."

"You know what I meant. You have magical…stuff."

He slanted closer, his voice deepening. "Stuff?"

"Come on, work with me here."

"I would, but I'm not certain what precisely you're trying to accomplish."

"We need to convince Brad to forget he ever saw us. Unless you'd care to explain to Travis how we resurrected a corpse using a healing vortex powered by a copper-addicted leprechaun. He's having enough trouble with the psychedelic light show in the cave."

"His confusion is irrelevant. I expend no energy on sorting out mortal affairs." He slid his gaze down my body and back up to my face, and in the wake of his appraisal, excitement sizzled over my skin. "Except for yours. I am acutely aware of everything to do with you."

"Brad's rebirth concerns me." All of a sudden, I could hardly catch my breath. "I need your expertise."

He edged closer, backing me into a tree, and placed his arms on trunk, bracketing my head. "My powers are bound to my duties."

Surrounded, I had no choice but to meet his gaze, inhale his scent, absorb the heat of him. "You enchant people to check for freaky supernatural thingies. Couldn't you enchant Brad for me?"

He recoiled, his upper lip twitching. After a few seconds of staring hard at me, he pushed away from the tree. "My duty does not involve enchanting men."

"I'm not asking you to kiss him. Just put him in a trance or whatever, to make him open to suggestion. You can do that, right?"

He grumbled, frowning and plucking at the buttons of his shirt.

"Please, Nevan, I need you to try. If you can't make it work, fine. But at least give it a shot." I linked my hands in a pleading gesture. "I will be forever grateful if you do this for me."

He threw a quick glance at Brad. His face pinched in disgust, but he nodded.

I hopped up to kiss his cheek. "Thank you so, so, so much."

With a grunt, he stalked to Brad. The shoplifter floundered backward a half step. Nevan snapped his fingers in Brad's face, drawing the man's attention to him. Nevan's eyes began to swirl, erupting with bright metallic ribbons of color. Brad's mouth formed an O. His eyes went wide, his entire body slackening and swaying. Lips twisted, Nevan cast me a sidelong look before he took hold of the other man's shoulders to steady him.

"Listen to my voice," Nevan said, "and look into my eyes."

His tone hushed yet potent, he spoke to Brad in a language I didn't recognize, one brimming with exotic vowels and lilting beauty. Transfixed by his voice, I studied his face and the way his lips moved as he enunciated his words, recalling those nimble lips on mine, imagining how his mouth might explore my body.

Nevan let go of Brad and said, "It's done."

"What?" Ripped from my reverie, I stared blankly at him. "Already?"

"The man was quite easy to control. Weak willed, this one." Nevan ambled toward me. "I believe I've proved I will do anything for you."

Even enchant a man, despite his distaste for the task. He'd done it for me. Because I asked. I could've kissed him—if not for my no-kissing rule.

Movement behind him snagged my attention and I spotted Brad the erstwhile thief shambling past the stone benches, down the trail to the shop. His eyes were glassy, his expression vacant.

"Is he okay?" I asked Nevan.

"He will be. The enchantment will fade within moments, long enough for him to reach the shop. He will have no memory of either of us, or of what transpired here."

"Good." I watched Brad until the woods engulfed him. "Um, are you sure he'll be all right?"

"Yes."

The syllable was clipped. I glanced up at Nevan, but he'd gone stone-faced again. He did that when he was anxious, I'd come to realize. In spite of his assurances to the contrary, he must've worried his magic might damage Brad—and maybe he worried about the same thing with Sandy, with every woman he enchanted. How could anyone, even an immortal like him, live with the consequences of wielding such power, if it might harm another? I couldn't fathom the fear and guilt it must engender.

On top of that, Nevan was bound to a nasty piece of work like Skeiron. Forced to do the king's bidding. Yet somehow, he disobeyed those orders with me. He hypnotized Brad for me too. His statement from a moment ago echoed in my mind.

I believe I've proved I will do anything for you.

Would I do anything for him? The skin at my nape prickled, the sensation sweeping down my arms. I lifted my face to Nevan's, but he was staring down the path where Brad had disappeared from view. His watchful gaze shifted to scan the woods around us, though he remained motionless and silent. He truly was a guardian. Rather than protecting Skeiron's interests, he now watched over me.

My chest seemed to swell under the pressure of a dull ache behind my ribs. My heart felt full, on the verge of overflowing with emotions I couldn't name. Wouldn't name. I'd known this man for two days. And yet...

Unwilling to finish the thought, I threaded my fingers through his. "Walk me back to the shop?"

"Anything for you."

A figure tromped out of the trees behind the vortex. Travis meandered around the stone benches, looking dazed, and turned in a circle before dropping onto one of the benches. His eyes were bleary and aimed at the spot where Brad had lain moments earlier.

He lifted his head as if it weighed fifty pounds and looked at me. "That man was dead. I saw him in the morgue. His friends identified the body."

I took a couple halting steps toward him, but his stark expression stopped me. "How much did you see?"

"Everything." Travis's unfocused gaze veered to Nevan and back to the ground. "How'd you bring him back to life?"

"With the—"

He flung up a hand. "Never mind. I don't wanna know."

Behind me, Nevan muttered with disgust, "Shall I enchant the sheriff as well?"

"No." I knelt beside Travis. "Magic is real. I know it's a huge pill to swallow, but you have to accept the truth."

"Magic?" He spoke the word in a hushed tone. "I need to be alone. To think about all this."

"Come back to the shop with us. Please."

He erupted, his race flashing red, his voice echoing off the trees. "Leave me the fuck alone!"

I jumped up, reeling backward into Nevan.

"Let him be," Nevan said quietly. "Let me escort you back to the shop."

As Nevan led me away, I kept looking back at Travis until the woods obscured my view of him. His reaction to the reality of magic was the polar opposite of mine and I couldn't understand his fury about it. His behavior over the past few days mystified me.

Well, at least he hadn't arrested me.

We crossed the rock garden in silence, our footfalls crunching on the gravel path, and rounded the corner of the shop building. His hand stayed firmly swaddled around mine. Ever the watcher, he kept surveying the woods—for Brennus, no doubt, the harbinger of everything bad.

Awareness shivered down my spine and I checked the sky for a raven, but saw nothing except a few puffy clouds. The eerie recognition of eyes tracking me slithered over my skin, so much like the intuition that affected me two days ago, right before I found the dead man, I couldn't shake the feeling I was missing something vital. In the car, I'd heard Calder's voice in my head, but that must've been anxiety induced. Not real. It couldn't have been what it seemed to be.

I stopped dead, pulling Nevan with me. He scrutinized my face, concern evident in his eyes, and said, "You've gone pale as death, love. What is it?"

What the hell. Might as well ask him, the only one who might know. "Are ghosts real?"

"Ghosts?" He brushed his thumb across my cheek. "Why would ye ask?"

"Sylphs and leprechauns are real, but ghosts can't possibly exist?"

"They exist. Not in the way mortals believe, but I fail to see the relevance."

Part of me resisted confiding in him, but most of me wanted to, badly. "Is it possible Calder, the man I shot and killed, is haunting me?"

He pulled his head back, chin tucked. "What leads you to believe he is?"

I explained what happened in the sheriff's car. "I keep having this creepy feeling someone is watching me. I'm nuts, right?"

"Never would I describe you as insane. Ghosts do not generally flit about at will, they're bound to a specific location, generally the place where they died, and only until they complete their unfinished business." He leaned in, his forehead touching mine. "However, if you sense a malevolent presence, I trust in your instincts."

"It's nice to have someone who believes me." *And understands me, and makes me feel again.* I wound a spiraling lock of his hair around my finger, loving the slick softness of it. "We have to do something about Skeiron, don't we?"

"Skeiron is my problem, not yours. Vow you will stay far from these woods until I resolve the matter."

"I am not hiding. I'm probably fired by now, so I have nowhere else to be." *Except with you.* "Take me with you or I'll sneak up behind you anyway."

"Which you did with remarkable stealth two days ago. I required mere seconds to detect your approach."

I dropped the lock of his hair. "Probably the same way I sense you coming. Magic is cheating."

"Magic is the essence of every elemental being." He patted my behind and gave me a little push in the direction of the shop. "Go. Tend to customers. And stay away from the woods."

"Ugh. You are so boss—"

An excited shriek pierced the seclusion of the garden. Raucous voices and laughter ensued, blasting over us in an auditory tide of human revelry.

Nevan gave me a questioning look. I shrugged.

Taking my hand again, he ushered me out of the rock garden and along the gravel path toward the shop. As we rounded the bend into the parking lot, I saw it was crammed with cars of varying sizes, most gray or black, the cherry red of my Malibu the only spot of color.

Well, not quite the only one.

My gaze fell upon a rainbow-colored behemoth. The motor home squatted alongside the entrance to the parking lot, behind a row of tall SUVs and pickup trucks, its garish paint job gleaming in the sun.

I shut my eyes, exhaling a whimpery moan. "They're here."

Nevan squeezed my hand. "Is it the ghost?"

"No, it's not a ghost. It's my family."

Nevan let go of my hand. "I suppose I should depart."

"Why?"

He appraised me with a curious expression. "I assumed you would not wish your family to see me. I am…difficult to explain."

At the moment, his appearance was moderately normal, though still striking. "Travis may have freaked out when he saw what you really are, but trust me. My family can handle it."

He eyed me with wary eyes. "Are you certain you wouldn't prefer I left?"

"Positive." Sort of. He expected me to shoo him away, to stop my family from seeing him. Part of me really, really wanted to sequester him from the rest of my life, but another piece of me longed to escort him straight over to the motor home, knock on the door, and introduce him to my parents.

Nevan stepped backward, shoulders square.

I recognized the movement and the way his gaze went distant, like he was visualizing another place. He intended to poof away to who-knew-where any second.

He swallowed visibly, his lips compressing.

My God. I recognized that too, a manifestation of shame, similar to what I'd witnessed when he enchanted Sandy. He honestly believed I wanted him to go, and the knowledge pained him.

Which bothered me a lot more than I liked.

Static electricity rushed over me, faint yet distinct.

Pivoting toward him, I held up a hand to halt his departure. "Wait. I said I want you to stay."

"You informed me your family could handle my appearance." He sighed with exaggerated drama. "In point of fact, you have not said you wish me to remain here."

"Stay, dammit." My turn to sigh, with irritation. "I want you to meet my family."

Laughter echoed from around the front of the building. Hand in hand, Nevan and I ventured a little further into the parking lot. A group of people milled near the shop entrance, gesticulating and smiling, their cheery voices merging into a melee of sounds. I noticed the familiar backside of a curly mass of chestnut-brown hair, attached to a woman at the center of the hubbub.

My mother pivoted our way, as if she'd sensed my approach. Delight lit up her face and she waved her hand with fierce energy.

Where was Dad? I searched the faces of the people surrounding Mom, but he wasn't among them.

Nevan grasped my arm, pulling me up short. He pointed to another, smaller throng gathered in front of the Porter family's monstrosity on wheels. "What is this?"

The half dozen people gathered there formed a semicircle around someone sitting on the ground. I tilted my head left and right, struggling to see past the bodies. A blonde young woman shuffled sideways to hook her arm around her male companion's waist. The woman was Sandy. She smiled brightly, but the person on the ground must've done something, because her eyes went wide and her mouth opened on an *oooh*. Her companion watched the spectacle, whatever it was, with equal awe.

What on earth was happening over there?

The answer revealed itself an instant later. Another onlooker moved aside, granting me an unimpeded view of the man seated cross-legged on the gravel at the center of crowd. His gray hair—cut in a short, military-type style—fringed a round face etched with wrinkles. Though I couldn't see his eyes from here, I knew they were an ice-blue echo of mine. His wrists rested on his knees, palms up, the thumb and forefinger of each hand touching to form a little loop. The lotus position. The breeze carried his litany of soft *ohmmm*'s across the parking lot.

My father was meditating in the middle of a freaking parking lot at the rock shop where I worked.

"Do you know him?" Nevan asked.

"Sort of." I watched Sandy crouch down to speak to my father, who responded with a beatific smile. "He's my dad."

Just then, someone hollered from across the parking lot. "What the hell is going on out here?"

I cringed at the sound of Stan's gravelly voice. With no explanation for my hours of being gone, I expected to be fired on sight.

Stan stormed down the path into the parking lot. His face flamed a particularly disturbing shade of maroon. His head jerked left and right until his gaze slammed into me. His arm shot up, one finger zeroing in on me. "Porter!"

His voice thundered even louder, reverberating off the trees, the metal building, the motor home. I sidled up to Nevan, grateful beyond measure when he hooked an arm around my shoulders.

My father paused in his *ohmmm*'ing to stare at Stan. Ken Porter set his hands on his thighs, fingertips curling over his kneecaps. He said something to my boss, who stopped short. Stan glanced around, seeming almost embarrassed, and squatted beside my father. After a quick discussion, the two men exchanged smiles and Stan assumed the lotus position.

Stan Lagorio was meditating. *Ohm*'s and all.

The shock of seeing blustering Stan chilling out with my dad left me immobile. I'd intended to trot over there and greet my parents, but all of a sudden I couldn't summon the will to move away from Nevan and relinquish the bizarre security he provided.

"Do you fear your family?" Nevan asked.

"No, of course not. I love them, really, I do. But they are unusual. And most people don't like unusual, especially if it comes packaged with chanting and incense burning and crystal talismans."

He rubbed my arm, the gesture so tender my heart sped up at the implications of it. I couldn't think that way, though because he was forbidden to get involved in mortal affairs.

Except he was involved in the affairs of one mortal.

Nevan tucked one finger under my chin, angling my face up to him. "I'm unusual myself, and not inclined to be judgmental about talismans or chanting."

So true. He was a supernatural being. Of course he wouldn't balk at my family's devotion to all things New Age. He was, in a way, the embodiment of their beliefs.

Which meant I was a complete jerk. I'd pooh-poohed my family's lifestyle since I hit puberty, and it turned out they'd been right. The supernatural did exist. I found myself, in this very moment, nestled under the arm of an elemental spirit.

"Perhaps," Nevan said, "you're not truly worried about my reaction to your family, but rather about their reaction to me."

Hmm, yes. There was the issue of Nevan, who even in his demure, mortalesque form exuded a sensual confidence—and oh my heavens, he was jaw-droppingly hot either way. Then there was the lingering desire that sizzled over my skin, inflamed by the slightest touch, even from his hand quite chastely holding mine or his arm looped around me.

Rein it in, Lindsey.

I bound up my sexual urges, but I couldn't bear to pull away from Nevan. No harm in accepting comfort from him.

Without moving my head, I glanced at my father, still seated lotus-style smack in the middle of the parking lot. Would my parents notice the sexual tension crackling between me and Nevan? Did it matter? I supposed I cared what they thought because I wasn't entirely sure what I was doing. Cavorting with a magical being. At least nobody had seen me with him in his natural form.

Travis had seen—too much, too soon—and it sent him on a trip to la-la-land.

He couldn't handle the truth about the supernatural. My parents were predisposed to believe.

"Would ye prefer I whisk ye away from here?" Nevan asked.

"No." Dammit, I refused to be a coward. I gripped his hand harder, maybe a bit too hard, but he didn't flinch. "I want to see them, but you have to understand. I gave up on the New Age lifestyle, then I ran off to

Texas and got into trouble and, well…It's complicated. I told them Calder dumped me for another woman. They know nothing about what happened to me three years ago."

Neither did Nevan, but in spite of the curiosity evident in his gaze, he refrained from asking.

"I'll introduce you," I told him. "Just do me a favor. Promise not to be your usual scoundrel-ish self."

"I promise to behave in the presence of your kin. I've already made the sacrifice of covering myself, so as not to embarrass you." He inclined toward me, his lips near enough to kiss. For a heartbeat, I thought he would kiss me—and he did, sort of. He pecked the tip of my nose. "I shall support and protect as necessary. You have my word."

"Thank you."

His lips contorted, as if he fought against grinning or frowning. I couldn't decide which. "You were doing so well with not thanking me. I gather your family's arrival is disquieting and has made you forgetful."

"Sorry, it comes out of my mouth all on its own. Blame my parents. Those bastards, they raised me to be courteous and thoughtful of others' feelings."

He threaded his fingers through mine, his mortalesque eyes glimmering with a hint of the sylphesque fire masked within them. "You do love your family, don't you?"

"Of course I do." My eyes found Dad again, and an old feeling resurfaced to pluck at my heart. I'd missed my family. "They've always been there for me, when I'd let them. They're good people."

"They'd have to be, to raise a daughter like you."

Aw hell. Every time he paid me a compliment, the urge to smack one on him got harder and harder to suppress.

A child's gleeful cry split the air. "Zeeeee!"

Nevan's mouth dropped open a smidgen, his eyes flaring wide for a split second as he caught sight of my little brother. Ash Porter was hurtling across the parking lot, arms flung out, a silly grin on his face.

"What is that?" Nevan said, with the disbelief of a man who'd never met a ten-year-old New Age devotee.

Before I could respond, Ash was there, hurling himself up at me. I caught my brother in midair and he clamped his arms around my neck. His golden-brown hair, cut short like my dad's, tickled my cheek.

He kicked his feet in an airborne happy dance. "Zee, it's you!"

Since Ash was all but choking me, I unclamped his arms from my neck and set him on the ground. He latched onto my left hand. I tousled his hair and he giggled. "Who else would I be, Ash? Do you throw your arms around every girl you see?"

"No, I'm not stupid," he said, rolling his eyes. "I haven't seen you in months and months and months." My brother scrutinized me with an adorable look of concentration, his tongue poking out between his lips. "You look different. What'd you do to yourself?"

"Nothing. I emailed you a picture of me last week." But I hadn't seen my family in person for over three years. Wow. Three years. "You've gotten bigger, though."

He puffed up, lifting his chin. "One point two inches taller than my last report."

"Impressive." Yeah, my brother gave me regular reports on his growth, texted straight to my phone. Little boys were weird.

Ash appraised Nevan with youthful seriousness, tongue protruding again, and crossed his arms over his chest, partly obscuring the Superman cartoon on his T-shirt. Nevan raised a brow. Ash puckered his lips. "Dude, are you Lindsey's boyfriend?"

I opened my mouth to say no.

Nevan leaped in ahead of me. "Yes, in fact, I am."

CHAPTER THIRTEEN

Y NAME IS NEVAN." HE OFFERED HIS HAND TO MY BROTHER, WHO AC-
cepted it. "And you are?"

"I'm Ash. So you're, like, really Zee's boyfriend?"

"Zee?" Nevan scrunched his whole face.

I got out one syllable before my brother bulldozed over me.

"It's what I call Lindsey."

"Why?" Nevan asked.

Ash rolled his eyes and dropped his head back. "Duh, it's from her name. Lind-*zee*. Get it? Everybody should have a wicked-cool nickname. She hated it at first, but I think she's starting to like it."

"I see," Nevan said.

Ash grabbed my hand and Nevan's, leaning his weight into it as he urged us to follow him. He half dragged us across the parking, swinging our hands, skipping and peppering us with questions he rarely gave us time to answer.

"Dude, you need a nickname," Ash told Nevan. "I mean, if you're gonna be part of our family, it's kinda required."

"He's not—" I cut myself off before I rejected Ash's suggestion about Nevan joining our family. Instead, I jumped into yet another lie. "Nevan and I haven't been seeing each other that long."

Okay, not entirely a lie.

Nevan raised my hand to his lips, feathering a kiss across my knuckles. "I am, however, immensely fond of your sister."

Nevan was immensely fond of me?

"Awesome." My brother tugged our hands, ensuring we'd continue trailing him across the parking lot. He released our hands as we reached my father and his circle of admirers. "Dad, I've got totally sick news. Lindsey's got a boyfriend."

And of course, he spoke the last part in a mocking, sing-song tone.

Nevan bent close to me to murmur, "I thought he was happy about this news, but he called it sick. Does he find me nauseating?"

"To a kid, sick means it's great."

"I...see." He straightened, but seemed to have developed a permanent crease in his forehead.

Ash took off, dancing around us as we approached the motor home, taunting me with his chant of "Lindsey's got a boyfriend, Lindsey's got a boyfriend."

When my dad approached us, I introduced him to my sort-of boyfriend. After sizing up Nevan with a dubious expression, my father thrust out a hand to shake Nevan's with shocking vigor.

"Nice to meet you, son." Dad sealed his other hand around Nevan's, tugging him closer. "If you hurt my daughter, I'll hunt you down and blow a hole through your skull the size of my fist. Understand?"

To his credit, Nevan stayed placid. "You have my word, sir. I've no intention of bringing harm to Lindsey, or of letting anyone else harm her. I stake my life on that promise."

Dad scowled at Nevan for several seconds, during which my pulse rocketed to levels no human should endure. At last, Ken Porter smiled and set my would-be boyfriend free. "Welcome to the family, Nevan."

I gaped at my father. Welcome to the family? I barely knew Nevan. Yet everyone assumed this was a relationship, and more than that, a serious relationship.

The three men in my life—Nevan, Dad, and Ash—glommed onto each other, plunging into an animated conversation. Nevan laughed at some joke my father told. Ash danced on his toes.

Dumbfounded, I could do nothing more than stare at the trio.

My mom, having disentangled herself from the crowd by the shop entrance, trotted up to our group. My mind had slipped into neutral, but somehow I managed to introduce my mother to Nevan. She snared him in a bear hug.

I stood immobile, hip-deep in shock. Mom never hugged anyone except family members and very close friends. When I'd introduced her to Calder, she'd barely shaken his hand. Calder was gorgeous and charming too, yet my family never took to him this way.

Maybe they'd sensed what I'd blinded myself to—that Calder was not right, on a fundamental level. I should've seen it. Unused to the attention, I'd been snowed by his innocent sweetness, his casual confidence, and his keen interest in me. Was I making the same mistake with Nevan?

Mom finally relinquished her hold on him, chortling at whatever he'd said. I couldn't take my eyes off his face, that beautiful grin, those mesmerizing eyes.

Dad slapped Nevan on the back. Ash hopped up and down, assailing Nevan with more questions.

My mother moseyed over to me. "A boyfriend? Since when?"

"It's a recent development. Sorry I didn't tell you."

"You like him more than Calder."

"Not sure yet."

"Pshaw. It's plain to see you do." She picked lint off my shirt. Or maybe it was otherworld moss. "It's okay, I like him."

"You—do?"

"Hooey, do I ever." She fanned her face with one hand. "He is gorgeous, a real hunk. That boy could make an old woman swoon. And he clearly adores you."

"Don't you think he's…odd?"

She tsked. "I trust my intuition, sweetie. Trust yours."

My shoulders caved in, as if great pressure compressed me. "I don't know. What if this thing with Nevan doesn't work out? What if he changes, like—" *Like Calder.* But I couldn't say it, because my family knew nothing about Calder's transformation or what he'd done to me. "What if Nevan turns out to be something other than what he seems?"

"You'll leave him." She formed a gun with her fingers. "And he if lays a finger on you, I'll off him."

Yeah, my entire family subscribed to the notion of shoot first, dispose of the body later. Only in self-defense, of course, or in the defense of another. Mom told me once she believed in the essential goodness of mankind, but sometimes a man needed a reminder to be kind delivered at the business end of a Smith & Wesson .357 Magnum revolver.

Mom owned one of those. She stashed it in her purse. Cindy Porter had also given her only daughter a Bond Arms Mini derringer. For my birthday. Along with a crystal pendant designed to calm negative energies.

For the first time, I understood the juxtaposition. A woman could believe in the supernatural and carry a loaded gun inside her waistband.

My gaze drifted to Nevan, where he was still chumming it up with Ash and my father. Despite years of scoffing at New Age stuff, deep down I had never stopped believing. I let popular opinion sway me into denying it, but I'd always believed. Even before I met Nevan. That's why I'd accepted everything he told me and showed me.

And yet I'd spent years scoffing at my family.

"Jeez." I scrubbed my face with my hands. "I am such a jerk. All these years, I've treated my own family like a band of kooks. You must hate me."

Mom kneaded my shoulders, freeing tension I hadn't realized was there. "Lindsey, you are not a jerk, and of course we don't hate you."

"I'm being punished. Karma's a bitch, right?"

Her fingers stilled. "What do you think you're being punished for?"

Damn. Freudian slips were real too.

"Tell me," she said, "how you feel you've been punished."

"I meant because of this crappy job. Karma hates me. I thumbed my nose at it and now I'm suffering for my arrogance."

My mother snorted. "Poppycock."

Against my will, my lips broke into a smile. "Thanks for the vote of confidence, but I'm not sure I deserve it."

Mom swung a finger past me, off to my right. "Your karma is standing right in front of you."

Tracking the line of her finger pointing, my gaze fell on Nevan.

He sat cross-legged on the gravel, one-third of a circle completed by my dad and Ash. Eyes closed, they appeared deep in meditation. Nevan seemed more relaxed than I'd ever seen him. His serene expression triggered a pang of something I'd buried deep inside me, under a mountain of pain, locked behind that damn vault door.

Nevan opened one eye, peering at me from under lush, dark lashes. His sweet smile devastated me, tearing into the mountain inside me, easing a long-held burden. Tears pricked my eyes and I hauled in a quaking breath.

I pushed away from the motor home, a coil of dread winding tight in my stomach. Though I looked away, I sensed Nevan's gaze on me. He couldn't be my karmic reward. It was crazy.

Nevan rose in a smooth movement, spoke to my dad and Stan—bidding them goodbye, apparently, since they waved—and strolled up to me.

To my mother, he said, "May I steal your daughter for a bit?"

"Go right ahead, dear."

Nevan slipped his hand into mine, guiding me around the end of the RV and the way to the other side of the vehicle. In the shade of the behemoth motor home, he drew me into his embrace. I closed my eyes, my cheek on his chest, and sighed with a contentment I hadn't experienced…ever. Until I met him.

"I wish to be alone with you," he murmured. "Quite alone."

"Sounds good." I folded my arms around him. "Please take me away."

"My pleasure."

He whisked us both away.

———

WE TOUCHED DOWN IN THE WOODS. MY EARS RANG, THANKS TO OUR trip through the carnivorous tunnel, which had me holding my breath. Having glued my eyes shut for the journey, I wrenched my lids apart as soon as we landed on solid ground.

Nevan kept his arms around me for a few more seconds, as I regained my footing. The tips of knee-high weeds swiped across my jeans. We huddled within a grove of pines and aspens, with a solitary birch standing sentinel behind Nevan, its white bark like a beam of light in the gloaming of the woods.

He stepped back a couple paces and frowned at the weeds. "This won't do."

"For what?"

Whether he hadn't heard me or heard but chose to ignore me, I couldn't say. He lifted one hand parallel to the ground, palm down, and moved it in a swirling motion. A breeze wafted through the clearing, rustling the vegetation. The weeds collapsed to the ground, flat as they would've been right after snow melt, compressed by a winter's worth of snow.

Nevan nodded, his smile one of satisfaction.

"Worried about ticks?" I asked.

"Ticks?" He hit the word hard, as if he couldn't quite grasp its meaning.

"Yeah. Tiny, blood-sucking insects that love tall weeds and carry diseases. We mere mortals prefer to avoid them."

"I know nothing of such creatures."

Pointing at the squished weeds, I asked, "Why'd you do that?"

As he advanced on me, he raked his gaze over my body from head to toe and back again. Desire darkened his features, fired up in his eyes, and roughened his voice. "I was striving for a more pleasurable atmosphere."

I responded the only way I knew how—with evasion. "Why did you tell my brother you're my boyfriend?"

"We have kissed, and we've spent the better part of three days in each other's company. What would you call me?"

Confusing. Enthralling. Frightening, at times. "I don't know."

"You trust me. You want me. We are involved, are we not?"

Involved? The word came with so many implications. "Technically, I guess we are."

"Well then." He ensnared my wrists with his hands, rubbing the pulse points there, his eyes burning and swirling in a maelstrom of living, breathing color. "Let's enjoy the pleasures of involvement."

The heat of his skin penetrated mine, rushing up my arms and through my entire body. My breaths quickened, my nipples shot hard, my breasts felt achy and constricted inside my bra. He skimmed his hands up my arms, inch by inch, tempting and teasing along the way with light strokes of his fingers.

His hands crested my shoulders, gliding up my throat to dive into my hair. His sure fingers massaged and explored, slid down to my nape, caressed and erased the tension bound up in my muscles. I couldn't stop my head from lolling backward into his touch, nor could I silence my breathy moan. I'd never experienced anything so damn good, and yet a need swelled inside me, a craving for more than this. Much more.

Losing control, losing my mind, losing my—

I snapped out of the haze as if someone had dumped a bucket of ice water over my head. Breathing hard, I staggered backward. I'd been on the verge of letting him do anything he wanted to me, of letting him take my virginity. Hell, I would've handed it over gift wrapped with a nice little thank-you card on top. To a man—a being—I'd known for less than three days. Christ.

Nevan raised one brow, his lips curving slightly in a devilish smile.

I coughed, shifting from one foot to the other. Could he read my mind? God, I hoped not.

He strode one step closer.

I scuttled backward, and for the second time since I'd met him, backed my stupid ass right into a tree. *Gah.* Why was I backing away from him, anyway? Not because I worried about losing control at the feel of his skin on mine or the intoxicating fever of his kiss. No, not because of that.

Nevan crossed those impressive arms over his chest, inexorably pulling my gaze to the landscape of sculpted sinews on his arms, and lower, to his taut abs and the trail chiseled out by those muscles, where it plunged beneath his loincloth.

One more step. Arms falling to his sides. Tongue sliding over his lips.

Plastered to the tree, I fought to catch my breath, to take in enough oxygen, but my scalp had begun to tingle.

Another step, those hips swaying.

Breath, stolen. Thoughts, scattered. I huddled against the tree, stiff and paralyzed.

With one final movement, he penned me between his body and the tree. He planted his hands on the wide trunk of the tree, at either side of my head. My heart fluttered, my stomach too. I crooked my fingers into the bark, desperate for a handhold to buttress me.

Nevan regarded me without expression, consuming my view so the entirety of my world consisted of him and only him. "Stars in heaven, love. Ye look ready to crumble. I didn't think a mortal could be this tense."

I'd built up enough tension to hold up a suspension bridge. "I've had a rough week."

"That's not the reason." He leaned in, his chest meeting my breasts, and suddenly the barrier of my clothing seemed flimsy and worthless. "Ye weren't this tense until I brought you here. With me. Alone."

The delicate pressure of his muscles against my rigid nipples coursed a painful desire straight down to my sex. I'd never survive this if I didn't cool things down. Right. Piece of cake. Moist, decadent cake dripping with warm, dark fudge sauce.

My mouth watered. *Damn.*

I drummed my left foot on the patch of purple wildflowers beneath my boots, pulverizing the petals.

Nevan shook his head. "How can ye stand to be this pent up?"

"Excuse me?"

"Perhaps repressed is a better term."

Repressed? Pent up? I ratcheted my spine even straighter and elevated my chin. "I am not repressed."

Except I had a mental vault where I locked up my emotions. But that wasn't the same as repressing them. *Pathetic, pathetic, pathetic.*

"It was an observation," he said, "not a judgment. You conceal your most powerful feelings quite masterfully."

"Said the pot to the kettle."

"And which would I be?"

"Does it matter?"

He dipped his head to mine, his lips within licking distance. Not that I wanted to lick him—them. As if he'd perceived my lust, he wet his lips with a slow glide of his tongue. His voice vibrated through me like distant thunder. "You are definitely the pot. A kettle releases it steam, but you've got yours sealed under a tight lid."

"I'm not sure that's the correct definition a pot or a kettle."

"Ye won't distract me with semantics, love." He settled a finger on my lips. "I can feel the steam trapped within ye."

"But I'm not angry."

He dragged his finger across my mouth, swept it back to center of my lips, nudged it between them until I tasted his skin. "Not that kind of steam."

Too late I understood, and my insides went warm and liquid. My shoulders sank against the tree. My head fell back, exposing my throat. Every labored breath pushed my breasts into him, chafing my nipples, turning my nerves into high-tension wires, the current fierce and almost unbearable.

Where was the frigging grip I'd gotten hold of a minute ago? I must've dropped it here somewhere.

Fumbling for my mental armor, I cleared my throat. "Maybe I do hold things in, but you're one to talk. I'm onto you, buster. This whole happy-go-lucky Irishman thing is an act, because you're just as repressed as I am, only in a different way."

"I'm not on the brink of snapping under the pressure of it."

Couldn't help smirking. "You just admitted you are pent up."

He bent his elbows, laying his forearms against the tree, bringing his body and lips to within a hair's breadth of mine. "I maintain control because I must."

I dared not move, else I'd be kissing him without intending to. Probably not intending it. I tried to scowl, but his proximity kept me on edge—a thrilling edge, beyond which lay forbidden pleasures. Failing to muster any anger, I clutched at the tree's bark, scraping off bits. "For you, it's control. For me, it's repression. Hmph."

"Am I to know what *hmph* means?"

I squirmed and my hips rubbed across his erection. Swallowing hard, I said, "*Hmph* means if this is your idea of flirting, you need an intensive workshop in seduction."

He smiled, white teeth bared, eyes crinkled at the corners. "Seduction. Is that what you're wanting, love?"

Shit, shit, shit. Why did I never learn to shut my trap?

"No." The petulance in my voice disheartened me. I pressed myself harder into the tree, and the bark scratched at me through my T-shirt. "Not what I meant. I do not want you to…um…do that."

His fingers, poised at either side of my head, toyed with my hair. Wispy locks feathered over my skin as he rumbled, "I will gladly study your desires and memorize all the ways I might tempt you."

Had to change the subject. Immediately. "Tell me more about the Unseen realm. Are bargains and debts the only things I have to worry about?"

Interest glimmered behind the firestorm in his eyes. "Are ye planning on spending more time in my world?"

"I don't—not really. I mean, if the need arises—"

He rocked his hips into me, his arousal hard and hot against my belly. "If what need arises? Ah, never mind. I can imagine."

"Keep your *imagination* in your pants, please."

His hair tickled my face as he tilted his head to the side. He dashed little kisses over my neck, working his way back to my face until his breaths ghosted over my mouth and I swore I felt the barest caress of his lips.

My eyes flew open. I shoved my hand between our mouths. "No kissing, you promised."

"I did not kiss you." He drew his head back and frowned. "I can tell when you're thinking of him. That Calder person. I recognize the grieved look."

"I'm not sorry he's gone."

"But you grieve for your innocence. It can't be regained." Though his face had retreated, his body was still molded to mine as he circled a fingertip over my temple. "I can show you a more rewarding state of mind, and body, if you wish it. One certain to erase bad memories."

"It's not that easy."

"Nothing worthwhile ever is."

His mouth hovered close to mine, yet never touched me. He must've possessed incredible control to keep a distance of millimeters without slipping. The nearness of him, the risk of accidental contact, excited me more than I'd ever admit aloud.

"Your heart is racing," he said against my throat. "Are you afraid of me?"

"No."

"Then you must be excited."

Christ, was I ever. More than I'd dreamed I could be.

A question popped into my brain, and I had to ask, since we seemed to be constantly negotiating one thing or another. "Do bargains and debts have any real power in this world?"

"No, not here."

"Magic doesn't force you to stick to our no-kissing agreement."

"I choose to abide by it."

His admission relaxed me more than anything else he might've done. Without magical repercussions to coerce him, he nevertheless stuck to our bargain. I wondered why for a brief moment, until he silenced my inner voice, skating his hand up my arm, hovering it just above the skin, exciting the fine hairs and stimulating the nerves beneath the surface. It felt like he'd flicked a thousand tiny switches inside me, to unleash pathways never before opened. I sighed, flooded with a satisfaction so intense my body slackened.

I was aroused and unwound all at once. Electrified and soothed. Starved and sated. It seemed impossible, but like many things I'd learned of late, this impossibility proved all too possible.

"I have to go," I said, "back to the shop. My family deserves an explanation. I owe them several of those, actually." A cold blade of anxiety pierced my heart. "I need to tell them about Calder."

He watched me, immovable as a boulder, his mood unreadable.

I waved a hand. "Step aside, please."

"You'll need to release me first."

"What?"

He nodded at my hands.

They were on his hips, my fingers gripping him.

I yanked my hands away and clamped them under my arms. I flailed for my thoughts, which spun out away from me. Somehow, this man—sylph, elemental, whatever—could shatter my composure without doing a blessed thing.

"Shall I transport you back to the shop?" he asked.

I roamed my gaze over the surroundings. "How far away are we?"

"Perhaps a five-minute walk."

"I'd rather walk, if you don't mind." A little time to clear my head, away from the influence of his proximity. Unbridled desires led to only one outcome.

Pain. Suffering. Tragedy.

I ducked around Nevan, marching toward the other side of the clearing.

He cleared his throat, gesturing in the opposite direction. "It's this way, darlin'."

"Oh." I spun on my heels and stalked past him down a narrow deer trail.

Alone.

CHAPTER FOURTEEN

MY SOLITUDE LASTED TEN SECONDS. THE SLAPPING OF BARE FEET ON earth signified Nevan had caught up to me.

I sighed when he came up alongside me. "Said I wanted to be alone."

"You said you'd rather walk. No mention of wishing me gone."

"I don't wish you gone. I wanted a little time to myself, that's all."

"Beginning to think you don't know what you really want."

Once again, he delved right down to my soul to expose a truth I couldn't deny. "Maybe I don't know what I want. But I'm too tired for penetrating insights, okay?"

He slipped an arm around my waist. "Am I penetrating you?"

"Ugh." I dared to glance at him, dismayed by his playful smile. "I just keep setting myself up for your double entendres, don't I?"

"Repressed longings are bound to slip out now and again."

Opting to let that comment go, because I absolutely did not want to discuss my pent-up emotions, I walked faster. He removed his arm but kept pace with me as we traveled in silence, his strides sure and purposeful while mine were shuffling. With anyone else, the lack of conversation would've made me uneasy, yet with him it seemed natural to be in each other's company without small talk.

A couple minutes later, as we approached the healing vortex, my gut twisted into tight little knots at the thought of what I needed to do. Tell my family about the supernatural nightmare my life had become. I resisted the urge to chew my nails, a bad habit I'd never suffered from before, and shoved my hands in my jeans pockets.

Nevan slid a hand down the underside of my wrist, easing my hand out of my pocket and into his palm.

I closed my fingers around his. "Tell me something about you. Something you wouldn't tell anyone else."

He stopped. His hold on my hand halted me too. We angled toward each other like two magnets whose poles sought to align.

"I was mortal once," he said.

"Was it a punishment, like getting suspended from school?"

"No." His fingers fidgeted around mine but he held onto my hand. "I was born a mortal and died one as well. My people had engaged in a long-standing war with a neighboring clan. I suffered a grievous injury during the last battle I fought. I was dying, I knew this." His fingers grasped mine harder, then loosened, his thumb massaging the back of my hand. "I had collapsed on the shores of a lake, my blood flowing into the waters, sinking down to the bottom where a portal to the otherworld lay. As it turned out, I had a bit of the Unseen realm in me. My blood unlocked the doorway."

Questions bounced in my head, but I squelched them. *Later.*

He raised our joined hands to his chest level, capturing me in his hold. Seeking comfort. Seeking connection. I recognized the need, since I'd suffered from it my entire life. Until I'd met this man, I'd failed to find the thing for which I longed the most. Its name whispered in the recesses of my mind, but still, I could not speak it even in my own thoughts.

No, I couldn't have fulfilled that need. Not yet. Not after three days with him.

I pulled our hands to my breast, sealing them together with my free hand. My heart beat a bit faster, with his skin glued to mine in the valley between my breasts, and my heart lightened.

Too soon, way too soon.

And yet, I could not let go of his hands.

"The sylph king, Notus, came to me," Nevan said.

"Skeiron hasn't always been king?"

"He ascended to the throne after a lengthy and violent war with Notus." A shadow seemed to fall over him—a shadow from the past. "At one time, Skeiron was an admirable warrior, the leader of the sylph army, a faithful servant to the king. Notus became depraved, though, just as Skeiron has."

Skeiron a decent guy? Unbelievable.

He appeared haggard now, burdened with the memories he recounted. "Notus offered me a choice—to die a natural, mortal death, or to be forged into a sylph. You see, elemental beings may produce offspring through biological reproduction but many deem it unseemly. We connive to increase our numbers through a method that's easier for our kind but far more perilous for the one who undergoes the forging."

I didn't like the way he said *we*, including himself in the statement. "Are you saying you've convinced mortals to go through this forging thing?"

"No." A pained look passed over his features, fading swiftly. "I would never encourage another to undertake it."

Good. I couldn't stand to think of him tricking mortals that way. Skeiron, for sure. But not Nevan. "How do elementals get people to do it?"

"We appeal to the fear of death ingrained in most humans." He gave a sharp, bitter laugh. "It worked on me. I accepted Notus's offer, though I had no notion of what it entailed. Believing in an afterlife does not, as I discovered, negate a weak soul's fear of dying."

"You are not weak." My questions must've been exposed on my face, because his mouth formed a sad smile.

"Pain and blood, that's what it entails," he told me. "The forging process demands a hefty price in suffering. I pray you never comprehend the depth of it."

My soul ached for him. The worst I could imagine was horrific, yet I sensed the truth in his prayer for me. I couldn't fathom the agony he'd lived through during his transformation.

"When an elemental offers immortality," he said, "the mortal has no conception of what awaits him."

"They leave out the bad parts, eh? Guess nobody would take the deal if they were transparent about the specifics."

"Indeed." He inched closer and my heart ticked even faster. "Since then, I've learned to be more cautious when entering into bargains."

"Why is it," I said, gazing up into his eyes, "you always smell like earth and thunderstorms?"

He extricated one of his hands from mine, plunging it into my hair to cup my nape. "I told you, I was forged from the earth and the air, imbued with everything in nature."

"There's no dirt in the air."

"Certainly there is." He tipped my head back, as if he meant to kiss me, and my lips parted in anticipation. "All of the elements are swept into the atmosphere. Water, earth, fire—you'll find particles of each in the air that surrounds, fills, and enlivens your mortal body." He dived his head down to mine, our mouths a breath apart. "Your soft, delectable mortal body."

My skin thrummed, alive with the promise implicit in his movements and his words.

He pulled away, strode backward one pace, and gestured down the trail. "After you."

Bereft of his touch, I huffed out a breath. "Do you enjoy torturing me?"

"Your ban on kissing remains in effect." His smug smile irked me. "So in actuality, it is you torturing me."

I breezed past him down the path toward the vortex. "Don't get too pleased with yourself. It's not like I threw myself at you."

"Perhaps not, but you wanted me to kiss you. Licked those ripe lips of yours and opened them in invitation."

"I did not." I had, but not on purpose. My stupid lips had a mind of their own these days.

He smiled brightly, chuckling. "Console yourself however ye like."

"Thank you. I will."

My statement garnered another chuckle. We walked in the comfortable silence I'd come to appreciate, the chattering of squirrels the only disruption to the arboreal serenity. A sky of deep azure peeked out from behind the treetops, and even the humidity sticking to my skin couldn't dampen the spark that still crackled inside me.

We passed the vortex and wended through the rock garden. Up ahead, I caught sight of the shop through the last stand of screening trees. Anxiety trickled down my nerves.

Nevan laid a hand on my wrist. "Don't go spoiling my hard work by tensing up again."

"Oh no," I drawled, "I wouldn't dream of inconveniencing you with my stark panic."

"Shall I accompany you, to offer support when you speak to your family?"

"I appreciate the offer." And I did, with all my heart. "But no. I'd better handle this on my own."

"Of course."

I glanced in the direction of the shop, its roof just visible behind the trees. "Will you be, uh, handling your own business while I'm occupied?"

He pinched the bridge of his nose. "Although I should return to my duties, I find I can't quite motivate myself."

"It's all right. I don't m—" I almost said I didn't mind, which was a lie. "I understand you have a duty and an angry king to satisfy. If you're hesitating because of me, it's not necessary. Don't let me stand in your way."

"You stand in the way of nothing."

"The men I've known would leap at the chance to kiss women for a living."

"After a century of it, they too would grow weary of the task." He kicked at a pebble half embedded in the dirt. "And it's not as if these women come to me of their own volition, or as if I choose them for myself. The desire they feel is engendered by magic, required by my bargain with Skeiron, and the kiss is vacant of meaning or pleasure."

I'd realized he hated his job, but the depth of his distaste for it never sank in until now. "You must kiss other women, for your own...enjoyment. Sexy elemental chicks must line up for the chance."

"No elemental woman will speak to me, much less proffer her lips to mine." He raked a hand through his hair. "And I suddenly find I cannot abide the notion of touching any woman other than you."

His admission stopped me. Telling my brother he was immensely fond of me was one thing. Losing interest in all other females signified a feeling deeper than simple affection, if I let myself believe it. He wouldn't lie, I knew that much.

I glanced around—looking for what, I didn't know. Anything to evade his gaze and the honesty in it. Desperate to change the subject, I asked, "Why won't elemental women touch you? Are they brain damaged, or just completely frigid?"

His dark brows elevated over his preternatural eyes. "Your confidence in me is greatly appreciated, but no. They avoid me because I engage in intimate contact with mortal woman. I am tainted."

"By measly kisses?"

"The mere touch of a hand taints me in the eyes of elemental females. What I've done with you would scandalize them."

My spirits lifted at the notion I'd scandalized supernatural females. *Score one for the mortal.* "Well, if you're not planning to fulfill your duty, what will you do while I'm gone?"

"Await you in your home." He ran a hand up and down his jaw. "If you'll permit me to enter in your absence."

"Please, feel free. I can give you a key—"

Nevan poofed away.

Politeness really was a foreign concept to elementals.

By the time I reached the RV, my parents had opened the door for me and waited on the top step.

No more chickening out.

"I need to come clean with you," I said, my voice surprisingly steady, "about a lot of things. To start with, I need to tell you the truth about Calder."

THE DOOR CLAPPED SHUT BEHIND ME AND I SLUMPED AGAINST IT, GRATE-ful for the twilit tranquility of my apartment. The draft from the air conditioning chilled my skin, drying the sweat and humidity stuck to me.

A shiver of awareness swept over me. Darkness cloaked the room, but the secondhand glow from outside filtered through the blinds, outlining a suspiciously familiar shape on the sofa.

"Nevan," I said, pushing away from the door.

Despite knowing what I'd find, when I hit the switch and light inundated the space, my pulse jumped at the sudden sight of Nevan reclined on the sofa, ankles crossed, feet braced on the worn carpeting. On spotting me, he slung an arm across the sofa's back as if waiting for me to snuggle against him.

I scuffled toward the end of the sofa. "You're still here."

"Naturally." He studied me with measured curiosity for a moment, then patted the sofa, inviting me to cuddle under his arm. "You look exhausted. Sit, before you collapse."

I tossed my purse on the floor. My car keys jangled inside it. Fatigue had seeped into every cell of my being, weighing me down and smearing grit in my eyes. Rubbing them, I clambered onto the sofa and curled up against him as he secured his arm around me. Knees tucked under me, I rested my head in the hollow of his shoulder.

"How did your confession go?" he asked, in a tone that implied he didn't care either way. Under the nonchalance, however, I discerned a sharp taint of darker emotion. Was he jealous I'd told my parents the truth and not him?

Hmm. Interesting.

I sketched curving lines on his chest with my fingertips, focused on the expanse of skin that became my canvas. "My parents needed to hear the story first."

He fiddled with the hem of my sleeve, staring into the vacant space between the sofa and my bedroom door.

"I was planning on telling you," I said, "after I talked to my family. This is after."

His gaze wandered over the meager contents of my apartment. Though he appeared unconcerned, I felt his body stiffen.

I spread my palm on his chest, propping my chin on his shoulder so I could watch his face. "I'm going to tell you about Calder, unless you're not interested anymore."

His fingers stilled. His eyes rotated my way, and though his expression stayed neutral, his lips tightened the slightest bit. "I assumed you wouldn't share the tale with me."

"You assume an awful lot, pal. Maybe you don't understand me as thoroughly as you think."

Without a trace of glibness, he said, "I admit it's possible."

"Are you offended I didn't tell you first?"

"Why should I be? I've no claim on you."

Yes you do. Sometimes I hated it, sometimes I longed to drown myself in it, but always I knew—if nothing else, on a subconscious level—he had staked a claim.

"Calder was Travis's brother, but I guess you know that already." An iron ball congealed in my gut and I laid my cheek on his shoulder, dreading what I must say. "I met Travis five years ago, when I got a paralegal job in Texas. We were friends, I thought. Not besties forever and ever, but we had nice conversations. Until his brother showed up."

This was where everything got complicated, and I took a moment to compose my thoughts. I needed Nevan to understand, maybe because I needed someone, anyone, to absolve me. As if it were possible. What I'd done could not be erased.

I snaked my arm across his broad torso, like I had any hope of holding him here if he decided to vanish again. "Calder had gone to New York after college to find himself, or some such nonsense. He came back humiliated, a failure in his own eyes. I could relate. From the moment we met, we just kind of...clicked."

Nevan stiffened a teensy bit, but he planted a tender kiss atop my head.

The story flowed out of me now, an unstoppable river of words. "I don't know why, but Travis did not like me dating his brother. He loved Calder, they'd been very close until I got in the way. Didn't mean to, but somehow I did." Memories unreeled in my mind fueling my voice with half-forgotten fears. "Calder was charming, sweet, intelligent, polite, and completely infatuated with me. I'd never been the object of anyone's affection before. He didn't even care I'm a moldy old virgin."

Nevan grunted. I hesitated, thinking he might speak, but he kept silent.

"I was with Calder for six months," I told him. "When he asked me to marry him, I said yes without reservation. Everything was good—until I decided to sleep with him."

With my ear to Nevan's chest, I counted the thump-thumps of his heart. They sped up a bit, as if he sensed what was coming. I fastened my arm tighter around him, praying his body could ground me to the present while I careened into the past.

"I told him I wanted to, you know, go all the way with him. We made a date for that night, but he stood me up, which was not like him at all." I drew me knees up, curling into myself while sheltered by Nevan. He enfolded me in his arms, the embrace protective and more comforting than I could articulate.

"He texted me," I continued, "saying he was sorry but his car broke down and he couldn't make it. We rescheduled for the next night, at eight o'clock. I went shopping in the morning, bought sexy lingerie, and I cooked a fancy meal for our candlelit date. I was so excited, so happy. But he didn't show. Again."

I crossed my arms over my knees, resting my chin on them. My insides quivered with a cold fear, a ghost of that night when everything changed.

"Take your time," Nevan murmured. "Or tell me no more. Your choice."

His understanding buoyed me to go on. "I fell asleep, in my sexy lingerie, still waiting for him after three hours. I woke up choking, with Calder's hands around my throat."

Nevan hooked a hand under my knees and eased me onto his lap. I huddled there, protected by his strong limbs, and let the tears pour out in silence. They oozed down my cheeks, hot and fast, streams of pain and regret that singed my skin. I didn't want to finish the story, but knew I had to do it. He needed to hear the rest. I needed him to hear it. Right here, right now, my future seemed to hinge on his reaction.

"Calder was all wild energy and mad conviction. I don't know how else to describe it. He'd gotten in with the key I gave him. But this wasn't the man I knew, the one I thought I loved. He was like a demon, with his crazy-wild eyes and his insane strength, and I realized he was going to rape me or kill me—or both."

Nevan caressed my hair, his face buried in the locks. The heat of his breaths rolled over my scalp.

"He tried to tie me up, to blindfold me. I kicked him in the nuts, which slowed him down for about a nanosecond. He tore my nightie, threw me onto the floor, clawed at me, and then—" I clutched Nevan's hand, but he didn't even wince when my nails cut into his skin. "He bit me. Repeatedly."

Nevan growled, a half-strangled noise, and hugged me tight.

I couldn't manage more than a whisper. "His teeth cut my ear the worst. He had his hands around my throat again, so tight I couldn't breathe. The whole time, he was babbling nonsense about blood being the key and I had to die to be stronger, to be his mate forever."

When I'd recounted the story to my parents, I hadn't cried. I'd held my emotions locked up, like always, because I never would've gotten through the ordeal of telling them otherwise. But here, with Nevan, the steel walls of my mental vault crumbled away into dust. The anguish and terror rushed through me with the same force they had that night.

"I had a semiautomatic pistol in my bedside table. When I grabbed the gun, Calder looked at it and laughed. I'll never forget the last thing he said. 'Mine forever, sweet thing, or no one's.' Then he rushed at me and I didn't have time to think, I knew I'd be dead unless—" I gritted my teeth, inhaling sharply through my nose. "I shot him seven times, six in the chest and once in the head. I emptied an entire clip into him and killed the man I was going to marry. That was the first time I saw a dead body."

The image of Brad's limp and bloodied form reared up in my mind. My stomach seemed to surge up into my throat. "When I found the dead guy the other day, I kept expecting Calder to jump out at me. Don't know why. He's gone, he has to be, I killed him."

Like a statue in an ancient temple, Nevan remained unmoving and seemingly unmoved. I knew better, though. Beneath his calm exterior, he contained a sea of emotions.

"It was my fault," I said. "I'd made Calder wait for…you know, sex. Made him wait too long and it pushed him over the edge. I wrecked him, and then I murdered him."

At last, Nevan spoke. "You murdered no one, sweet Lindsey. You shot him in self-defense. I imagine the sheriff convinced you withholding sex drove his brother to insanity."

"It's why he calls me ice princess. I'm so cold I freeze men's balls off, that's what he said at the time."

Nevan muttered something under his breath that might've been a curse in another language. "There's more, isn't there?"

A gentle query. I bent my head back to gaze at him. "After I shot Calder, I sat there shaking and crying for I don't know how long. I finally called nine-one-one, then I stumbled into the bathroom to throw up and put on some clothes. By the time the cops arrived, Calder's body was gone."

Nevan betrayed no surprise, no reaction at all, except for the gentle motion of his hand smoothing my hair, over and over, in slow sweeps. "You loved him."

"Thought I did. Not sure anymore. Maybe I don't really know what love is."

"You'll know it when you feel it." He turned me toward him so he could capture my gaze with his own. "Listen to me. Lack of sex does not compel a man to assault any woman, much less the one he claims to love. I know this for a fact."

I supposed he did, after a century of forced celibacy, but still…

As if he'd read my mind, Nevan grasped my face in his hands and said in a fierce voice, "You did not drive him mad. Besides, you were about to give yourself to him, so why would he choose that moment to snap?"

"Don't know. The snowball effect, I guess, and I decided too late—"

"No." He bent closer, our eyes level, his scorching with unnamed emotions. "You did nothing. He was weak. You are strong and good and deserve happiness."

I could no nothing except stare at him. He kept telling me how amazing I was, while I kept questioning everything, expecting him to change the way Calder had. But he wasn't Calder. Swimming in the whirlpool of Nevan's eyes, I finally understood this one fact. I knew Nevan's nature, because he'd never hidden it from me—from the jovial pseudo-Irishman to the primal warrior to the intensely sensual man, I'd witnessed every aspect of him.

I wanted to share my revelation with him, but when I opened my mouth, instead of speaking I yawned.

"Stressful day," I said around my big, loud yawn.

Nevan rose to his feet, taking me with him. In a dangerously hushed voice, he said, "If I had the power, I would travel back to that night and tear the man's head off with my bare hands before he had a chance to harm you."

I believed he both could and would do it, if given the chance. Settling my palm on his cheek, my fingertips on his temple, I felt a vein throbbing there. "The battle's long over. You can't do anything to change it and neither can I."

His eyes hooded, he turned his face into my palm. I skimmed my thumb over his mouth. His lips moved under my thumb, his tongue flicked out to sample my flesh.

Nevan stepped back, a sure sign he was about leave.

"Stay," I said. "Please. I don't want to be alone."

He nodded.

"Just let me change into my nightie first."

I hurried into the bedroom and called Nevan into the room. He strode to the dilapidated wooden chair in the corner by the window, plucked my satin robe off the seat, and lowered his lithe body onto the chair. The robe he draped over his lap, his fingers stroking the fabric.

I snatched my nightie off the bed and marched into the bathroom, kicking the door shut. I banged my knees on the sink, twice, while stripping off my clothes. The bathroom had just enough space between the sink and the wall to accommodate me, but no more than that, which was why I preferred changing in the bedroom. Not an option tonight.

When I emerged, Nevan grinned with wolfish delight.

His gaze heated when he soaked in the sight of me in my satin nightie.

The thing was skimpy, but nobody was supposed to see it. I liked the satin fabric on my skin. The spaghetti straps and mid-thigh hem kept me cool on these hot summer nights. I wore the nightie for me, not for leering sylphs.

He wasn't leering, though. He admired me, his gaze exploring the length of my body. By the time he finished his assessment, arousal had me in its velvety grip and I had to clamp my thighs together to quell the wet pulsing there. It didn't help. No man had ever looked at me the way he did. Like he wanted to devour every inch of my body.

"You are lovely," he said, petting my robe. "My tasty little morsel."

"Tasty morsel? I am not food."

"But you are delectable." He crooked his fingers into the robe, as if kneading flesh. "I know the taste of your kiss, love, sweet and spiced with all those luscious desires you keep bottled up. When you let go at last, I will feast on the rest of you as well."

For several seconds, I couldn't move or breathe. Feast on the rest of me. Though I tried so hard not to, I envisioned all the ways he might do just that.

I scuttled to the bed, flinging the covers back.

Nevan lifted my robe to his face and inhaled. His smile took on a predatory slant. "This garment smells of you, of honeysuckle and sunshine."

My knees bumped the mattress. "Baloney. Sunshine has no scent and I don't smell like honeysuckle."

"Ah, but you do. And you taste of strawberries."

Snorting, I sat on the bed. "Haven't eaten a strawberry in weeks."

"Nevertheless, you taste of them. Elementals can detect aromas and flavors mortals can't. Human men have no idea what they're missing." He frisked the satin across his lips. "You leave a fragment of your essence on everything you touch."

"Guess that means you're stuck smelling like me."

He let the robe tumble to the floor, where it puddled around his feet. "If I could, I'd bathe in your scent so I might enjoy it every moment of the day."

If he'd walked over here, I would've dragged him down onto the bed on top of me. My annoying brain, however, preferred to torture me with fear. "What about my family? Will Brennus go after them?"

My question shattered his rapture. "I don't know."

"You need to guard them."

"I will not leave you."

"Please, Nevan, I'm begging you. Watch over my family. They have no clue what's going on."

He worked his lips, finally settling on a lopsided frown. "I will not leave you alone all night, but I'll pop over every so often to check on your family. Satisfied?"

"Thank you."

He rolled his eyes heavenward. "Your manners will be the death of us yet."

I crawled under the covers, pulling them up to my neck. The cotton sheet and acrylic blanket failed to dull the effect of Nevan's gaze on me.

"Sleep well, my scrumptious mortal," he said, with humor in his voice.

"Yeah-yeah, good night."

I shut off the bedside lamp. Shadows descended, obscuring Nevan, obscuring anything that might be hiding nearby, invisible. He was a silhouette in the moonlight seeping through the lace curtains, his eyes simmering with muted amber.

Rolling onto my side, facing away from him, I began the fruitless battle for sleep. Memories of Calder and Skeiron and Brennus tormented me. With a huff, I flipped over to the other side, only to endure another replay of past horrors. I flipped back the other way. All the while, I was acutely aware of Nevan's gaze tickling my skin.

I punched my pillow. "Unh."

"Something the matter?"

"Can't sleep. No idea why, there's only a supernatural assassin stalking me at this very moment."

The wood chair he sat on creaked. As the shuffling of bare feet on carpeting came nearer, I resisted the instinct to glance over my shoulder. His presence had become a tangible thing, a light caress against my soul, both terrifying and thrilling me.

His weight settled onto the bed, rocking me a little. His firm, hot body nestled up against my backside as he sprawled an arm over my hip, letting it fall across my belly. His fingertips teased me through the fabric of my nightie.

"I will protect you," he said, "if you'll allow me to."

The strange part? Those were the most enticing words he'd spoken. "Still can't sleep."

He feathered his fingers over my belly. "I will watch over you."

My gaze inexorably moved to the deeper shadows in the corners.

Nevan withdrew his hand from under the sheet. "Perhaps a bit of illumination will ease your mind."

I expected him to switch on the lamp, but instead, he raised his hand in the air and flourished his fingers. A spark ignited in his palm, enlarging into a fist-size ball of incandescent, glittering light. He tossed the orb into the air and it hovered near the ceiling, directly over the bed, casting a delicate glow. Tiny sparks floated down from the orb, disintegrating before they touched us.

"What is that?" I asked.

"A fairy light," he said, tucking his hand under the blanket again, right over my womb. "A fae owed me a favor and gifted me with fairy lights in return. Sleep now."

The orb's glow was oddly comforting and I couldn't prevent myself from going limp as I exhaled out the tension. Cocooned by his body, enveloped in his supple flesh and tough sinew, I floated down from consciousness toward slumber.

His kiss intoxicated me. But this…I could get so addicted.

Nevan murmured to me, sweet and hushed. "Dream of me, Lindsey."

As if I could dream of anything else.

CHAPTER FIFTEEN

The chattering of squirrels roused me at sunrise. Eyes closed, I luxuriated in the softness of my sheets, the fluffiness of my pillow, and the whooshing of cool air through the vents. Thank heavens I'd found an apartment with central air. This heatwave would've killed me without a retreat.

Safe in Nevan's arms last night, I'd fallen into a dreamless sleep and not woken until morning. He'd said I was exhausted, and man, was he right. Soulbaring could really tax a girl. My long night's rest had recharged me for the day ahead and whatever new surprises it might bring.

I was alone in the bed this morning. The chair by the window sat empty. Nevan must've popped out to check on my family. I silently thanked him, stretching my arms above my head as I yawned.

Unease crept into me. My gaze migrated past the curtains to the gloom in the corner near the foot of the bed. I shivered at the unearthly sensation of invisible fingers probing my skin, and tugged the blanket up to my chin.

The darkness shifted.

Something is there.

I pushed up onto one elbow. "Nevan?"

Tentacles of energy, unseen and oily, stretched out to me, licking at my body as if testing the flavor. Whenever I sensed Nevan, his presence aroused and yet calmed me. This energy slithered over my skin. It seeped into my pores, infesting my psyche.

I heaved my body up into sitting position. The blanket slumped down to puddle around my hips. The tentacles fused to my flesh, to my bones, to my soul. Not Nevan. His presence activated my senses, nothing like this engulfing blackness.

"Who are you?" My voice came out strained, my throat was parched and tight.

The curtains billowed. An icy draft churned through the room.

My clammy hands dampened the sheet. The window was shut.

"Show yourself." As if I held any sway over supernatural beings. If Nevan refused to obey me, why should this entity? Still, I couldn't huddle on the bed praying the thing might vacate the premises. "What do you want?"

The darkness seethed. It siphoned fragments of light from the shaft of sunshine that warmed my skin. The bright and the black coiled, spun, coalesced into a tall figure.

A man.

I clutched the blanket to my breast, abruptly aware of the my nightie's low-cut neckline.

He moved away from the wall. His knee-length white toga swished around his thighs and the curtains fluttered behind him. Blades of sunlight scraped away the shadows enshrouding him to unmask his tall, muscle-bound frame. The light coated his olive skin with a golden sheen. His platinum-blond hair blazed as if set afire by the sunshine. Energy spun out from his body to entwine me in its frigid, slick embrace.

The being eyed me with detached interest, like a scientist examining a petri dish full of multiplying bacteria.

My ears rang. Darkness invaded my vision. I realized I'd stopped breathing and hauled in a lungful of air tainted with the sharp odor of something vile and indefinable. This was the man I'd met in the shop two days ago, the one who warned me the guardian was bound to him.

This was Skeiron, the king of the sylphs.

I fought to break eye contact but I couldn't blink, much less avert my gaze.

The immortal being before me bent his head back. "Are you the one?"

I struggled to speak, but my voice had frozen, along with the rest of me.

In one stride, he crossed to the bed. His mass towered over me, eclipsing the light and, as if on command, I raised my face to him.

He grasped my chin in one massive hand.

"You," he said, his voice cool and even, "have lured my best guardian away from his task. If you are the one, and he is concealing the truth from me..."

"Guardian?" He must've meant Nevan, the only guardian I knew, but I couldn't summon the brainpower to interpret Skeiron's words. His presence overwhelmed all else—the surroundings, my thoughts, my ability to feel anything save for his alien touch.

Skeiron's eyes shrank to slits, his mouth became a slash. "You know of whom I speak. You have spent three days with him, seducing the guardian into forsaking his duty for you."

Black hair. Swirling metallic eyes. The memory of Nevan rushed through me, sweeping my mind clean. "I haven't seduced anybody. Nevan does what he wants."

The sylph king tightened his grip on my chin the slightest bit. Flames of hellfire red erupted within his irises.

I scuttled backward, away from the pull of this creature's gravity.

Serpents of power whipped and snarled around me, unseen yet tangible, biting into my skin with every lash. I swatted at my arms and face, driven by the impulse to sanitize my flesh, but the spectral serpents tore at my flesh, firing shocks of pain into me.

The assault cut off with a jolt. The energy snapped back into the humanoid being who loomed over my bed.

Between gasps, I croaked, "I know who you are. Skeiron."

His nostrils flared, his eyes too. "A mortal may not speak my name. It is forbidden."

The nerve. I opened my mouth to spit out a snide retort, but snapped my jaw shut. This bastard stole into my home, into my bedroom, and accused me of luring Nevan away from his job of enchanting gorgeous, hapless women. Yet I was forbidden? I gulped back the hysterical laughter rising in my throat.

Skeiron exuded everything dark—anger, envy, greed, and a hunger I preferred not to examine. My stomach twisted into razor-sharp knots. I clambered backward, away from him, and jumped off the bed's opposite side to barricade myself with its bulk. As if that would deter an elemental creature.

The king's top lip wrenched upward in a nasty expression. "I will root out the truth. If you are the one, I shall have you."

"I don't understand."

Skeiron flew across the bed to slam down in front me. On his knees on the mattress, inches away, he seared me with his glower. "Another seeks you, but he will not be as restrained as I."

He exploded into a black tornado the size of a man. It reeled through the room, knocking me off my feet. I cried out as my hip smacked into the dresser, my body ricocheted off it, and I crumpled to the floor.

The man-size twister plowed into the window. Glass shattered, raining into the room with a harsh tinkling sound. A final gust ripped through the space.

In the stillness that followed, I blew hair from my eyes. With both hands, I grabbed the mattress and hauled my ass off the floor. On my knees, bent over into the bed, I gaped at the shattered window. Bits of glass stuck to the wooden frame, which had splintered into multiple pieces. The curtains hung in tatters.

Nevan had alerted me to the danger, but I refused to listen. Refused to believe. Here, in my own home, the king of the sylphs had thrown down a gauntlet at my feet. And I still had no clue what Skeiron wanted from me.

Thunder boomed overhead. The building rattled around me and the floor trembled.

I staggered to my feet, bumbling sideways into the bedside table. Water sloshed in the glass I'd left there last night.

My battle with Calder nearly destroyed me, but at least my foe had been human—if deranged. This time, I floundered for the words to describe my predicament. Somehow I'd earned an enemy with unspeakable power and motives beyond my comprehension.

Skeiron's voice bellowed on the wind. "The guardian shall not have you. Your power belongs to me."

He thought I had power? This guy was terrifying *and* insane.

A bolt of dark power sliced through me. Nausea twisted my gut. Tears burst from my eyes, borne on a retching sob as the agony of Skeiron's energy clawed at my soul, and I clutched at my stomach, doubled over on another body-wrenching sob. A single thought seared my mind, a frantic call sent out through the ether, on a wavelength I'd never imagined existed. Maybe it didn't. Maybe I was freaking out from the knowledge I was about to die, but my mind—my heart—screamed the plea.

Nevan, I need you.

Thunder detonated overhead. The building trembled. Bits of paint and plaster showered down from the ceiling. The quaking escalated into a bone-jarring crescendo as framed photos bounced off the wall, striking the floor one by one. Glass cracked. The bed jounced.

The ceiling collapsed on top of me.

CHAPTER SIXTEEN

TICK, TICK, TICK. THE SOUND ROUSED ME FROM A FOG OF DIZZINESS and exhaustion. Darkness encased me, though I swore it had been morning a few minutes ago. My head pulsated with pain.

Flat on my stomach, I lifted my head. The floor tilted and spun.

Tick, tick.

The noise originated overhead. I pushed up onto my knees, but my muscles gave out and I collapsed again. Dust plumed up into my nose and eyes. I coughed, sneezed, panted. A heavy object pinned my feet, and though I jiggled them, I could not free my ankles. Resting my cheek on the floor, I blinked to clear the watering of my eyes. The ticking battered my eardrums like hammer blows.

I crawled my fingers across the floor, hunting for the source of the sound. My fingers bumped into a cold, metal object. I closed my hand around it and dragged the thing close to my face. The ticking got louder, its relentless rhythm apparent now. I held my alarm clock, an old-fashioned kind with hands that counted off the seconds and minutes. I was still in my bedroom.

Duh. A psycho with supernatural powers attempted to murder me, with my own bedroom as the weapon.

When I stretched one arm up over my head, my fingertips grazed popcorn-like balls. My muddled brain spit out one lucid thought. The balls came from the ceiling. Skeiron had stomped his proverbial, or perhaps literal, foot down on a pesky, eensy bug—aka, me.

I huddled under a large hunk of the ceiling. It pitched down at an angle, the higher end wedged on my bed, the lower pinning my ankles. I shoved against the ceiling chunk. No movement. I twisted around to push with both my hands, but succeeded only in punching pains into my shoulders and neck, straight up into my skull.

Trapped.

My chest morphed into a granite block crushing me. My breaths panted, shallow and unhelpful. Numbness tingled through my face and spread out into my body. I was hyperventilating. If I passed out, and the super-scary king of the sylphs came back, I'd be thoroughly screwed.

"Help!" My scream echoed in the space around me. My ears hurt from the noise. My eyes hurt too. Every muscle in my body burned or ached or quivered, or some combination of the three. My breaths puffed shallower and faster, the numbness sweeping down my limbs. "Somebody help me!"

My hoarse shriek set off a fit of hacking. I crumpled onto my stomach, cheek on the floor, hot tears streaming down my nose to drip onto the floor. No one was coming. I'd hyperventilate myself to death, if that was possible, or die in some other, more horrific way.

A weight thumped onto the pile above me. The debris shivered. Dust and fragments of plaster pelted me.

I spit out the dusty gunk that collected on my lips. What if Skeiron was back?

The ringing in my ears escalated into a chorus of off-key bells that deafened me. Black dots in my vision merged into a margin of darkness encroaching on my mind. *Don't pass out, don't pass out.*

The debris shifted. I squeezed my eyes shut against the cascade of detritus. It infiltrated my mouth, mutating into a dry, chalky paste on my tongue.

Rattling and clattering erupted overhead. A whooshing sound preceded a cracking splat.

The pressure on my ankles released with an almost painful rush. Cool air rushed over me. Light shimmered behind my lids, but I could not make my eyes open, immobilized by a primal terror. I sensed a figure above me and a familiar energy sizzled over my skin, but my adrenaline-addled brain denied my instincts, denied what I'd prayed for with the last scraps of my strength. I couldn't stop the fear from whispering in my ear a warning someone else might be impersonating my sylph, right down to the sensations I experienced when he was near but out of my sight.

When my rescuer moved closer, blocking the light, I sucked my lips between my teeth and squeezed my lids tight enough to wring tears from my eyes.

"Lindsey," a familiar voice said. "Love, can ye hear me?"

"Nevan?" I pried my eyelids apart. Through the tears and dust blending to blur my vision, I spied a person kneeling beside me. A large, bare-chested person. I inhaled, but drew in plaster dust and dirt, hacking until my throat was raw.

A hand stroked my forehead. "Shh, love, it's all right. Let me help you off the floor."

Nevan's voice flooded me with relief. The intensity of it pulverized my thoughts and wilted my body. One of his muscular arms locked around my waist to lift and turn me until he could hook his other arm under my knees. He scooped me up into his embrace, my head on his firm chest. His heartbeat hammered under my ear. My ears still rang, my breaths came quick and shallow.

"Easy now," he said. "Try to take slow, deep breaths. You're safe."

With my entire being, I trusted his words and clung to them like a life preserver. Though it consumed all my energy and concentration, I dragged in one long, slow breath after another. The ringing subsided. The numbness drained away, replaced by the warmth of his flesh against mine. I cuddled into him, relishing his earthy scent and the solidity of his body. *Safe.* Lord, for the first time in years I felt protected.

He nuzzled my hair. "Better?"

"Yeah." I dared to glance at my surroundings. Sunshine poured down through the hole where the ceiling had been, and rubble buried my bed. "I think your boss tried to smother me with a building."

He went rigid. I swung my gaze up to his face, inches from mine. The stutter in my pulse had nothing to do with shock. The stark look in his eyes, coupled with the strained slant of his mouth, pierced my heart. Without even thinking about it, I laid my hand on his cheek.

A weak smile trembled on his lips.

I caressed his face, stretching out my index finger to graze his temple. "I'm okay."

"The king spares no thought for mortals. Are you certain he did this?"

"Positive. Mr. Creepy didn't introduce himself, but I recognized him from the shop. He said a mortal shouldn't speak his name. He also said you couldn't have me."

Nevan set me down on my feet. He swept a tangled lock of hair from my face.

I rubbed my arms, overcome by an inner chill. "Your king's a real sweetheart. What's he got against me anyway? He sends a bird to spy on me, then he tries to murder me."

"If Skeiron meant to kill you, I'd be collecting the pieces of your remains from this debris."

"He dropped a freaking roof on me."

Nevan stared down at my bare feet, his arms slack at his sides.

My toes wiggled, as if they were showing off for him. Saucy little digits. I couldn't control my own toes around him.

He ground his teeth. "I failed to track down Brennus. Perhaps I could've stopped this if I had caught him."

"This is not your fault."

"It is." Nevan ran a hand over his mouth. "I've been selfish and reckless, abandoning my duty to be close to you. In the process, I've pulled you into the center of my debacle."

"Listen up." I waited until he looked me in the eye. "I wanted to be with you. I chose to go with you into the Unseen. Brennus has been spying on me, I knew it, and I decided it was worth the risk."

"To be with me?" he asked, his tone uncertain.

Just as I started to reply, a black shape spiraled down from the sky, right through the hole in the ceiling. I yelped, but Nevan glanced up with disinterest.

The grackle dove low over our heads before soaring up and away.

Nevan arched a brow at me. "Why so frightened? It was far too small for a raven."

"Excuse me for being a tad jumpy after my visit from His Royal Scariness."

"What else did Skeiron say to you?"

"Oh, nothing much." I shrugged halfheartedly, feigning indifference. "If you're the one then you'll be mine, I'm a big baddie, blah-blah-blah."

Nevan spewed a volley of what must've been curses, given his tone, but in that alien language he'd used before. He grasped the back of his neck in both hands. "Brennus may simply be observing you, but that is dangerous enough. He reports to the king. If Brennus has seen you with me, Skeiron also knows about our...relationship."

"Yeah, he probably heard you tell my brother you're my boyfriend."

"Possibly."

Boosting up on my tiptoes, I tapped my finger on his nose. "I notice you haven't asked if I'm your girlfriend."

"Such a presumption would be indelicate."

"Presuming you're my boyfriend isn't?"

"Ah..." Nevan grimaced, then swept his gaze over me. One corner of his mouth pinched.

I glanced down to discover dust and dirt coated me from head to toe and those little popcorn balls from the ceiling stuck to my skin and hair. I took hold of my nightgown between my thumb and forefinger, shaking the fabric. Dust clouded around me. Bits of debris plopped onto Nevan's feet. "If Skeiron didn't want me dead, what was the big show about?"

"It was a message. For me." Nevan focused on my shoulders, as he picked ceiling popcorn off my skin. His fingers nudged the spaghetti strap of my satin nightie. Its neckline dipped low over my breasts, exposing the upper slopes. His fingertips skimmed over my collarbone, to the juncture at the hollow of my throat. I imagined his hand dipping lower to cover my breast. My skin tightened, every nerve energized.

How could I fantasize about him touching me at a time like this?

Nevan's fingertips skated down my breastbone, into the valley of my cleavage. My nipples shot hard. His eyes widened at the sight of the taut buds poking through the flimsy fabric.

He snatched his hand away and coughed into his fist.

I rubbed my arms, shoulders bunching. "What kind of message was your king sending?"

"No matter now." He squeezed my shoulders, patted my upper arms, and lowered his hands to his sides. "What's done is done."

"Come on, I was almost a pancake. Don't you think I deserve an explanation?"

He took one big step backward, as the pained look on his face morphed into bleak resolve and his gaze focused on the wall past my shoulder. "I must leave you and I shall not return this time."

"I've lost my fascinating appeal, eh?"

"Never." His gaze fastened to mine, his eyes dazzling kaleidoscopes. "I was mistaken to believe I could have one thing for myself. How selfish I've been. I only wanted…" His hand floated up, near my arm, his fingertips teasing the gossamer hairs and triggering a flurry of goosebumps. "You'll be safe once I am gone."

A reckless impulse seized me. I grasped his hands and dragged him to me, our bodies mashed together, my breasts crushed against the planes of his muscles.

A smirk threatened to bust out, twitching his lips, but he banished it. His eyes flared hot, then darkened to a smolder. When I lifted my head, he dipped his closer to mine. Our breaths mingled, and for a blessed heartbeat I imagined our souls had mingled too. He glided his finger up my wrist, massaging lightly. Our lips hovered dangerously close.

I gave in to the lure of his magical eyes, indulged in the carnal allure of his body pressed to mine and the firm line of his erection against my belly.

"A few days ago," he murmured, his voice rough, "you ordered me to stay away. You're free of me at last. Is that not what you wanted?"

"Not anymore." I probed his eyes for some clue to his motivations, his intentions. "I am your girlfriend, Nevan. Please don't leave me."

He grazed his cheek across mine. I drank in his presence, my mind whirling from the intoxication of it. He dragged his lips down my skin, toward my mouth, and in a husky whisper said, "Goodbye, my sweet Lindsey."

My eyelids fluttered shut in anticipation of the kiss, my lips tingled, liquid fire gathered between my thighs. He wanted me. And God help me, I wanted him.

A breeze cooled my skin where his flesh had warmed me. My eyes flew open.

Nevan had disappeared.

Even as he abandoned me, apparently forever, he respected my no-kissing decree.

An unsatisfied yearning ached inside me. More than the physical need, though, I longed for the safety and connection he imbued into me. I didn't understand it. I'd never wanted it. Yet somehow, I needed it more than any-thing.

Sirens wailed outside, echoing the sorrow in my heart.

***

I DUG THROUGH THE WRECKAGE OF MY BEDROOM IN SEARCH OF MY robe while racking my brain for a reasonable explanation for this calamity. The sirens whined ever nearer and the cops would be here soon. When my fingers found my satin robe, I wrestled it out of the debris. Ripped and dirt-stained, it would have to do. A portion of the wall had caved into my closet and my dresser lay smashed under an avalanche of ceiling debris.

As I shook out my robe, my thoughts rewound to the first time I'd met Nevan. He caught me when I tripped. Distracted me from a dead body. Whisked me away to another world so we could get Brad resur-rected. He rescued me when his king tossed a ceiling on my head. Most of all, he made me feel—period.

Car doors banged shut outside.

Pins and needles pricked at the backs of my eyes, manifesting tears. I squeezed my eyes shut, but the tears pooled anyway. I swiped at my eyes, rolled my shoulders back, and lifted my chin. I could not afford to break down. There would be questions from the authorities, most likely Travis, and I'd need all my wits to survive the onslaught. I shoved down my terror and pain, along with every other strong emotion roiling inside me, and caged them in the steel-reinforced vault of my mind, secured with three deadbolts and a massive combination lock. My passions were death row inmates.

Even prisoners condemned to death got a chance at appealing the con-viction. Maybe I could, someday, release my emotions. Nevan kept encour-aging me to do it, and with him I'd wanted to so badly, but I'd waited too long. He was gone, forever.

I fumbled with my robe, finally pulling it on, and clambered over the debris pile, through the doorway, into the darkened living room.

The front door quaked with the pounding of an angry fist.

"Open the goddamn door, Porter," Travis shouted. "Before I break it down."

Another blow rattled the door.

I switched on the lamp by the sofa as I hurried past it. Light flared out into the gloom, dousing the blackest shadows. I swung the door open, re-membering a moment too late I was wearing my sexy nightie, with my robe unfastened to reveal the plunging neckline and high hem.

Travis's jaw dropped. His eyes all but popped out of his head. Behind him burned the sulfurous glow from the lights posted outside each door of the apartment complex. Stray beams glanced off the badge on his chest.

I whipped my robe closed, tugging the sash around my waist to knot it over my belly.

He swallowed with a visible effort. As his eyes shrank into a squint, he lurched into the doorway, inches from me. "Are you hurt?"

"No. The ceiling fell on me, but I was lucky. The bed protected me."

"What in the hell went on here, Lindsey?" He clapped his hands on either side of his head and clawed his scalp with his fingers. "How—why—" His hands fell away, his jaw trembled. The pitch of his voice rose. "Ceilings don't collapse for no reason, but I ain't seen a tornado."

A scary-angry supernatural beastie ate my house. Uh, no. Not saying that, particularly given his agitated state. I offered up the best hogwash I could. "Maybe it was a downburst or a straight-line wind."

Travis bared his clenched teeth. "How stupid do you think I am?"

"I don't think you're stupid."

He smacked his hands on the doorframe, and braced there, he pitched toward me. A current of black fury rippled through his deceptively soft voice. "Tell me the truth. After everything we've been through together, you owe me that much." He angled his neck down to level our faces. The anger radiating out of him mixed with another emotion, something far more personal. "You coulda died, and I wanna know what the fuck is going on here. The truth. *Now.*"

Or what? I didn't ask, certain I wouldn't like the answer. "It's better if you don't know."

I'd hated it when Nevan refused to tell me stuff, and here I was shoveling the same crap onto Travis. No wonder he was pissed.

He glared into my eyes. "Not good enough."

More sirens ululated outside. Past his shoulder, I glimpsed the strobing, multicolored lights of emergency vehicles. The beams lashed across the balcony to hurl their colors onto Travis with a sinister glow that matched the drilling intensity of his gaze.

I locked my hands over my belly and took one step back. "Please, Travis, let this go. It's weird and dangerous and completely crazy. You're better off not—"

He shackled his arms around me, pinning my arms to my sides, mashing me into his chest. The thick stench of booze made my stomach lurch. His mouth bore down on mine, stifling my shocked cry, the kiss hot and sloppy and soaked in alcohol. He towed me closer, his fingers punching into the flesh of my upper arms, and tried to shove his tongue between my lips.

Oh, like hell you will. I rammed my knee up into his groin.

My mouth muffled his grunt. His fingers loosened and I took advantage, slugging him in the only soft part of his belly. Air exploded from his lungs as he doubled over, and I swung my fist up into the vulnerable underside of his chin, wrenching his jaw shut with a crack. He cried out, staggered backward into the door jamb, and slumped against it. Breathing hard, he raised his face to me.

The light from outside slashed across his features, revealing tableau of drunkenness. His bloodshot eyes were glassy, his eyelids droopy. He looked dazed, his face flushed, and perspiration beaded on his forehead. His sheriff's uniform fared no better, creased with a multitude of wrinkles, his shirt partly untucked, and his belt off kilter. His holster was empty, the Sig nowhere on his person.

Travis shook his head, a palm plastered to his forehead. "Jesus Christ, what have I done? I don't know how that—why that—"

His voice evidenced the faintest slur.

Words pushed against my paralyzed vocal chords, scrabbling to get out. Angry, vulgar epithets. And a few creative suggestions for what he could do with himself.

"Lindsey," he said, reaching a hand toward me then snatching it back. "God, I'm so sorry."

I shoved him out the door and slammed it in his face.

My hand over my mouth, I fell to my knees on the rough carpeting and huddled there until the first responders banged on the door. Then I collected myself and let them inside.

Nevan did not materialize to comfort me. From here on, I was on my own.

CHAPTER SEVENTEEN

I DRAGGED THROUGH THE DAY AS IF MY FEET WERE ENCASED IN CE-
ment and I was spiraling down into the depths of an icy river, the undertow
dragging me out to sea. When I'd moseyed in at 10:14 a.m., Stan was manning
the counter, his scowl entrenched deeper than usual. Catching sight of me, he
trotted out from behind the counter and squeezed out a tight smile.

"How are you feeling?"

Wow, he actually sounded concerned. What alternate universe had I
stumbled into? "I'm fine. Thank you for asking."

He shoved his hands in his pants pockets, danced in place, and then
jerked his hands free, the fingers shimmying in a wild rhythm. He cast his
gaze down to the floor. "I, uh, need to apologize to you. My wife can be
difficult, even jealous, and she didn't like me hiring a woman. I took my
frustration with her out on you. I'm sorry."

"Thank you," I said slowly.

"If you need a place to stay, my brother can put you up in his motel—my
treat." And then he spoke the words that shattered all my previously held
beliefs about the world I lived in. "I appreciate everything you do here. I
know I can be difficult, but you don't complain and I'm very grateful to
have you working here."

With his bombshell detonated on my head, he sprinted for his office. The
door clapped shut behind him. After about an hour of pure shock, I convinced myself I hadn't hallucinated the whole encounter with Stan.

As I observed the smattering of customers in the shop, the stomping
of footfalls made me glance at the shop entrance. Travis moseyed inside,
halting across the counter from me. He smoothed his hands over the wood
surface, studying the grain as he addressed me.

"Hey, how are you?" he asked, as if we exchanged pleasantries every
morning. As if he hadn't made a drunken pass at me mere hours ago.

I had to deal with Travis eventually. Might as well get it over with.

"How am I?" I rolled my shoulders back in an attempt to iron out the kinks and appear more assured. "My apartment imploded. And what was your sympathetic response? Oh yeah. You shoved your bourbon-soaked tongue down my throat."

He tugged at the collar of his uniform shirt. "Yeah, I know."

"What the hell were you thinking last night? Drunk on the job? A sheriff's supposed to be a role model, or at least a law-abiding citizen."

"You don't know much about cops."

His superior tone ticked me off, inflaming the fury I'd bottled deep inside—only a part of it related to him, but I didn't care. Pressure throbbed in my chest. How fantastic it would be to pop that cork and spew my anger and betrayal all over Travis. Maybe it would scorch some sense into him and make me feel better.

I couldn't risk it.

"I was off duty," he said, "not drinking on the job."

"What a relief."

Color rose in his cheeks, and he coughed into his fist. "I can never apologize enough, but shit. The things I've seen, they're unreal, and I ain't handled it well."

"What you've seen? Oh, you mean when you were spying on me outside my apartment." I felt hot all over, and not in a good way. In the steaming-pot-about-to-burst way. "The self-righteous cop turned into a stalker."

"It ain't like that. Somebody's gotta protect you."

"Protect me?" His claim derailed my train of thought for several seconds, as I tried in vain to understand any of this. "You hate me. Why on earth would you be concerned with watching out for me?"

He mumbled, scratching his forehead.

"Come off it, Travis. You know what Calder did to me." I wished I had my derringer, but the holster wouldn't fit under this top. Skeiron had trashed my wardrobe, leaving me only a tight-fitting T-shirt with short sleeves, a pair of low-slung jeans, and undergarments. I'd stowed my gun and its holster under the passenger seat of my car, along with two boxes of ammo. "I shot Calder in self-defense."

Travis's head bobbed in a weak nod, his gaze still downcast.

I hesitated, gathering the right words. "When you grabbed me last night and…did what you did, it was like I'd time-warped back to that night with Calder. It's like you became him."

Travis's head fell into his hands. "Jesus. Please forgive me, I didn't think."

And therein lay the problem. He hadn't thought, because he'd been drunk. For the longest minute of my life, I glared at him and he eyed me like he'd never seen me before. With a shapeshifting assassin and his crazy king after me, I had no energy to waste on despising Travis. He seemed genuinely horrified by his actions, so I made the best decision I could.

I exhaled out my anger. "Fine, I forgive you. Let's move on."

He looked so relieved I half expected him to collapse into a weeping lump on the concrete floor. Instead, eyes shiny with moisture, he gave me a lopsided, shaky smile. "Thank you, Lindsey. God, thank you so much."

He hustled out of the shop, rubbing at his eyes.

I had no clue why he cared so much that I forgave him. Another mystery to add to my growing pile of the unsolved.

At lunchtime, my parents showed up to force food on me, which I dutifully ate despite not being the least bit hungry. The afternoon wore on, heavy and suffocated by humidity. By three o-clock, I'd begun to daydream about a double bed in a nice, air-conditioned motel room.

All the while, memories of Nevan haunted me. Memories of our…whatever it had been. The thing I hadn't wanted anyway. Or so I'd told myself. How could I grieve for a relationship that had never been? What had we shared, really? One all-consuming kiss. Flirting galore.

I wandered down the aisles of the shop, distracting my brain and my heart by reciting the names of the rocks in the bins as I tapped them. I kept my voice quiet, a tick above silence. "Snow quartz. Fossil agate. Float copper. Red sandstone."

A presence tickled my sixth sense. My pulse quickened, butterflies flapped away in my stomach. It couldn't be. But my heart whispered *please, please, please.*

"Have ye forgotten the name of this particular stone?"

My breath hitched. I knew that voice, like I knew my own thoughts.

Nevan's hands glided up and down my arms. He bent his head to my shoulder. "Well, love, do ye know the name?"

His voice in my ear sent an exhilarating shiver down my spine. "It's called star moonstone."

"And what does it signify?"

"It's associated with—" I picked up one of the silvery gray moonstones, running my thumb over its polished surface. "It signifies love and passion."

He slid a palm down my arm, past my wrist, to close his hand around mine and trap the moonstone in my palm. "I tried to stay away from you, but it's like trying to stop gravity from holding my feet on the ground. I don't understand this. I've never wanted any woman the way I want you, Lindsey. Being without you is impossible."

I leaned back into him and the steel knot of fear and anger wedged inside my heart unraveled. "You keep saying you shouldn't be here."

"Still true, but alas, I do not always do as I should. Not anymore. Not with you." His lips covered my earlobe, his breath tantalized the hairs on my cheek. "I missed you. My sweet, mortal miracle."

That broke me. I spun around and threw my arms around his neck. "I missed you, Nevan."

Had he called me a miracle? Yes, he had. *Huh.*

Nevan's arms lashed me to him. I soared on a natural high induced by the soul-stirring, utterly impossible connection that bound me to him and him to me.

The moonstone slipped out of my hand, clattering to the floor. He murmured to me in that esoteric language and I dissolved into him, my lids shuttering on their own, my thoughts scattering into infinity. This was belonging.

"Why are you smiling?" he asked.

"Am I?"

"You are. I can see half your face. It's the kind of smile that implies you've got a lovely secret." His hand roamed up my spine to the base of my neck, his fingers plied my flesh with sensual delicacy. "Care to reveal your secret to me?"

"I'm glad you're here."

"As am I." He spread his palms over my shoulder blades. "We should talk about Skeiron."

"Can it wait until after my shift?"

"I suppose it can." An exasperated sigh rushed out of him. "You are intent upon keeping this ridiculous job, aren't you?"

"It may be a crappy job with crappy pay, but it's all I've got at the moment. Stan let me come in late this morning, but I don't feel like testing his newfound generosity."

"As you wish. I will visit with your family until you're free."

"Deal." For once, I didn't overthink my actions. I simply raised onto my tiptoes and planted a kiss on his cheek.

He smirked, of course.

Reluctantly, I let go of his hand. "See you at six."

"I'll be counting the minutes."

He flashed me a sizzling smile and sauntered out of the shop.

That's when I finally registered his appearance. He wore golden brown slacks and a white dress shirt with the sleeves rolled up to just below his elbows and the top two buttons undone, exposing his tanned flesh. Though he'd once again toned down the coloring of his skin and eyes, he nevertheless made a striking figure as he exited the building.

A twenty-something girl clad in a Hello Kitty T-shirt gaped at Nevan, blinking repeatedly at the sight of him.

Yeah, those muscles were not toned down for mortal consumption. The girl looked ready to pounce on him, and I could've done the same. He was devastatingly gorgeous, even with his supernatural traits muted.

When he walked out of sight, I tried to go back to work. Worries about Skeiron chilled me, so I warmed up by engaging in some choice fantasies about what might transpire later, when I met with Nevan in private.

Make love to me, Nevan. My body ached for it. For him.

Would the damn clock ever read six?

———

I SKIPPED UP THE STEPS INTO THE MOTOR HOME, INTO THE WONDERFULLY cool air inside. I found my parents, my brother, and Nevan all seated around the dining table, laughing at a joke I'd missed. I plopped my purse onto the nearest chair.

The four of them swiveled their heads to me almost in unison.

"Your cheeks are pink," Mom said.

"It's been a long, hot day," I said, "and I'm exhausted."

Nevan uncoiled his long body and moved to my side, gathering me under his arm. I rested my head on his chest.

My mother gave me a knowing smile.

I tried to smile in return, but it came out crimped.

Her lips crooked up on one side, carving out a dimple. She appraised Nevan from top to bottom and I didn't miss the appreciative, but subtle, lift of her eyebrows. If she thought I'd had sex with Nevan, she clearly had no problem with it. My entire family adored him.

Nevan's fingers traveled up and down the bare skin of my arm. "If ye don't mind me stealing your daughter for a bit, I'd like to take Lindsey for a stroll back to the falls."

Mom's irritating, knowing smile reemerged. "Oh, how romantic."

Dad wore a smugly pleased expression. "Lindsey needs a break after what she's been through. Make sure she takes it easy."

"I'll take good care of our girl," Nevan said.

My parents nodded their approval and waved goodbye as we exited the bus. Nevan kept his arm around me during our journey across the parking lot. We passed by the concrete statues in the rock garden, picking up speed as we entered the woods. A bird screeched overhead. My stomach flip-flopped, but then I glimpsed the creature—a hawk, not a raven.

Nevan squeezed my hand. "If Brennus is in the vicinity, he hasn't located us yet. And I've thrown out a little spell to confuse him."

"Like what you did to Travis and his men?"

"Similar, yes."

We lapsed into silence, strolling along like any couple out for a romantic walk. After a few minutes, when we'd bypassed the vortex and rounded the bend just before the falls, he halted us.

"I spoke with Skeiron," he said. "He confirmed he attacked you as a message for me, though not for the reason I'd assumed. My interference in mortal affairs is trifle to him." Nevan hesitated, his gaze clouding. "He wants you."

"Why? I'm nobody."

"I've no idea why. Our conversation ended rather abruptly, when Skeiron ejected me from his fortress."

"Ejected? Do you mean physically?"

"Yes."

"Are you hurt?"

"No." He scratched his ear, glancing at the ground. "Wish I could tell you more. Skeiron wants you, that's all I learned."

He trailed a fingertip down my nose and onto my lips, his gaze fixated on my mouth. Desire sizzled on my lips, on my skin, and in the deepest, most secret part of me.

Seeming to rein in his own passions, he took a seat on the nearest stone bench and gestured toward the adjacent one.

I parked my butt on the hard rock, startled by the unexpected chill of it, and wondered if magic kept the summer heat from affecting the stone. The last time I'd sat here, an odd energy had healed the wounds Brennus inflicted on me in his raven form. Today, I suffered from the exhaustion of stress—caused by Skeiron, and to a lesser extent, Travis.

The mystical forces that lived in this place suffused me with cool, soothing currents. The first time, I'd nearly fallen down from dizziness. This time, the power of the magic flowed through me and around me, invisible yet palpable.

The healing energies wash over you like a cool breeze, infusing your body with ancient wisdom.

How many times I'd recited the spiel. Although the vortex didn't seem to be imparting any wisdom, it was washing energy into me, refreshing and gentle as a spring breeze. Though my muscles unwound, I couldn't stop worrying about what frequent exposure to mystical energies might do to me. Would I grow a second head? What if my skin turned scaly and purple? It was dumb, I knew, but the thoughts kept coming.

Nevan knelt beside me and cupped a hand over my knee. "Are you fretting about Skeiron?"

"Not right this minute."

"Why so despondent?"

"I'm not despondent." I had been after he left me this morning, and I cringed inwardly at the memory of my reaction. "Thing is, I never believed in the healing vortex. I made snide comments about it and assumed anybody who did believe was a fool. Now here I am, sitting inside the frigging vortex, feeling the exact effects I swore did not exist."

Mouth set in a hard line, he flicked his eyes back and forth, up and down, examining every inch of me.

"What are you doing?" I asked.

"You said you're feeling the effects of the vortex. That only happens if you need healing."

"I'm wiped out, that's all."

"Are you certain?"

Striving for a calming expression, I captured his hands with mine. "I didn't mean to scare you. I'm fine, I swear, no real damage. The vortex is kind of ironing out the kinks and I got a little weirded out by it is all."

He sagged a bit, shutting his eyes briefly. "Don't do that to me again, love. It...bothers me."

"Sorry." I stretched, groaning as my muscles loosened up. "Skeiron dumping a building on me was bad enough, but then Travis had to go and make a sloppy pass at me. Being kissed by a drunk was not on my to-do list."

Nevan shot straight and stiff as a telephone pole, his eyes ablaze with angry colors. He lifted his gaze above my head, shoulders back, and focused on a sight only he could see.

I recognized the signs. He was about to skedaddle, the elemental way.

"Hold up," I said.

Though he didn't vanish, he stayed in position, ready to go.

"Where are you going?" I asked.

"I shall go wherever the sheriff is and have a chat with him." He snarled the words sheriff and chat.

"No you will not."

"He must be castigated."

I jumped up. "No. He was drunk and stupid, but I already yelled at him for it—and slugged him good. I can take care of myself."

Nevan rushed to me, lightning quick. His hands grasped my shoulders, hauling me into him, and his mouth dove perilously close to mine.

"I don't like aggressive men," I said, though my body roused with a surge of desire.

He closed his lips over the sensitive spot where my jaw met my neck. He ravished my skin with all the passion and abandon he'd lavished on my mouth during our one and only lip-lock, and I threw my head back on a long, low moan.

"You're mine," he said, his mouth quivering the flesh of my throat. "You told me so."

"Goes both ways."

"Mmm...yes. I am yours, my sweet."

I groaned as he dragged his mouth down my neck, his teeth nipping at my flesh, his scorching lips journeying ever downward until they found the side of one breast. He lapped at my skin with his skillful tongue, savoring me, winding me up until I succumbed to the sheer pleasure of it, wrapping my arms around his head to hold him to my breast.

He whipped his head up, strode backward, and said, "But the sheriff must be castigated."

Before I could speak, he was gone.

The flapping of wings pulled my attention skyward. A raven circled overhead, diving low over the clearing. My instincts warned me it was no ordinary raven.

Brennus plummeted toward me with terrifying velocity.

I clambered to my feet, intending to run, but the bird's wings whacked me sideways and bowled me over smack onto my ass.

The instant his feet touched down, the raven transformed into the black-skinned, blue-tinged, monstrous man I'd met yesterday. Brennus, his face cold and hard, twisted his lips into a grotesque version of a smile. His voice boomed like nothing of this earth.

"Mortal," he said, "you have defied him for the last time."

"Get away from her."

Nevan's voice roared from behind me, invested with a rage that raised the hairs on my nape. He stalked up beside me, where I lay sprawled on the ground. With one hand, he snagged both of mine and pulled me to my feet. Cracking his knuckles, he confronted Brennus.

The raven-man smiled again.

"Guardian," Brennus said, "you have disobeyed Skeiron once too often. He sends me to deliver a final warning. Give up the mortal woman, or be forced to watch as His Majesty extracts the essence from your female and disassembles her piece by piece."

Disassemble? A gruesome image raced through my mind.

"You have until the sun sets in the mortal realm," Brennus continued. "Discard the female or Skeiron will eliminate the distraction for you."

Discard the female? I wasn't a piece of lint to be chucked in the trash.

"Deliver the woman to Skeiron," Brennus said, "or he will take her himself and his wrath shall lay waste to this realm."

I clenched my fists. "Lay waste to my world? The hell he will."

Nevan narrowed his eyes on me, rotating his head in my direction while his mouth sharpened into a scowl. Even I, a foolish and often dense mortal, comprehended his meaning—*shut the hell up, woman.*

Being foolish and often dense, however, I forged ahead anyway. "Tell your master not to bother with all the raping and pillaging, because I'm not the one he wants. He's confused me with somebody else."

The raven-man glanced at me like I was an ant crapping on his toes and told Nevan, "The king has realized she holds the power. Why else would you, guardian of the falls and seeker of the Janusite, protect this puny mortal female?"

"I will do what must be done."

A couple days ago, I might've worried Nevan had been sizing me up this whole time, to ferret out whether I did indeed have whatever power everybody wanted so damn badly. Though it made no sense, I trusted him now and I recognized he'd stated exactly what he meant. He would do what was necessary—but he'd omitted the "to protect my puny mortal female" part.

I pushed in front of Nevan, face to face with Brennus. "This *puny mortal* has a few questions."

"The deadline is sunset," Brennus said.

He shimmered and disappeared.

"Aw, come on." I spun toward face Nevan. "He can do the poofing thing too?"

Nevan shrugged.

"That's so unfair." I latched my arms around me, but my skin still crawled from our encounter with Brennus. "Am I misinterpreting this, or did a freaky raven-man just threaten to cut me up in itty-bitty pieces?"

"Skeiron would be the one to disassemble you, but only after he extracts your power."

"Oh great." I threw my hands up and let them flop back down. "Your boss wants to suck me dry and chop me up like hamburger. I feel much better. And what's the deal with Skeiron thinking I have some kind of power?"

He slipped his hand around mine, but his attention wandered, his eyes losing focus.

"Nevan?"

His gaze snapped back into focus, trained on me, and he released my hand. "I've no idea why Skeiron believes you possess great power. I've sensed something in you, suppressed and difficult to identify, yet nothing worth killing for."

"I don't have any goddamn supernatural energy inside me."

He canted his head. "Are ye certain of that?"

Was I? Despite longing to say yes, I couldn't. Not anymore. "You said a lot of humans have a touch of the Unseen in them. Maybe that's what I've got, but it's buried for some reason."

"If that were true, my enchantment would've worked."

"Maybe you're not as enthralling as you think."

He lips curved in a tender smile. "I believe we've demonstrated quite definitively that I enthrall you in other, non-magical ways."

My body chose that moment to thrust me into a whirlwind, sense-memory recap of our first kiss, segueing into a replay of his mouth on my throat earlier and the way he'd licked a path down my breast.

Nevan surrounded my hands with his and tugged me close, our hands pinned between my breasts and his torso. "You recall, don't ye?"

His voice was a seductive murmur. I struggled not to respond, but everything inside me betrayed my wishes.

"Your pupils are dilating," he said, "your breaths are quickening, and your body is yielding to me. Admit it. You are enchanted, in your own way, without magic."

"If that's the criteria, you're just as enchanted as I am."

"I'll concede the point." His voice was thick with a need rivaling my own.

My lips yearned for his. The faint caress a second ago had not been enough. I craved full contact. His lips. His tongue. His...everything.

Through the haze of desire, a thought surfaced. "What did you do to Travis?"

"Nothing. I hadn't reached him yet when I sensed you were in danger and returned."

He sensed I was in danger? I had no time to ponder the ramifications of that, because a shriek punctured the silence, ululating with blood-curdling effect.

Nevan jerked his head in the direction of the scream.

Another shriek resounded through the woods.

"That's coming from the direction of the shop," I said, overwhelmed by a mounting dread. "My parents. Ash."

Nevan hauled me into his arms and whisked us away.

CHAPTER EIGHTEEN

WE POPPED OUT WITHIN SIGHT OF THE SHOP, BEHIND A WIDE PINE TREE. In the parking lot, Sandy was gaping at the closed trunk of my car, hands raised. Her body impeded my view, but her shrill cries pierced my eardrums.

I tore down the hill into the parking lot.

Sandy's boyfriend sprinted out of the shop toward her. At the same time I reached her, he grasped her shoulders and spun her around, pressing her face into his chest, his hand cradling the back of her head.

My shoes slipped on the gravel, tripping me up.

Sandy pointed a trembling finger at the trunk, directly above the license plate.

I pushed around the young couple, tiptoeing to the trunk. A dark red liquid dripped from the undercarriage onto the gravel. Crushed in the seam where the trunk lid met the car's body was a human finger.

The world telescoped down, blackness encroaching to shut out everything except the finger jutting from the trunk of my car. The air was redolent with the stench of blood. I covered my mouth and nose with one palm, but the sheer horror of the bloody appendage and what it signified nailed me in place.

Maybe it was only a finger, not a whole body. Maybe the finger was fake.

"Porter! Open the goddamn trunk or I'll blast it open."

Travis's hollering ripped me out of my panicked thoughts, but I could not look away from the blood-soaked finger.

Nevan secured his arms around my waist, and in the back of my mind, I knew he meant to whisk me away. Numb, I wrenched out of his grasp and trudged to the driver's door. I hadn't locked the car this morning, so I swung the door out and lunged a hand under the dashboard to click the trunk release. A *clunk* told me the trunk had popped open. I shuffled back to Nevan, my ears ringing faintly.

His arms came around me, pulling me into the shelter of his body.

"Don't look, love," he said. "Please don't look."

The stench of blood. The acrid taste of bile in my mouth. I couldn't stand here, immobilized, and wait for someone else to sort this out. It was my life on the line here.

I broke free of Nevan, spinning around.

Sandy fainted into her boyfriend's arms.

Travis glanced at me, his expression inscrutable but his face a touch ashen. I imagined my face must've been pasty too, and I hadn't seen what everyone else had—yet. Travis held the trunk lid at full extension, his fingers in a death grip, knuckles white from the effort. I scuffled closer, hands locked over my belly, until the trunk's interior came into view.

I reeled backward into Nevan.

A dead man lay crumpled in the trunk, limbs bent at unnatural angles, as if someone had stuffed him into the space in a hurry. But the most sickening sight was not the body. The head had been cleaved from the body.

It lay perpendicular to the neck. Blood and spinal fluid gushed out of the severed neck, filtering down through a crack in the car's metal hull to drip onto the gravel.

The dead man's face consumed my focus. His red hair. Green eyes.

"Oh shit," I croaked. "It's Brad."

Travis yanked the handcuffs from his belt. They jingled as he brandished them at me, partly due to a tremor in his hands. "Got no choice this time."

I shook my head, my gaze glued to the body. To Brad. I never even knew his last name.

Travis stalked up to me, grabbing for my wrists. "Lindsey Porter, you are under arrest for—"

Nevan threw his arms around me and catapulted us into the void.

The real world winked out as we careened in a free-fall through the abysmal tunnel, tumbling out into the world again totally out of control. Nevan lost his grip on me. I ricocheted off the ground, rolling over and over. My spine cracked into a tree. Vertigo spun my head, mutating the ground into a carnival ride.

After several seconds, the nausea-inducing motion inside my head settled down. I scrambled to my feet, a little unsteady. Nevan had come to rest a few yards away, flat on his back. I hurried to him, offering my hands. He made a face, but accepted my aid in separating his body from the ground.

We were in the woods. Where, I couldn't tell. Wild blackberry bushes bloomed nearby, their white flowers giving off a caramel aroma. The scent soothed my nerves, but nowhere near enough to obliterate the riot of thoughts in my head. Travis planned on arresting me. I understood he had little choice, but I couldn't go to jail. Whoever had framed me before had done it again, with more conviction this time.

Something Tris had told me resurfaced. He'd said Brad could be resurrected as long as his head hadn't been "lopped off." The snarky leprechaun couldn't be responsible for this. He had zero motive. The only one with a clear intent to destroy me was Skeiron.

Nevan tucked a lock of hair behind my ear. "All right?"

"I'm not going to barf or pass out, if that's what you mean." I wanted to hide under a bed somewhere, but otherwise I was peachy. "There's nothing all right about the situation, though."

Nevan's gaze hardened, his expression too. "I will not allow the sheriff to take you."

"He has no choice. Somebody put a dead—" The visual exploded in my mind as if I'd been hurled back in time to relive it. Blood. Brad. Headless. *Don't think about it.* I slammed the lid on the memory, my panic, everything. Sometimes repression was necessary. "Who killed Brad this time?"

"I've no clue."

"What about Skeiron?"

"As I said before, Skeiron doesn't muck about with corpses, much less mortal ones."

"His Nutbar Majesty wants me dead," I said. "Disassembled, remember? This might be part of his plan."

"To have you convicted of murder? What are you suggesting, he'll wait for you to be executed by the mortal system of justice so he might cackle at your funeral?" Nevan scoffed, shaking his head. "Skeiron is neither that subtle nor that patient."

"Yeah, I guess you're right." I let my head fall back, staring at the swathe of blue sky visible between the treetops. Every moment, the sun descended further toward the horizon, a silent countdown to my doom. "When is sunset?"

"When it is."

"How terribly helpful." I slouched, drained by the day's events and by our fruitless conversation. "God, I wish I had my gun."

"It would do you no good against an elemental."

"Unless you can give me an endued weapon, it's the best I've got. I bet two .357 rounds between the eyes would give him a bitch of a migraine." I gnawed the inside of my lip, chewing on the problem in a literal fashion. "If I had my purse, I could check the time on my phone. At least then we'd know how long we have."

Nevan blipped out.

Seconds elapsed, ticked off by a gigantic, phantom clock in my head. I was about to holler for him when he reappeared in the exact spot where he'd stood a moment ago. My purse dangled off his shoulder. He held my gun, in its holster, in one hand and m two boxes of ammo in the other.

"Wow," I said, smiling with real admiration, "I'm about two seconds away from having sex with you right here in the woods."

Clearly trying not to smirk, he tossed my purse to me. "Perhaps we should wait until our heads are no longer in matching nooses."

I dug around inside the main compartment or my purse for my phone. I plucked it out with an "ah-ah!" and danced it in the air in front of his face. He arched one brow and almost smiled. I checked the weather app on my phone. "Sunset is at 8:47 PM and it's 7:20 right now." I plunked the phone back in my purse. "We have a little over an hour to figure out…something."

Nevan handed me my gun and its accoutrements. By the time I'd reloaded the barrel with .357 rounds, my insides had morphed into a simmering cauldron of all my worst fears come to pass. An innocent man had died and because of me. "Somebody wants to drive me over the edge, that's why Brad was killed. If it's not Calder's ghost, I don't know who it is. Travis is having a meltdown, maybe it's him."

"Unrequited desires can turn into resentment, in a weak-willed man."

"What on earth are you talking about? Travis has no desires for me."

A muscle in his jaw ticked. "He kissed you."

"Ugh. He was drunk."

"You are blind to it, aren't you?" Nevan guided me toward a tree with a hand on my elbow. He sat down—back against the trunk, legs outstretched—and patted his thigh in invitation. I crawled onto his lap, unsure why, knowing only that I needed the contact. He linked his arms around my hips. "Think about it. The sheriff despises me. He knew you before you became involved with his brother and, by your own account, he became withdrawn and angry after his brother won you."

"Nobody won me. I'm not a raffle prize."

"You are deflecting." He gave me a squeeze, rocking my hips on his lap. "You know of what I speak."

"Afraid I don't."

"The sheriff is in love with you."

"Wha—" I jerked my head back to gape at him. "That's crazy."

Except it might not have been. When I reflected on my entire acquaintance with Travis, I recalled small clues I'd once dismissed as nothing. He had changed after Calder showed up, for reasons I never could puzzle out. He'd tracked me down in Michigan. He'd almost said he was here to protect me, before he corrected himself to say he had to protect the world from me. Travis had also pleaded with me to stay with him instead of going with Nevan, not to mention he kissed me—and begged me to forgive him for it.

Oh God. It was true.

I must've looked shocked, because Nevan smiled tenderly. "You see it, don't you? He is quite desperately in love with you. Can't blame him."

Desperately. In love. With me.

Nevan skirted my cheekbone with his fingertips. "Whatever his failings, I sincerely doubt the sheriff would harm you on purpose."

"Who then? The murderer went out of his way to implicate me. It's got to be personal."

He gazed into the distance, lips tight. "I do not believe your enemy is mortal."

"You said Skeiron isn't the guy."

"There are countless elementals in the Unseen." He lifted us both to our feet. "We should cross the veil and seek help there."

"From who?"

Nevan considered me for a moment, motionless, unreadable. He hooked his hands around my upper arms. "Skeiron must believe you are the Janusite."

"What? Why?" I clutched a handful of his shirt. "He can't. I'm not."

"It's my fault." He scrubbed his face with one hand. "When I reconsider everything Skeiron and Brennus have said, I can reach but one conclusion. Skeiron decided there is one reason and only one reason why I would shirk my duty to pursue and protect a mortal woman. You are the Janusite."

"But you can't know that, right? You said all the girls you, uh, test have to be taken to Skeiron so he can figure out if they're the one."

The sylph king's voice blared in my memory. *Are you the one?* he'd asked me. Holy hell in a giant frigging basket. He'd thought I might be the Janusite even then.

"You are correct," Nevan said, "normally that would be the case. But I took you through the falls. Brennus witnessed it. Skeiron has no idea of where I took you or why and so, of course, he's decided I spirited you away to an oracle for confirmation you are the Janusite. And now, according to his estimation, I intend to harness your power for my own gain."

"Why are you protecting me?"

Bowing his head, he scratched his neck. "I don't know."

He kept saying that, but it rang false. After I made him enchant Brad, he told me he that proved he'd do anything for me—and he swore he'd protect me from Skeiron. When he'd declared Travis was desperately in love with me, what had he said?

Can't blame him.

Goose bumps prickled my arms. I couldn't deal with another epiphany about one of the men in my life, not with Skeiron's deadline fast approaching. Whatever Nevan had meant, I had to put it aside for later.

I had more urgent questions. "You mentioned an oracle."

"Yes, the oracle is the only one who can identify the Janusite."

"When you say *the* oracle, do you mean there's just one?"

"No, there are quite a few. This oracle is the one who issued the Janusite prophecy." He frowned at the grass. "The oracle will speak only to

Skeiron. No one else is permitted to know where he lives. But perhaps I can persuade a fae to aid us, for a price."

"No bargains, remember? Bargains are bad."

"For you, yes. I have considerably more experience in negotiating them."

"Desperation is not a good starting place for making a deal, even I know that." I shoved my hands in my pockets. "Let's say you do bargain for the oracle's location and he deigns to speak to you. If he says I am the one, then what?"

"One step at a time."

"Which means you don't know."

He growled a sigh. "For once, can ye just agree and let it drop?"

"Maybe." I flashed back to the scene in the parking lot earlier today, when the Porter clan had arrived. "I can't leave my family hanging. They'll worry."

"Time is running short for us."

"We've got about an hour. Help me get to my family, let me show them I'm okay, and I'll do whatever you say."

His lips crept into a smirk. "Whatever I say?"

"Within reason."

"As you wish." When I opened my mouth, he held up a hand to silence me. "Let me check the way is clear before I take you to them."

"Hurry up."

He popped out and popped back in a few seconds later. "They are in their large, wheeled home. I instructed them to lock the door, to prevent us being surprised by the sheriff."

"You let them see you poof in?" Once was bad enough, but twice?

"They seemed well adjusted to the concept."

"Well adjusted? What the hell were you think—"

He swept me into his arms and rushed us away.

An hourglass glimmered in my mind's eye, the sand sifting away bit by bit. One hour and a smattering of minutes. One hour…

Until my personal Armageddon.

———

MY MOTHER SEIZED ME IN A BEAR HUG, CLINCHING ME HARD ENOUGH I expected to hear my ribs cracking. When she finally released me, I was relieved to find all my bones intact. Nevan had materialized us right in front of my parents and Ash, without bothering to ask me if I cared where we landed. Considering what I planned to tell them, I supposed it made no difference.

Besides, my parents and my brother acted like nothing bizarre had occurred, as if visitors blipped into their RV every day. For the first time in a very long time, I realized the benefits of having a family obsessed with the metaphysical.

Mom grabbed Nevan's face and smacked a firm kiss on his cheek. "Thank you for taking care of our baby."

"I am not a baby," I said. "I'm thirty-two years old. And I need to talk to you."

Nevan's eyebrows rose when I pointed a finger at him.

Snaring his hand, I dragged him down the little hallway into the bedroom my parents had allotted to me until I could find a new apartment. They'd been using the room for storage, but now it was filled with the remnants of my personal belongings. In the cramped space, made more cramped by my boxes of stuff, I couldn't get more than three feet away Nevan.

Clapping the door shut, I planted my hands on my hips, fingers tapping. "Poof in right in front of my parents? I told you not to do that."

"No, darlin', ye didn't."

He smirked with a mixture of affectionate humor and sarcasm, which made me want to kick him. And kiss him. And kick him again.

Maybe I hadn't actually told him. The past few days had become a mental blur.

"Besides, your family seems quite fine with my preferred mode of travel. In fact, they seem fine with magic in general." He rubbed his chin between his thumb and forefinger. "Why does it vex you?"

"Because it's—" I flapped my arms, as if I might pump rational thoughts into my brain. Didn't work. I threw my head back, letting my arms flop down. "Unh."

"Unh?" Nevan repeated my noise with a tinkle of amusement. "You'll have to be more articulate if you expect me to understand."

Head bent back, I let a crack in a ceiling tile absorb my focus. Thinking was too damn hard. I didn't notice Nevan coming closer until his lips brushed my throat, just below my jaw. His breaths excited my skin, unfurling tendrils of desire through my body.

"Never have I seen another mortal who contains as much stress inside as you do." His voice was sultry, his lips warm and soft, feathering across my skin in delicious little kisses. "Shall I relax you?"

He stole my breath with an open-mouth kiss on my pulse point, nipping and licking, his soft groan vibrating my flesh. I resisted leaning into him for as long as I could—about two seconds. "We have a deadline, remember?"

"All the more reason to let me give you pleasure."

"Thanks, but no." My body screamed *yes, yes, yes.*

Trailing his lips across my cheek, he took hold of my hips and rocked me into him. "Are ye certain?"

"Uh-huh." *Maybe.*

One of his large hands wandered to the small of my back, while the other cradled the back of my head, slanting it forward until our gazes converged. "You don't sound certain."

"My parents are right outside."

His fingers massaged my scalp, slow and sensual. Oh good heavens. He really did have a talent for melting me. "You're saying you would let me do this, if we were elsewhere."

Aw hell. Why bother lying anymore? "Yes."

The hand on my back skated up and over to my side, just under my breast, and with his thumb he traced the band of my bra. I barely suppressed a moan as he rumbled, "Ahhh…There is hope then."

But why was he seducing here and now? We were about to embark on Operation Destroy a Vengeful Godlike Being, which might well result in both of us being "disassembled." I couldn't fathom the impetus for his behavior, for his need to show me pleasure before we took off on a dangerous mission.

Ohhhh no. I did understand.

And the lovely fog of lust evaporated in an instant. "You think we're going to die, don't you? That's the real reason for the porn show. You're saying goodbye."

The stark sadness in his eyes told me everything I needed to know. He backed away.

Robbed of his touch, of his hands and lips and breaths on my skin, I ached in ways I hadn't known I could.

"We still have no plan," I said. "Other than going to the world of don't trust anyone, never say please or thank you, and try not to accidentally bargain your way into enslavement."

"I can think of nothing else to do." The starkness had infected his voice, but he kept his gaze squarely on me. "I will go alone. You will cross the boundary where you will be safe."

"Like I told you before, I am not hiding," I said. "We go together. Got it?"

He nodded, looking as defeated as anyone I'd ever seen. With his usual whiplash-inducing speed, he switched back into Aloof Nevan mode. Glancing around the room, he asked, "Was there a reason you brought me in here?"

"Of course." Good. I could focus on this instead of impending horrific death. I cleared my throat. "I want to tell my parents everything, which means telling them about you. What you can do. What you are."

"Do as you must."

"You don't mind?"

"No, but you clearly do."

I chewed on that for a moment before heaving out a sigh. "Might as well get this over with. Let me do the talking, okay?"

He shrugged, but the tightness around his eyes belied his nonchalance.

Pushing the door open, he swept his hand in a grand gesture for me to exit first. As we emerged into the living area, he kept one hand on the small of my back. Although my parents hadn't moved, Ash was skipping up and down the aisle. He stopped when he saw me and bounced on his heels.

Nevan lingered a pace behind me. His hand on my back comforted me more than I would've expected and I leaned a fraction into the contact, grateful for his warmth.

I drew a fortifying breath and looked at my family. "I'm sure you've noticed some strange things happening around here lately. Inexplicable things."

Ash had ceased bouncing. All three of them nodded, solemn and silent.

"Well, here goes."

I launched into a recap of the past few days, of my discovery of the body and of Nevan's first appearance, of the corpse vanishing and Nevan reappearing to corroborate my story for Travis. The raven stalking me. The leprechaun. The resurrection. Skeiron and the roof collapse and poor Brad's second demise and the Janusite and the deadline looming ahead of us. I left out Nevan's gentle seductions and the details of his "duty," though I told them he'd been tasked with finding the Janusite.

When I finished, my dad said, "Lindsey, you're in a pickle for sure."

I almost laughed. Almost.

He glanced at Nevan, then me. "How can we help?"

"Get the hell out of here." I felt Nevan inch closer, his hand drifting down to grasp my hip. I settled my hand over his. "I can't worry about you while we're off in another world searching for answers. Please, drive as far away from here as you can get."

My parents rose, Dad looping a protective arm around Mom's shoulders. "We'll leave, but we won't go too far. Our baby's in trouble and Porters don't run out on family."

Nevan whispered in my ear, "The boundary."

Oh. Duh. "Just promise me you'll stay at least one mile away from the shop."

Dad's brow crinkled, but soon realization smoothed it out. "You mean stay outside this invisible line you mentioned. The one the whatsits can't cross."

"Right."

"And water," Nevan said. "Lakes, rivers, ponds, streams, waterfalls. Any naturally occurring bodies of water may provide an avenue for a portal to open. Each has its own boundary."

First I'd heard about that. "Yeah, like Nevan says, stay a mile away from water."

"Kind of hard to do," Dad said. "This place is full of hidden waterfalls and streams."

"We'll do our best," Mom said to me. "Don't worry, sweetie."

Relief rushed through me, leaving me a bit weak. Jeez, I was massively tense, like Nevan said. "Be careful."

My mother broke free of Dad's embrace to march straight up to Nevan. Her neck craned back to meet his gaze, she aimed her sternest mother's look at him. "You better keep her safe, son. If anything happens to my daughter, I'm coming after you with every weapon in my arsenal. And believe me, I've got plenty of ammo."

Nevan wore a grave expression as he told her, "Your daughter's life means more to me than my own, Mrs. Porter. I shall protect her at any cost."

With a smile, my mother raised onto her toes to peck another kiss on Nevan's cheek. "Good boy."

She returned to Dad's side, taking his hand.

Ash stood somberly beside them. "Are you gonna come back, Zee?"

I knelt before him to level our eyes and gave him my best brave smile. "Of course I am. Don't think I'd let you eat all the chocolate pudding, do you?"

He shook his head, eyes glistening with unshed tears.

I tousled his hair and tried to sound casual. "See you later, brat."

Turning away from my family, I marched straight to Nevan. My eyes burned and my lips trembled. Nausea roiled in my stomach. If I died, at least my family would be safe outside the boundary.

Nevan enfolded me in his arms, his chin on the crown of my head, and spirited us away.

CHAPTER NINETEEN

W E REAPPEARED INSIDE THE HEALING VORTEX, THE ONRUSHING gloom of night turning the woods into a haunted forest from a Grimm fairytale. Shadows slashed across the stone benches, speckled with wan sunlight that dimmed with every passing second. Nevan kept his arms around me, holding me close. My holster must've poked into him, since it poked into me, but he gave no indication of noticing. The old stoic mask had shuttered his features.

He swallowed visibly, the solitary sign of emotion.

No, not the only sign. The way he held me, as if I might float away if he loosened his grip, it told me more than any words. I was damn glad he'd retrieved my derringer for me. If he was scared…

I looked up at the darkened treetops swaying in a wind I couldn't feel, shielded by the woods around us. "Why'd you bring us here instead of closer to the falls? We are in a hurry."

His hesitation spurred me to look at him. Though his expression betrayed nothing, his eyes were shot through with cold, pure white. "I—tried to take us there. Something prevented it."

The cold fear in his eyes seemed to rush through our touching skin straight into my veins. "Something? Do you think Skeiron…"

I couldn't finish the thought, praying he'd refute it until he decimated that hope with his next words.

"Most likely." He shut his eyes briefly and I swore his heated skin cooled a few degrees. "I sense a magical barrier walling off the falls and its vicinity. We cannot reach the portal."

"What do we do?"

He pressed a kiss to my forehead, his lips lingering there as he spoke. "Skeiron waits inside the barrier. For me."

"For us." I tipped my head back until I could see his eyes. "I'm with you. Whatever happens."

I couldn't have torn my gaze from his if I'd wanted to, but I had no inclination to sever the connection. Not for anything.

"The clock is ticking," he whispered. "Go outside the boundary. Please."

"I won't leave you to fight Skeiron alone."

Without another word, he clamped his hand around mine and half dragged me down the path toward the falls. The healing vortex receded behind us, devoured by the woods. His bare feet slapped and my boots clomped on the dirt path, a dark river ferrying us through the trees. We traveled at a brisk walk, verging on a run, with Nevan a stiff and almost robotic guide, his expression stern, his eyes focused on what lay straight ahead.

My anxiety ratcheted higher with every step, triggering a flood of adrenaline that burned in my veins and heightened my senses. Wings flapped overhead, but I didn't dare glance up, not with Nevan urging me onward at a merciless pace. The winged visitor would be Brennus, tracking us for his master.

I couldn't be the Janusite. I'd never mattered that much to the world—any world.

Nevan pulled us up short at the clearing beside the waterfall. His eyes flashed crimson and steely silver in the twilight, a muscle jumped in his jaw, and those massive shoulders rolled back in readiness for a fight.

He dropped my hand.

My throat went dry and tight. "Skeiron's here, isn't he?"

"Yes."

Wind gusted through the treetops, rattling branches and raining leaves down on us. As the greenery fluttered to the earth around us, bits catching in our hair and on our bodies, the ground beneath us quivered. A gale ripped through the clearing, and borne on the tempest, a voice deep and resonant roared.

Nevan yanked me to him, his arms steel bars around my back.

The gale blustered around us in whirling eddies. I strained to see Nevan through the ropes of my own hair lashing my face.

The wind ceased. One second blasting us, the next dead calm.

I tipped my face up to Nevan, praying he had an answer, knowing there was no magic solution this time. "I'm sorry, love. I can't take us away from here. He strengthened the magical barrier around this area to stop either of us from leaving. He banked on you coming with me."

"It's not your fault. We had no choice, Nevan."

"Where the blame rests hardly matters." He pulled his hand free and backed up two steps. With a flourish of his hand, he conjured an object.

I blinked repeatedly, sure I must be hallucinating. But it was real.

Nevan grasped a sword—long, thick, fashioned from polished, silvery metal laced with bronze. The grip was sheathed in leather, the hilt carved with ornate spiral designs. He lifted the weapon and the ambient light glinted on its blade.

"Listen carefully," he said, holding the sword at his side, blade down. "Skeiron will show himself any moment, once he's done menacing us. He will attempt to take you, but I will not allow it. I must fight him. He has an endued sword, which means I will die, but I'll make certain he goes with me."

I snaked a hand under my shirt, closing it around the butt of my gun.

"You are correct, guardian, on one point."

The voice boomed from across the clearing. Nevan and I turned as one to face the being at the edge of the pool, positioned between us and the falls.

Skeiron sneered at us, his onyx eyes seething with vile green and orange. He wielded a sword too, one forged from obsidian metal shot through with indigo. In lieu of his white robe, kilt of dark gold swathed his hips and thighs. The fabric hung low, slightly askew, exposing the top edge of his hip bones. His muscular chest rivaled Nevan's, his skin a darker shade of suntan, burnished with copper.

Heat rippled through the air, carrying with it the odor of sulfur.

"Would you care to know," Skeiron asked, "on which point you are correct?"

Nevan glowered at his king, the fingers of his free hand twitching.

"You will die, guardian," Skeiron said, "that is a certainty. But I shall not join you. The mortal wench will be mine."

The bastard called me a wench?

"If she is the one, I shall extract the power from her and discard the lifeless remnants of her pitiful—if enticing—human body. If she is not the one, I'll mine what pleasure I can from her and then slowly disassemble her mortal form."

My nails bit into my palms as I fisted my hands tight. "Like hell you will, you psychotic son of a—"

"Silence, wench!"

Ohhh, I was damn sick of him calling me that. "Somebody needs to disassemble your ass."

Nevan surged forward, sidestepping to block my view of the sylph king. Feet planted wide, he raised the sword. I swore I glimpsed a slight uptick of his lips.

"We end this the old way," Nevan said. "With physical might."

They launched into action, barreling toward each other, swords flashing. Their blades collided with an explosive clang that reverberated in the air and in my eardrums. I winced and clapped my hands over my ears to mute the crashing of their swords. Their movements came with such ferocious speed the scene turned into one big blur of motion. The clashing of metal on metal punctuated their grunts and shouts. Feet scuffled across earth, tore grass, uprooted weeds, kicked up clods of dirt.

The battle held me transfixed, my body frozen, my breaths caught in my throat. I ought to help, somehow. What could a puny mortal wench do? I'd be shredded if I dived into the melee of super-speed swordplay. What was happening? Who was winning? I could hardly distinguish Nevan from Skeiron anymore.

One of them flew backward across the clearing and slammed into a thick pine tree. The wet *thwack* of the impact echoed in the clearing.

Nevan slumped to the ground, legs askew. The sword tumbled out of his hand. His breaths panted out of his gaping mouth and blood streamed from slashes on his face, arms, and chest.

Skeiron had reopened the scar over Nevan's heart.

Between gasps, he shouted at Skeiron. "Using magic? You have no honor left, do you, Your Majesty?"

Nevan transformed the word majesty into the worst insult.

Skeiron's lips peeled back in a vicious grin, and in slow motion, his devil-bright eyes zeroed in on me.

Nevan scrambled to rise, lost his balance, clawed at the tree for support.

The king stormed toward me.

I yanked out my derringer, fired both rounds straight into his chest, and flipped open the barrel to reload.

Skeiron paused mid step, eying the wounds. He swept his hands down his chest as if brushing off insects, his eyes slitted, and rushed at me.

I jammed the rounds into the barrel and snapped it shut, but I pulled the trigger too late. A single copper-sheened hand seized my throat, knocking my aim off target. The shot punctured a tree.

Leaping to his feet, teetering for an unnerving second, Nevan snatched up his sword. "Release her."

His command thundered like the voice of an ancient god.

Skeiron strangled me. The gun popped out of my grasp. I gurgled, clawed at his hand, kicked at him, but he merely hoisted me off the ground and smiled at Nevan. Blackness licked at the edges of my vision. I battled for breath, lungs on fire, but my limbs stopped responding and my arms and legs went limp. The abyss beckoned me with sweet relief from the stabbing, searing agony. The blackness encroached further and further and—

A force hurled me sideways. The vise around my neck popped free.

I tumbled to the ground, wheezing. Brightness burst through the darkness in my vision. Ringing in my ears deafened me. I rubbed my throat, as the scene around me snapped into focus.

Nevan and Skeiron wrestled on the ground a dozen feet away. Nevan's sword lay on the grass beside me, while Skeiron's was wedged against a sapling, sharp end up. Skeiron punched Nevan in the chest. Stunned, he gasped for air.

The king pounced on the opening. He vaulted to his feet with super-natural agility and flung one hand out, fingers spread. His sword dislodged from the sapling, somersaulting through the air straight into his waiting palm. He flipped the sword vertical, blade down. Grasped it in both hands. Raised it over Nevan.

And rammed it into his chest.

"No!" I screamed.

Skeiron ripped the sword out. Blood drenched the blade, dripping off the tip onto Nevan's belly. Blood poured from the chest wound.

The drumbeat of my heart battered my eardrums. A fury like nothing I'd ever known exploded inside me, scorching and irresistible, fueling a sensation of mounting physical strength. I knew the feeling was false, but I didn't give a damn.

I closed one hand around the grip of Nevan's sword.

Skeiron was focused on Nevan, his glee enlivening his features with manic effect. He lifted the sword to his mouth and licked the blade, savoring the blood.

I pushed onto my knees and tightened my grip on Nevan's sword.

Skeiron sniggered. "Your essence tastes of weakness, guardian."

Nevan gurgled, flailing one arm. His eyes were flat, the bronze tint gone from his skin, driven out by a growing pallor. And his lips. Oh God, his lips were turning blue.

"Next," Skeiron said, "I shall taste the blood of your precious mortal wench."

I sprang to my feet, brandishing the sword.

Skeiron's gaze flicked to me, the sword, me. His eyes flew wide for an instant, but then a nasty grin split his lips.

I bolted toward him, howling with rage and terror. Before he could react, I jammed the sword into his side. I shoved with all my might until the blade sank in to the hilt and my fingernails scraped his flesh.

Hot liquid flowed over my skin.

I jerked my hand away. Blood soaked my fingers. Despite the tremors racking me, despite how the world tilted around me, I fell to my knees at Nevan's head, his crumpled body laid out before me, and thrust my arms under his. I struggled to lift him, but he was too heavy.

His hand sealed around the sword's hilt, he collapsed to his knees. "Brennus!"

The call roared on the wind that blustered over us all. A raven squawked overhead. Brennus touched down fifteen feet away, morphing into his humanoid form—but not quite as I'd seen him before. Talons curled from the tips of his fingers, sharp and glistening. When he bared his teeth, I glimpsed razor-like points.

An awareness tingled over me. Something had changed.

Nevan dragged in a breath crackling with wetness.

The world winked out.

It winked back an instant later, but we weren't in the woods anymore. Nevan had whisked us to the parking lot of the rock shop, landing us smack beside my car. The last tendrils of sunset reeled back into the horizon, casting us in sickly, ever-diminishing light. Even in the onrushing gloom, I saw the blood. The gaping wound.

"Oh God, Nevan." I clasped his face in both hands, gazing at him upside-down through a haze of tears. "What do I do? Can a doctor help you?"

"No." The wet crackle was there again and an invisible fist gripped my heart. "The barrier dropped…when you…injured him."

That was how he could transport us here. How long would Skeiron stay debilitated?

"I—" Nevan hacked, spraying bloody spittle. "Sorry I couldn't…take us further. Too weak."

Shaking my head, I stroked his cheeks. "It's okay. You did great."

He choked on a cough. Blood trickled from the corner of his mouth.

Oh Jesus, no. I had to stay calm because this was not over. Skeiron had unleashed Brennus on us and the raven would not stop until he hunted us down.

I tore off my T-shirt, leaving only my bra to cover me. I balled up the shirt and pressed it to Nevan's wound.

"No," he croaked. "Too late."

"Like hell."

In the woods, a raven screamed.

Car keys. I needed them *now.*

Fumbling in my pocket, I dug them out, scrabbled to my feet, unlocked the driver's door, and flipped the switch to unlock the others.

The flapping of wings drew ever closer.

I ripped the back door open and fell to my knees beside Nevan. The vehemence in my tone was not an act. "You are going to help me get you into the car. Understand me?"

His eye rolled shut.

I slapped him.

He cracked his lids. His lips quivered as he formed a faint smirk. "Still with the…questions. Eh, love?"

My heart swelled. If he could joke, then goddammit, he could help me move him.

I grabbed his hand and pulled. "Sit up, you arrogant sylph."

He grimaced and gasped as he levered his torso off the ground. I pulled with every iota of strength I had left, grinding my teeth against the pains webbing out through my shoulders and back. When he achieved a semi-erect sitting position, I waddled to his side and threw his arm around my shoulders, linking us with my arm around his waist.

He flailed a hand out to brace himself on the car and, with our combined strength, we hefted him to his feet. His wheezing had gotten worse. After much grunting and shuffling of feet, we got him to the back door. I pushed him inside and he flopped onto the seat on his back. His feet stuck out the door, so I shoved them inside, urging him to bend his knees.

He gazed at me with bloodshot, bleary eyes. "This is pointless. I'm… already d—"

"No. You are not dead yet, buster, so don't go giving up on me." I straightened, my hand on the door. "And that is a command."

I slammed the door.

Something whooshed overhead.

I glanced up to see a raven spiraling down toward me.

By the time I shut the driver's door and cranked the key in the ignition, Brennus had landed in the parking lot, morphing into humanoid form in a heartbeat. He positioned his gigantic bulk directly in front of the car.

I jammed the gear shift lever into reverse and floored the accelerator. The car rocketed backward. Gravel pelted the undercarriage. I jammed the car into drive and rammed my foot down, wrenching the wheel to the left as the car shot forward.

The front bumper nicked Brennus.

We blasted out of the parking lot onto the highway.

In the rearview mirror, I watched Brennus morph back into a bird and take off after us. How fast could a magical raven fly? I was about to find out.

The boundary. I only had to get us past the boundary.

Which would kill Nevan.

I pounded my fist on the wheel. What the fuck was I supposed to do?

For the first time, I prayed Skeiron was right. I prayed to be the Janusite.

A weight crashed onto the car above my head, denting it inward. A talon punched through the roof.

The speedometer breezed past seventy, then eighty, as the car rocketed down the highway. The yellow lines blurred, the trees blurred, everything mutated into a surreal blankness. Less than a mile to go.

The raven hurtled into the driver's window. The glass fractured into a gummy screen.

Through the blur surrounding the car, I spotted a familiar yellow shape. The highway sign. The mile marker.

Brennus struck the glass one more time. His talons pierced the gummy mass, then retracted.

We barreled past the boundary.

CHAPTER TWENTY

I GRIPPED THE STEERING WHEEL IN BOTH HANDS, HANGING ON AS I VEERED around a curve too fast. The car swerved over the center line, but I wrenched the wheel in the other direction, my muscles burning from the strain of it, and the car eased back into the right lane. I checked the rearview mirror.

Brennus, no longer a bird, hulked in the center of the road near the highway marker, just inside the mystical border. We'd passed the boundary—safe, for the moment.

I wrenched the wheel and jammed the brake pedal down to the floorboard. The car fishtailed and stopped amid a hail of gravel. I twisted around to peer into the backseat.

Nevan lay prone with his eyes shut and both knees bent, legs askew, one arm hanging off the seat. I snatched up his hand and felt for a pulse in his wrist. It thumped against my fingers, weak but there. What the hell was I going to do now? I'd had no time to formulate a plan. Sheer panic had driven me to action.

A healing vortex. That's what I needed.

We'd resurrected Brad with the one at the shop, but I didn't dare go back inside the boundary. Not that particular boundary, anyway. One very ticked-off sylph lay in wait for me there. I should've shot him in the head, right between the eyes. It might not have killed him, but it could've bought me more time.

Nevan had told my parents there were other portals, near other water features. I knew of another waterfall a few miles from here. Christ. *Miles.* Did Nevan have that much time?

No choice.

I floored the accelerator and the car hurtled onto the asphalt. The force of our takeoff pinned me to my seat. The car weaved, the wheel jerking in my hands, until I got a firm grip and evened out the vehicle's trajectory. Scenery zipped past. The headlights punched through the darkness like twin swords annihilating the night, though at the periphery, shadows of every shape and size lurked. They seemed to writhe and jump from the car's dizzying speed. At first, I jumped at each faux surprise—until a strange numbness set in, affecting me down to my bones. I navigated on autopilot, my mind incapable of any thought except getting to the waterfall.

Roaring around a curve, I spun the wheel to slalom my car around another vehicle. My body was slung one way, then the other. Back in my lane, I risked a quick glance into the backseat.

Nevan was sprawled as before. Eyes shut. Lifeless.

No, not lifeless. Unconscious. *Remember that. You can't afford to freak out every time you look at him.*

I concentrated on the road, both hands on the wheel, my knuckles white. Nobody was losing anybody tonight.

How far had I driven? The miles blurred the same as the road. I let up on the gas pedal and the speedometer eased downward. Seventy. Sixty.

The landscape was familiar. Not far now.

Nudging the accelerator, I pushed the car back up to eighty. The road curved left and right, forcing me to ease off the gas. My heart pounded. A cold sweat dribbled down my temples. Almost there.

The headlights flared across an asphalt driveway up ahead. A big, blue road sign announced "Rest Stop." This time I stood on the brake pedal, terrified to miss the turn and have to double back in the dark, on this narrow highway. I veered the car into the semicircular drive and parked it in front of the shed that housed the restrooms. The car was angled across three parking spaces, but nobody was here in the dead of night. By rote, I shifted the car into park, shut off the engine, and stuffed the keys in my pants pocket. The headlights stayed on, but outside their reach, full-on dark had swallowed the earth.

I retrieved a flashlight from the glove compartment, kicked the driver's door open, leaped out, and tore the passenger door open.

Nevan lay so still. His head lolled. One arm dangled off the seat with his fingertips grazing the floorboard. Blood still trickled from his wound, down his side and onto the floor.

When I shoved a finger into his neck at the pulse point, a weak beat pushed against my flesh. Relief nearly toppled me to the ground.

I needed to move him, but how? I hadn't been able to carry him by myself before, and even with his aid it had taken all my strength. A fatigue deeper than any I'd known before weakened my limbs, far worse than before. The adrenaline spike I'd experienced back in the clearing had drained away when I needed it the most.

"No!" I screamed it into the night, collapsing against the door, and glared up at the stars. "I could use some fucking help down here!"

As the echoes of my screams spiraled down into silence, I detected another sound.

The soft rumble of a waterfall.

I jerked upright. *Of course, you moron, that's why you came here.*

To heal Brad, we'd required a leprechaun's help. And elementals—fae, whatever—possessed far more strength than I did, not to mention nifty magical powers for zipping here and there. Locating a leprechaun meant traveling into the other realm on my own. Could I even open a portal without Nevan's help?

Well, I'd transported Nevan across the boundary and he was still alive. Maybe I was the Janusite, or maybe things weren't as black-and-white as these supernatural types believed. I had to try.

My gaze lanced down to Nevan. I'd have to leave him here, alone, while I hunted down a willing elemental.

A sharp pain stabbed at the back of my throat.

Bent over the seat with one knee on the floorboards, I brushed my fingers over Nevan's cheek. My hair fell around his head like a curtain. His customary heat was fading, with a chill seeping in behind it.

"I'll be back soon. Don't you go anywhere." Though his face was blank, I imagined his smirk and that sultry chuckle every time he'd teased me for saying dopey things. I touched my lips to his forehead. "I'll fix this, promise."

Without allowing myself to think anymore, I shut the door and clicked on the flashlight as I ran for the waterfall. No trail led down to it. Instead, a railing made of driftwood barred the way and a big wooden sign offered historical information on the site. I clambered over the barrier. My left boot caught on the uneven wood. I cursed, the noise bouncing off the trees, and shook my foot loose.

I bolted toward the falls. The water cascaded down from maybe ten feet above the ground, onto a flat landing of sorts that tapered into a small, shallow pool.

My boots slid on the slick rock as I sidled across the landing, my back flat against the cliff. In my left hand I clutched the flashlight, while with my right I clawed at the rock wall in search of support I didn't really need. At the falls, I stepped away from the cliff and squinted into the darkness. My flashlight penetrated the thin veil of water.

No cave. A solid wall of rock backed the falls.

My head spun, and for more seconds than my wits could stand, I waited out the vertigo. I still felt lightheaded, but at least I wouldn't trip and crack my skull on the rock landing.

You should exercise more care, darlin', or you'll crack that lovely head of yours.

Nevan's words to me the first time I'd seen him replayed in my brain. A sharp sob burst out of me. The flashlight clattered to the ground. I slapped both palms on the cliff face, through the water, oblivious to the cold liquid that sprayed up in my face and inundated my hands, my arms, my ankles, my boots.

Water is the doorway. Nevan had said that too.

Not *the waterfall is the door*, but water itself. Had that been what he meant?

I pushed away from the wall. Snagged the flashlight. Clamped my hand around it. Turned away from the falls.

The pool appeared shallow, probably similar to the deep end of a swimming pool. I really could crack my skull, if I was wrong about this. Time for a genuine leap of faith.

Drawing in a long breath, I held it. Now or never.

I leaped into the water.

My feet punched through the surface. Water erupted around me. I plunged into the pool, sinking deeper and deeper, flailing my arms, struggling against the overpowering urge to suck in a breath.

Up, down, left, right—my mind fought to sort out the directions but failed. I twirled round and round, starved for air, chest aching from my thunderous heartbeat and the urgency to breathe. Oh God, I would die here, in this pool, alone.

Images flashed in my mind, bright and fast. My parents. My baby brother. The rock shop. Travis. Nevan.

He would die because of me. Because I failed.

My lungs screamed for oxygen. I released the breath I'd held, shooting out a cloud of bubbles. Pressure built inside me until I feared my lungs might explode. One final, anguished plea echoed in my mind. *I don't want to die.*

A vision of Nevan's face hovered in front of me, glowing with ethereal light. The soothing energy of his presence streamed into me.

The beam of my flashlight, still gripped in my hand, speared down to the pool's bottom.

I fought the impulse to inhale, but it grew stronger every second.

Open up, you stupid portal.

As my body dived toward the bottom, the ground crumbled away below me. An oily blackness churned like a whirlpool, its spiraling eddies interwoven with iridescent green and purple. The pull of the portal dragged me down faster, faster, as my limbs stretched taut and pain coruscated through me. Just as I lost the battle to not breathe, I launched through the surface into the open air, bobbing like an empty bottle. I gulped in mouthfuls of air. Nothing had ever tasted so delicious or felt so wonderful. Water streamed off my hair, rolling down my face in rivulets. I blinked to clear my eyes.

Night enveloped me, but a faint, milky glow sifted through it.

Head bent back, I panted and stared at the double moons—one large, one small—smiling down at me from a sky speckled with more stars than I'd ever seen from the mortal realm.

I swam to shore. My flashlight lanced across the alien landscape and straight up into the sky. A new burst of energy shored up my body, fueling my muscles as I hauled myself out of the water and onto my feet.

Now to find a damn leprechaun.

My jaw hurt, which made me realize I was gritting my teeth. I chewed my lip instead, drilling my brain for answers. I knew of one leprechaun, but we'd found Tris by going through the other waterfall. Everything looked different here.

When I'd screamed for Nevan, he'd heard me and come to my rescue. Might the same tactic work with a different elemental?

I threw my head back and yelled, "Tris, you obnoxious little twerp, get your ass out here this instant."

Seconds that dragged like minutes ticked by on my mental clock. Ten. Fifteen. Nothing happened.

Nevan was dying, all alone on the other side. I'd gotten him past the boundary, halting Brennus's pursuit.

The boundary.

Everything inside me froze. Since I'd brought him to another waterfall, that meant we'd traveled inside another boundary. Brennus and Skeiron might've found him already.

No. They couldn't have guessed which waterfall I'd taken Nevan to, or that I took him to any kind of portal. I needed to cling to the positive thought, because otherwise I'd fall apart.

I shined my flashlight into the inky woods. No leprechaun yet.

Screw this.

I screamed, like a teenage girl riding her first roller coaster. I shrieked Tris's name, railing epithets into the night.

My cries slid back into wordless, blood-curdling screams, the likes of which had never busted out of me before in my life. I screamed until my throat burned, until my voice cracked, until—

Tris materialized in front of me.

Gasping for breath, I choked off my wail. My throat scorched like sandpaper set on fire.

The leprechaun screwed up his mouth, brows knit and lowered in a sullen expression. "What the hell do you want, lady? You're waking up the whole neighborhood."

"To hell with your friends," I croaked. "You're the only one I need."

"Here I thought you were hot for the sylph. Hate to break it to you, sister, but you ain't my type." He waved at my breasts. "Too busty."

"You little worm." I stomped straight up to him, stabbing my finger into his chest. He winced the tiniest bit. "I don't have time for your bullshit. Nevan is dying."

His brows smoothed out and an emotion flickered across his face, but I had no brainpower left to decipher it. He stuffed his hands in the pockets of his ripped jeans. "What's it got to do with me?"

I bent to glare into his eyes, our faces so close my breaths reflected off his skin. "You are going to heal him with the vortex."

"Ain't no vortex here, lady."

I shuffled back a step. "What?"

"No vortex." He enunciated with exaggerated care, as if speaking to a dimwit.

I felt dimwitted at this moment, and devoid of all hope. But I could not—would not—give up. "There's a waterfall. I brought him here, I nearly drowned crossing the fucking veil, and you're telling me it was all for nothing?" I grabbed the collar of his flannel shirt, hauling him into me. My lips scraped his as I hissed words at him. "You find a way to heal him or I will rip your dried-up, repulsive, festering little heart right out of your chest."

He stopped blinking. Stopped breathing. Stopped fighting and just stared at me.

"Do you hear me?" I shook him hard enough to rattle his brain. "Do you?"

"Yeah," he said slowly, his voice hushed. "I hear you, but…"

"What?"

He shrank a little, shoulders bunching. "There really ain't a vortex here, I'm sorry. We'd have to somehow get him to where there is one."

"Not the one where I first met you. Skeiron is there, or he was, and he's pissed." Understatement of the millennium. "I don't think Skeiron's dead, but even if he is, Brennus would be waiting for us there."

"Skeiron? Brennus? Holy cripes, lady, feed me to the hell hounds and get it over with. I can't fight those two."

"You don't have to." A retched thought took hold and I squinted at Tris. "Are you working for Skeiron? Is that why you won't save Nevan?"

"Working for him?" Tris blew air through his lips. "He massacred a whole coven of fae witches to steal their power. No fae helps him—ever."

"Unless he tricked you into a bargain."

One corner of his mouth ticked up in a half smirk. "He can't. We made a group bargain not to deal with Skeiron, and trust me, we worded it so no stinking sylph can get around it."

Though I couldn't focus on his words, though part of me understood.

I shoved him away. "Get Nevan to another vortex and *fix him*."

"Yeah-yeah, okay." Tris raised his hands, palms out. "I know of another one, a good strong vortex. I'll have to, um…" He twirled one finger in the air. "You know, uh, kinda get us there the magical way."

"Whisk us through the tunnel thingy. Fine, I don't give a damn, just do it."

"Well, ya see, I ain't eaten lately."

I shook my fists in the air. "Then eat some goddamn copper."

"Got none."

"Nevan is dying."

"Sorry, I can't do nothing without fuel." He cringed, as if expecting me to explode.

Which I'd done constantly since summoning him. I drew in a breath, letting it out little by little, and fought for self-control. Easier said than done. My entire body had begun to shake with a combination of terror and fury. Still, I managed a calmer tone when I spoke again. "Zip over to the rock shop, you'll find plenty of copper there."

"All right." He eyed me askance, leaning back. "You better come with me. Never know who you might've woken up with your hollering."

The thought of Nevan breached my panic. He'd be as safe where he was as anywhere, and besides, I had no other options.

Tris cautiously stretched out a hand to me. I took it. Nevan had always embraced me for traveling this way, but the instant my hand touched Tris's, he zipped us away. We materialized in the darkened shop, my flashlight illuminating the interior.

My trip with Tris proved Nevan hadn't needed to hug me for traveling. He must've wanted to do it that way. The realization made my chest ache.

Tris and I scurried around the shop gathering every kind of copper available—nuggets, fist-size chunks, jewelry fashioned from the stuff, and a pair of copper ore bookends like the ones Brad stole.

Brad. He was dead forever this time.

Nevan would be soon too, if we didn't hurry the hell up.

In one hand, Tris grasped the plastic shopping bag we'd laden with copper items. Before I could pester him, he snagged my hand and transported us to my car, where it was parked at the rest stop. I tore the back door open and knelt at Nevan's head. Tears fuzzed my vision and tightened my throat. I clamped my teeth over both lips, clasped Nevan's cold hand in mine, and looked at Tris. His hand still held mine.

"The vortex," I said through my teeth. "Now."

No griping. No eye rolling. He zipped us away from the car, into a forest much like the one around the shop and the other waterfall. Were we still in the Keweenaw? In Michigan? I didn't give a crap anymore. Nothing mattered except saving Nevan.

He lay at my feet, crumpled on the ground. The moss-covered earth squished under my boots as I moved to Nevan's side and crouched there, his hand still enclosed in mine. I clasped our hands to my heart.

Tris inched backward away from me.

Wherever we were, this clearing had no sign declaring the area a healing vortex, no stone benches, nothing except empty space ringed by the woods.

The leprechaun squatted, ripping open the shopping bag. He wolfed down copper ore in whole chunks, only resorting to biting off mouthfuls when he got down to the bookends. Ore dust rained from his lips, coating his clothing and sprinkling onto the mossy ground, as his teeth pulverized the rock in quick time. When he'd finished, he wadded up the bag and jammed it in his pocket. Then he rose and rolled back his shoulders.

His blue eyes gleamed, twin supernovas of cobalt blue.

And he just stood there.

My frustration exploded out of me on a breath. I flapped my arms, trying to get his attention, but he gazed off into nothing. "What is wrong with you? Wake up, dammit."

"Something hinky's going on," he said, sounding drugged. "Funky energy's interfering, and I can't get past it." His gaze cleared and zeroed in on me. "It's you."

"That's—" I stopped, my mouth still open. Nevan said time passed slower in the Unseen because magic must've been interfering with it. He'd suggested the energy he sensed in me had been responsible. Now Tris made a similar claim, but I didn't give a damn what the cause was. "How can we fix this?"

"No frigging clue. Maybe a b—" The color flooded out of his face. "Forget it. There ain't no way."

I slunk closer to him. "A bargain. That's what you almost said."

"No way." He blundered backward, tripped on a rock. "If I power up the vortex from this side of the water, I have to pull in a piece of the Unseen realm to do it. In essence, we are in my world."

So a bargain...*Shit.*

"Can't let you do it, lady." He twisted his shirt around his fingers, glancing down at Nevan. "He'd kill me if I did."

My gaze fell to Nevan. His pale face. Those sensual lips now a frightening shade of blue-white. The blood on his chest. The gaping wound.

Flashbacks raced through my mind. Nevan taking me away when Travis was chasing me. Nevan's body curled around mine as I slept. The way he insisted I eat and brought me tempting foods to ensure I did. His lips on mine, tender and then ravenous with passion. The vow he'd made to my mother, that he would protect me at any cost. I squeezed my hands around his. If his death was the cost, I could not let him pay it. My hands trembled. *Nothing else matters.*

I rolled my eyes up to fixate on Tris. "If you heal him, I will give you anything you want."

"Aw, lady, are you nuts?"

"Probably. Do we have a deal?"

Tris's gaze darted to Nevan and doubt flickered on his face. His shoulders hunched. "Oh man, if I let you do this, he'll murder me for sure."

"I won't let him." I lifted my chin, trying for self-assurance I didn't feel. "Here's the bargain. If you restore Nevan to his normal state, healing all his wounds and bringing him back to consciousness, I will give you anything you want and I'll stop Nevan from hurting you. Agreed?"

"You sure about this?"

"Quit hemming and hawing."

He gave a curt nod. "I accept your terms."

A tether of power whipped between me and Tris, the unseen ends latching onto us with a jolt. Bargain sealed.

"Do it already," I said. "Uphold your end."

Tris closed his eyes.

Energy roiled off him in coppery, glittering tentacles. They nipped at my skin, zapped into me down to the core of my being. The tentacles gyrated around the three of us, diving into the ground, spewing out of it again, encompassing Nevan until the shimmering energy obscured his entire body, except for the arm I clutched to my breast.

I shut my eyes and prayed, like I never had before. I infused my silent prayers with every ounce of anguish and hope I harbored inside me.

Nevan's hand warmed in mine.

The snapping energy dissipated.

I cracked my eyelids to peek out through my lashes. Nevan rested on the ground as before, but his bronze coloring had returned. His hand in mine had grown warmer, feeding into me that precious, intoxicating heat.

My tears flowed, unfettered.

Tris cleared his throat. "Seeing how my job's done, I'm gonna split. He can get you wherever you need to be."

Without looking away from Nevan, I said, "Okay. Thank you."

"For crying out loud, lady. Gratitude too? You better keep up your end, 'cause if he comes after me, I'm calling in your debt."

He vanished.

Nevan's fingers twitched. I lifted them to my lips and kissed them one by one.

A moan emanated from him.

Was he still injured? Damn that leprechaun. I spread my palms on his chest, running them over his skin in broad circles. The wound was gone. Only the old scar over his heart remained.

My tears splattered onto his chest.

"Why are you crying, love?"

At his words, I burst into a fit of weeping.

Nevan sat up, folding his arms around me, and pulled me onto his lap. I hugged my hands to my chest, burying my face in his neck, and let his heat banish the chill. He stroked my hair and rocked me as he murmured soothing sounds. Gradually, my weeping subsided. He kept rocking me, his arms firm but gentle around my shoulders.

His body squashed my arms to my chest. I wrestled my hands free to hold his face in my palms. "You're alive."

"Was I dead? Didn't feel like it."

"Not quite, but—" His hands traveled down to my hips. I couldn't move my hands, his skin felt too good under them. "It took so long to get you here, to this vortex. I got us away from Brennus, but then I had to find Tris and he needed copper and—"

His fingers kneading my flesh scattered my thoughts.

"It's all right." His voice was a low rumble, unbelievably sexy. "I'm quite impressed you got me here without Skeiron beheading us both." He ran his hands over my shoulders and down my arms—searching for wounds, I supposed. "Did he or Brennus hurt you in any way?"

"I'm fine." I raked my hands up the back of his neck and into his hair, my fingers splayed over his scalp. "How are you?"

"I feel quite well, very alive."

The way he accentuated the last word flashed heat through me, from my lips straight down between my thighs. I wriggled on his lap, relishing the sensation of hard muscle as it rubbed against my aching core. An impulse hit me and I had no willpower left to resist.

I drew his head down to mine and crushed my lips to his. He yielded to me without hesitation, his lips parting for me. I forged deep inside, lost to the sensations of his tongue, his mouth, his hands anchoring my waist. He groaned into my mouth. I devoured him as if our essences could merge through our lips joining and our tongues tangling. I kissed him like nothing else in the universe mattered to me, nothing except him and this heady passion.

He broke the kiss, his flaming eyes locked on mine.

Dazed, I couldn't prevent the words from spilling out unbidden, hushed enough he couldn't have heard. "Rein it in, Lindsey."

He leaped to his feet, carrying me up with him. I landed flat on my feet.

The flashlight's beam sprayed across the ground in a wedge of illumination, aimed right at Nevan. I backed away, bereft from the loss of contact, but I needed to see him, all of him, to be sure.

The flashlight flickered and extinguished. I snatched it up, shook it, thumped the heel of my hand against it. Nothing. I made an unladylike, disgusted noise.

"What is the matter, my sweet mortal morsel?"

"Flashlight's dead. I can't see a thing."

"I can see you." The statement, his teasing but sensual tone, tickled me in the most intimate way.

"You might still be injured. I need to..." How could I phrase this without sounding salacious? Oh hell, who cared. "I need to get a good look at you. Please."

"If you insist."

Balls of light popped into existence in his palms. They swelled into softball-size orbs, bluish and sparkling with the purest white.

Fairy lights.

He tossed them into the air, where they floated above our heads. He conjured a half dozen more, tossing them into the air so we were immersed in the shimmering glow.

And I saw him. All of him.

"Here I am, love," he said, devouring me with his hot gaze. "What will you do with me now?"

CHAPTER TWENTY-ONE

THE FAIRY LIGHTS TWINKLED ABOVE OUR HEADS, BATHING US BOTH IN silvery light. The six feet of space separating us glittered with incandescence, from the droplets of energy showering down from the lights. The air sizzled faintly.

And there, like a mirage in the forest, stood Nevan.

I roamed my gaze up and down his length, soaking in every muscular inch of bare flesh. I'd intended do nothing more than verify his wounds had healed, but I couldn't stop the heat pooling inside me, low down, in places I'd ignored for far too long. My attention wandered to his chest, that dazzling expanse of bronzed skin. My hands ached to explore him, to map out the contours of his body with my fingertips. I licked my lower lip, slowly, envisioning my tongue on his neck, licking my way down to—

"Are ye quite finished, love?"

Nevan's voice, rife with self-satisfaction, snapped me back to reality. Sort of. The damned fire in my nether regions had coalesced into a deep, throbbing tingle. The sensation robbed me of my breath and stripped away my senses, until I had a hell of a time hauling my mind out of the fantasy. Maybe it didn't have to stay a fantasy. Just for tonight, maybe I could release my fears and dive into Nevan's embrace, into his kiss, into…everything. Maybe.

An old saying popped into my head, the phrase sailors of the olden days used to describe what lay beyond the horizon—*there be monsters here*. The ghost of Calder, real or imagined, was my monster. Nevan was my horizon, but I was too chicken to go there.

I folded my arms over my chest, proud of my physical composure in the face of hormone overload, and gestured at him with one finger. "You look fine."

But oh, he looked way better than fine.

A memory exploded in my mind—Nevan, prostrate on the ground, a sword jammed into his chest, blood pouring out. A jolt of dizziness rocked me and I zeroed in on his torso again. Though I saw nothing aside from his scar, not a scratch or scrape, doubt niggled in my gut. "Is the pain gone? Are you sure you're completely healed?"

"I told ye already, I'm quite fine." He flashed a wicked grin. "But hadn't ye better check for yourself? I understand mortals conduct physical examinations after an injury."

"I—well yes, but—" A blush fired up in my cheeks, so hot aliens on distant planets must've spotted the glow. *Rein it in, Lindsey.* "I'll take your word for it."

Nevan shook his head, rolled his eyes, and sighed. I struggled to hold back a smile. He did "exasperation personified" so well.

Hands clasped behind his back, he began to pace in a circle around me, his strides long and purposeful, fluid and masculine. The hunter stalking his prey. He watched me with each step, and even when he crossed behind me, his gaze flared across my skin, stoking an awareness deep inside. Half of me relished the thought of being the sole focus of his concentration. The other half wanted to bolt, hide, pretend I hadn't broken my own decree that we never kiss again. I'd thrown myself at him in the most humiliating way. I'd done more than kiss him. I'd drowned myself in him.

And lord, had it felt *good.*

But it was a mistake. Calder had taught me that lesson.

Nevan's footfalls shooshed on the grass, the skin of his ankles glistening with dew. He circled around me again, and again, and again, inching closer with each circuit. The playful sylph had retreated, submerged beneath the ancient warrior. Though I'd glimpsed this part of him a few times, when others provoked him, now I had triggered his feral, possessive instincts.

I fidgeted, but did not move my feet. "What are you doing?"

"Thinking."

"About…"

"You." He smiled, that thousand-watt smile, the one that zapped me with an electrical shock every time he beamed it at me. "I've thought of little else since first I saw you."

"Which would be three months ago, when you were pretending to be somebody else."

"Nice try." He crossed behind me, out of sight, yet I felt him prowling ever closer. "I won't let you reshape this conversation to your own comfort. This will unfold as I design it, not you."

"Whatever you say, Mr. Bossy Pants."

Though he arched an eyebrow, he kept pacing. *Shoosh, shoosh, shoosh.*

I let myself admire the view when he passed in front of me again. Never before had I enjoyed an unimpeded, uninterrupted view of him in motion, those muscular thighs working, his loincloth shifting a little with each step, stretching taut over the bulge of his cock.

The shooshing stopped. He stopped. Behind me. Watching.

Every cell on the backside of me electrified, a million microscopic circuits zinging an erotic current straight down to my core. I gulped, not sure why, and bundled my arms around myself, then dropped them to my sides, my fingers twitching in a restless rhythm. "What are you doing?"

"What would you like me to be doing?"

"I don't know."

He stepped into my peripheral vision. I wanted to look, but my head refused to budge. He exhaled a long, languid sigh that rippled shivers down my spine. When he spoke, his tone was thick and molten. "You kissed me."

I snorted out a nervous laugh. "Yeah, I'm aware of that."

Damn if my voice didn't quiver the slightest bit. *Get a grip, woman.*

In two long strides, he moved in front of me, turned, and whirled on me. Ten feet, maybe twelve, separated our bodies, yet the gravity of his presence pulled at my atoms.

He canted his head. "You made me vow never to kiss you again, to keep my lips away from yours at all times. Then you kissed me, and not a simple kiss, but the wanton kind that compels a man to reach certain conclusions."

"I didn't mean to lead you on."

"You've led me nowhere. I've been dragging you here by the hair."

I did a double take. Seriously, I did. He dragged me? Never. He'd been gentle, careful, respectful. And yes, erotic as hell. But never, ever rough with me. Yet to him our little dance had clearly seemed like an ordeal. He didn't look annoyed, though. Curious, maybe. Predatory. Possessive, in a way that liquefied my resolve.

He ran his tongue over his lower lip, slowly, sensuously. "You broke your own vow. I want to know why."

"Maybe I changed my mind."

"You realize what this means."

Yeah, I'm a lust-drunk moron. "Why don't you spit out whatever it is you're trying to say and stop making me guess."

"You want me."

I laughed, but it came out as a frantic giggle. Even the densest man would've picked up on the subtle clues to the non-mystery of my attraction to him.

He shrugged one shoulder, undulating all that taut flesh. "It's all right. I want you too. Which is why I'm not letting you 'rein it in' this time."

My heart stopped. I know it did. I'm pretty sure every clock on earth stopped ticking too. He must've heard me mumble those words—*rein it in*—under my breath, to myself, after I kissed him.

"Let it go." His voice was the purring of a cougar.

My heart started up again with an agonizing thud.

Nevan strode toward me, narrowing the gap between us to inches. The vision of him, of his muscles pulsating with each movement and the tiny loincloth straining to cover him, devoured my focus. For the first time in my life, I craved a man with a passion so intense nothing could quench it. Nothing except for his body.

An icy ribbon of fear unfurled in my chest. I teetered on the precipice, more than ever before, nudged there by lust and…affection? Yeah, okay, I liked him. Hard not to like a man who'd taken a sword to the chest for me. It was nothing more than…a mild fondness and immense gratitude. Expressing either sentiment posed risks I didn't care to take.

He lifted a hand, grazing it over my arm with the barest touch, and my breath caught. The heat of him radiated over my skin as he wrapped his arms around me, tugging me tight into his lithe, firm body. I drew in a long breath, savoring the scent of him—earth and grass, with a hint of sharp sweetness evocative of onrushing thunderstorms. He always smelled of the elements, but then what did I expect from a sylph? He was, he'd told me, forged from the air and earth. I should've pulled away, the impulse pulled at me, but a stronger need overpowered it. The need to relent. Drop those blasted reins. Give in.

His breaths caressed my ear as his voice murmured, "You're tensing up again. Why must you do that? Do ye really believe I'll harm ye?"

"No." I said it without thinking. And my eyes were closed. Damn, when did that happen? I commanded my lids to open, but they disobeyed.

His lips brushed the shell of my ear, his breath teasing the inside, while his hands skimmed the hairs on my arms. "You are glorious, Lindsey, a goddess in disguise. Instead of hiding under this brittle armor, you ought to shake it off and bask in the sun. With me." His mouth slid lower, his teeth nipping my lobe. "How about it?"

"I—" Christ. I'd made so many mistakes, survived too many disasters, to believe losing control had no consequences. "You might change your mind."

"About what?" His voice was low, sultry.

"Me. I'm not…like this. Not like all those other women you've been with."

"The others were nothing compared to you."

"I'm a repressed, scaredy-cat virgin. Remember?"

He laughed, his lips trembling over the skin under my ear. "You are strong and clever, braver than the most powerful elemental, and—" He cupped one hand on my right cheek, turning my face into his. My lips met his cheek, sending a flaming shudder down my body. "And you are the most desirable woman in any realm. If you stop holding back, you'll realize just how glorious you are. Unleash your passion. I won't let you fall."

My heart pounded so hard and fast I thought the blood might burst my veins. "You don't know what you're asking. I'm not capable of it."

His head moved, his hands too, releasing me. "Open your eyes."

I did. Though measured in inches, the gulf between us seemed wider than the universe.

Nevan studied me with thoughtful interest, his gaze roaming the length and breadth of me. "You seem quite capable to me."

His eyes lured me in and bound my focus to him.

I stuffed my hands in my jeans pockets. Anything to stop my fingers from stretching out to explore his flesh. I had to step away, right this second, but my legs disagreed. "Look, I know you'll panic if I express any you-know-what, but you did save my life and, well, I…" Struggling for a way to thank him without thanking him, I grumbled. "Screw this. We're still in my world, so I'm going to say it. Thank—"

His mouth smothered my words. His lips moved over mine, pressing and releasing, capturing my lower lip, then setting it free. My traitorous hands twitched in my pockets, hungry for the feel of his skin. I wanted him. I needed control. I ached to unleash my body and soul. I had to shield myself.

Nevan parted his lips from mine, though just enough to speak. "Do you recall the pot and the kettle?"

"Yes." Our previous conversation, about pots calling kettles black, didn't seem relevant here.

He backed away one pace. I fought the urge to haul him back, and as if he sensed my inner battle, his mouth slid into a knowing smile. "What does the kettle do, love?"

"Huh?" In my head, I ran a quick replay of our earlier discussion. "Oh. Right. It steams. But I don't understand why we're talking about this."

"That's why. Because you don't understand." He slanted his head, eying my breasts with a ravenous gleam. "A kettle releases its steam. You're a pot, keeping everything locked under a tight lid, boiling away, building up pressure. What you don't seem to comprehend is that you've got to let some of it off, or the pressure will blow you apart." His focus shifted to my eyes, intent and unwavering. "I'd hate to see that happen to you."

"I can't change what I am."

"Sure ye can. Decide to become a kettle."

I huffed out an annoyed sigh. "This is the most ridiculous metaphor ever and I'm sorry I ever mentioned pots or kettles. I'm a person, a very, very screwed up person who can't just decide to become a—" I threw my hands up. "A kettle or whatever. Pots are pots, end of story. I wouldn't even know how to do what you're suggesting."

"Losing control is easy, darlin'. With the proper motivation."

Without taking a single step, he reached across the distance and dragged me into his arms, pinning my hands to his chest between our bodies. One of his arms locked me there. The other raised as he thrust a hand into my hair and forced me to look up at him. "You, my glorious goddess, can be anything you choose to be."

"Why do you care what I am?"

Amusement sparkled in his eyes and dimpled his cheeks. "Because you matter."

I yearned to believe he meant what my heart prayed he did, but his vagueness left too much doubt. "I matter because your king wants to kill me. Otherwise, someone like you wouldn't look once at me, much less twice."

"I've looked at you a thousand times, seeing the woman, the goddess, the frightened little rabbit, and everything else in between."

"But why? Why me?"

"I'll tell ye later, when you'll be receptive to the answer." His tongue danced across my lips.

"Uhhh..." It was all I could manage to say.

All around us, a breeze rustled the aspen trees. Their leaves rattled, pattering like rain. The sensual sound rippled the tingling through my entire body, from my loins to my scalp, and straight down to my toes. His fingers massaged my scalp in lazy, gentle strokes. His voice dropped to a seductive whisper. "Steam for me, Lindsey."

I drank in the sound of the words, letting them course through my veins, intoxicating me with every syllable. *Steam for me.* The heat pulsed inside me, a driving force too powerful to fight, and I didn't want to anymore, the craving was too intense, the pressure more than I could stand. I let his body brace me, my knees trembling, and for once, I didn't even try to clamp a lid on the passion escalating inside me.

Nevan stroked his hands up and down my back, dipping his head to whisper his breaths over my mouth. I lowered my head to his chest, grazing my lips over the centuries-old scar across his heart. He shuddered. This big, strong, elemental man—my bronzed god, the hero who'd saved my life over and over—shuddered at my touch.

I tilted my head back to gaze at his face, at the lines fanning out from his half-closed eyes. He'd gone stiff, his hands tense as they settled on my hips. Maybe I'd embarrassed him by touching his scar in that way. But no, I could not believe I had the power to embarrass a man who lived in a loincloth and excited every nerve in my body simply by speaking my name in a sultry, husky voice. Just in case I was wrong, in case he was the one in need of relaxation this time, I tapped his chest with one finger. "Is your heart still in there? I mean, you said Skeiron cut you when he cursed your heart, so..."

His chuckle rumbled in his chest, vibrating into me. The tension softened, his hands tugging my hips into him. "Yes, darlin', I've still got the bloody thing."

"Why is your heart a bloody thing?"

"Because it's given me naught save agony. Until tonight." He hooked his thumb under my chin, lifting it, and ducked his head near to mine. His breaths, hot and enticing, teased me and I burned to taste him, to take his breath into my body and meld with him. He bent closer, our lips brushing. "Let's not start with the questions again. I can think of other, more interesting things we might do together."

No words. No thoughts. Only him.

"Say it, love."

"What?"

"You know what. The words I told ye never to speak again unless you agreed with my interpretation."

"Don't remember the words."

"Yes you do." He slipped his tongue between my lips, then withdrew. "Say it."

I did know what he was asking. He'd promised me if I spoke a certain phrase one more time, he'd accept the offer, though at the time I hadn't meant the words the way he'd implied. Right here, in this moment, I understood exactly what he needed from me. Permission.

A choice. A precipice.

I jumped.

"Nevan...take me."

His voice growled, his lips dangerously close to mine. "I will do just that, for as long as it takes, as many times as it takes, until you break apart for me and only me. Not because your fear has cracked you, but because I have won you, body and soul."

Need catapulted through me with such force I swayed in his arms. He clinched me tighter against him. His flesh scorched mine through the fabric of my T-shirt, exciting my every nerve, until my nipples hardened against him. For the first time in—oh God, how many years?—I confronted the hunger burgeoning inside me without a shred of shame to taint it.

No more fear. This is your chance to come alive again. Seize it.

I bent my head to scrape my tongue across his scar.

He tensed again.

Don't chicken out now. I dragged my tongue across the faint line of rough skin once more, tracing a damp path up his chest, over his collarbone, into the hollow above it.

He groaned.

A thrill coursed through me. He liked it. No, he *loved* it. I held power over him, despite the glib facade he often retreated into, despite the fact he could crush me with his elemental magic with a single flick of his wrist. In this moment, *I* controlled *him*. My touch ignited his passion. Why he was rock hard, and not in the way I wanted him hard, baffled me. I'd given in, hadn't I? That's what he wanted.

I skated my hands up his chest. "Shall I help you...relax?"

He hissed out a shaky breath. I had no doubts he remembered the precise context of the moment when he'd posed the same question to me.

Still, he said nothing.

I bounced up onto my tiptoes. Our eyes leveled. Currents of bronze, gold, and silver swirled within his irises, a vortex of molten metal sparking with bright red pinpoints. I let the sight entrance me for a moment, reveling in the strange beauty and naked desire in his eyes. Then I draped my arms around his neck. Shut my eyes. Hauled in a deep breath. And crushed my mouth to his.

His teeth clamped shut, blocking my tongue.

I peeled my mouth away and squinted at him.

"No," he said, without a hint of emotion.

My heart thudded and my head reeled, but not from desire. A cold emptiness sucked all the passion out of me, leaving me speechless.

His expression softened, his body relaxing at last. "I didn't mean no, darlin'."

"Well, you *said* no. And I swear if you start arguing semantics with me—"

The tips of his fingers sealed my lips. "I meant not this way. You're trying to control the situation again, and while I enjoy your efforts immensely, we're doing this my way." He danced his finger over my mouth, as his other hand massaged my hip in an intoxicating rhythm. "You, my little kettle, will be the one losing control. This time."

He skimmed his hand across my cheek without touching my skin, his fingers awakening every little hair, and I turned my face into his palm, flicking my tongue across it. He shifted his hand down to my neck, hovering his flesh an aching millimeter from mine. Last time, I'd stopped him. This time…

This time. He'd said I'd be the one to lose control this time. Did that mean next time—

He swept his lips across mine, shattering my thoughts. His mouth claimed mine, and with one thrust of his tongue, I was gone, consumed by the passion exploding between us. He sank his hand into my hair and bent my head back, delving deeper into my mouth, his tongue soft and slick, demanding my surrender. I relinquished everything to him, giddy with the freedom of it, exploring him with wild strokes of my tongue.

He released my hair and grasped my buttocks. His mouth fused to mine, he hoisted me off the ground, my hips pinned to his groin. A long, low moan resonated inside my chest, up my throat, straight into his mouth. His chest heaved. One of his hands lunged under my shirt. The rasping of his palm against my skin shot a white-hot bolt of desire into my core. I raked my hands through his hair, gripping the back of his head, forcing him closer as I feasted on the flavor of him.

His arousal swelled against my sensitive mound, activating all my nerves at once. I flung my legs around him, desperate to take him inside, even through my jeans. I didn't care, couldn't think, my every inhibition flapping around me in tatters.

He tore his mouth from mine, panting, his cock jutting into me. "This won't do at all. Can't have ye screaming my name in the woods again, for anyone to hear." He ground his hips into me and I gasped. "Only for me."

The world vanished. He whisked me through the tunnel of clawing darkness, so fast I had no time to process the journey, and out again into the moonlit night. Droplets of cold water sprayed our bodies as I clung to him. The falls rumbled beside us, silencing any question I might've asked, if I'd retained the capacity for speech or rational thought. Gripping my bottom with one hand, he slid the other up my back to secure me to him. In one swift motion, he turned and leaped through the cascade.

We touched down in the cave. Or he did. My feet dangled above the stone floor. He set me down, freeing one hand, but maintained his firm grip on my ass with the other, staking a claim and ensuring I wouldn't forget his intentions. As if I could. The proof of his intentions rubbed against me.

He waved the fingers of one outstretched hand. The doorway to the Unseen realm spiraled open, swelling and roiling. The sight of the oily, writhing blackness, and its iridescent curls of energy, constricted my throat. I'd seen it before, walked through it with him, but the portal still creeped me out.

I jerked out of his grasp. Bad idea. Now I could see every glistening inch of him, as well as the beads of water rolling down his body to drip onto the floor. It took all my willpower to resist the urge to dry him off with my mouth. "Where are you taking me?"

"To my home. Where I can keep you safe."

"You have a home?"

He glanced at me sideways. "Did ye think I lived in the bushes?"

"I never actually thought about it." Too distracted by sensual fantasies, and the occasional threat of imminent death. "Is it like a house or a cave? Maybe an underground lair?"

His full attention snapped to me, my stomach fluttering at the intensity of his stare. He curled his fingers closed. The doorway telescoped shut.

I cleared my throat. "Uh, you know, I don't think this portal thingy likes me, so maybe we should go back to the woods. Or forget the whole thing. Yeah, that's the smartest move, let's shake hands and say good night."

"No." His tone brooked no argument.

But I argued anyway. "We barely know each other, and as you've pointed out so many times, I'm horribly pent up. We should think about this."

"That's the problem. You're thinking too much." He marched to me, grabbed my ass, and hefted me off the ground. "I can remedy that."

A chill washed over me, eradicated in an instant by the fire of his flesh against my bare skin.

My bare skin? What?

I glanced down. "Oh!"

My clothes—every scrap, from the T-shirt to my panties, even my boots and socks—were gone. His loincloth had melted away too. I wobbled in his grasp and locked my arms around his shoulders for support. The friction of his skin on mine unfurled sinuous tendrils of desire in me. I was naked. With him. Against him. On him.

He exerted a light pressure to spread my thighs a few inches. It was enough. His erection slipped between my already damp thighs, torturing the swollen, aching flesh at my core. I gasped, digging my nails into his shoulders. He rocked his hips to torment me more. I tried to open myself to him, but his hands kept me locked in place. His face had turned to a mask of control, his eyes narrowed, the rest of his body as rigid as his shaft.

"Nevan." I whimpered his name.

With a faint groan, he rushed forward until my back slapped against the rock wall. His teeth nipped at the hollow of my throat, tracking down my skin with every little nip, edging nearer to the swell of my breasts. He let go, bent his head, and covered my nipple with his mouth, suckling fiercely, stunning a cry out of me. He nipped me, laved his tongue over me, sucked so hard the pleasure burst through my sex like fireworks inside me. I arched into his touch, expecting—praying—he would drive into me at long last and end my torment.

Instead, he took hold of my left thigh and hitched it over his shoulder, then did the same with the other leg. Perched on him, his face perilously close to my throbbing core, I slapped my hands on the wall, clawing for purchase but finding none. He eased me toward him, his mouth so close to my flesh, excitement intensifying every sensation. What the hell was he doing to me? I tried to squirm out of his grasp, but he held on.

"Nevan?" Fear tightened my voice.

His eyes met mine, burning, swirling, promising everything I'd denied myself—and he uttered two syllables that annihilated my inhibitions. "Trust me."

I stopped squirming. Let my body go limp. And closed my eyes.

He cradled my hips in his hands, tipped me toward him, raked his tongue across my rigid nub. Pleasure broke through me, so hot it almost hurt. His tongue licked and stroked with merciless precision, and his mouth closed over my nub to suckle with ruthless strength. I bucked against him, clutching at him, my hands digging into his hair, his scalp, urging him deeper into me. He worked his way down my cleft, inch by inch, stroke by stroke, traversing the length of me with his lips and tongue. I lost all sense of reality, as my guttural moans and feral cries echoed off the walls. Pressure escalated inside me, squeezing out whimpering pleas. His tongue thrust into me and twirled, propelled me higher, consuming me with one thrust after another, delving deeper and harder as my nails scraped his scalp.

My body convulsed with a thunderous orgasm, wave after wave of earth-shattering ecstasy ripped through me. As the exquisite pleasure settled into a dull ache, I floated away on a cloud of endorphins, higher than the moon. I was dimly aware of Nevan moving, picking me up, carrying me. By the time I drifted back down, we stood before the pulsating doorway, with me cradled in his arms. Still naked.

"Where are my clothes?" I asked absently, not really caring anymore.

"I sent them to my home. But you won't be needing clothes tonight."

My body responded to his promise, but my head battled to sort out what I'd just done. Or rather, what I'd let him do. "That was…I don't know what it was, actually. Unexpected, for sure."

"Lindsey, my love." He kissed the tip of my nose. "That's how you let go."

I grinned. Couldn't help it, though I must've looked like an idiot. I was beyond caring. Nevan had liberated me from a terrible burden, and tonight I soared with a freedom I'd never known before.

The grim concentration on his face told me how much he'd restrained in the last few minutes. I brushed my hand over his cheek. I needed to tell him something before he took me through the veil and I couldn't say it anymore. "This might sound idiotic, but I'm going to say it anyway. Thank you."

He smirked with what I took for masculine satisfaction. "Save the gratitude for after I'm finished with you."

"Finished?" It came out whiny. "Are you…That sounds kind of final."

"Ye must stop thinking the worst. I meant finished for tonight." He adjusted my weight in his arms and his erection grazed my buttocks. "I'll never be completely done with you, not if we both live to eternity."

"Okay." Two distinct syllables, divided by my crumbling will.

"What happened a moment ago, that was for you." His voice had grown raspy, strained. "Now it's my turn."

He strode through the portal.

CHAPTER TWENTY-TWO

WHISKED AWAY THE MOMENT WE EXITED THE PORTAL, I SQUEEZED MY eyes shut against the gnawing chill of the tunnel. Nevan's arms bound me to him, cradling me to his body, and I knew without any doubt he would keep his vow and never let me fall.

Light extinguished the darkness as we exited the tunnel, into the Unseen realm. Radiant warmth washed over me.

I cracked my eyes open. We stood inside a windowless room, hewn from solid rock, with smooth walls and an earthen floor. Oil lamps affixed to the walls kindled a golden glow within the space, but shadows lurked beyond the doorway at the far end of the oval-shaped chamber.

Nevan settled me onto a long bed precisely the size of one tall, sexy sylph. My feet hung suspended several inches above the floor. My bottom sank into the bedding, fashioned from something thick and plush, with a fur blanket on top. I combed my fingers through the lush, silky hairs of the blanket, loving the way my skin sensitized at the feel of it. I registered nothing else beyond the bed, thanks to the man poised before me, an arm's length away.

With no conscious intent, I touched my fingertips to my lips. The faint rush of air escaping them tickled my skin. I beheld him with unabashed fascination, taking in the panorama of his stunning, nude body and the luster of water droplets that clung to him. The flames of the oil lamps licked at his skin, exactly the way I wanted to lick him. Everywhere. Over and over. *Right now.*

His rigid shaft rose up at my eye level. Desire shimmered through me, warm and familiar, electric and silken at the same time. God, I wanted him. And after what he'd done to me—for me—behind the falls, I'd shed any guilt or shame about craving this man. This elemental spirit. My Nevan.

Mine.

The thought fired an erotic missile down my body, from my lips into my nipples, and straight down to my sex. No wonder he relished calling me his, if he experienced anything like this when he spoke, or even thought, the word.

He delved a hand into my hair, stroking my scalp. I leaned into his touch, eyes half closed, but the bliss disintegrated with a single memory that slashed through my mind. Skeiron. A sword. Blood.

"You're thinking again, love." Nevan's voice lured my gaze to his with an inexorable pull. "You're thinking of reasons to stop."

His fingers trailed down my neck, across my shoulder. I longed to tilt my head back and offer my throat up for his ministrations, but he was right. The memory of Skeiron's attack had me doubting everything again.

Nevan dragged the backs of his fingers down my arm. "You're not stopping now."

I wanted tonight to stretch on to eternity, with the two of us holed up in his lair, entangled in every way. But could we afford to ignore the threats looming outside this protected haven?

"Skeiron," I said, battling to ignore the storm of sensations triggered by his fingers as they skated down to wrist. "He's out there, hunting for us."

"Not yet." Nevan lowered onto one knee, his face level with mine. He took my hand and feathered kisses across my knuckles one by one. "The king was grievously injured, at the hand of my courageous love, and he will require a good deal of time to recover."

"Tris told me the fae won't help him, because he murdered their witches."

"It is true." Nevan turned my hand over, flittering his lips over my palm, up to my wrist. His tongue teased my tender skin, and all the while, his gaze held mine. "But I would rather discuss what I want to do to you tonight."

"Oh." I couldn't break eye contact, my body overwhelmed with a riot of sensations set off by every word he spoke and every whisper of his skin on mine. "Tell me."

"Perhaps I should show you." His thumb massaged the inside of my wrist, while his other hand coasted up and down my arm. He pressed a damp kiss to the hollow of my shoulder and I sighed with pleasure, helpless against the onslaught of his touch. His lips curved up in a gentle smile. "You, my little kettle, truly could drive a man mad by looking at him the way you're looking at me."

His hand on my wrist moved up to my inner elbow. His thumb manipulated the flesh there as his lips found my throat, lingering on my skin until I let out a long, breathy moan.

"Forget Skeiron," he breathed onto my throat. "Forget everything for this one night. You hunger for me and I hunger for you—your mind, your voice, your lips, every part of your luscious body."

"Me too," I groaned. "Want yours, I mean."

His chuckle liquefied what little remained of my willpower. He ran his tongue up my throat to the spot just under my ear, then took my lobe between his teeth, flicking his tongue across it. I sagged into him, powerless to move or speak or breathe as he breezed his lips down my jaw to my chin. He pulled in a harsh breath, his voice going rough with barely contained passion. "I need to be inside you."

"Oh…" I arched my back as his lips found the corner of my mouth. "Nevan, yes, now."

"On your back, love." He drew his head back to meet my gaze. "Please."

An odd sensation rippled through me, a cross between static electricity and faint needle pricks. I stiffened. "What was that? Did you feel it?"

"Yes." He nuzzled my cheek, my hair, my neck. "Don't worry. I asked permission, which is a kind of debt—a very small one."

"Permission. You mean saying pl—the P-word?"

"Correct."

"Why would you do that?"

I felt him smile against my throat. "You seem to have an obsession with politeness." He swept a hand up my belly, between my breasts, to spread his palm over my heart. "And I need to make certain you feel no compulsion to give yourself to me."

A tendril of ice coiled around my heart. "Magic?"

"No." His hand stayed on my chest, its heat penetrating my skin, but his lips ghosted over mine in brief, light kisses. "As you may have noticed, I can be rather demanding."

"Right." I dared to rest my hands on his back, sliding them over taut muscles. "You are bossy. But since you asked nicely…"

I stretched out on the bed with my arms above my head, exposed more than I'd ever been before, with anyone. "You're the first man who's seen me naked."

His tongue slicked over his bottom lip, his eyes burned a brilliant shade of brandy. "I want to be your first and your last. Your only lover."

I linked my hands over my head, wondering how I could ever be with another man after him. He did things to me, without removing a stitch of clothing, I couldn't have imagined were possible. Not because he was a sylph. Because he was Nevan.

His weight settled onto the bed, eliciting a soft creak, as he straddled my legs. The entirety of his body towered above me, transformed into a golden statue by the sensual lighting and the tension in his muscles. Soon he would touch me, take me, do everything I'd longed for him to do to me.

My mouth went dry. Sex with a supernatural being. Was I ready for this? Was it safe?

Nevan's gentle smile slanted downward. His brow crinkled. "What is it?"

Hugging myself, I averted my gaze to the wall beside us.

Nevan kissed my forehead, the bridge of my nose, the tip of it, the little dent above my mouth. I couldn't stop my eyes from seeking his, but a pang pinched the back of my throat.

"Tell me," he said, without a trace of demand, only a tenderness infused with an unspoken plea.

Hands joined over my belly, I caught my bottom lip between my teeth. If I wanted him to make love to me, if I wanted some kind of relationship with him, I'd have to learn to express my concerns. Not my strong suit. "Well...I was wondering if it's dangerous for a mortal to have sex with an elemental."

Gold and silver flecks glimmered in his irises as he tugged at my lip with his teeth, encouraging me to free it. When I at last loosened my hold on my lip, he drew it into his mouth, swiping his tongue across it, releasing it little by little—so gradually I felt his smooth flesh sliding over mine. "Ah, you do fret about everything. Don't ye, darlin'?"

"And this is news to you?"

"Hardly." He hooked an arm under me and flipped us over. I yelped, suddenly on top of him. The lightning-fast movement ensured I wound up straddling him with his knees bent behind me for support. His rock-hard arousal was trapped underneath me, between my thighs, the ridge of it pressed into my cleft with the head jutting out over his stomach.

He hit me with that devastatingly wicked grin. "You're in control, to do with me as you wish."

My mouth opened, but my voice had abandoned me.

His big hands came up to curl around my hips. "No harm will come to you. Countless elementals have bedded countless mortals. Even gods may engage in relations with humans."

My hands rested on my thighs, though I yearned to explore his body. "You're at my mercy?"

"I am." He rocked my hips forward, pushing my swollen flesh into his shaft. "Do with me as you will."

"That may be the hottest thing anyone's ever said to me." I gazed down upon the raw maleness laid out beneath me and wrung my brain for some sexy thing to do, but I came up empty. *Dammit.*

"You look perplexed, love." He frisked his hands down my thighs to where my hands rested, encircling my wrists, lifting my hands, threading his fingers loosely through mine. "Touch me."

I stared at his chest, longing to do as he suggested but uncertain how to do it. I had no experience with seduction.

He let go of my wrists and curled his hands over my hips again. "You've avoided touching me, for the most part. But when you did, you drove me wild." He rotated his hips, grinding his arousal into me. "Give it a go."

Excitement rushed over my skin, raising the fine hairs, as I splayed my hands over his chest, relishing the feel of his smooth, supple skin contrasted with firm sinews. *Do with me as you will,* he'd said. All right then.

I spread my hands and began painting swirls on his pectoral muscles with my palms and fingertips, exploring the canvas laid out beneath me, a masterpiece of muscle and skin and bone. For the second time tonight, I set my mind loose, shedding all my worry, doubt, and inhibitions. I let my body take over, moving without conscious thought. My hands wandered up his throat to his face, my thumbs glanced over his lips before my fingers covered his mouth, the tips playing with his pliant flesh. His lips were warm and full, sinfully lush. His breaths whispered over my fingers, sneaking out between his slightly parted lips, and when his tongue flicked out to taste my fingertips, I froze for a moment, paralyzed by the sudden rush of liquid fire between my thighs.

He must've felt my wetness on his erection, nestled against my sex, because he groaned softly, his eyes fluttering half closed and his breaths growing heavier.

My body had come alive from head to toe, awakened to every sensation like never before. I plowed my hands into his hair, plying his scalp, delicately at first, but then harder and faster in time with my quickening pulse. I skimmed my fingers down his face and throat, into the uncharted territory of his body. Earlier, I'd fantasized about mapping out his flesh. Now, I charted every inch of his sculpted muscles and soft flesh, kneading and stroking, as stimulated by it as he was—evidenced by his pulsating shaft and shortening breaths. His eyes, though hooded, ignited with fiery shades of scarlet and amber.

I moved to elevate my hips, but his hands bound me to him.

"Not yet," he rasped.

"You're a glutton for punishment?"

He rolled my hips forward, grinding my sex down on his cock, choking back a hoarse groan. "Your naked body on mine is not punishment. It…Ahhh, it is the most exquisite reward."

Another rock of my hips. His fingers sank into my hips, urging me into a rhythm. My slick flesh slid over his shaft, back and forth, inflaming my need and propelling my body toward climax. Panting, gasping, I slapped my hands onto the blanket at either side of his head and dived my head down to his. Our lips collided. We ravished each other's mouths with velvet strokes and desperate moans, starved for the taste of each other, lost to the craving that would not be denied. His hands raked up my back. I crushed my body to his, my taut nipples scraping on his skin as everything inside me clenched, hurtling toward release.

I wrenched my lips from his, breathless, aching and throbbing deep inside for a the release I'd denied us both. "Not like this."

Nevan growled, "Like what?"

I swatted his chest. "Don't get grumpy."

He took a long breath, seeming to collect himself as he exhaled. "What is it?"

"You said—" My panting derailed my words. I took a few precious seconds to catch my breath. "I thought we were going to, you know, have sex."

"That's what we're doing."

"No, I mean…" I leaned back against his raised knees, needing the space between us but hating it at the same time. "I don't want it halfway. All the way or nothing."

"We'll get there." He walked his fingers down my thighs. "We have all night."

"I know you like to play, but I've been waiting a long time for this."

Understanding curved his lips and lit his eyes. "And you want to get right to it. Play later."

"Exactly."

He raised onto his elbows. "I've no objections to taking you right now."

The sheer sensuality of his tone made my sex throb. But I had one more matter to settle first. "I need to ask a very important question."

His groan resonated through his torso, straight into my groin. "If you must."

With a little huff, I shifted my weight to ease the tension building again between my thighs. The movement did not help. "In my world, we have something called safe sex."

"I told ye, my kind and yours enjoy pleasurable relations with no injury—"

"That's not what I meant." I screwed my face up with irritation, which made him grin. "Do elementals have birth control? You know, ways to prevent pregnancy."

"Ah, I see." He boosted his hips up, rubbing his erection into me. "I can't impregnate you without exercising a conscious decision to do so."

"Really?" When he nodded, I couldn't help laughing. "Damn. Wish we had that option over on my side of the falls. For mortals, it's very complicated. I mean, there's pregnancy and then you have STDs—sexually transmitted diseases."

"No wonder your kind are so repressed. It's a wonder you ever loosened up for me."

"Watch it, buddy." I thumped his thigh, but that only made his grin broaden and his eyes twinkle. "So about diseases…"

He pushed up on one arm, half sitting, and captured my wrist with the other hand. Drawing it to his mouth, he tormented the inside of my wrist with his deft tongue. "I'm immortal, love, which means I suffer from no natural diseases or illnesses of any kind."

"Oh. Good." I felt my lips pucker. "But you're not invincible. You could catch a magical disease."

He slapped a palm on his forehead. "Thunder and hail. Do ye ever quit the worrying?"

"Not really."

"Hmm." Both hands on my back, he hauled me down to his chest and murmured seductively in my ear. "In that case, you know what I have to do."

With dizzying swiftness, he flipped us over and took my mouth in a sweet, sensual kiss that went on and on. When he pulled away, he lowered his body over me, bracing himself with both hands at either side of my shoulders, his neck inches from my face. The heat and scent of him radiated across the gap between us and I couldn't breathe, overwhelmed by the knowledge of what was to come. I knew, but lord, I didn't know. How he would take me. How he would stoke me. How his shaft would fill me to bursting. How I would fling my self-control out the window and cling to him with all my strength, riding out the storm.

These were fantasies, nothing more. Any second, I would experience the reality.

When he nuzzled my ear, I sucked in a lungful of blessed oxygen, arching into him as his hair tickled my skin. He moved lower, peppering feathery kisses across vulnerable flesh, eliciting sighs from me that ruffled his hair. He raised his head to gaze at me with a tenderness that floored me. Not just sex. Not for either of us.

He kissed the corner of my mouth. "Everything with you is a revelation. *You* are a revelation."

"What does that mean?"

"It means shut up, Lindsey." He uttered the decree without a hint of sarcasm or annoyance, but with a gravelly tone that testified to the passion flaming in his eyes, darkening his expression, tensing his body.

I shut up.

He levered himself up on one arm, his erection skimming my belly, and settled a hand on my throat, the fingers loose and relaxed. I must've flinched a bit at the position of his hand, because he murmured wordless encouragements. My muscles slackened of their own volition, my body answering his every call without hesitation. He covered my body with his, easing my thighs apart with his knees. His head was above mine, his cheek against the crown of my head, so that my hair muffled his voice. "Are you ready?"

Helpless to speak, I answered by throwing my arms around him, my hands on his back fisting and loosening, fisting and loosening, my mind senseless from the feel of his muscles undulating beneath my palms. I buried my face in his neck, nibbled his shoulder, crooked my fingers until my nails dug into his skin.

"Take that as a yes," he said, his cracking from the sheer power of his need.

"Nevan." His name tumbled from my lips, chased by breathless little noises. "Yes."

Poised above me, propped on his straight arms, he admired me with rapt wonder, as if my body offered the solution to a great cosmic mystery. I started to ask a question, but he stunned me into silence with a punishing kiss, ravaging my mouth with his tongue and his lips, at once enticing and demanding. Without a word, he pulled away and lifted my hips off the bed. Exhaled a raspy breath. Rolled his hips back. And finally, plunged into me.

He moved inside me, delicate and slow, rocking in and out in with a purpose and strength that stripped away every vestige of my inhibitions. The velvet softness of the bedding electrified my bare skin with each movement. He bent to suckle my earlobe, his breaths soft groans against my flesh. I clenched his hair in my fist, arched my neck to inhale the earthy scent of him. The silky texture of his hair sparked through my nerves, spurring me to unleash a string of mindless noises. He showered kisses down my neck, across my throat, up the opposite side to nip at my jaw, and all the while he thrust in and out, each stroke forceful and controlled.

"Lindsey, my love…"

A strange pain gripped my heart. He was mine and I was his. All the pain of past betrayals fled the instant he'd spoken those two beautiful words. *My love.* I'd barely noticed the first time he spoke the phrase back in the cave, but in this moment the lilting declaration struck me full force. My hands fell to his shoulders, squeezing and releasing in a fierce rhythm, in time with his thrusts.

"Nevan." His name was a plea and a demand, punctuated by my teeth rasping across his shoulder. "Don't hold back. I let go for you, and oh God, I need you to let go for me."

A guttural, almost feral sound rumbled in his chest. I crushed my open mouth to his throat, to take in the vibrations of his vocal chords, seized by an insatiable need to merge with him in every way imaginable.

Nevan rose into a crouch, pulling out of me, running his hands down the insides of my thighs to my knees. "I cannot deny you anything."

He braced his hands at either side of my shoulders and drove into me, filling me with exquisite pressure, diving deep with one breathtaking thrust. I trussed my legs around him, secured by my locked ankles, and held on for the ride. His length consumed me as he pounded into my flesh again and again, sweat beading on his forehead. I nearly shattered into a million shards, writhing against him like a wild thing, heedless of the senseless pleas bubbling out of me, the speed and desperation of my cries quickening along with his movements until the bed thumped against the floor, counting out the frantic pace of our love-making.

Dropping onto his elbows, his mouth against my ear, he whispered exotic words I couldn't decipher. The beautiful phrases flowed into me like warm liquid, softening my need just enough to keep me teetering on the edge.

My gaze was riveted to him, my mind exclusively focused on the experience of his body—hips pumping, muscles straining, burnished skin glistening—as he tortured me with an ecstasy beyond comprehension. I bucked my hips to force him deeper, lost in the fervor he conjured within me, clawing at his back to pull him closer.

My release racked my entire body. I screamed, heart thrashing in my chest as he shouted with his own climax, plunging into me once, twice, three times before collapsing on top of me, startling a strangled cry from me. He rolled onto his side next to me, balanced near the bed's edge.

Robbed of breath, I struggled to compose myself, to no avail. This man had wrecked me. My self-control, gone. My inhibitions, gone. My fear and shame, gone.

My heart…gone. I'd handed it over to him, without even realizing it, the second I granted him permission to ravish me. And oh boy, had he ravished me thoroughly.

His arm around my waist, Nevan pressed his lips to my forehead. "You are indeed a revelation, my sweet mortal angel."

I felt a smile stretch my lips and dimple my cheeks. "No one's ever called me an angel before. I like it." I roved my hand over his muscular arm. "But I'd really like to know what you mean when you say I'm a revelation."

"You've performed a miracle. You resurrected my heart."

My pulse stuttered. For several seconds, I stared at him. My face probably resembled a cartoon character's version of shock, though his expression revealed no disgust or amusement, only adoration.

He guided my hand to the scar on his chest, my fingers over the mark. "I thought Skeiron destroyed my heart forever. For a century, I felt nothing more than surface emotions. No passion, no fire, only an emptiness that made me ache for what I knew could never be." He brought my hand to his lips, kissing my palm. "You proved me wrong. You awakened my heart and showed me how to care for another above myself. And you introduced me to true passion, like none I've experienced in my entire existence. That is why you are a revelation."

Speechless, I could do no more than gape at him.

"No need to speak." He held my palm to his cheek. "I wanted to tell you, that's all, to help you understand why I'm here with you."

My brain sputtered to life at last, spitting out a jumble of thoughts. "Is this the thing you wouldn't tell me until I was receptive to the answer?"

He shook his head once.

I turned onto my side, facing him, and looped my arm around his back to pull him close. He obliged, molding his body to mine. I snuggled my face into his neck. "Mmm…Tell me the other thing. I'm feeling very receptive at the moment."

"Later. Sleep, love. You're exhausted." He pinched my bottom. "Partly my fault."

"Don't think I can sleep."

"Try."

His hands caressed my back in slow circles, light and calming. I relaxed into him, into the fur beneath us, and—despite myself, despite the horrors lying in wait outside this little sanctuary—I slept.

CHAPTER TWENTY-THREE

I WOKE ALONE IN THE NEVAN-SIZE BED, THE FUR BLANKET ENSHROUDING me. Yawning, I sat up and stretched. The blanket slipped off to gather around my waist. I flipped it away, to the foot of the bed, and swung my feet over the side. Despite my nudity, I felt no chill. The air inside this underground bubble stayed skin temperature, apparently. My skin temperature. Nevan must've adjusted his…thermostat, for lack of a better term, to suit my body. His flesh ran considerably hotter than mine.

Hot skin. On me. His body pinning me into the bed. His hips undulating, driving him deep inside me. My body sizzled from the memory, a damp ache burgeoning between my thighs.

Last night, when he lay on top of me with our bodies in full contact, he'd shown me astounding passion and a tenderness that stirred a silly, girlie part of me to wish for things I couldn't have. He was a super-powerful sylph from a world of magic, I was an underemployed ex-paralegal from plain old Earth. Where could this go? Nowhere.

I rubbed my arms, but the chill frosting through me originated within, not without. Skeiron was still out there. If we survived his wrath…

We still came from different worlds, literally.

I glanced around the softly lit room, wondering where the source of the light was, unable to trace the diffuse glow to any particular spot. But I wondered about something else with more urgency. Where the hell was Nevan?

What if Skeiron exerted his magical influence to drag Nevan away from me? Or what if Nevan went willingly, to conspire with his king? No, I refused to believe that. Yet his bargain with Skeiron bound him to do his king's bidding, and really, I knew so little about the immortal warrior who'd become my lover. I couldn't compete with supernaturally enforced fealty. I needed to know either way.

I took a big breath and shouted with all my lung power. "Nevan!"

Silence, broken only by the thumping of my heartbeat.

If Skeiron had lured Nevan out into the open…Last time they'd fought, Nevan got skewered and I almost died saving him. Skeiron might kill him this time, for good, with me locked up in this underground hole and helpless to stop it. *Not again, please, not again.*

"Nevan!" I shouted.

This screaming-for-my-man stuff was absolutely not me, yet I'd resorted to it more than once in the past few days. Maybe I didn't know myself as well as I thought. Then again, it was the only method at my disposal for contacting Nevan.

I hollered his name once more, empowering the cry with all my frustrations.

Nevan winked into view right in front of me, his loincloth-clad groin smack in front of my face. He crouched down, his hands coming to rest on my thighs. "What is it?"

"Are you serious? Asking what's wrong?" I kneed his chest, but he didn't react. "I was afraid Skeiron tricked you into meeting him and he—You weren't here and I didn't know what to think."

His left hand lingered on my thigh as the right one cradled my cheek. "You worry far too much."

"Yeah, we've had this conversation before." I shut my eyes, leaning my face into his touch. "I can't stop worrying until we've dealt with Skeiron and all this Janusite crap."

"I know." His thumb traced the seam of my lips. "I hate to see you tying yourself up in knots again, after I worked so diligently to unravel them."

The sincerity in his tone, and the sensual promise implied by them, unraveled me all over again. Enveloped in his presence, I reveled in the sense of safety he'd imbued into me last night, with his body and his words. One thing I knew for certain. This man could never turn on me, not willingly, and even under duress he'd fight it to his last breath.

"Did you believe I'd abandoned you?" he asked, without inflection, his face unreadable.

"Of course not. I don't want to have to save you again is all." My teasing tone must've bypassed him, because his expression fell into resignation and his head drooped, leaving me to gaze at his hair. "That was a stupid joke, my backwards way of saying I was worried about you. I know you wouldn't abandon me. I trust you."

His head sprang up, making my hand slip down to his cheek. "You must never trust me."

I went cold inside at the finality of his tone. "Last night, you asked me to trust you. This morning, you tell me not to. What gives?"

"Then, we were in your world. Now, we are in mine." He fastened his hands around my waist and brought us both to our feet, keeping me close. "Vow you will never trust me on this side of the falls."

"I won't say it. I can't."

"Lindsey."

"Don't *Lindsey* me." I shook off his hands. "It would be a lie. I will trust you, no matter what."

"Then you will die."

"Stop being so melodramatic." I squared my shoulders and lifted my chin, which probably didn't look as resolute when I was naked. "The subject is closed."

He blew out three short, erratic breaths, his gaze bouncing around the room as if he couldn't quite focus on any one thing—until he aimed his eyes, now flat and dull brown, at me. "Fine. We must talk about our other problems."

At the moment, he seemed anxious and irritated with me over my refusal to un-trust him. Yesterday, he'd told my brother he was immensely fond of me. Last night, he claimed I'd resurrected his heart, though I'd seen zero evidence his emotions had ever shriveled up, mummified by the so-called curse. Skeiron might've lied about imprecating Nevan's heart. Since Nevan disliked talking about it, I was left to draw my own conclusions.

Skeiron was a mass murderer. I could totally believe he'd lie about cursing someone.

The truth might lie in whatever it was he'd refused to tell me last night.

I crooked my fingers around the bed's edge, one finger tapping. "Are you sure Skeiron cursed you? I mean, what proof did he have?"

"It was magic, love. There's no concrete evidence. The proof was in my inability to feel for a century." He caught my hands, gently prying them from the bed's frame to surround them with his hands. "Until you, that is."

"Oh please." I tried to lean away from him, but his hold on my hands inhibited movement. "I'm not convinced you ever were cursed. I think Skeiron played on your guilt about his daughter and used the power of suggestion to make you believe he'd stripped you of your emotions."

He scrutinized my fingers, brushing his thumbs over my knuckles. "Perhaps."

"What does it take to imprecate a heart, anyway?"

"I'm not certain." He pursed his lips as if deep in thought, silent for a moment. "Fae magic, I presume. A great deal of it."

"Ah-ha." At his dubious look, I straightened and lifted my chin. "Tris told me Skeiron massacred the fae witches and no fae is allowed to help him. You confirmed that. So how could he get his hands on a fae curse?"

Nevan's face blanked and his hands fell away from mine, and for several seconds I thought he wouldn't answer. At last, he leveled his shocked gaze at me and spoke. "He couldn't."

"See." I sat back, arms folded over my breasts. "I was right."

His smile was shaky, as if he couldn't quite believe I'd been correct on this. Or maybe he couldn't quite believe for a century he'd languished in the self-delusion, instigated by Skeiron, that he'd been cursed.

"By the stars," he said in a hushed voice, gaining strength with each word. "I've been such a bloody fool, all these years."

"Hey, don't beat yourself up about it. Skeiron is one wickedly scary son of a bitch." I laid a hand over my heart. "If he told me he'd cursed my heart, I'd probably buy into it."

"Still, I might never have realized the truth without you."

"I don't know about that. Some other chickie would've come along eventually and—"

"No." The force of his declaration resonated within the room.

"Take it easy." I lowered my hands to my bare thighs. "It doesn't matter either way. You were never cursed."

"It does matter." In one stride, he bridged the gap between us and dropped to his knees before me, settling his hands over mine. "You matter."

I squirmed, searching for the courage to ask the question that plagued me. "Will you tell me the thing you wouldn't say last night?"

"Perhaps you are receptive."

"Let me decide that." I slanted toward him, my breasts waving above his face. "I'm receptive."

He stared at my breasts, the tip of his tongue slipping out between his lips. My nipples went taut under his intent gaze and he swallowed visibly. I leaned back, which seemed to break the spell.

Nevan clasped my hands to his heart, right over his scar. "You saved my heart and my life. I would've died, but you risked your safety to restore me."

His voice had gone husky—this time, with deep emotion rather than lust.

I couldn't speak or tear my gaze away from his.

"My heart may not have been cursed, but I'd been unable to care for anything or anyone, trapped in a hell of my own making." He let his head fall forward onto my lap. But then an uncertain laugh rumbled out of him and he tilted his head to gaze up at me. "You saved my soul, Lindsey. I owe you a debt I can never repay, though I'll spend the rest of my existence trying to."

A tether snapped taut between us, pulsing with fervent energy. I'd felt a similar, but far less intense, binding when I promised Tris anything if he'd save Nevan. This time, the energy burned with more than the power of a debt. It shimmered with the unquenchable fire of passion and devotion.

Nevan mashed my hands into his flesh. "Thank you."

The tether pulsated, hot and hard, driving his commitment into me with such force I lost my breath. No, my debt to Tris couldn't compare with this. Nevan owed me his heart, his life...his soul.

A one-sided commitment meant nothing. I owed him everything. "You've saved me too, Nevan. I owe—"

He silenced me with two fingers on my lips. "Don't. Let the debt stand, love, please. You may need it."

"I don't understand. Why can't I express you-know-what like you did?"

"Because when two parties each owe the other in equal proportion, it cancels out both debts. I do not believe your gratitude to me is equal to mine, but I won't risk it. You may soon have need of the bond."

"You've said that twice. Why would I need you to owe me?"

"It's a life debt. The most potent sort." He rose and took a step backward. "A life debt supersedes all other obligations and bargains. In fact, there is little else capable of overriding the debt levied by saving a life—except accomplishing the same feat in return."

"You would have to save my life the way I saved yours."

"Precisely. A life for a life."

"And you're sure," I said, "nothing else can override it."

His forehead crimped into deeply etched lines. "Once, I would have said no without hesitation. But I'm beginning to wonder if there is another force more powerful than any debt."

"Like what?"

He gazed at me with what I could only describe as longing. "I'll let you know when I figure that out."

Realizing he would say no more, I heaved my body off the bed and rubbed my temples. My brain was starting to hurt. "What kind of influence does the person holding the debt have over the person who owes them?"

"You will have nearly unlimited sway over me." He moved closer, his hands coming up to grasp my hips. "I am at your command, a virtual slave to your desires."

A languid, molten heat unfurled through my body, pooling low in my belly. Oh God, how did he infuse every syllable of that statement with simmering sensuality?

Because he was Nevan, that's how. And I loved everything he did to me. No more denials.

I wound my arms around his waist, my body flush against his. "My slave, huh? Think I'm going to like this life debt stuff."

"A debt has never been so pleasurable." He rubbed his hands up my back and down again to the upper curve of my buttocks. "But beware. Even if another saves your life, you must never admit to the obligation or you will be at the whim of the debt-holder forever, unless they incur an equal debt to you."

"Yes, sir. Any other orders?"

"Several come to mind, but we haven't the time. "

Memories of last night—of our bodies entwined, of the rapture he'd given me—replayed in my mind, too vivid to allow coherent thought. With a great feat of willpower, I ignored the fresh desire smoldering within me. "How does it work? This debt thing, I mean. If you're a slave to my whims, do I just holler your name and, whoosh, you appear to do my bidding?"

"Whoosh?" The laughter in his voice matched the affectionate amusement on his face.

"Yeah. Whoosh." I rolled my hips into him and he winced, though I recognized it had nothing to do with pain and everything to do with his swelling erection. "Is that how it works?"

"Essentially, your colorful description is accurate." He palmed both my buttocks, kneading my flesh. "The owed party must consciously invoke the debt and speak the words in the form of a command. Then and only then will the full magical power of the debt be invoked."

"Hmm. These magical rules are damn confusing." I freed one arm, reaching up to comb my hand through his hair. "If I can't use the G word or the T phrase, then I'll have to be more creative. I was a terrified, pent-up mess. You should've walked away, but you didn't. You freed me from a burden I've carried for way too long, and oh yeah, you rescued me—repeatedly. You're my hero."

He groaned, scrunching up his face.

I tickled his scalp.

His lips ticked up at the corners, but he pulled away, turning his back to me. "We should be talking about your future."

"What about it?"

"Your future is uncertain as long as you stay in my world, or within the portal boundaries in your world."

"Why bring me here if it's so dangerous?"

I couldn't see his face anymore—confronted with his uninformative, though mouth-watering, backside—but I spotted the slight hunching of his shoulders and the way his head lowered a smidgen. He spoke in a quiet voice I had to strain to hear. "I tried to let you go, Lindsey, but I cannot do it. Skeiron has attempted to kill you twice and yet I cannot push you away. My sanity has left me, but I don't care, so long as I have you."

I padded up behind him to drape my arms around his waist, my cheek on the rippling muscles of his upper back. His chest inflated on a deep breath, then deflated as the air hissed out of him.

Rubbing my cheek on his skin, I said, "Can't let you go either. When you were dying, I wanted to die too. I did some stupid things, I almost killed us both by losing control of the car, but I had to make it to another waterfall. It was the only chance." I hugged him tighter, needing the intimacy more than ever. "So you see, we're both a little crazy."

He spun around, grasping my shoulders. His eyes darted back and forth, hunting for something in my expression or my eyes. His mouth had set in a stern line.

I tried to smooth away the lines on his forehead, but they were too entrenched.

"Tell me," he said, "exactly what happened after Skeiron defeated me."

A storm cloud had invaded his eyes. They darkened, the colors washed out by a cold, gray fear. He squeezed me until I flinched, then loosened his grip just enough to let me breathe again.

I touched his cheek. "What's wrong?"

"You mentioned another waterfall. When I woke, I assumed we were in the same woods as before."

I thought back to last night, after Tris left us. Nevan and I had been in the throes of passion, clamoring to get inside each other, and he had whisked me away to the waterfall. Our waterfall. Not the one I'd penetrated to get to the Unseen realm and beg Tris for help. Nevan took me to the falls behind the rock shop, because he hadn't realized we were in a different place.

Guess sylphs didn't have GPS.

Nevan pulled me close, his gaze boring into me. "There is no other waterfall within one mile of the falls I guard."

"Duh. You whisked us to my car and we got you inside, remember? You passed out, I think. I improvised."

"Crossing the boundary should've destroyed me."

"It didn't and I had no choice, what with Brennus on our tails. You were bleeding to death and I drove super-fast. Maybe we outran the boundary thingy." Idiotic, but all I could think of to explain it. Except for the option I still could not accept.

Nevan had the grace to ignore the obvious conclusion, for the moment.

His eyes narrowed. "What else did you do to save me?"

Uh-oh. "What do you mean?"

"You mentioned doing stupid things, plural." He angled his head until our lips grazed each other. "What else did you do?"

His proximity overpowered my brain, my body, everything. He knew the effect he had on me and exploited it to his advantage whenever necessary. I had to admire his tenacity, but in this moment I could've slugged him for it. If I'd retained control of my limbs. Which I hadn't.

Without meaning to, I melted against him, my chin braced on his chest, slanting my face up to bring our mouths into full contact.

He rasped his tongue across the seam of my lips. "Tell me."

"I…made a deal with Tris."

His head jerked up, eyes flaming. "You what?"

I studied the scar on his chest and nibbled my lip. "You were dying. I couldn't stand by and let that happen. I couldn't lose you. But the only way I knew to save you was a healing vortex and I couldn't go back to the one by the shop because Skeiron might've been there, or Brennus, so I took you to another waterfall in hopes it also had a vortex and a doorway." I inhaled, breathless from my long-winded explanation. "Somehow, the portal opened for me, even without you there to do it, and I went through."

No need to mention the almost-drowning portion of my evening, I decided.

Frowning, Nevan held perfectly still.

"And then I found Tris," I said. *Screamed his name until the blasted leprechaun paid attention.* "I begged him to heal you. I said I'd be, um, grateful."

Nevan shut his eyes, his mouth twisting into a grimace. "How grateful?"

"I may have promised him anything if he healed you."

"Anything?" He gaped at me as if I'd vowed to have kinky sex with the leprechaun and bear his arrogant little spawn. "Were those your literal words? You would give him *anything*?"

"I said, and I quote, if you heal him I will give you anything you want."

I watched Nevan's jaw grind. His nostrils flared.

"You have no right to be mad," I said. "You'd be dead if I hadn't bargained with Tris."

His shoulders flagged, a breath rushing out of him, and he let his head fall onto my shoulder. "I am not mad. I'm afraid for you."

"I won't apologize. Given the same choice, I'd do it all again."

"You've indebted yourself to a powerful elemental. Tris may call in the debt anytime he likes, in whatever manner he likes."

"I really don't think he'll do anything bad."

"You've known him for less time than you've known me. How can you be certain?"

"Intuition." And yeah, I believed in that crap now. "I was right to trust you, and I'm right about Tris. He's not as bad as he wants everyone to think. In fact, he seemed genuinely upset at the idea of you dying."

Nevan barked a derisive laugh.

"You used to be friends," I said. "Why is it so hard to believe he still cares if you live or die?"

"Perhaps he does. Satisfied?"

"Yes."

Nevan stared past my head, his gaze distant. "Did you say the portal opened for you?"

"Yep."

"Are you certain Tris didn't open it? I imagine you were screaming *his* name this time."

"Jealous?" I teased. "But no, I didn't yell for him until after I went through."

His gaze swiveled back to me and he pushed me away, only a matter of inches, but enough to get my attention. He kept his hands on my upper arms. "Are you certain? The portal admitted you without any magical being to assist you?"

I flung my arms out, forcing his hands away. "Yes, dammit, I'm certain. What's wrong with you?"

He opened and closed his mouth several times before finally speaking. "I know of but one way it could be possible. Even mortals with a touch of the Unseen in them can't command a portal to open."

"Okay. How'd I do it?"

"Lindsey...you are the Janusite."

Chapter Twenty-Four

NEVAN INSISTED WE EAT BEFORE DISCUSSING HIS OUTRAGEOUS CLAIM any further and my stomach had chosen that moment to growl, so I deferred to him this once. He took me into his kitchen, where I observed from atop a high stool while he moved this way and that, preparing a meal even more enticing than the one he'd brought me that first night.

I couldn't remember the last time I'd eaten, or what I'd eaten. The meal he whipped up for me this morning roused my taste buds with decadent flavors and sumptuous textures, laced with hints of the exotic, every bite of it designed to make me moan with pleasure. Lord, the man could cook.

Throughout the meal, he picked at his food, pretending to partake—for my benefit, no doubt. He kept frowning, only for a second each time, and rubbing the back of his neck. The tension mounting in him was subtle yet definite, but I was too starved to pause for an interrogation. Once I'd wolfed down the last of my meal, I wiped my mouth with the silky napkin he'd provided, realigning my butt on the stool to face him.

"Something's bothering you," I said, setting the napkin on the counter. Yeah, I was avoiding the Janusite discussion, but for a good reason. "What happened while you were gone earlier? Where did you go?"

He turned away, leaned against the counter behind him, and clamped his fingers over its edge.

I watched him stand there like a statue for several minutes, his profile offering no clues to his agitation, until I could take the silence no longer. "You need to practice your sharing skills."

He grunted.

Jumping off the stool, I marched in front of him. "Explain."

I phrased it as a command rather than a request, to sidestep the danger of saying please and all that craziness. Besides, I was getting damn tired of begging him to be honest with me.

Nevan let his head fall back, his eyes directed at the ceiling but his gaze retreating somewhere much further away.

I roped my arms around his neck, my hands at his nape, and pressed my entire body to his. God, the feel of his skin on mine never failed to crackle desire through me.

His breath hitched.

I lavished an open-mouth kiss on his throat, determined to lure him back from his thoughts, rewarded by his eyes homing in on mine. "Come on, you know I won't back down until you tell me."

After a pause, he said, "I went out to assess the danger, to determine if Skeiron has healed yet. I came upon a battalion of his soldiers."

When he fell silent again, I prodded, "And?"

"I overheard them discussing the king's swift recovery and their orders to hunt down both of us. I was about to leave when—" He squeezed his eyes shut, grimacing. "One of them spotted me. I'd cloaked myself, becoming invisible, but the glamour must've slipped. Or I slipped." He opened his eyes and shook his head. "I failed you yet again."

"You have never failed me."

His hands fell to his sides, his entire body slumped. "They nearly caught me. I escaped, as your kind would say, by the skin of my teeth."

"But you did escape. That's the important thing."

Though he nodded, my gut told me he didn't truly believe it.

He stomped out of the kitchen.

Totally confused, I stared after him for a moment before I took off at a trot to catch up. He'd gone into the living area, halting at its center. My gaze wandered to the bed, rumpled from our passion the previous night.

Nevan stood tall and stiff, hands fisted at his sides, his jaw tight enough to grind diamonds to powder. "Skeiron is hunting for us as we speak."

I approached him from the side, reaching out a tentative hand to touch his arm. "We'll face him together."

"You will stay here." He rolled his shoulders back, lifting his chin to stared down at me. "I will destroy him. Alone."

"You tried that already. He came way too close to killing you." Realization raised all the hairs on my arms. "Quit trying to get rid of me. I won't hide. And you can't seriously expect me to stay here, in this underground lair, while you go fight the bad guys."

"I do. And you will."

"Like hell I will." I tipped my own chin up. "I am going with you."

"No. I will not permit it."

I drew back, feeling as if he'd struck me. "You will not permit it? I'm not your sex slave, who you can lock up in this dungeon until the next time you get horny."

"Lindsey—"

"Quit saying my name like that." I jabbed a finger in the air near his chest. A different kind of fire raged inside me, one borne of fury. "I'm not a child. And I make up my own mind about what risks to take."

"You are only safe as long as you remain within the wards. They are magical spells that prevent anyone else from entering my home." He threw his hands up, eyes going wild and sparking with electric blue and searing white. The colors of fear. He shook his head and his dark hair quivered around his face. "I cannot protect you out there."

"You said you'd never abandon me."

He jerked his head up, eyes intent on me. "I will return for you."

I moved closer but did not touch him. His fear unnerved me, and a compelling urge to soothe him flowed through me, softening my voice. "Nevan, think about it. What happens if Skeiron kills you this time? I'll be stuck here with no way out."

Though he didn't react, I glimpsed something indefinable in his eyes that told me he'd recognized the truth of our situation and knew I was right.

I reached for him, but he spun away from me, clutching his head in his hands as he stalked back and forth across the room, his pace increasing with each circuit. He thrashed his head, muttering things I couldn't make out. He might've been speaking another language, or just mumbling nonsense. When his pace turned frenetic, I thrust out a hand to halt him.

My fingers curled around his bicep, I stroked my thumb over his skin. "There's a risk either way. If I go with you, at least I'll know what happens to you—and vice versa."

He turned his face up to me, the anguish there tearing at my heart.

I threaded my fingers between his. "I want to be with you, whatever happens."

A moment—maybe two or three or ten—in which neither of us spoke or moved. We regarded each other, fingers and gazes entwined, unwilling to sever the connection yet unable to bridge the gap between us. Just when I feared he'd zip away, leaving me here alone, he folded me into his arms and said, "I wish to be with you as well. Whatever comes."

"Good. Because I'm way too stubborn to let you have your way."

"I suppose I must accept that." He swaddled me tighter in his arms. "You cannot ignore the truth any longer. You are the Janusite."

"That's ridiculous." Plastered to him, I suddenly became aware of our nudity. Of my nudity. I scrambled out of his embrace and said, "I can't fight Skeiron in the buff. Where are my clothes?"

He waved toward a cushy chair. My clothes were stacked on the seat, neat and clean.

As I hurried toward my clothing, Nevan remained glued in place. I yanked my clothes on with violent movements, my hands shaking faintly—whether from fear of the battle to come or fear of considering the possibility I was the Janusite, I couldn't say. By the time I had my boots laced, I remembered my derringer and began frantically combing the room for it, going to so far as to drop to my knees and peer under the bed. When I came up empty, I clambered to my feet and muttered. "Shit."

Nevan flew to me—whoosh, he was there. "What is it?"

"I lost my gun."

He held out one hand and my gun poofed into his palm, tucked inside its holster.

I plucked the holster from his hand, slipping it inside my waist band and clipping it onto my jeans.

"You feel safer with it," he said.

"Sure. I like my gun." I rose onto tiptoes to peck his cheek. "But I don't really feel safe unless I'm with you."

He studied me as if I'd babbled in gibberish.

I smoothed my shirt, but the outline of my holster still showed. "Time to fight Skeiron, eh? Guess we better get moving. Don't suppose you have a plan this time."

"In a manner of speaking." He cranked one corner of his mouth into an expression of dismay. "I rid the world of Skeiron whatever the cost, and if necessary, I will bargain with him to save you."

"Bargain? No. I forbid you to do it."

"Alas, I don't always do as I'm told." He ran a finger down my jawline, to tap my chin. "I will give up my freedom, my life, my soul, for one reason alone. For you."

"I don't want you to. You're already enslaved, who knows what Skeiron would demand for this. And if I'm the Janusite, he won't bargain at all."

"Perhaps. But I will try—for you." He edged closer, until I had to bend my head back to meet his gaze, and said, "Not for the Janusite. For you. Lindsey Astrid Porter."

I screwed up my mouth. "How do you know my middle name?"

"Your mother told me."

"Never say it again. It's goofy."

"But it's charming. Do you know its meaning?" When I shrugged, he told me, "It means beloved goddess."

"If you say so."

"You are a goddess," he said, "in every way. And you are beloved, by your family and friends."

His eyes grew…misty? Dear lord.

"And by me as well," he added.

Nevan's confession set my stomach to fluttering, hardly a useful state to be in considering the upcoming battle. "Getting back to Skeiron, we need some kind of plan."

Nevan let out a frustrated grumble. "What would you have me do? I have no chance of acquiring an endued weapon before we encounter Skeiron."

"I'm not exactly unarmed." I patted the holster inside my jeans. "I know you'd rather I hide under the bed, but I was helpful last time you went to war with Skeiron."

"Helpful? You came close to dying and indebted yourself to a leprechaun."

"Well," I said, "have you got a better idea?"

"I have no ideas."

He sounded so desolate, I longed to pull him into my arms and kiss away his anguish. "How about if I give you permission to whisk me away anytime you deem it necessary, provided I'm in serious danger?"

"That would be acceptable, though not preferable."

"In that case, you have my permission—exactly as I outlined it." I considered my options for a moment, then said, "I've got an idea."

One of his brows arched. "I imagine I won't approve."

"Probably not." I slanted toward him, angling my head back to meet his gaze. "But look at it his way. You've got no other options, so you might as well try my crazy idea."

"Which is?"

"Gather *my* allies."

His lip curled as his head popped backward. "Mortals? Against the king of the sylphs?"

"Hey!" I nudged his shin with my boot. "This mortal saved your ass. Don't get snooty about it."

"Snooty?"

"Yeah, it means uppity." I lifted my shirt hem to reveal my holstered derringer. "I have a gun and my parents are well armed. The sheriff owes me a big one. Hell, we might even get some heavy artillery, if I play the guilt card heavy enough."

"Four mortals will not be enough—"

"And there's Tris." At Nevan's disbelieving look, I explained, "I'm positive he will help. The kid's not all that bad."

Nevan sniffed, with a haughty bob of his head. "I stand corrected. Four mortals, an irritating fae, and me. Salvation, at last."

"Better odds than last time, at least."

He scratched his head. His face twisted into a mixture of agony and severe annoyance. Finally, he threw his head back and groaned. "All right. We try your plan."

"Good." I extended my hand to him. "Let's go."

"One moment."

I started to balk, but his look of intense concentration stopped me. He stared into nothing, eyes distant, body taut and erect.

Metal plates materialized around his limbs.

I choked on a gasp. He'd conjured a freaking suit of armor.

The metal shone bright silver, with feathery veins of bronze and gold shot through it. A matching helmet appeared on his head, with the face plate flipped up, and leather boots affixed with plates forged from the same metal encased his feet and ankles. His sword, the one I'd used on Skeiron, took shape in his hand.

I slid my tongue over my lower lips as I scanned him from head to toe. "If you want to have sex again before we go, I'm game."

His smile was sensual and very, very intimate. "Later."

When he held his hand out to me, I took it. He zipped us out of his home.

My feet touched down on solid earth, in the woods, at the base of a low hill. "Barely even felt it this time."

"Perhaps you are adjusting."

I squinted into the darkness. "Where are we?"

"Outside my home." He hugged me tight. His armor fit so well it was like a much harder version of his skin. "We should have appeared at the portal."

His confused tone rippled dread through me.

"Why didn't we?" I asked.

"I've no idea." He canted his head, as if listening. "I felt energy fire through me. Only once before have I experienced anything like…"

"What is it?" I whispered, though I wasn't sure why.

"We must go."

He vanished.

I staggered a step, off balance from the loss of his support. Even more than his body, though, the loss of him echoed through a hollow space in my soul. He'd abandoned me.

No. He would not desert me.

I felt energy fire through me, he'd said.

A surge of air blasted over me, setting off an electric thrill of anticipation. "Nevan!"

I whirled around—and came face to face with Skeiron.

The king of the sylphs regarded me with a warped smile and eyes bright with cold blues and greens. "I'm afraid Nevan cannot return to you. Unless I command it."

I spun away.

He catapulted his body toward me. His arms cinched tight around my torso, strapping my arms to my sides. "Nevan, come here."

Nevan materialized in front of us, his armor gone.

Posture stiff, face blank, eyes dull and still as a stagnant pond, he directed his gaze at his king.

Awaiting orders. Bound to heed his master's whims.

I struggled in Skeiron's grasp, but he only tightened his arms around me.

"You see," he said, "Nevan belongs to me. He serves my will, not yours—and not his own."

Skeiron shoved me toward Nevan. "Hold her."

Nevan shackled me in his brawny arms, and for the first time, being pinioned to his body shot an arctic chill through me.

The sylph king waved a hand. "Strangle her."

Nevan clamped a single hand around my throat and squeezed until I sputtered, choking on every attempt to inhale. Stars burst in my vision, but blackness swept in from the edges to consume my vision bit by bit. I clawed at Nevan's hand, kicked at his shins. He lifted me off the ground, cranking his hand tighter and tighter. I couldn't breathe, couldn't gurgle, couldn't shake his grip no matter how hard I thrashed. A final, desperate ploy exploded like a bomb in my mind.

Stop, Nevan, you're killing me.

When Skeiron dropped a ceiling on me, I'd called to Nevan with my thoughts and he rushed to my side. Now, the solitary response was a weak flicker of red in his eyes and a slight downward tick of his mouth.

My lungs were on fire. My vision telescoped down until all I could see was Nevan's eyes.

"Enough," Skeiron said, his tone bored. "I need her alive."

Releasing my throat, Nevan restrained me with his arms again, holding my feet off the ground. I hacked until my chest throbbed, knowing I could not escape.

"Show her to me," the king said, and damn, did he have the authoritative, kingly arrogance thing down pat.

Nevan flipped me around, barring one arm over my hips and the other across my chest, buckling my arms down. I had no leeway to struggle, except with my feet. When I thrashed them, he locked one powerful leg around both of mine, constraining me while balanced on one foot. If he were mortal, I could've knocked him off balance, but his preternatural agility kept him steady even when I struggled in his grasp.

Skeiron sauntered to us, his freaky eyes on me. "Are you the Janusite?"

"Does it look like I am?"

One side of his mouth slanted upward as he slid a finger down my jaw. "Mortals are so predictable. Fighting the inevitable, believing they can win."

"What about you? Searching for a lowly human female to escort you across the boundary, because you're too impotent to do it yourself."

"Watch your tongue, mortal."

"My name is Lindsey Astrid Porter."

Skeiron kept his gaze nailed to mine but no longer spoke to me. "Nevan, have you witnessed any evidence she is the Janusite?"

Nevan's muscles went rigid around me, his fingers crooking into my flesh. In a dead voice, he replied, "Yes."

"Tell me."

One of his fingers jerked, pressing into my hip. "She—transported me across the boundary."

My stomach plummeted through the ground, but then I heard the faintest wisp of tension in his voice and hope sparked to life inside me. Though he'd ratted on me, he hadn't mentioned I wasn't touching him when we crossed the boundary. Important or not, the fact would've interested Skeiron for sure. Maybe Nevan was fighting his bargain after all.

"What else?" the king asked, his voice hushed but thick with a seething fury.

Nevan's foot fell away from my legs, no longer binding them. "She opened a portal without assistance."

"Is that all the evidence you've seen which identifies her as the Janusite?"

"Yes."

The spark of hope blossomed into a full-blown flame. He hadn't said a thing about the strange energy he sensed in me, or about me calling Tris to help resurrect him. He was still in there, rebelling against his king's hold on him.

It wasn't enough.

"Take her to the dungeon," Skeiron said.

Nevan rocketed us away.

CHAPTER TWENTY-FIVE

A HORDE OF FOOTFALLS THUMPED FROM SOMEWHERE IN THE DIS- tance, growing nearer with every *thud-thud* of synchronized feet. I stared at the doorway of my cell, a gaping maw in the smooth walls hewn from pale bedrock. Were they coming for me?

Goose bumps prickled my arms and I swept my hands up and down them to banish the chill. A few minutes earlier, after Skeiron and Nevan left me alone here, I'd tried to walk out the doorway—only to smack into an invisible barrier. My head still hurt from the impact and the strangely electrical jolt it zapped through me.

I was a prisoner. Nevan had brought me to my cell.

You must never trust me, he'd told me this morning. *On this side of the falls* had been the qualification. I'd scoffed at the idea because, though he'd confided the details of his bargain with Skeiron and warned me about magical debts, part of me still couldn't accept the reality of it all. Mortals broke their promises every day. No one died from it.

But I might die today. And Nevan might be forced to kill me.

I paced the length of the oval room, maybe a dozen feet across, my body crackling with nervous energy as the thudding footsteps outside receded. *Relax*, I commanded myself. As if that ever worked. Minutes ticked by in my head, each second pounding like a hammer striking an anvil. I checked my watch each time I reached the doorway, before I spun on my heels and started the circuit over again. Ten minutes bled into twenty, then thirty.

I tried shouting for Nevan. No response.

Forty-three minutes into my incarceration, my feet aching from repetitive impacts with the hard stone floor, I gave up and slumped against the wall.

Had I lost Nevan for good? He belonged to Skeiron, or so the king said. But Nevan had defied his king at every turn since the moment we met—until today. I longed to believe his bargain with Skeiron had weakened somehow, granting him a measure of freedom, but then I flashed back to his vacant face when he shackled me in his arms and abducted me to this hellhole—all because the king commanded it.

Christ, I didn't understand this magic malarkey anywhere near good enough. I was lost in this world.

Weariness engulfed me and I sank down the wall to the floor. Knees bent to my chest, I let my head droop.

Thunderous footfalls reverberated in the corridor, growing louder and sharper, advancing on my cell.

Pushing up onto my feet, I pressed my back to the wall and sneaked a hand under my shirt to rest it on my derringer's grip. Skeiron either hadn't known what a gun was or dismissed it as no threat, since he'd given it no more than a cursory glance. I'd considered firing a shot at the force field in the doorway, but decided I'd accomplish nothing except deafening myself for several minutes. If the soldiers, or whatever they were, approaching now stopped in for a little chat, maybe I could blast holes in their foreheads and at least incapacitate them long enough to escape.

I had two rounds in my gun, having lost my ammo boxes somewhere along the way. Based on the racket out there, I was dealing with more than two sylph soldiers. I inched closer to the doorway to peek outside.

Two by two, the soldiers tromped past my cell door, clad in obsidian armor gilded with metallic ruby streaks. Matching helmets with face shields disguised their faces, and not one of them deigned to glance at me. Maybe Skeiron had tricked all of them into bargains, making them automatons bound to his will.

Nevan had looked like that. Robotic. Dead. I knew what he was, but he'd never seemed inhuman—until today.

Soldiers filed past.

I counted fourteen, every one as tall as Nevan, some taller, and every one of them built like a pro wrestler on steroids.

For once, I was quite happy to be ignored.

As the last pair goose-stepped past, an image flared in my mind—Nevan in his armor. It had glistened with bright colors, with life and light, not the obsidian darkness of Skeiron's army.

I trudged to the center of my cell, turning in a circle, studying the smooth alabaster of the ceiling.

Why hadn't Nevan come when I hollered? He owed me a life debt. That superseded all other magic, according to him, which should've meant he could penetrate any protection ward Skeiron erected around this underground bunker. Yet Nevan ignored me.

He wouldn't. If I called, and if he could come, he'd be here in a flash.

If he could.

I struggled to recall everything he'd told me about life debts. Only another life debt could erase it, and the debt-holder had nearly unlimited power over the debtor. *A virtual slave*, he'd said, which sounded sexy as hell at the time. He'd cautioned me to never admit to such an obligation or I'd be at the whim of the debt-holder forever, unless they owed me an equal debt in return. Nevan had sealed his life debt to me with his beautiful words of gratitude and he hadn't saved my life since then. No equal debt.

He still owed me. He was bound to me, at my command.

I'd asked how it worked, if the debt-holder simply thought about the debtor would the other person appear, like whoosh, to do their bidding. I remembered Nevan's laughter at my use of the word whoosh, his face full of affectionate humor.

My throat tightened. What had Nevan said after that?

The owed party must consciously invoke the debt and speak the words in the form of a command. Then and only then will the full magical power of the debt be invoked.

Duh. I'd screamed his name, but not invoked the debt. Back in his cave home, I'd told him to take me with him, but I hadn't consciously invoked the debt then either.

I threw my head back, shook my fists in the air, and shouted so loud my throat burned and my voice cracked.

"Nevan, you get down here this instant! You owe me and I command you to poof your freaking ass in here immediately, don't care what you're doing, just get your goddamn self here!"

Breathing hard, pulse pounding behind my eardrums, I dropped my arms to my sides and listened. Waited.

After a couple agonizing seconds, I could take it no longer. "Nevan! I said get your—"

"There's no need to shriek at me, love."

I yelped and spun around.

Nevan leaned against the wall, arms crossed over his chest, head cocked and lips ticking up at the corners.

I wagged a finger at him. "You scared me half to death."

The little smile faltered. "Don't speak of death, even in jest."

A knot inside me loosened at the sight of him, sagging my shoulders. "I finally figured out how to make you do what I want."

With one thrust of his arm, he separated from the wall and spanned the distance between us. His hot gaze liquefied me but he held back, by a degree of inches. His hands floated up, as if to touch me, but flopped down to hang at his sides. "I've been waiting an eternity for you to call me."

"I only figured out how to make it work a minute ago. Doesn't Skeiron have wards? How'd you get through them?"

"I was still within the wards. Awaiting the king's next order."

"Well, you're free of him now." I swung my gaze to the doorway, then back to Nevan. "I saw a bunch of soldiers go by. Is Skeiron preparing for war?"

"A king is always preparing for war. Another sylph might rise up to usurp the throne, as Skeiron did to Notus. Then there are the other elementals and, of course, the troublesome fae."

"No rest for the wicked, eh?"

"Even the righteous must be ever vigilant." He watched me for a long moment, uncertainty flickering in his eyes. "I would have killed you, Skeiron commanded it." He gritted his teeth, unwilling to meet my eyes. "If I had taken your life, I would never have forgiven myself. Lindsey, I—"

"Shut up. I'm not forgiving you because there's nothing to forgive. You were enslaved to his will."

"Until you freed me." At last, he enfolded me in his arms, surrounding me with his strength and warmth and earthy scent. My eyelids closed and I nestled into him, cheek to chest. He threaded his fingers through my hair, stroking my scalp, feathering hair over my neck. "What will you have me do next?"

"If I ordered you to raze this creepy compound, could you do it?"

"Given my life debt, I would be forced to try. However, I am not an earth elemental. I lack the power of a gnome, the only type of creature that might succeed in destroying Skeiron's palace."

"Palace? It's drafty and barren, not opulent."

"You have seen but a portion of it." He kissed the top of my head, and I heard a sniff as he sampled the scent of my hair. "As always, you smell of everything sweet and wonderful."

Propping my chin on his collarbone, I gazed up at him. "What should we do?"

"I don't know. For days, I should've been formulating a strategy, but I could think of nothing outside of you."

"Well…I have an addendum to my original plan."

His mouth compressed. "I imagine I won't approve of this idea either."

"Probably not."

"No more of your schemes. Now that you have freed me from his control, I will confront Skeiron."

"Screw that idea." I placed my hands on his shoulders. "You're a virtual slave to my will, right? So listen up. You will not fight Skeiron unless he attacks you first. That's an order."

He bared his clenched teeth. "Lindsey."

"I mean it. Keep away from Skeiron."

Another voice chuckled from the doorway. "Sage advice from your mortal whore, guardian."

I whirled on Skeiron, fueled by a sudden and irresistible rage. "I am not a whore, you whacked-out son of a bitch."

Skeiron waved a hand, the invisible barrier glittered, and he strolled into the chamber. "You've brought the guardian to me. Excellent." He flashed me a sneer at me and focused on Nevan. "You will suffer for your disobedience, old friend. And you will watch as I strip the power from your mortal plaything."

I seized Nevan's hand. "Get us the hell out of here."

He pulled me into his arms.

Skeiron raised a single finger. "I have your brother, Lindsey Astrid Porter."

Clinging to Nevan, I glowered at Skeiron. "You're lying."

"Ash—that is his name, is it not?—sits in my bedchamber, guarded by my most steadfast follower, Brennus."

"I don't believe you."

He motioned for me to exit the room. "Come. I will show you."

Nevan clenched me tighter.

Skeiron arched a brow. "You may always command your slave to remove you from this place at any time. He clearly owes you a debt of overarching magnitude." He made a disgusted little huff, throwing a sidelong look at Nevan. "What service did she perform to earn such gratitude?"

Nevan squinted at his king, anger flaming in his eyes. I curled my fingers on his chest, scraping my nails to gain his attention. When his eyes flicked down to me, I said, "Let it go."

He acknowledged the command in my voice with a curt nod.

Skeiron strode out the doorway. Nevan gathered me under his arm and led me out into the corridor under the shield of his body.

"You have my permission," I whispered to him, "to get me out of here whenever you feel it's appropriate—once we get my brother."

He gave me a quick squeeze, the only indication he'd understood me. His gaze was nailed to the back of Skeiron's head as the king ushered us down corridor after corridor, and finally, up a sloping passageway. The cold, pale rock of the lower level segued into a rich, brown stone shot through with green veins. The walls were still smooth, but here polished so the oil lamps on the walls shimmered golden light across the surface. The further we traveled, the drier my mouth grew. I sensed...I don't know. Something very bad on the way.

Ash was not here. He couldn't be. My parents took him outside the boundary.

Skeiron shepherded us around a curving corner. We halted in front of a wooden door engraved with symbols I didn't recognize and Skeiron twisted the knob to swing the door inward.

Unease crawled over my skin, pricking like a thousand tiny claws.

There, perched on the edge of a large bed, sat my brother.

Ash swung his head up, training his gaze on the doorway. His face lit up with relief and excitement, and he propelled himself off the bed toward me.

Brennus the raven-man sprang out from beside the doorway, inside the room, to block Ash's path.

My brother hopped up and down, trying to see around the massive shapeshifter. "Zee! Are you okay? Where are Mom and Dad?"

"I'm okay." I tried to move toward him, but instead of letting me go, Nevan inched us both closer to the door. I forced a smile for Ash. "Everything'll be okay, I promise. I'll find Mom and Dad. I'm sure they're okay too."

If I said "okay" one more time, it would stop sounding like a word.

Skeiron nodded to Brennus. The raven-man slammed the door shut in our faces.

Ash shouted to me, his cry muted by the wood. "Lindsey!"

I wanted to attack someone, anyone, or at least beat my fists on the door. It would do no good. Channeling my anguish and fury into something useful, that was a better option.

Confronting Skeiron, I demanded, "What did you do to my parents?"

"They remained on the other side of the boundary." His arrogant smile had me battling not to whip out my gun and shoot him between the eyes. "Your brother's room in the—what do you call such establishments?—in the motel was a few feet within the limit." He gave me look of mock pity. "You see, there is more water in your world than you recognize. The motel lies near a spring which is hidden from view in a remote section of the forest."

Hidden springs? How the hell was I supposed to protect my family when I couldn't see the dangers?

Skeiron's arm shifted. Metal glinted.

He'd conjured a goddamn sword. The one he'd rammed through Nevan's chest.

In a heartbeat, I understood his intention.

Shoving Nevan away, I commanded him with every ounce of conscious effort I had. "Get out of here!"

He vanished, the instant before Skeiron's sword slashed the air where he'd stood.

Skeiron seized me by the throat, yanking me off my feet. "Clever wench. I will destroy him, but first I will drain you of every trace of Janusite magic."

We teleported us away from the room where Ash was held, into a dank and gloomy chamber with rough walls. The air was redolent with the stench of blood and pain.

He dropped me.

I stumbled into a hole, regained my footing, and whirled on the sylph king.

With a flourish of his hand, he summoned another man who emerged from the shadows behind him.

"This," the king said, "is the mage who will extract the power from you. It will be painful, and it will not end until you are dead."

The mage shuffled toward me, his grimy hands outstretched. His stained, red robes dragged across the floor. Scars etched across his face cinched his eyes and mouth into a perpetual grimace.

I snaked a hand under my shirt's hem, going for my derringer.

Skeiron flicked his wrist.

An unseen force hurled me into the wall, suspending me there, my feet off the floor.

The mage shambled to me. He grasped my head in hands that stank of filth. His fetid breath choked me. His purple eyes seared into mine, his irises shot through with a dark light dredged from the depths of the grave. My grave.

He spewed a string of noises, some kind of incantation in a long-extinct language.

A million tiny teeth tore at my brain.

I refused to scream. No way would I give Skeiron the satisfaction. Agony shredded me, from my head down to the soles of my feet, in slicing waves that wrenched my body, but I gritted my teeth and clenched my fists until my nails punctured my flesh. Blackness pitted my vision, the room twirled around me, and I knew I would die here—buried inside the earth, with a skeletal mage sucking my soul dry—unless I mustered the brainpower to save myself.

I longed to call for Nevan, but I could not risk Skeiron attacking him. The fates of two worlds depended on one of us surviving, and with his powers, he was far more useful than I was.

Save the worlds, Nevan, for me.

It was my last thought, as a final wave of magic towed me under to drown.

The mage gasped. His hands flew away from my head and he staggered backward, eye bulging.

My agony relented, permitting me one long inhalation, a breath so cleansing I nearly sobbed from the bliss of it. The ringing in my ears waned and the blackness receded.

The mage lifted one long-nailed finger to me in accusation. On a wheezing breath, he said, "The power, she protects it. She hoards it. No magic of any realm may breach the mind of the Janusite."

Skeiron punched his fist into the wall. Chunks of stone crumbled away to patter on the floor.

My knees buckled as the mage's hold on me evaporated, and I flailed at the wall for support, my hand at last slapping flat on solid rock. Damned if I'd collapse in front of Skeiron.

"You swore to me," the king said, seizing the mage's robes with both hands, "you could extract the power and feed it into me."

The mage sputtered. "I tried, your majesty. But she is neither elemental nor human. A fragment of Janus's essence lives inside her." His pallid face turned sickly gray when Skeiron clamped a hand around his neck. "My liege, it took the combined power of the gods to scatter Janus's energy to the Four Winds. Perhaps they could..."

Skeiron rattled the mage with a violent shake. Spittle sprayed from his lips as he said, "You suggest I appeal to the gods?"

"N-no." The mage mewled. "I tell you what I learn from her, nothing more. Please release me from my bargain. I've done all you required of me."

"Have you?" The king sneered, his tone caustic. "Our bargain was for you to mine the Janusite's power and transfer it to me." Skeiron cinched his fist tighter around the mage's neck, making the man gurgle. "You have voided the bargain. Your life is forfeit."

With a sickening crunch, Skeiron crushed the mage's windpipe.

I winced, shutting my eyes until I heard the mage's body thump to the floor.

The sylph king rounded on me.

Without a thought, without conscious decision, I tore the gun out of its holster and fired both .357 rounds into Skeiron's chest. I'd almost aimed for his head, but I wasn't sure I could hit the target with adrenaline ripping through my veins.

The rounds slammed into his chest. Blood spurted.

He jerked, stumbled away from me.

I opened my mouth to shout, but got out only a squeak.

Nevan appeared beside me. He collected me in his arms and spirited us away. High-voltage shocks racked my body, snapping and crackling around and within us both. This was not the rollercoaster through hell. It was a torment of fire and power that tore at the center of my being.

We landed in the forest. I didn't know where and I didn't care.

Shoving away from Nevan, I said, "Go get my brother. Hurry!"

He shook his head, his mouth a grim line.

"Nevan, I command you to retrieve Ash."

He shut his eyes for heartbeat before zeroing in on me. "I can't."

I beat my fists on his chest. "Save him, dammit. Save my brother."

"Lindsey, I—" His shoulders caved in and the misery on his face stopped me. "Oh, love, I can't save anyone."

I slapped him in the face. He did not move or react. I slugged him in the jaw. "Are you working for Skeiron? Is that it?"

"No."

"Then go get my brother."

"I cannot." His tone was solemn and heartbreakingly certain. "I would retrieve your brother, you know I would, but I can do nothing anymore. I'm prevented from action."

"But this fucking debt overrides all magic. You told me that. You swore it."

"I was truthful but—You must have felt it during our transit. The energy firing through me must have affected you as well." His glowing amber irises had faded into a dirty brown. "We barely made it here. Skeiron stripped my powers."

The seconds ticked by, counted out by the rapid beating of my heart. Re-holstering my gun, I stomped back and forth across the little clearing, faster and faster with each ten-foot circuit, perspiration oozing down my temples.

I should never have let Nevan take me out of there. I should've command-ed him to retrieve Ash first, then get me. What kind of a sister abandoned her baby brother in the lair of a psycho elemental being?

Nevan had shown up before I called him and took me away before I had a chance to demand he get my brother first.

"Why did you command me to leave you with Skeiron?" Nevan asked.

"He had a sword. He was about to skewer you again." I kicked a tree so hard the concussion lanced up my ankle into my shin. Dancing on one foot, I cursed myself blue. "You should've taken Ash, not me. He's just a kid."

"I sensed your suffering. You had granted me permission to remove you from the palace if I deemed it necessary, if you were in danger, but I had no power to pierce the ward caging in your brother."

"Did you even try?"

Nevan took hold of my shoulders, rotating me toward him. Despite his haunted expression, a hint of the old confidence sparked there. "We will rescue your brother. I vow it."

A metaphysical bond, more slender than the life debt but still palpable, snapped taut between us. He'd cemented his vow with magic, willingly.

God, I loved him.

And the revelation didn't even scare me. I was in love with a sylph from another world. Maybe it never could work out between us, but for this one day, I'd welcome the experience of loving him.

Hands crossed over my chest, I leaned into Nevan, resting my cheek on his skin. "I am the Janusite. Skeiron brought in a mage to prove it. Turns out I've got a piece of Janus's essence inside me, though nobody seems to know what that means." Entranced by the thumping of his heart, I relished his warmth. "We're screwed, aren't we?"

The sunlight percolating through the treetops speckled his skin with light and shadow. He fastened his arms around me. "Forgive me."

"For what?"

Nevan released the longest groaning sigh I'd ever heard. "I cannot whoosh you anywhere, or conjure anything, or protect you in any manner. I am impotent and utterly useless."

"Bullshit."

He scuffled away from me. "We are far from the portal to your world and the only way back is to walk. Skeiron will have his army searching for us. Leave this place. Quickly. You may make it to the portal before Skeiron catches up to you."

"And what about you?"

"Since I am of no further use, you must leave me here. I have vowed to retrieve your brother and I shall keep my promise."

"Your plan sucks," I said. "I veto it."

He hissed a breath out his nose, eyes squinted. "I am useless."

"You, Nevan, are not in any way impotent, with or without magical abilities."

"Currently, I am but a man. Unable to defend you."

"Oh please." I shook my head. "You are not a man, as you've told me so many times. You're a hot sylph with cool armor and a wicked sword."

"Even if I had my sword and armor, without powers I am—"

"Not useless." I punctuated each word with a thump of my fist on his chest. "I need you in warrior mode, not moping like a fairy."

A small, tight smile stretched his mouth. "Warrior mode is pointless without armor and a sword."

"Maybe I can help you with that."

His smile changed into one of bemused interest. "In what manner?"

"Well, I've got all this power, right?" I swept a hand up and down, indicating myself. "I'm so strong, the mage couldn't suck the magic out of me. I've got serious power."

Nevan got that dubious look again, the one that said he knew I was about to suggest something wacky and he wouldn't like it, but he'd give me a chance to explain anyway. "Janus was the god of doorways, which is why you can open the portal and transport immortals across the boundaries in the mortal realm. Not helpful in—"

"Shush." I took a breath, rolling my shoulders back. "Think. I have Janus's power. He was the god of doorways, yes, but also of beginnings and endings, and of transitions."

"Information I gave you."

"Zip it. I'm not finished."

He mimed zipping his lips shut. Cheeky sylph.

"This Janus guy was tough, right?" I gnawed the inside of my cheek, flipping through the pages of my mental book for answers. "You said Janus was so powerful the other immortals feared him and so the gods banded together to destroy him. But they couldn't get rid of his power, so they scattered it into the winds."

"The Four Winds, which are not winds as you know them. They are both avatars and guardians of energy and magic."

"Doesn't that mean they must've been the ones who put Janus's essence inside me?"

"I suppose," Nevan said slowly. "Not directly, however, since Janus was destroyed eons ago. They must've set things in motion. Why does it matter?"

"They imbued me with magical powers, right?"

"Yes."

"Here's my plan." I paused—not to be dramatic, but because I also feared my plan might be too crazy. "Step one, I make use of my Janusite magic to re-empower you."

From the look on his face, I could tell he really, really wanted to *Lindsey* me. "I doubt that is possible."

"You're awfully pessimistic at the moment, so I'll go with my instincts this time." I walked straight up to him, bounced up on my toes, and leveled our gazes. "I'm giving you back however much of your power I can, whether you like it or not. The life debt ought to smooth the way."

His arms went limp as he gave a tiny shake of his head. "I've come to realize I cannot stop you, when you've set your mind to a task."

"Smart man."

"Do I want to know about step two?"

I sank back down onto my heels, patting his chest. "Step two, I'm going to give Skeiron exactly what he wants."

Nevan flinched away as if I'd shot him. "You will not surrender to Skeiron."

"I have to. He has Ash." I tugged his hands and he shuffled closer. "Besides, after I've shared my magic with you, I'm counting on you to crash through the wards, empowered by your debt to me. In fact, I hereby command you to rescue me and Ash once I've found him."

"Let us pray the life debt is strong enough for that. What is the rest of your plan?"

"I invite Skeiron to take a jaunt across the boundary with me. If we pull it off, this little field trip will be one Skeiron won't enjoy."

He covered his face with his hands for a second, and then let them drop away. "Your plan sounds exceedingly dangerous—and it requires you to be alone with the king. Even with an infusion of your power, I rather doubt I'll be strong enough to aid you if things should go awry."

I placed a kiss over the scar on his chest. "You are smart, resourceful, stubborn, and brave. With or without magic, you have what it takes to help me defeat Skeiron."

Nevan stopped blinking, his cheeks faintly pink. "I am yours to command."

We stared at each other, unspoken things hovering between us, things we both wanted to express but each held back for different reasons. Or maybe the same reason. Fear.

At last, he said, "Explain to me how transporting Skeiron across the boundary will end anything. You took me through the barrier and I am quite alive."

Okay. Honesty time. "We both know why I was able to take you over the boundary, without even touching you."

"Do we?"

I didn't pull away from him, but I did squirm and start counting the swirls in his eyes. "It's not about sex, Nevan. It's about you. How I feel."

He searched my face, his brow pinched above his nose.

"The point is," I explained, "I could take you over the boundary because we have a…um…"

"Connection." No inflection, no smirk, a simple statement of fact.

I nodded. "My magic was awakened by my desperation to save you. I don't have that connection with Skeiron. If I take him across the line—"

"He will be destroyed."

"That's the idea. He doesn't understand why my powers worked with you. He believes I can take him over the boundary."

Nevan gazed at me with admiration. "You are a genius."

I rolled my eyes.

He kissed my forehead. "I will do as you ask."

"About damn time." I ran my hands over his chest. "I wish I could give you all your powers back. Make you whole again. But I think partway is the most I can do."

He thrust a hand into my hair, angling my face up to his. "I was whole again the moment you looked at me in the forest that first day, when you saw me as I truly am and looked on at me without fear or disgust."

"That moment changed me too." A better confession clamored to get out and I no longer saw any reason not to tell him. "I love you, Nevan."

"I love you, Lindsey Astrid Porter."

He kissed me long and slow, with a tenderness and yearning equal to mine, and I relinquished my body and soul to him yet again, within the confines of this bubble we always erected around ourselves whenever we touched. When our lips parted, I cleared my throat, still feeling the slickness of his mouth on mine.

Energy tingled over my skin, diving under the surface to suffuse my entire being. I crushed my mouth to his again, willing my power to infuse him too. He made a surprised noise deep in his throat, his body tensing and then relaxing.

Metal materialized between us.

I moved back a step, smiling when I caught sight of the armor shielding his body and the sword gripped in his hand.

A rustling, faint but distinct, lured my attention to the woods behind me. An instinct stirred inside me, warning of Skeiron's approach.

"Go," I told Nevan. "Skeiron's almost here, I can feel it. Find Tris, he'll help. Find my parents and Travis. Gather our allies, Nevan."

"I will." He laid a hand on my cheek. "Be careful, my love."

He turned and jogged off into the woods. Despite his armor, he made little noise as he slipped away into the night.

I walked in the opposite direction, into the deeper shadows where the forest canopy thickened. Strange insects chirped, orange specks danced in the bushes and trees, and the moss-like ground cover squished under my boots. I ducked a hand under my shirt to touch my holster. With no bullets, the gun was useless—yet reaffirming its presence comforted me somehow.

A raven swooped down from the trees to land in front of me.

Brennus rose, a rippling, roiling shadow that transformed into a man-like creature. His black eyes locked on me. "You are without your guardian."

"And you're without your king."

The weight of another gaze prickled my skin. I spun to face Skeiron.

"He is my scout," the king said. "But never out of contact with me."

"Does he want to serve you, or do you have something on him?"

"There is no difference." Skeiron strode up to me. "Your guardian will not save you this time."

"Don't count him out yet. You may have stripped his magic, but he's still ten times the man you are."

"He is powerless, no better than a mortal." Skeiron nodded to Brennus. "Find Nevan and kill him."

The assassin morphed back into a bird and launched into the sky. His cackling echoed down through the forest.

Nevan, please, run fast.

CHAPTER TWENTY-SIX

SKEIRON ZIPPED ME BACK TO HIS SUBTERRANEAN PALACE, STRAIGHT into the room where he was holding Ash. The instant we materialized, my brother flew off the bed where he'd been sitting cross-legged and tackled me. I staggered backward but clung to him as fiercely as he clung to me.

"Zee!" Ash clinched me hard enough to make me gasp. "I knew you'd come back. Can we go home?"

"Soon, I promise."

His saucer eyes latched onto my gaze. "I don't like it here."

"I know." With a pointed look at Skeiron, I told Ash, "I have to talk to our host first, but then we are going home."

Possibly to die.

I pulled Ash tighter to me and kissed the top of his head. Then I said something I'd never said before to my brother. "I love you, Ash."

His head popped up again, his eyes no longer wide but squinted with befuddlement. I tried to clap the old lid on my emotions, but my hazmat-level containment had fractured. My face must've revealed everything—my guilt at failing to protect my family, uncertainty about what was to come, and so much more—but my brother noted only the fact of what I'd said.

A grin broke out on Ash's face. "I love you too, Zee."

I mustered a smile, weak but genuine. "I need you to trust me, sweetie. I will get you home, but first, I have go outside for a few minutes."

His eyes widened again as he bit down on his lower lip.

"I'll be back," I said. "Just a few minutes."

Ash nodded, eyes glistening with unshed tears. He scampered over to the bed, hopped onto it, and dangled his feet over the edge. The heels of his sneakers bumped the wooden bed frame with each swing of his feet.

A shadow shifted in the far corner, and I abruptly noticed the obsidian-armored sylph posted there.

I led Skeiron out into the corridor.

He shut the door. His expression revealed nothing, but he watched me as if waiting for me to initiate our discussion.

Trying for nonchalance, I let my arms hang slack, my shoulders relaxed and rolled back, resting my weight on one hip. The mistake I'd made before was allowing Skeiron to witness my fear and anger. *Time to rein it in again, Lindsey.*

This part of my plan required cool detachment and clear thinking. I hadn't shared the details about this phase with Nevan, because he would never have agreed to my surrendering to the king if he knew. I needed him far away, gathering our allies in the relative safety of the mortal world. Of course, he couldn't breach the boundary on his own, which left him vulnerable.

To Brennus. To whoever framed me for murder. To Skeiron and his freaking army of sylph warriors, all armed with magic while Nevan had none.

Focus, Lindsey. You've got the power here, remember?

I deliberately met Skeiron's gaze, ignoring the cold that slithered through me at the eye contact. "I want to make a bargain with you."

No reaction. "What sort of bargain?"

"You want me to help you cross the boundary." My fingers had started to twitch. I closed them into loose fists. "I want a few things in return."

"Bargains are formal agreements with magical power."

"That goes both ways, you know."

He crept closer, bending forward to loom over me.

I squelched the impulse to back away. This was it.

His eyes glinted with pure white and seethed with putrid green. "Speak your demands."

"You release my brother and agree to never kidnap, harass, injure, or kill any member of my family ever again. They are safe from you and everyone who is, was, or will be associated with you."

He slanted lower, descending over me. His odor, sharp and sulfurous, suffocated me. I fought back a retch as he plunged his head down to sear his gaze into mine. "In return, you will share the power of the Janusite with me and only me. You serve my will, without question."

"As long as you're king."

He blew a breath out his nose. "As long as I am king. You will also remain with me, physically present at my side, for the remainder of your life."

"Or the remainder of yours, whichever ends first."

"Agreed." He smirked, clearly certain he'd outlive me.

"One more thing." I resisted the urge to scuffle backward, to escape his vile presence. "You will call off Brennus. No harm will come to Nevan for the rest of his existence and you'll return him to his full power, releasing him from any and all bargains he made with you, as well as from the curse on his heart."

I didn't believe Skeiron had really cursed Nevan, and Nevan believed I'd broken the curse anyway, but I wanted nothing omitted from this bargain.

Skeiron's tongue snaked out to moisten his lips. "Nevan has no value to me anymore, so I accept your conditions. In return, you will have no contact with Nevan for the duration of your bargain with me." He snatched up a lock of my hair, coiling it around his index finger, and pulled it taut. "Our bargain will last forever, you realize, as I am immortal."

But not invincible. The king had no idea Nevan apprised me of that fact.

I squared my shoulders, clearing my throat. "Do we have a deal? Based on the parameters we've outlined since the moment I initiated the process by stating my clear intention to strike a bargain."

He brought his finger to his lips, my hair wrapped around it, and inserted his long finger into his mouth, lips puckering around it as he sucked. His face contorted in disgust. He spit out my hair. "You taste of *him*."

"Do we have a deal, Skeiron?"

He straightened, a tower of muscle and menace. "Yes. A bargain is struck."

Magic shot through me, fire lashed with ice, electricity sparked by rain. The ground trembled, or maybe my legs quivered. I struggled to keep my footing as the power of the bargain coursed through me.

The energy faded into a simmering discomfort and I regained my equilibrium.

Brennus appeared beside Skeiron. "I was a feather's breadth from capturing the guardian. Why have you commanded me to return?"

"I have struck a bargain with the Janusite."

Though I supposed Janusite was an improvement over wench, I still fumed at the moniker. "I have a name."

Skeiron sniffed. "I've no use for mortal names. You are a tool, not a comrade."

A tool. Fabulous. I prayed I'd done the right thing, instead of just royally screwing myself and everyone who mattered to me. The one thing I'd most wanted to ask for had been the one thing I could not request.

That he leave the mortal world alone.

Skeiron would never have made such a vast concession, what with multi-world domination tops on his to-do list. Saving my family and Nevan was the most I could ask for and I was banking on my ability to craft a solid bargain— and on the hope Skeiron wouldn't finagle a way around my terms. I bore sole responsibility for saving the world.

Not entirely accurate. I had my allies. My well-armed family, a tough sheriff, and one testy fae. My best hope for rallying those allies lay with a singular sylph clad in armor, who wielded a magnificent sword.

Nevan believed his current lack of power made him useless. I would've bet on him in any fight—unpowered, unarmed, with both hands tied behind his back. But my deal with Skeiron, sealed by our mutual agreement, ensured Nevan would regain his full power.

I pointed toward the doorway. "My brother."

"Will accompany us to the portal, which you will open. Once we are through, your brother may return to your family."

"And Nevan?"

"He has been restored."

I'd have to trust him on that point, since I'd agreed to stay away from Nevan for the duration of our bargain. An ache throbbed in my chest, squeezing my heart. I'd couldn't see Nevan again, much less touch him. And God, how I yearned for the comfort of his arms around me. *Out of reach forever.*

Unless I succeeded. Unless I liberated two worlds from a tyrant.

Me. The one-time man-killer who'd hidden out in a rock shop for three years, too afraid to deal with the past.

Nevan's voice echoed in my mind. *You are a goddess, in every way.* Time to act like one.

I was more than the frigging Janusite. I was Lindsey Astrid Porter, daughter of gun-toting hippies, girlfriend of an immortal elemental warrior from the Bronze Age, and the tough chick who'd blasted .357 rounds at a sylph king and bridged two worlds to resurrect my lover. Plus, I'd talked a powerful being into agreeing to every one of my demands.

No time for basking in my accomplishments. The greatest risk of all was ahead of me.

The door pivoted inward and Ash trotted out, escorted by his sylph guard.

"Let's get moving," I said. "We've got a boundary to cross."

———

I PUNCHED THROUGH THE FALLS AND SIDESTEPPED ONTO THE LEDGE, MY hair glued to my face and my clothes dripping. Goose bumps pebbled my skin, chilled by frigid water. I threw a hand up to shield them from the brilliant sunlight, as my eyes slowly adjusted. Humid summer heat blanketed me, turning my drenched self into a clammy mess.

Ash tumbled out of the falls. I snagged his hand and urged him onto the ledge beside me, scooting sideways to make room.

Skeiron leaped out next, lithe as a cougar, far more agile than either of us mortals. With one smooth stride he penetrated the cascade and pivoted to march onto the ledge, pushing past me and Ash. We crushed ourselves to the cliff to avoid getting shoved off into the deep pool below us.

When Nevan had taken me through the waterfall, he whisked me onto and off of the ledge. Skeiron made no effort to aid us. He leaped across the wide gap between the ledge and the wooden railing, vaulting over the barrier onto the dirt path where I'd first seen Nevan. Hand in hand, Ash and I inched along the shelf.

Brennus hurtled through the cascade in raven form, wings spread wide, water spraying out. His wings whooshed as he soared past us, high into the sky and out of sight behind the trees.

Ash and I reached the ledge's limit. A good fifteen feet out and six feet down separated us from solid ground, with the railing in the way. Skeiron waited on the path, gaze fixated on me.

"Need a hand?"

I yelped at the familiar voice. Ash jumped, reeling into me, and the momentum thrust us forward, our feet skidding on the wet stone.

A rangy body swung out in front of us, halting our fall.

Tris frowned at me. "So ya do need a hand. Eh, lady?"

"You scared the hell out of us." I slapped his arm. He moved past me to hover in the air just beyond the ledge's end.

He was floating. Actually *floating.*

"Whoa," Ash said, staring wide-eyed at Tris. "Who's he?"

"A leprechaun," I told him. "Tris, about my brother…"

"Got a safe place to hide him." Tris rubbed his neck and grumbled. "Nevan wanted to come get you, but he couldn't. Something about bleeping foolish mortal women. I'm paraphrasing. Nevan's powers are back, but cripes, that dude still has issues—and he knows about your new bargain."

The deal with Skeiron prevented me having any contact with Nevan. He must've sensed the prohibition, much the way he sensed when I was in trouble back in the palace. "Nevan sent you?"

"Yep." Tris offered me his hand. I took it, and since I was holding Ash's hand, the three of us winked out of and back into the real world, our feet now on the path about twenty feet from Skeiron. Tris cast a wary glance at the king and hunched his shoulders, jamming his hands in his jeans pockets. "Nevan don't know the details of your bargain, but he ain't a happy camper."

"Tell him to trust me, stop bitching, and do what I told him."

The leprechaun grinned. "Sure. Love to."

Without so much as a wave goodbye, Tris grabbed my brother's arm and they vanished.

The sylph king watched with arrogant satisfaction as I approached him. "Your fae friend will not save you. Nevan cannot save you. The bargain you entered into binds you to me forever."

Our deal stated it remained in effect until one of us died. He assumed I'd die first and my enslavement would last essentially forever, in mortal terms. Good. My plan relied on his misconceptions.

Skeiron herded me down the path, past the vortex, and through the rock garden into the parking lot. The Porter family motor home hunkered there, parked near the exit onto the highway, but the shop seemed oddly deserted. I wondered why he hadn't poofed us straight to the boundary. This death march of ours made worms wriggle in my gut.

But it was more than the walk. Everything seemed off. I struggled to figure out why, when the truth hit me.

Silence. No birds twittered. No cars hummed on the highway. Even the rumble of the fans inside the shop had gone quiet.

The door of the motor home burst open. My parents rushed out, their arms loaded with—well, arms. My father had slung a rifle over his shoulder and wore a gun belt with a holstered semiautomatic pistol on his hip and extra ammo clips attached to the belt. Mom gripped a shotgun, with her favorite .357 revolver and its speed loaders clipped to her belt, ready to reload on the fly. She had another handgun berthed in a shoulder holster, while Dad carried a second rifle in a sheath strapped to his back.

I'd never loved them more than in that moment.

My parents stopped halfway across the parking lot, their stances wide, their gazes and expressions hardened into steel.

Skeiron tipped his chin up, sweeping his haughty gaze over them. "If you wish no harm to come to your daughter, lay down your weapons."

Mom targeted her 12-gauge shotgun at Skeiron. "Touch my daughter and I'll blow enough holes in you to make your head spin for a good long while."

"He won't hurt her," Dad said, resting his hand on his holstered pistol. "He needs her alive. We're just here to make a point."

"And what point is that, puny mortal?" Skeiron asked.

Nevan materialized in front of my parents. His impressive armor glittered in the sunshine. He set his mouth in a determined line, his eyes twin supernovas, his body a vision of sinuous muscle and contained fury.

"The point," Nevan said coolly, "is to show you Lindsey will never be alone."

How the hell was he here? The bargain—

Nevan winked at me, his eyes glittering.

And that's when I understood. He held a trump card nothing could outplay. He owed me his life. Though I remained bound to Skeiron, the part of our deal forbidding me from seeing Nevan could not override the life debt. I'd granted him permission to come to me whenever he deemed it necessary.

A flash of movement drew my attention to the shop's entrance.

Travis sauntered down the walkway, his strides long and purposeful, one hand firmly on the gun on holstered on his hip, the other gripped around the barrel of a rifle. He wore his sheriff's uniform and his eyes were clear, his face molded into a stern expression.

Stan marched out of the shop behind Travis. His tie-dyed shirt and rumpled khakis clashed with the M-16 rifle he held in both hands.

My allies. My army. Pride swelled in my chest for this ragtag group of family, friends...and Nevan.

Without thinking, I took a step toward him.

An invisible force yanked me back. I grunted in surprise, stumbled, caught myself.

Skeiron sniggered. "You belong to me, wench."

Wench again? Oh, he'd suffer for that. "Let's go to the fucking boundary already."

"Not yet." His arctic smile frosted my blood. "It's time to teach you a lesson about bargains."

I recoiled a step, gravel crunching under my boots.

"Did you believe," he snarled, "*you* could outwit *me*, the king of the sylphs? I have negotiated bargains since before your kind learned to paint outlines of their hands on cave walls."

My gaze shot to my parents and then to Nevan, who'd switched into warrior mode, stoic and rock-still.

"Your family is safe from me and my associates," Skeiron said. He pointed a finger straight up, indicating the sky. "But not from the elements."

I stared up at the heavens, a ceiling of deep azure arching over our heads. A gray blob appeared, swelling and churning, transmuting into a writhing mass of purple and black. The air thickened, charged with a faint current that crackled over my skin. The humidity choked my lungs.

The storm cloud swallowed the sky, plunging us into a false twilight. Lightning slashed the air. Thunder detonated, the ground shook, and balls of sizzling, white plasma disgorged from the clouds. They bounced along the gravel to fizzle out at our feet.

I waved my arms above my head. "Get inside!"

My parents retreated into the RV. Travis and Stan bolted for the store.

Nevan remained steadfast in his position twenty feet from me and Skeiron, the sword in his hand, its tip directed at the ground.

The storm unleashed a torrent of rain. It inundated us and clogged my vision, but bound to Skeiron, I couldn't move unless he bid it. Tiny hailstones pecked my face, arms, chest, stinging my skin.

The sky mutated to grayish green, washing the world in an eerie light, and a clattering, rumbling racket erupted overhead.

Skeiron seized me, and in the instant he teleported us away, I glimpsed the source of the tumult.

A tornado was descending on the heads of everyone I loved.

CHAPTER TWENTY-SEVEN

WE CRASHED DOWN ON U.S. 41, SMACK ON THE DOUBLE YELLOW LINE. SKEI-ron was behind me, his hands shackling my upper arms. He yanked me back against his body, the fabric of his toga scraping over my exposed skin.

Straight ahead of us, sunlight set the mile marker sign ablaze.

Behind us, thunder boomed. Lightning cracked. I twisted my head around to look back and panic surged in my chest. The thunderstorm overwhelmed the horizon and half the sky above us, and I could just make out the gray-blue rope of the tornado whipping side to side, spiraling ever downward.

Skeiron spun us both around to face the storm. "Your loved ones will be destroyed in a matter of moments. Know you belong to me and there is no one left in any realm who can rescue you."

Metal screeched and clanged. Wood cracked. I couldn't see the shop or the RV, but I realized the tornado was chewing them up. It spat debris in a whirling-dervish cloud. My mind jumped to the worst conclusions, but I did what I do best. I bottled up the terror, the images of mangled bodies, and locked it all away in my mental vault.

Tears streamed down my cheeks, but I hauled in a breath and steeled my soul. I had to finish this.

Power sizzled in the air.

A phalanx of black-armored sylph soldiers materialized before us, two rows of ten each. Another phalanx appeared beside the first. Then another. And another. I counted the groups as they popped into view, until the last one emerged and Skeiron leaned in to growl in my ear.

"This is one battalion. I have twenty more."

I'd counted a hundred soldiers in this battalion. Twenty more? That would make...

Two thousand soldiers.

If they survived the tornado, I had my parents, Nevan, Travis, Stan, and—if he showed up—Tris. Seven of us against way too many of them. If any of my family and friends were still alive.

My gaze flew to the tornado. The ripping, banging, freight-train racket reverberated in my ears.

Skeiron wheeled us back around toward the mile marker sign. "This is the boundary, delineated by the post there. The energy licks at me even here, thirty paces from the line." He thrust me toward the sign, making me stumble a few steps. "It is time, Janusite."

A *pow* ripped through the air, originating from the sky behind us.

I whipped my head around.

The tornado scattered. The thundercloud dissipated, like smoke blown away by a hair dryer.

Nevan. Somehow I knew he was responsible, though I had no clue how.

Skeiron clapped a hand on my shoulder, wrenching it backward. I bit back a grunt.

"The boundary," he said. "Now."

Oh God, please let this work.

I took a deep breath, straightened, lifted my chin, and marched down the highway with Skeiron trailing behind me. When we reached the mile marker sign, I hesitated long enough for him to catch up. I took hold of his hand, cringing inwardly at the contact, and led him across the boundary.

Heat flashed over me. I tripped, halted, gasping for air as pressure mounted in my chest.

Skeiron freed my hand and clutched his head in both palms. His eyes went wide, his mouth was agape, and his entire body shuddered violently. Sparks of energy seared his skin.

He crumpled to his knees, his features distorted in agony.

I scrambled away from, toward the boundary. A bizarre mixture of glee and horror tore through me, propelling me forward again to crouch beside Skeiron. I didn't care that my voice came out harsh, not like me at all, rife with an anger I'd suppressed for too long. "I promised to stay with you as long as you're alive and still king."

He bellowed at me.

"Sucks, doesn't it?" I bent closer and the power ripping him apart singed my skin. "You made a bad bargain and you made one too many assumptions. You should've asked me how I managed to take Nevan across the line."

Energy arced over his flesh, into his nostrils and open mouth. He gagged. "You will suffer. My army—"

"Will be stuck on the other side of the boundary, you stupid bastard." I gulped down my gorge, sickened by the blood pouring from his nostrils. I forged on anyway, hungry for a vengeance I hadn't realized I needed. "Let me tell you how this works. I brought Nevan across the line because he matters to me. Love empowers my magic, you sadistic bastard."

The king screamed.

A curtain of white, electrical energy enveloped him. His body seemed to blur and boil, bits of him splitting off to spiral out into the air, forming an ever-growing mist. The realization of what I was witnessing struck me. I staggered backward a few more steps, my hand flying to my mouth.

His body was being disassembled atom by atom.

Thunder exploded just down the road behind me.

As the remnants of Skeiron drifted into an amorphous cloud above my head, I risked a glance back down the highway.

The sylph army was advancing on me, swords brandished.

Gulping down the lump in my throat, I stared up at the cloud composed of Skeiron's essence. It floated up, expanding, dispersing. A gust of wind worthy of a hurricane blasted over me. I teetered toward the boundary but held my ground.

The wind scattered the cloud, scattered Skeiron to the Four Winds.

Gone. No longer king, no longer alive.

Our bargain shattered with a palpable tearing sensation. I hissed at the pain, though it was blessedly brief.

The sylph army halted at the boundary, an arm's length from me.

I raised an arm to indicate the last vestiges of the Skeiron cloud. "Your king is gone. You can't cross the boundary, which means there will be no conquest of the mortal realm. Go home."

They didn't move.

What did I have to do to get rid of these creeps?

"It doesn't work that way, love."

Relief gushed through me at the sound of Nevan's voice. Moving only my eyes, I searched the area for Nevan and found him a few feet to my left, angle sideways to me on the opposite side of the boundary. His armor glistened and sunlight bounced off the blade of his sword, gripped in his muscular hand.

"Need a bit of help, darlin'?" he asked with a grin.

"The damn army won't go away."

"I'm afraid they'll have no intention of giving up." He swept his gaze over the army poised a dozen feet from him. "They will complete their mission, even without a king."

I nabbed his hand and towed him over the boundary. As I twined my fingers tightly with his, I said, "It's safer over here. Is my family okay?"

"They are unharmed, as is your employer." He hesitated, then added, "And the sheriff."

"What got rid of the storm?"

"I did."

"I knew it." Though I longed to kiss him, I wouldn't do it in front of the sylph army. "How did you do it?"

"I am an air elemental—and my full power has been restored, which I believe you are responsible for. Aren't ye?"

"Absolutely." Hell with the army. I sealed my lips over his for a firm kiss. "Best deal I ever made."

He brushed the backs of his fingers down my jaw. "I underestimated you. What you did, crafting such a cunning bargain...You will do fine in my world."

"Thanks." A warm glow enveloped me from the inside out. The glow of victory, yes, but mostly it stemmed from his compliment. "I never realized how incredibly powerful you are in your full glory. You are magnificent, Nevan."

He puffed up a little, his closed-mouth smile one of pride and well-earned satisfaction.

My gaze wandered to the army standing motionless mere feet from us. "What mission are they waiting to finish?"

"To destroy me and your family, then take you back to the Unseen realm. They must avenge their king."

"I thought killing him would end this."

"Sorry, love." He sighed. "It's only the first stage."

"What else is there? Do you have a plan?"

"Nothing as foolhardy as yours." He sounded annoyed but his gaze was soft, his eyes muted by worry.

"My ideas are always crazy," I said. "But it worked. Skeiron is no more."

"Yes, I saw what you did." He let out a long sigh, and I swore a burden physically lifted from his shoulders, squaring them. "You freed me, Lindsey. Thank you."

"Are you back at one hundred percent? I mean, did my bargain with Skeiron get undone when I undid him?"

"Agreements previously fulfilled remain and we are both freed from our vows to him. But for the record, you have not yet experienced my full glory." He hit me with his best sensual smile and a pulse of sweet, erotic energy shot through me. "I'll demonstrate it for ye later, in private."

If what he'd shown me so far represented less than his full glory...Another pulse of desire rippled through me.

He dipped his head and pulled me closer. "Think ye can handle me, unrestrained?"

"Absolutely." I swept my hand through the air, indicating the sylph battalion. "You had a plan?"

A soldier separated from the throng and approached the boundary. His face shield revealed only his eyes, but he spoke in a voice gravelly and cold. "Surrender the Janusite or we will slaughter every human within the confines of the boundary."

Without releasing my hand, Nevan rose to full height, shoulders back, head high. He looked so regal, so powerful, so virile. *Magnificent.*

I observed him—okay, gazed in rapt adoration at him—as he addressed the army.

"Skeiron is no more," he announced, his voice echoing off the trees. "He cannot protect or empower you. All of you have seen what the Janusite can do. The king possessed more power than all of you combined, and yet she—" Nevan swept a hand in my direction, flashing me a surreptitious wink. "—destroyed him without a single weapon, wielding only the power of the Janusite. Do you dare challenge her?"

All but a dozen of the soldiers vanished.

"If you will not surrender," the leader of the army said, "the battle begins."

Nevan's posture went taut, his demeanor shifted into predator mode. His voice became a soft threat. "So be it."

I nudged him with my shoulder. "This is your plan? Interdimensional war?"

"Trust me." He voiced it as a statement, but uncertainty flickered in his eyes, as if he still couldn't quite believe I did trust him.

"I was just curious," I said. "But I've got complete faith in you."

"As do I, in you."

Someone blipped into view to my right. I blinked at the late-comer.

Tris slouched with arms slack at his sides and scowled at us. To Nevan, he said, "We doing this or what?"

"We are."

I glanced from Tris to Nevan three times before pinning my gaze to the sylph holding my hand. "What the hell is going on?"

At least a dozen men and women appeared, one after the other, individuals of various ages, shapes, and sizes. They wore casual attire, as if they'd just come from the mall—everything from jeans and T-shirts to crop tops and corduroys. One young woman sported a mini skirt.

Every one of them carried a weapon. Daggers. Maces. Swords. Bows and arrows.

"We got this covered," Tris said. "We've endued your team's weapons, temporarily, to give you mortals a leg up with the sylphs at the shop. Ya might wanna go help them, while me and my team cast a little spell."

"A spell?" I said, totally confused.

Nevan hooked an arm around my shoulders. "They will erase the soldiers' memories so they forget both their mission and why they sought you."

"Ah…" I looked at Tris, speechless.

Nevan spoke for me. "She's trying to say she appreciates the fae's assistance."

Tris shrugged, making a noncommittal noise.

"Don't worry," Nevan murmured to me. "Only Tris knows you are the Janusite. The other fae have no idea."

Thank heavens for that. I glanced up at the sky, issuing a prayer for more good fortune. "I need to see my family. Take me, Nevan, please."

He took me. And he didn't even make an off-color joke about my word choice.

The gunshots battered my eardrums in the instant before the world blurred into view. The explosive noise made my ears ring, deafening me.

Over by the RV, Mom and Dad unleashed a volley of gunfire at two sylph warriors. The soldiers flinched at the impact of the bullets but did not relent as bore down on my family.

Stan huddled against the shop building, pinned down by a trio of sylphs. He squeezed off round after round, sweeping his M-16 left and right to hit all three soldiers. One dropped to his knees and clutched at his neck, blood streaming out from between his fingers.

A weak spot. Hallelujah.

Stan's lips moved as he shouted something to Travis and my parents.

From his vantage in the driveway, Travis fired off a shot. The sylph in his path lunged at him, clamping one hand around his shooting arm and wrenching it. Pain contorted his features. He must've cried out, but I couldn't hear a damn thing. The gunfire ricocheting off the metal shop building reverberated off the trees in a feedback loop that amplified the ringing in my ears.

Nevan threw an arm around me, his sword brandished in his other hand. My own voice sounded muffled when I told him, "Go. Help them."

I had no idea how sylph hearing worked but I prayed he could still make out my words, by lip reading if nothing else. He nodded, started to leave, and turned back to me. He offered his open palm to me and two objects appeared in his hand. A box of ammo for my derringer. I took the gift.

Nevan stalked off into the melee.

Heart pounding, I yanked my gun free of the holster inside my waistband, popped open the barrel, dumped out the empty shells, and dropped in two .357 shells. As I clicked the barrel shut, I caught sight of Nevan.

With his back to me, he clashed swords with a sylph taller and broader than he was. Their blades locked as the soldier drove Nevan backward.

My mom shot a sylph in the neck. Blood spurted. The warrior tumbled backward onto the ground.

The gigantic soldier battling Nevan swung his sword back and slashed it at Nevan, who thrust his own blade up to meet the assault. The other sylph pounded his sword into Nevan's with brutal force, knocking Nevan off balance. He lost his footing and his knees smacked into ground.

With deadly precision, the other sylph hefted his sword up, aimed the tip down, and drove the blade toward Nevan's throat, exposed above his metal breastplate.

I pulled the trigger on my derringer, slamming both .357 rounds into the soldier. One round fractured his collarbone, blood running down his breastplate. His head jerked as the second round slammed into his neck. His sword veered sideways to puncture the ground beside Nevan's head.

The warrior collapsed, face down in the gravel.

With one hand, Nevan braced his sword on the ground and levered his body off the gravel. I rose with him, oblivious to the battle raging around us.

Nevan shoved me behind him and thrust his sword straight into the sylph who'd been targeting me with his own blade—the soldier I hadn't seen coming. Nevan's blade pierced the warrior's neck, nearly decapitating him, and he fell down dead.

Travis dispatched the last soldier with a shot to the larynx.

Blood stained Nevan's armor and his sword. My gaze traveled around the parking lot, taking in the blood pooling around the dead sylphs, the red stains on the clothing of my friends and family. I was the only one not marked by the battle. My stomach twisted, at the gore and at the realization the ones I loved most in the world had risked their lives to protect me.

Even Travis, the man who'd harassed me for three years, had stood by me in this fight. Of course, I now realized he'd been in love with me for years. I scratched my arms, plagued by a sudden itching all over me. Travis loved me. I had no idea how to deal with that, but the time had come to stop hiding from life and the problems it handed me.

I holstered my gun.

None of this would've happened if I weren't the Janusite. Nobody asked me if I wanted this burden. I was stuck with it, though, and I still had no conception of what the job entailed—or what I might become.

Shedding his armor, vanishing it to wherever he sent his possessions, Nevan drew me into his arms. I wrapped mine around him and buried my face against his chest, the heat of him comforting me like it always did, though I needed it even more today. The ringing in my ears died away and I noticed sounds. My parents, Travis, and Stan chattering. The *ka-chunk* of rounds being chambered into firearms. The *thump-thump* of Nevan's heart.

We both needed a cuddle. And damn, we'd earned it this time.

"Is everyone okay?" I called out, unwilling to peel myself away from Nevan yet.

"Fine," said Mom, Dad, Travis, and Stan.

My head shot up and, without relinquishing my hold on Nevan, I twisted my head around to study my parents. "Where's Ash?"

On cue, Tris and Ash poofed in. The leprechaun shrugged and poofed out again, as my brother exploded with glee. "Whoa, Zee, that was awesome! Teleportation rocks."

I resettled my head on Nevan's chest. Warm. Solid. Velvety against my cheek. "Thank you, Nevan. For saving my life—again."

"You saved my life as well." He combed a hand through my hair. "Once again, we're even on the gratitude front."

"I like equality. Then I know you're here because you want to be, not because you owe me."

"Never doubt that, love."

"But we need to zip on over to the other side of the falls and officially cancel out your life debt."

"We will. Later."

A *whoosh-whoosh-whoosh* made all of us glance skyward.

Brennus, the raven, soared overhead in a wide circle.

My dad swung his shotgun up and loosed three rounds. The bird cackled and swerved out of sight behind the trees.

We'd forgotten all about Skeiron's pet assassin.

The raven swooped down with stunning speed, his body a blur of motion. His talons sank into my shoulders. I clawed at them, but as swiftly as he'd descended, Brennus ripped me away from Nevan and launched into the sky with me in his clutches.

CHAPTER TWENTY-EIGHT

I SHUT MY EYES AGAINST THE WIND SCOURING MY FACE, GRABBED onto Brennus's talons, but no amount of scratching and pulling loosened his grip. I couldn't fight off a damn bird? So much for me being the most powerful muckety-muck ever. Plummeting to death from high above the earth appealed to me a hell of a lot more than whatever Brennus had planned. Daring to open my eyes, I choked back a scream.

We plunged through the sky, toward the woods below. My stomach heaved at the sudden drop. The air bit into me like teeth and lashed my hair around my face.

Brennus flew us straight toward a waterfall secluded deep in the overgrown forest. It stretched higher than the falls behind the rock shop. This cataract rumbled with menacing vigor, its water spraying up in a low-hanging cloud.

We plummeted into the cascade. I gagged as water pierced my nostrils and throat.

The raven-man released me. The momentum of our flight hurled me across the cave behind the falls, straight into the rear wall. My bones cracked against solid rock, my nerves screamed from the agony. The tang of blood dribbled down the back of my throat, into my mouth. I toppled backward onto the floor, striking with a lesser, but no less excruciating, blow.

My entire body burned, ached, throbbed in the worst way. I was fairly certain I'd broken multiple bones. I tried to move my legs but they didn't budge. I managed to lift my arms and palpate my head. My scalp was moist with a warm, viscous liquid spreading through my hair. I fought for each breath, wincing at the pain in my chest.

Brennus landed by my feet. He squawked once and morphed into his humanoid form, rising above me, his head inches from the high ceiling. He dragged me by my feet into the center of the cave. His black eyes, cold and empty, bored into me.

"You must die," he said, sounding vaguely regretful about it.

I rolled my eyes to glance around the cave. Based on my glimpses of the area outside, I'd determined this wasn't the falls behind the shop. Brennus had taken me far away and I had no idea how long it might take Nevan to find me.

I was a self-reliant woman, right? I could save myself.

Except I couldn't move my legs. Or my arms. Turning my head, even a smidgen, shot searing pain through my skull.

Brennus tilted his head side to side in a bird-like mannerism. "Thank you."

I stared at him, unblinking. "Excuse me?"

The wet rattling in my voice made my gut clench. *Running out of time.*

"You killed Skeiron," he said. "I was bound to the king by a bargain he tricked me into, which prevented me from harming him. Skeiron commanded, and I had no choice but to obey." He swiped a hand over his bald head. "He is gone, thanks to you. But, I'm afraid, you still must die."

"Why? You're free to do what you want." I coughed, spitting blood onto my chin. "I've done nothing to you."

He gave a slow nod that turned into a shake of his head. "Another has bound me with a debt beyond all others. He spared my life once and forced me to admit the debt I owe him." Brennus knelt beside me, laying a hand on my stomach. "For a thousand years, I have served the will of my king. But on this day, I must enact the will of my true master—as I did when I terminated the life of the red-haired mortal."

The truth shivered through me. "You killed Brad."

His eyes narrowed. "Brad? Was that the mortal's name?"

"Yes." I pulled in a crackling breath, my chest on fire with pain. "Who made you do it? Who is your true master?"

He shifted over me, straddling my thighs. "Enough of this talk. You must die, but first I must know. Will your power be scattered or will it be destroyed forever?"

"No fucking idea."

He grasped my chin and yanked my head left and right, inspecting me with a ruthless focus. "I cannot perceive your magic. Only the guardian was permitted that right." His nails dug into my skin, triggering the hot sting of blood. "I must risk it. He commands me to do so."

Brennus drew back one huge hand, like a baseball player about to pitch a ball. His fingers slimmed and sharpened into black talons.

You've got magic, girl. Use it.

Fueled by desperation, I reeled my thoughts back to the moment when my power first emerged, when Nevan kissed me in the woods to test me. The passion, the freedom, the burning connection between us—those elements awakened the magic. But it was trust and love that liberated my powers.

Brennus shredded my shirt with his talons. He tapped the curved point of one talon on my chest, over my heart. "I will take your heart and hex it to bind your magic to the Four Winds. No one shall ever recover your power."

"What is it with you guys and cursing hearts?"

"The heart is the seat of the soul."

He drew a circle on my flesh, marking out his path.

I concentrated all my thoughts, all my desires, on one objective. *I love you, Nevan.* Could he hear me? I didn't know, but the declaration blazed through me. The potency of it wrung tears from my eyes and flooded me with energy. Hot, snapping power. It scorched my veins, energized my body, overwhelmed the pain. The doors of my mind and my soul flung wide. I might die in a few minutes, but in this moment, I was empowered.

Brennus pressed his talon down to pierce my skin. His eyes rapt on the task, he parted his lips as if admiring his handiwork.

He drove his talon deep into my chest.

I swallowed my scream, because goddammit, I would not give him the satisfaction.

Nevan's energy poured into me. Warm. Spicy. Earthy. Just like him.

The talon fractured my ribs. I screamed and hurled everything I had at him, uncertain of what I was wielding or how it worked. A wave of glittering, ice-blue magic collided with the raven-man. His body jerked. His talon popped out of my chest. Another, stronger wave—a tsunami of power—bowled him over backward. He flipped end over end, flying through the air, to wham into the wall.

"Nobody curses my heart."

Speaking sent me into a fit of wet hacking. Liquid dribbled from my lips, accompanied by the bitter taste of blood. Blackness invaded my vision.

Nevan blipped into view beside me, his face wrenched with grief.

Yeah. I was dying. The idea bothered me less than I would've expected, lost as I was in a haze of numbness. I wanted to see my family, to be held by Nevan one more time.

From far away, I watched Nevan produce his sword, targeting Brennus.

"Don't kill him." I spoke the words, my voice rattling, though I felt detached from my own voice. "Someone else made him do it. A bargain."

Nevan stopped with his sword still raised over the assassin and glanced at me. "Who?"

Another figure materialized near my feet, on a diagonal to Nevan and Brennus. In a throaty Texas drawl, the newcomer said, "I made him do it."

A chill like none I'd ever experienced froze me from my skin straight down to my soul. I croaked, "Calder?"

"Howdy, angel." Hunched over, as if his spine had been permanently crooked, he extended a bony hand to point his claw-tipped finger at me. His eyes had no whites, only golden brown irises that filled the orbs, with black pupils dilated by the gloom in the cave. "Took me a long time to figure out how to get you, how to get the power to do it. You got no clue how many bargains I had to make."

Calder's voice scraped like sandpaper on granite. Long, wiry hairs sprouted from his arms, exposed by the ripped and filthy short-sleeve T-shirt that hung on his emaciated torso.

Nevan let his sword-holding arm fall, the tip of his blade lodging in the dirt. "This is Calder?"

My formerly dead ex-fiancé laughed, the sound sharp and rough as broken glass. "And you're her new honey. Sorry, but you lose. She's mine, forever."

Nevan gritted his teeth, forcing words out between them. "You made it appear she had murdered that man. Why?"

"You oughta know how it works." Calder dropped into a crouch, running his teeth over his bottom lip, revealing two sharp canines, inhuman in size and shape. "The forging has to be entered into willingly. She's gotta want to die."

I tried to sit up, but pain racked my body and forced me down again. "Forging? What are you talking about?"

"Why d'ya think I did all this?"

"Revenge. I shot you."

"Nah, you got it all wrong, sweetness." He trailed one claw up the inside of my calf, raking it over the denim of my jeans. "I was trying to tell ya that night. We can have eternity together, but only if you go through the forging. Like I did."

The forging. Puzzle pieces clicked into place in my mind, forming a vivid picture I'd never wanted to see. Nevan had told me how, as his mortal body lay dying, his blood had opened a portal and drawn the sylph king Notus to him. On the night I had shot Calder, he kept saying my blood was the key, and if I died, I'd be strong enough to become his mate forever.

Oh God. His mate.

I focused on his eyes, the odd coloring and the lack of whites. His wicked canines. The long hairs on his arms. He wasn't human anymore. He wasn't a ghost either. Nevan had told me it took enormous strength of character to survive the forging process intact. Why on earth would Calder have volunteered for it?

"I was attacked," he said, curling those clawed fingers over my knee. "I can tell you're wondering why I signed up for this. Well, I didn't—exactly. I went hiking in the woods and a damn cougar got me. I was dying, but I'd fallen next to a stream."

Water. A portal.

"All of a sudden," Calder said, "this man was there. Offered me a chance to live, but in a different way. I'd be immortal and powerful, practically invincible, and he swore I could still have you. But only if you went through the forging."

I coughed, wheezing for air, dizzy from blood loss and pain—and the stark reality of everything Calder had done. For me. No. For himself. "If you loved me, you would've let me go."

Nevan fell to his knees beside me, laying a palm on my forehead. He eyed Calder sideways. "She needs healing."

"Uh-uh." Calder flicked one claw at Brennus, who conjured Skeiron's endued sword and wedged the tip at the base of Nevan's skull. Calder wagged a finger, tsking. "She has to die, you know that. I'm getting my mate back and this is the only way. She's gotta be forged and become like me—like us."

Nevan's lip curled. "You and I are nothing alike. I'm a sylph. You are one of the kerkopes, a filthy shapeshifter, a monkey in a man's body. I can see why you chose the species, they are as vile as your soul."

Calder slammed his fist onto the rock floor. "Shut up! Lindsey was mine way before she ever met you. She wore my ring."

Nevan arched one eyebrow. "And yet she remained a virgin while with you. She gave herself to me after four days." His hand still on my forehead, he bent his fingers to caress me in a soothing gesture. "We both know which of us she chooses."

Calder leaped up, his bare feet lifting off the floor and smacking down again. His feet bracketed my thighs, inches from Nevan. Calder bent, then flexed, his fingers. "Lindsey, tell him. You choose the forging. You choose me."

My voice thin and reedy, I said, "Brennus said you wanted me dead."

Throwing his head back, Calder groaned. "The bird's being too literal. You have to die to be forged."

Nevan winced as Brennus prodded his neck with the sword. "She does not want—"

"Shut up!" Calder screeched, clutching his head in both hands, eyes wild. "You don't get to choose for her."

"And you believe you do?" The cold hatred in Nevan's voice made me look at him, but his face gave away nothing.

"I love her," Calder growled. "It's my right."

"Nobody decides for me," I said, lifting my head to meet Calder's gaze. "You tormented me for days, framing me for murder and sending Brennus to stalk me. You must've known Skeiron was after me, but you didn't do a damn thing about it. Guess who did." I smiled weakly at Nevan, then turned back to Calder. "Why on earth would I ever choose you? I'm sure as hell not dying to be with you, turning myself into a giant monkey-thing so I can be your mate."

Calder backed away from me, past my feet, hiding near the wall. "Then you die. For good, for real, no take-backs."

Nevan squinted at Calder. "I will never allow it."

"That's why you die first, lover boy."

Calder nodded to Brennus.

The assassin sliced Skeiron's sword down at Nevan's neck.

Nevan rolled out of the blade's trajectory, kicking at the sword with such strength it popped out of Brennus's grasp. Nevan snatched it up, bounded to his feet, and slashed the blade toward Brennus.

"Stop!" I said.

Nevan hesitated, the blade nicking Brennus's skin. A droplet of crimson blood trickled down the iridescent blue-black flesh of his throat. Nevan looked to me, a question in his eyes.

He'd stopped because he had to, thanks to the life debt.

"Don't kill him," I said. "You of all people should understand it's not his fault."

"But he'll kill us both. His debt to this one—" Nevan pointed the sword's tip at Calder. "—coerces him to do so."

I summoned the last ounce of my life energy, though it drained away on every drop of blood, to push up onto my elbows and address Calder. Pain coruscated through my nerves, my bones. "You signed up for the forging because you wanted power, didn't you? Not for me. Not out of love or a desire to stay with me. Anyone who loved me could never ask me to give up my humanity. And you're not even asking, you demand it."

Calder inched toward me. "If you love me, you'll do it."

A great sadness filled me, part grief over what had become of Calder, part regret for what I needed to say. "I never loved you, Calder. I wanted to, tried to, thought I should and even convinced myself I must have. It wasn't real. I'm sorry, but it's true."

He leaped forward in a crouch to squat on my midsection.

Nevan rushed toward me, but Brennus punched him in the chest, hurling him backward into the cave wall.

Calder scraped a sharp claw lightly down my throat. "You're dying, baby. Let me help you be reborn."

"I'm the Janusite. How do you know I can be forged?"

"Worth a shot." He leaned down to press his rough, cold lips to mine. "The sylph must've put a spell on you, to make you forget how much you love me. It's why you ran away to this nowhere place. But you can't escape destiny. The forging will free you."

The man I'd known—the sweet, charming man who swept me off my feet—had died three years ago, before I shot him. He chose eternal life and immense power over the peace of natural death. If I died here in this cave, my soul would move on and I would leave this world certain I'd achieve immortality through the memories of my family, my friends, and Nevan.

He'd shown me real love, forged from trust and respect—not a need to control and possess.

"Kill me," I said, "but I will never submit to the forging."

Chin quivering, Calder shook his head. "You'll change your mind when the time comes."

"I won't."

"You will." He raised his hand and his claw elongated, the tip sharpening into a thin, double-edged blade. "You will."

He lanced the claw across my throat. My arms gave out. I collapsed onto the floor, my head thudding on the stone floor. Lights flashed in my vision, then fizzled out.

Nevan roared. He tackled Calder, the two wrestling and grunting and thrashing their limbs.

My body had gone numb, the only sensation that of hot blood streaming down my throat. As my eyesight waned into a deepening darkness, the shapes of the battling elementals faded from view. The noise of their scuffling seemed far away.

Crunch.

Silence.

A final thought flitted through my mind. One of the men had snapped the other's neck, and somehow, I knew Nevan had emerged victorious.

The living world spun away from me as my consciousness receded toward a blessed emptiness and the void claimed me.

Chapter Twenty-Nine

Sensory details pierced the numb haze enveloping me, one at a time. Pins and needles prickling my flesh from head to toe. Cool air on my skin. Soft, damp grass under my body. Voices, their words indistinguishable.

A singular voice broke through, low and fierce. "Come back to me, love. Please. I need you."

Nothingness overwhelmed me.

Time passed—minutes, hours, days, who knew. My consciousness seemed to float back down into my body, and my mind roused from the deepest slumber. My eyes stayed closed, my lids too heavy to move.

Soft fabric slid across my bare arms as I shifted position, and a puffy pillow cradled my head. Warm light glowed beyond my eyelids and warmed my face. Traffic rumbled nearby, muffled and intermittent. I pulled in a long breath and exhaled bit by bit, cleansing some of the grogginess. A tentative stretch of my entire body brought no pain.

The scent of thunderstorms wafted over me.

A smile parted my lips as I cracked my lids open. Nevan reclined in the padded wooden chair in the corner of my bedroom in the motor home. His eyes were shut, his head leaning against the wall, both arms slack with one hand on each thigh. He wore his khaki pants and polo shirt. I lay on the bed, beneath the blue-and-green quilt.

I tossed the covers off me.

Nevan's head sprang up, his eyes flew open. His lips trembled with a smile struggling to form, hindered by the concern evident in his gaze as he surveyed my body.

Sitting forward, he asked in a tentative voice, "How do you feel?"

I stretched again, with more vigor, swiveling my hips and thrusting up my breasts. "Mmm. I feel wonderful."

And I did. How odd.

The image of Brennus shredding my shirt and ripping into my chest exploded in my mind, followed close behind by the memory of Calder slashing my throat. My ex had turned into a shapeshifting monkey-man. I rubbed my chest, uneasy at the memory, then noticed a sky-blue cotton shirt and gray sweatpants covered me—and my wounds had healed completely.

"How long—" Realization struck me, ushering in a relief that slackened my tight muscles. "The vortex. You got Tris to heal me."

"Yes. Repairing the damage required a great deal of energy. Tris will be resting for days to regain his strength, but he was more than willing to help." Nevan watched me as if I might disintegrate, as if he'd imagined me. "Are you certain you feel no pain? No remnants of your injuries?"

"Positive." I spread my arms wide, luxuriating in the softness of the satiny sheets. I felt alive, awake, vital. "Never felt better."

"Glad to hear it."

"Um…" I recoiled from the need to ask, but I had to know. "Is Calder dead? I mean, really dead?"

Nevan nodded, eyes downcast. "I snapped his neck, then Brennus handed me Skeiron's endued sword and I drove it through Calder's heart. He will never haunt you again."

"I hope he's at peace." I rolled onto my back, picking at the hem of my shirt. "Christ, I can't fathom why he volunteered to become a monkey-thing."

"Doubt he knew precisely what he'd become."

"What are kerkopes, anyway?"

Nevan braced his elbows on his knees. "The first kerkopes were a pair of mortals who angered Zeus and were cursed to become shapeshifting monkeys. Over thousands of years, they've recruited more humans through the forging process."

I considered his words for a moment. "Brennus is a shapeshifter, but he looks essentially human—except for his shimmery skin. Why did Calder seem so different?"

"Kerkopes inherit their physical traits from the original curse. They are unable to completely shift back into humanoid form."

"Creepy." I stretched my whole body, arms above my heads. "Let's talk about something more fun."

In the literal blink of an eye, he lay on top of me, kissing me, running his hands up and down my sides. "No talking."

His left hand grasped my hip, his right kneaded my breast. His mouth devoured me with a hunger borne of fear and desperation but fueled by joy, his tongue sweeping over mine, coiling around it, firing up my libido with record speed. I wrapped my arms around him and gave in to the passion, our bodies molded together, limbs entwined. My fingers wended through his hair. I inhaled his scent, savored his taste, thrusting my tongue into his mouth as he delved deep into mine.

The door latch clicked. "Oops!"

At the sound of my mother's voice, Nevan rolled off me onto his side, head bowed. I flailed for the covers—to hide myself, because in his fondling he'd shoved my shirt up and tugged one breast out of my bra.

I aimed a sheepish look at my mom, but I couldn't meet her gaze. Sheesh, I was like a teenager caught making out with her boyfriend. My lips still burned from the intensity of Nevan's kiss.

"I came to see if you're awake and I see you are," Mom said. Her gaze switched to Nevan and back to me. "I take it you're feeling better."

"One hundred percent."

"You must be starving." Her tone conveyed motherly concern, but her faint smirk suggested she knew exactly what would've happened if she hadn't interrupted us. "It's blueberry pancakes this morning."

She shut the door.

"Morning?" I pushed up onto my elbows. "How long was I asleep?"

"The remainder of yesterday and all night." Nevan traced a fingertip over my collarbone. "I feared you might never wake, in spite of Tris's valiant efforts."

I opened my mouth in a mock gape. "Did you just call Tris, the vile leprechaun, valiant?"

Nevan rolled his eyes. "You will not hear me speak the words again."

"Do you like blueberry pancakes?"

He stared at me for moment, as if I'd spoken a foreign language. Leaning down, he teased my mouth with swift brushes of his lips and quick laps of his tongue. "I will eat whatever your family offers me, because pleasing them pleases you." He nipped my lower lip. "And pleasing you is my prime objective."

I didn't know what to say to that, so I straightened my clothes and led him out into living room. We ate pancakes while my brother peppered us with questions about the Unseen realm, my status as Janusite, and the details of Skeiron's death. Nevan wolfed down the pancakes with obvious relish, even groaning his approval, and downed what must've amounted to a half gallon of milk. My mother kept offering him more of everything and smiled every time he complimented her cooking, her housekeeping, and especially her marksmanship and courage during the sylph battle.

When my dad started his interrogation, Nevan didn't even seem irritated at the questions. Dad asked if Nevan had used his "voodoo spells" to control me and even that question didn't faze my sylph. He simply stated, "I would never betray your daughter in such a way. If I can't win her without magic, I do not deserve her."

I couldn't stop watching him. His easy smiles, his honest answers, his charming quips and his obvious affection for my family. He handled my brother expertly, in spite of his incessant quizzing about the other world.

Nevan cared for my family. There was nothing sexier in the universe.

Mom noticed my infatuated stare and gave me one of those smiles only mothers could pull off, the kind that said she recognized the depth of my attachment to him and she approved.

After breakfast, Nevan and I wandered outside. The shop building had suffered worse than any of us. The roof had caved in and a big hole gaped in the wall facing the parking lot. Through the gap, I spied overturned tables, the contents of their bins scattered over the floor.

Things could be replaced. Saving lives, saving the ones I loved, that mattered more than property damage.

We met Stan and Travis on the path to the shop door, where the two men were talking and gesturing at various wounds on the building. Instead of his sheriff's uniform, Travis wore jeans and an Aerosmith T-shirt. He looked different in civilian clothes, younger somehow, and more like the man I'd been friends with for years, back before Calder wrecked us both.

I'd found my redemption. Maybe Travis would find his one day.

Nevan slipped an arm around my shoulders. "Are you disturbed?"

"Bad memories, that's all."

As if he sensed my attention on his back, Travis turned toward us. He looked frightened for a moment, but regained his composure and traipsed over to us. He flashed me a tight smile. "Lindsey."

One word conveyed more than I could interpret. Regret. Sorrow. Guilt. Maybe a tinge of hope.

He offered his hand to Nevan. After a quick shake, both men jerked their hands away. Not exactly friends, but no longer enemies.

Travis shifted his weight to one foot, then the other. He hooked his thumbs in the waistband of his jeans, hunching his shoulders. His gaze flitted from the ground to me, back and forth several times, before settling on my face. "Lindsey, I need to apologize, again. I got no excuse and you know I ain't a drinker under normal circumstances. I don't expect us to be friends, won't ask for it but—"

"Stop." I couldn't take his rambling. It made my skin itch. I realized what he wanted and I realized I needed to give it, for both our sakes. "I forgive you. Let's move on, okay?"

His shoulders relaxed. "Okay. Thanks."

I let Nevan shepherd me away. Stan smiled and waved, and I reciprocated. This whole craziness had brought positive changes to my life, like the way my relationship with my boss had improved.

Nevan and I moseyed down the trail to the falls, his arm around my shoulders, mine draped around his waist, my head on his shoulder. The normalcy of our stroll, of our comfortable intimacy, made warmth swell in my heart. I'd thought I would never find this, but it found me. And at last, I understood what it was.

We halted at the wooden railing that hemmed in the pool and the falls. The spray misted over us, dampening our skin and hair. Nevan pulled away to move in front of me, face to face. His expression was serious, almost wary, as he stroked his palms up and down my arms, the droplets from the falls lubricating the motion.

Nevan dragged me into his arms, but rather than kissing me, he zipped us to the ledge beside the waterfall and jumped through the water with me snug against him. We lighted on the rock floor, dripping, my short breaths heaving my bosom into his chest. He ravished my mouth with passion and hunger, our kiss a mutual declaration of everything we couldn't express in words. The kiss heated swiftly, our hands groping, our bodies melting into each other, desire bursting inside me in tiny explosions of pure pleasure.

Our lips still molded together, we dived through the portal and he whisked us to the clearing outside Nevan's home. He broke away, backing up several feet.

I waved toward the slope that concealed his lair. "Why didn't you blip us inside?"

"Blip?" His mouth quirked. "You do come up with the most interesting descriptions."

"It's a gift."

He ducked his head, scrubbing both hands in his hair. When he raised his head again, his face had gone impassive. "Stay with me."

"Are you asking me to move in with you?"

"Yes."

I was mute for several seconds, my thoughts adrift. "I can't live with you."

"Why not?"

"I've never lived with anyone other than my family. And besides, we hardly know each other."

His mouth tightened, his hands fisted. "But you love me."

"That doesn't mean I'm ready to move to the Unseen realm and shack up with you."

Nevan threw his head back and let out an exasperated growl.

"Ugh," I said. "You are so melodramatic when you don't get your way."

His gaze homed in on mine and his flaming eyes sent an erotic shiver through me. "I want you with me always, love. You feel the same, you told me so. Stay with me."

The intensity he imbued into the last sentence shot heat through me, a lightning bolt of desire that throbbed in my sex. I longed to say yes. The word lodged in my throat and I swallowed. "This is a big decision, Nevan. We've known each for what, a week? I need time."

One corner of his mouth ticked downward. "Time for what?"

"To think, dammit. I need time to think about this, about you, about us."

He nodded. "How much time?"

"I don't know."

Sighing, he shook his head. "I will grant you time to think. How much do you require?"

"Are we negotiating a bargain?"

His head drew back, his eyes narrowing. "You believe I would trick you into a bargain?"

"No." I rubbed my temples. "I'm sorry. You wouldn't do that to me."

"I simply want to know how long I must wait." His fingers wriggled, as if working out a muscle spasm. He was anxious. This powerful warrior from another world fretted about my answer to his request. He cleared his throat. "I promised you once I would never use magic on you without your express permission. You know I keep my vows."

And I did. Even without magic to bind the promises, he kept them anyway.

He coughed, glanced around, fixed his attention on me again.

I gathered my sopping hair in both hands and wrung it out. Water splattered the ground. "Two weeks."

The breath he must've been holding rushed out of him. "May I see you during this period?"

"Of course. That's kind of the point." I wrung out my shirt's hem. "I want us to get to know each other."

The old playfulness returned, sparkling in his eyes. "Starting now?"

"Sure." His tongue darted out to moisten his lips, his eyes zeroed in on my breasts, and I knew what he was thinking. "Oh no. There will be no sex today."

Disappointment flashed across his face for an instant. "Perhaps tomorrow. Or the next day."

"You don't mind waiting?"

I hadn't noticed when he'd switched his Eddie Bauer outfit for the loincloth, but I suddenly became aware of his near nudity. My cheeks heated. Ridiculous, after everything we'd done together while buck naked.

He cocked one hip, stretching the loincloth taut over his groin, reminding me of what he could do with the asset hidden beneath the scrap of fabric. "Lindsey, my love, I am an immortal spirit. I have all the time in the world and I would wait until eternity for you."

"Tha—oops." I slapped my palms on my thighs. "Gah. Almost said the T-word. I've got work to do on the gratitude front."

"You'll be fine." He gave me an appreciative look. "Your bargaining skills have certainly improved. You outwitted Skeiron."

I squared my shoulders. "I did, didn't I? Maybe I am awesome after all."

"You awe me at every turn." He roved his gaze down my body and back up to my face, his lustful expression shifting into concern. "You seem worried."

"It's the debt. I don't want you staying with me because you have to come whenever I call."

"Never mind that."

"I will mind whatever I like." Hands on my hips, I drummed my fingers. "No more debts between us. You saved my life when Calder slit my throat. I owe you my life, just like you owe me yours. We're even."

The tether binding us in a one-sided debt snapped. The dissolution hit me with a jolt, like I'd touched an electrified fence. It passed in a split second, leaving behind a new, much softer bond. A genuine one, formed out of emotion.

"There," I said, letting my hands fall to my sides. "That's a relief."

Nevan swept me into his arms. His lips descended toward mine and I slapped a hand over his mouth. "No sex, remember?"

He licked my palm with leisurely strokes of his warm, slick tongue. When he peeled his mouth away from my hand, he left a damp trail across my skin. "I can do a great deal without removing your clothing." He slid my middle finger into his mouth and sucked. "Without even touching you."

I looped my arms around his neck and surrendered to his kiss. By the time we parted, I was breathing hard, flushed all over, and my swollen lips tingled. I pressed my lips to the corner of his mouth. "Show me your world."

A smile of unbridled elation illuminated his face. "My pleasure."

CHAPTER THIRTY

OR TWO WEEKS, I TRAVELED BACK AND FORTH BETWEEN THE
worlds—but only during my off hours. My job mattered to me, and
despite his grumbling, Nevan did not try to convince me to quit. When
Stan offered me a promotion to assistant manager, after a moment of head-
spinning shock, I accepted. When Stan informed I'd get a big raise, bumping my income up to twice what it had been, I stopped breathing for so long
my ears rang.

Everything had gotten better these days.

Every few days, Travis stopped in at the shop to say hi. At first, we endured awkward conversations about the weather, but eventually we found
a new dynamic for our relationship. We didn't talk about *that* night, or
about Calder. Travis and Nevan learned to tolerate each other, though I
held out no hopes they'd become best buds. As long as they weren't killing
each other, I was happy.

Nevan popped in everywhere I went—the shop, my parents' motor
home, my new apartment, the freaking grocery store. At least he had the
sense to wear normal clothes in public, but in my apartment, he made no
efforts to conceal his sylph-ness. I didn't want him to anyway. I'd grown
rather fond of his loincloth.

And yeah, we discovered I didn't need to escort him over the boundary as long as I was somewhere in the mortal realm at the time. When
I asked him how that could be, he'd given me the sweetest smile and
explained.

"You asked me once," he said, "if anything is stronger than a life debt. I
suggested one thing might be."

"I remember."

He touched his forehead to mine. "It's love, Lindsey. The force more
powerful than any magic. The one that allowed me to forgo my duty and

defy Skeiron. You told me love empowers your Janusite magic, and that's because it is the only unbreakable bond in the universe."

I almost balked, but my heart confirmed what he'd suggested. I no longer needed or wanted to deny the power of what we felt for each other. He was right, and the realization imbued me with a heady sensation of freedom and exultation.

At work a few days later, while Nevan was off with Ash and my dad doing heaven knew what, I looked up from restocking the fossil agate bin to find Tris observing me from the opposite end of the aisle.

Hand raised, I waggled my fingers at him. "Hi."

Tris scowled, glancing around as if afraid of getting caught. By mortals or his ilk, I had no idea. Apparently satisfied, he moseyed to me.

"Guess the healing stuck," he said.

"If you're asking how I am, I'm great. Thanks for your concern."

He flinched, probably more at my use of the dreaded T word than my sarcasm. "Yeah, whatever. Just don't go getting yourself mortally wounded again, pun intended. I ain't got enough energy to keep up with you and your boyfriend."

"I'll try." I patted his cheek. "You're very sweet to come check on me."

Tris scowled again, though with less sincerity.

"I've been wondering," I said, "why you got so wiped out from healing me and not from healing Nevan."

"You were way more damaged than him. Besides, repairing two almost-dead people in less than a day will tax any leprechaun."

"Ah." I'd forgotten how close together our near-deaths had come. "I appreciate you risking your own skin to save us. You're a good boy."

"Jeez, lady." Tris did an excellent impression of a snottily embarrassed teenager. "Quit calling me nice things. I got a rep to uphold."

"I'll be sure to spread it around you're a heartless little bastard."

He smiled, for real. "Could ya?"

"Absolve her this instant," said a deep voice from behind me.

My body awakened, responding to Nevan's voice even before I turned sideways to stay in view of both Tris and Nevan. My sylph wore tight jeans and a tan T-shirt, his every muscle on display.

I clasped his hand. The action had become instinctive. "What are you mad about this time? Tris hasn't done anything. Today."

"Hey!" Tris complained.

Nevan glared at the kid. "He's been hiding from me for days, because he knows what I'll do if I catch him. You still owe this leprechaun a debt."

"Don't care. Leave him alone."

Tris snorted. "I can handle a frigging sylph. They ain't so bad-ass as they think."

Nevan's voice dropped to a menacing whisper as he slanted forward just enough to loom over Tris. "I'm at full power, tiny fae."

I slapped a hand on Nevan's chest. "Cut that out."

He drew back, but the murderous glint in his eyes remained.

Tris hunched his shoulders, his gaze on the floor. "Chill out, Nev. I absolved your girlfriend right after I left her at the vortex with you, when you was still out cold after the healing." He looked straight at Nevan. "You two better get more careful."

I gave him a sly smile, a trick I'd learned from Nevan. "Why? Are you worried about us?"

"No." The petulance in his tone sounded forced.

Nevan squinted at Tris. "You truly absolved Lindsey of her entire debt to you?"

"Yeah-yeah, like I said." Tris nodded to me. "She'd feel it if she still owed me."

Thinking back to when my debt to Tris was sealed, and recalling the similar sensation when Nevan indebted himself to me, I recognized the truth. "He's right, Nevan. I don't feel it anymore."

Nevan relaxed, pulling me against him.

Tris shook his head. "I'm outta here. I'll spew copper sludge all over this floor if I have to watch you two make out."

He made a beeline for the back door. Once the leprechaun had walked out of sight, Nevan's lips found mine. His kiss was playful, sweet, and restrained.

Probably because we were in public and I'd chastised him for trying to ravish me in any way—with his mouth, his hands, or his other assets—in view of other beings, in either realm. He'd clearly disapproved of my need for privacy, but acquiesced to my demand.

These days, when he caved to my will, I could rest easy knowing magic played no part in his decision. He did it because he loved me.

He bent his head back. "Why are you smiling?"

"I need a reason?"

"No, I suppose not."

But it irked him not to know. I'd learned this about him over the past couple weeks.

"If you must know," I said, "I was thinking how wonderful you are."

A naughty grin spread across his face. He reached down to cup my behind with both hands. "What else were you thinking?"

I poked Nevan in the ribs. "No monkey business in public, remember?"

His lips flattened, but he removed his hands from my tush.

"About what I was thinking," I said, resting my hips against the bins. "Would you like to sleep with me tonight?" When his expression brightened, his eyes flaring hot, I amended, "No sex. Just sleep. With me."

I'd expected his excitement to wilt, at least a tad, but it didn't.

He cupped my cheek—the one on my face this time. "I'd love to sleep with ye, darlin'."

That night, I slipped into my slinky nightie and slid under the covers beside him. He enveloped me in his body, one arm draped over my belly, his fingertips dancing over the fabric to tease my skin, as he'd done the first night we slept together.

I awoke the next morning to the silky brush of his lips on mine. He kept it chaste, but even the light touch, the gentle questing, stoked me to white-hot awareness. I plowed my fingers into his hair and pulled his head closer. He groaned as I plunged into his mouth, intoxicated by the scent and flavor of him.

We kissed for an hour. I was late for work, but Stan made no comment, accepting my apology.

The fourteenth day arrived.

Nevan materialized at the foot of my bed at six a.m., his approach waking me before he entered the apartment. I switched on the bedside lamp and froze when I saw his face—the tension lining his forehead, the haggard tint of his skin, the dimmed colors in his eyes.

"I've been summoned," he said. "By the tribunal."

"The what?" I scrambled across the bed to kneel at the footboard where he stood. "I don't understand."

"My people are without a king. The tribunal demands a full accounting of Skeiron's demise and my role in it, before they appoint a new ruler."

"A full accounting?" I tried to lay my hands on his bare chest, but he shuffled backward. "Are you in trouble?"

"I aided in the demise of a king. I abandoned my duty and consorted with a mortal."

Though he kept his gaze squarely on me, the starkness in it carved a gulf between us. He'd done all of those things for me.

I slid off the foot of the bed to close the distance. "We can hide across the boundary."

"No, love." He ran his hands up my arms, drawing me closer. "We can't hide from this. I must confront the consequences of my actions."

I blinked away the first sting of tears, desperate to prolong this moment, to keep him here as long as possible. "Will you come back?"

"You have my vow, I will return."

"When?"

He pulled me into him, my face buried in his neck, his arms pinning me. "When I can, love. When I can."

"What if—"

Slanting my head back with a hand on my nape, he silenced my unfinished question with a tender kiss. "Hush, Lindsey. I will always come back to you, whatever the cost."

Before I could respond, he vanished.

Days crawled by, one after another after another. I crossed them off on the calendar in my kitchen, and with each stroke of my pen, a new pang lanced my heart. Five days and no sign of Nevan. Six days. Seven.

On the eighth day, I sat alone inside my parents' motor home, in a chair that swiveled left and right with the restless movements of my feet. I'd finally convinced my parents to go home to Kentucky, where they owned an actual house—the kind with a foundation and everything. Besides, this was August and the approach of autumn signaled the close of their annual summertime sojourn.

Nevan was gone. My parents and my brother were leaving. I had Stan and Travis, but as much as I liked them—yeah, I even liked Travis again—they served as pale substitutes for the people I loved.

I clapped my feet down on the floor. My chair halted with a creak. I slumped until my butt started to slide off the chair, staring vacantly at the breakfast nook across from me.

A familiar sensation rippled through me from deep within, triggered by the pulsating tingle of magical currents in the air. The fine hairs on my arms lifted as the aroma of earth and thunderstorms tantalized my senses and anticipation enlivened every cell of my being.

I bolted upright in my chair, hands clamped over my knees. A lightness rushed through me, banishing the malaise, and my gaze rotated toward the open doorway of the motor home.

A shadow elongated through the opening.

I leaped up, kicking over a pile of comic books on the floor, and sprinted for the stairs. I stopped short, my heart soaring at the vision awaiting me at the bottom of the steps.

Nevan grinned at me with the most brilliant joy I'd ever witnessed. Though he wore his toned-down-for-mortals glamour, he looked so good I wanted to throw myself at him and lick him from head to toe like a delicious, man-size lollipop.

"There ye are, darlin'," he said. "Aren't ye glad to see me?"

Glad? The term fell woefully short of describing the overpowering high hurtling through me at the sight of him.

I held off on the licking thing, but I hurled myself at him, sailing across the distance without touching one toe on the steps. He caught me, staggered backward, and whirled us both around with my feet flying through the air.

Our lips found each other in a kiss of sheer, unbridled passion. His tongue thrust into my mouth, devouring me with powerful strokes until I went soft in his arms. When we finally broke the kiss, he held me tight with my feet still off the ground. After a few minutes of silent rapture, basking in the feel of each other, he set me down. His hands lingered on my back, cradling me.

I splayed my hands over his chest, on the pale green shirt that disguised his jaw-dropping physique. Sort of disguised it. "How'd the meeting go?"

His lips kicked up, but he ironed out the amusement. "The meeting, as you call it, went much better than expected."

"No disassembly required?"

With a soft chuckle, he shook his head. "No punishment whatsoever. In fact, the tribunal was pleased to be rid of Skeiron."

A selfish thought reared its head and I had to ask, though I bit my lip and focused on the buttons of his shirt, fingering one. "Um, do they know I'm…"

"The Janusite?" At my anxious nod, he pressed a kiss to my forehead. "No one knows except you, me, Tris, and Brennus."

"No one else?" I pulled my head back, squinting up at him. "But the entire sylph army—"

"Only one battalion knew your identity and they have since forgotten, as ensured by the fae spell. The tribunal believes the Janusite is a myth."

"Thank heavens. I'd still like to know what being the Janusite means, in terms of the bigger picture."

"We will discover the truth together. I promise you this."

I cuddled up to him, my head on his chest, listening to the beat of his heart and the steady rise and fall of his breaths. We held each other for several minutes, silent and content in the warmth of each other. He moved his hands in slow circles on my back. I swirled my fingers over the back of his neck.

Finally, I said, "I owe you an answer."

"No, love. You owe me nothing."

"You're getting it anyway."

I ushered him into the motor home, shutting the door for privacy, and gestured for him to take a seat in the breakfast nook. I slid onto the bench beside him, our thighs pressed together. Hands on my lap, I braced for his reaction to what I was about to say.

"I can't live with you, Nevan."

Though his expression stayed placid, icy blue flashed in his eyes. "I see."

He moved to get up.

I grabbed his arm, urging him back down. "I'm not finished."

Mouth tight, he sat beside me again, stiff and straight, his eyes aimed out the windows across the aisle.

I scrubbed my hands on my thighs to wipe away the clamminess.

Nevan did not look at me, though one finger tapped on his thigh. "Continue."

His imperious tone bristled, but I recognized he was trying to appear unaffected because he was, in fact, very affected by my announcement.

"My family is in this world," I said. "I can't abandon them, but I want to be with you. I want us to have a relationship, like normal people."

"We are not normal."

"Yeah, but we can follow some normal customs." I grasped his hand, stilling his nervous finger. "This is called compromise, Nevan. If you want to be with me, you have to give a little."

His hand clinched mine. "All right. Compromise."

I let out the breath I'd been holding.

Angling sideways on the bench, he pulled me onto his lap. "You will spend every other night with me, in my home."

"Weekends only."

"I'll agree, as long as I spend the weeknights with you in your apartment."

"No." I rapped a finger on his chest. "That's living together."

Both hands on my hips, he tipped them into his burgeoning arousal. "I enjoy bargaining with you."

"I can tell." I wagged my finger at him. "Behave."

"Make your final offer."

"Weekends at your place. On weeknights, you can stay with me if I ask you to." I leaned in until my nose bumped his. "Agreed?"

His gaze seared into mine and a single word rolled of his tongue with sensuous promise. "Agreed."

"Thank you. Now please take me home and make love to me."

"My home or yours?"

"Don't care. Just take me."

He whisked us away. We emerged in my bedroom, where the closed curtains kept the room in twilight, even at midday.

"Tell me," he said, toying with the rivet on my jeans, "would you like to experience my full glory?"

The question rocked me. "Yes."

"I've never made love to a woman before."

"What?" I made an unladylike face. "You've been with lots of women—including me."

"I have enjoyed carnal relations with many females." He unhooked the rivet and eased the zipper down, the sound alone making my sex pulse. "I made love to none of them, because I loved none. Until you."

His hand stole inside my jeans, gliding inside my panties to palm my mound. One finger parted my folds and traced circles around the bundle of nerves at the apex of my thighs. I sucked in a breath.

"I am yours alone," he rasped, his breaths heavy. "Are you mine?"

"You know I am."

"Mmm," he murmured against my throat. "Will you be mine once I become king of the sylphs?"

Drunk on lust, I needed a few seconds to process what he'd said. As the meaning and import of it sank in, I caught his head in both my hands and forced him to look at me. "When you what?"

He moved his hand to cup my breast, and suddenly my bra felt constrictive. "The tribunal asked me to assume the mantle. I will ascend to the throne in a ceremony three days hence."

"Three days?" I tugged his face closer, peering into his eyes. "Will they let a king consort with a mere mortal?"

"I agreed to their proposal with one condition. They must accept you."

"And they said yippee, sure thing?"

"Not precisely." He raked his thumb over my rigid nipple. "But they acquiesced to my terms."

"Wow." I ran my hands down his neck, over his shoulders, fondling the muscles of his chest through his shirt. "I'm sleeping with a king."

His lips curved in a mischievous smile. "Shall I undress you slowly?"

That devious finger of his, wedged inside my panties, rubbed with strong, but mercilessly unhurried, strokes. His lips swept back and forth across my cheek, as I writhed in his hold, grinding my hips into him.

"Dammit, Nevan, vanish our clothes."

"Anything you wish, my sweet mortal goddess."

Our clothes dissolved. Cool air kissed my skin, tormenting my taut nipples. His hand dived lower and his thumb flicked across my nub, as his fingers explored my opening.

I moaned. Loudly.

He zipped us onto the bed, his hard body on top of mine. "It's time to show you all of what I can do."

CHAPTER THIRTY-ONE

HIS KISS WAS DEEP AND ALL-CONSUMING, RICH WITH HUNGER YET softened with tenderness. A contradiction, just like him. Warrior and jovial sylph. Bone-melting passion and aching gentleness. Eyes closed, I surrendered to anything he gave me.

Inch by breathtaking inch, he slid his swollen shaft inside me, penetrating my throbbing core. I arched into him and panted, "Faster."

His mouth consumed my protests. I clamped my arms around him as his shaft filled me to the hilt. He froze mid kiss, our tongues entangled. I clawed at his back, strapped my legs around his, and thrashed beneath him.

"Always eager," he growled. "I love your passion."

He drove into me, pounding into me with reckless desire, and I bowed up into each thrust, desperate to take him into me as far as possible. Locked in a fiery kiss, we were joined on every level. Even our powers were drawn to each other, the magics twirling around each other in a supernatural tango, colliding and separating in rhythm with our love-making. Through my eyelids, I spied a rainbow of lights exploding and sparkling around us, and I opened my eyes to see a constellation of fairy lights dancing around and above us, their sparks wafting through the air.

Even gravity seemed to give way to our passion and a lightness overtook me, a sense of weightlessness that amplified my arousal. His arms slipped under my body to bolster me as a climax of explosive power shattered me.

My cry wrenched our lips apart. I threw my head back to scream again, the ecstasy crashing through me again and again. At last sated, I clung to him as he plunged into me once, twice, and on the third thrust found his release. His own cry was half groan, half shout.

I shut my eyes, for fear I'd do something idiotic like weep. I'd never felt this close to anyone—and it wasn't only from the mind-blowing sex.

"Damn." My voice was breathless, my body tingling. "I hope that was your full glory, because anything more might kill me."

"Look down, love."

"Why?"

"Please, once, do as I ask without questions. You won't regret it."

I pried my lids apart, turned my head, and gasped. I belted my limbs around him. No way was I letting go.

We floated atop a white cloud outlined with silvery gray. The literal air bed hung suspended high above the earth, so far up I could glimpse Lake Superior, which lay twenty miles from my apartment complex. The building was tiny from this vantage, like a child's toy.

"Loosen your grip," Nevan said, his voice tight, "before I lose mine."

I struggled to make myself relax. "Better not drop me."

"Never. I meant I'd lose my grip on the magic that's holding us up here." He pecked a kiss on my lips. "Thank you for loosening up."

"You mean just now, or in general?" I gingerly stretched out one foot and tapped my big toe on the cloud. It billowed around my foot. "This isn't solid."

"It is and it isn't." He swept his fingers through the gaseous bedding, swirling it with ease. "And to answer your question, I meant both. If you hadn't loosened your grip, I might've sent us both plummeting to the ground. But I'm also grateful you let go of your emotions."

The cloud captured all my attention. "What do you mean it is and it isn't solid?"

"It's magic, my love. You'll have to get used to the contradictions."

"Will the cloud support me?"

His smile was as cryptic as his words. "It will and it won't. Go on and try it out. I won't let you fall."

I hesitated, then lowered one leg onto the cloud. My limb sank in a little, but somehow the cloud buoyed it. I let me other leg relax onto the billowy bed. Nevan's arms slackened around me and my whole body sank onto the cloud. It felt like the best waterbed ever, without the sloshing.

Nevan moved to roll off me. I stopped him with my arms around his back.

He gave me an odd look, a mixture of confusion and amazement. "Aren't I—how do you phrase it?—squishing you?"

"A little, but I like it."

"What would you have me do then?" He palmed one breast. "I am at your command."

"Make love to me again. And again." I swished my hand through the cloud. "And maybe again after that."

He laughed, the full-throated kind rife with such joy I couldn't help joining in. When our laughter faded away, he took my face in his free hand and stared into my eyes. "Are you sure you wish to have a relationship with me?"

"I hate to break it to you, but we're already having one."

His other hand kneaded my breast, his thumb raking over my nipple. "You know what I mean. Life with me will not be simple."

"You've got yourself a handful too."

Thunder rumbled in the distance. I glanced left, spying a storm cloud on the horizon. Lightning lanced up from the cloud top, straight out into space.

I slapped his behind. "Is that you? The thunderstorm?"

"Possibly. It won't be severe, nothing but a light show with some much-needed rain. This is my power. And you fuel it."

"Oh. That's, um, sweet. I think."

"Sweet is not the compliment I'm seeking at this moment." He ducked his head to capture my nipple in his mouth, giving it quick pull. "Would you care to amend your statement?"

"Arrogant sylph."

"I'll accept that."

By the time we came down, from the skies and from our next round of full-glory sex, the sun had dipped below the horizon. Lightning coruscated across the sky, the bolts slender and white-hot.

In my bed again, we snuggled under the covers. Nevan's thunderstorm produced a soft, steady rain that pattered on the roof.

From here on, our lives were merged and time itself could not sever the unbreakable magic of our love. Me and my sylph warrior, on a journey with no itinerary, because we'd make it up as we went along. With my ear to his chest, I counted the time between lightning bolts and thunder by the clock of his heartbeats.

However fast or slow the clock ticked, for me, he had nothing but time.

Did you love

Visit

AnnaDurand.com

to subscribe to her newsletter
for updates on forthcoming books in this series
&
to receive free gifts for signing up!

ANNA DURAND IS A BESTSELLING, MULTI-AWARD-WINNING AUTHOR OF contemporary and paranormal romance. Her books have earned bestseller status on every major retailer and wonderful reviews from readers around the world. But that's the boring spiel. Here are the really cool things you want to know about Anna!

Born on Lackland Air Force Base in Texas, Anna grew up moving here, there, and everywhere thanks to her dad's job as an instructor pilot. She's lived in Texas (twice), Mississippi, California (twice), Michigan (twice), and Alaska—and now Ohio.

As for her writing, Anna has always made up stories in her head, but she didn't write them down until her teen years. Those first awful books went into the trash can a few years later, though she learned a lot from those stories. Eventually, she would pen her first romance novel, the paranormal romance *Willpower*, and she's never looked back since.

Want even more details about Anna? Get access to her extended bio when you subscribe to her newsletter and download the free bonus ebook, *Hot Scots Confidential*. You'll also get hot deleted scenes, character interviews, fun facts, and more! Plus you'll receive the short story *Tempted by a Kiss* and mutliple bonus chapters in both ebook and audiobook formats.

VISIT ANNADURAND.COM TO SIGN UP.